One Little Sin

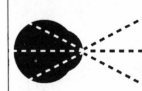

This Large Print Book carries the
Seal of Approval of N.A.V.H.

One Little Sin

Liz Carlyle

Thorndike Press • Waterville, Maine

Published in 2006 by arrangement with Pocket Books, a division of Simon & Schuster, Inc.

Thorndike Press® Large Print Core.

The tree indicium is a trademark of Thorndike Press.

The text of this Large Print edition is unabridged. Other aspects of the book may vary from the original edition.

Set in 16 pt. Plantin by Al Chase.

Printed in the United States on permanent paper.

Library of Congress Cataloging-in-Publication Data

Carlyle, Liz.
    One little sin / by Liz Carlyle.
      p. cm. — (Thorndike Press large print core)
    ISBN 0-7862-8470-6 (lg. print : hc : alk. paper)
    1. Large type books.   2. Single mothers — Fiction.
    3. London (England) — Fiction. I. Title. II. Thorndike
Press large print core series.
    PS3553.A739O54 2006
    813'.54—dc22   2005034501

To my agent, Nancy Yost,
with my deepest gratitude

As the Founder/CEO of NAVH, the only national health agency solely devoted to those who, although not totally blind, have an eye disease which could lead to serious visual impairment, I am pleased to recognize Thorndike Press* as one of the leading publishers in the large print field.

Founded in 1954 in San Francisco to prepare large print textbooks for partially seeing children, NAVH became the pioneer and standard setting agency in the preparation of large type.

Today, those publishers who meet our standards carry the prestigious "Seal of Approval" indicating high quality large print. We are delighted that Thorndike Press is one of the publishers whose titles meet these standards. We are also pleased to recognize the significant contribution Thorndike Press is making in this important and growing field.

Lorraine H. Marchi, L.H.D.
Founder/CEO
NAVH

* Thorndike Press encompasses the following imprints: Thorndike, Wheeler, Walker and Large Print Press.

Prologue

The Boxing Match

It was a sweltering afternoon in September when Sir Alasdair MacLachlan very nearly got what his Granny MacGregor had been promising him for at least the last three decades: *his comeuppance.* Nonetheless, for all its repetition, her admonishment had never been taken very seriously.

Until the age of eight, Alasdair had thought the old girl was saying *"come a pence,"* which he took to be just another Scottish prayer for good fortune, since Granny was notoriously clutch-fisted. So he'd simply tucked the aphorism away, along with all her other gems, such as *Sup with the devil, bring a long spoon,* and her perennial favorite, *Pride goeth before a fall, and a haughty spirit —*

Well, he couldn't quite recall what happened to a haughty spirit, nor did he much care to think about it, because, on this particular hot afternoon, Sir Alasdair's mind was elsewhere, and he was already deep in Bliss — Bliss being the name of the village blacksmith's wife — when the first gunshot rang out, and his comeuppance edged near.

"Oh, shite!" said Bliss, shoving him off. "Me 'usband!"

Tangled awkwardly in his trousers, Alasdair rolled down the pile of straw and came up spitting dust and flailing about for his braces.

"Awright, Bliss! I knows yer in 'ere somewhere!" The grim voice echoed through the cavernous stable. "Out w'you, now! And that bloody, backstabbin' Scot, too!"

"Gawd, not again," muttered Bliss wearily. By now, she'd hitched up her drawers, and was twitching her petticoat back down her rump. "Most times, I can stall 'im a bit," she whispered. "But you'd best climb over that wall and run for it. Will won't hurt *me.* You, he'll kill."

Hastily jamming in his shirttails, Alasdair grinned. "Will you grieve for me, my dear?"

Bliss shrugged. Easy come easy go, apparently. And Alasdair prided himself on being easy. Along the passageway between the box stalls, doors were screeching open, then slamming shut with ruthless efficiency. "Come on out, you fancy bastard!" the smithy bellowed. "There ain't but one way in, an' one way out, and that's by way o' me!"

Alasdair gave Bliss a smacking kiss, then hefted himself halfway up the box's wall. "Ta, love," he said, winking. "You were worth it."

Bliss shot him a cynical look, then threw back the stall door. With an artful fling of his legs, Alasdair swung himself up and over the planked wall, then dropped silently into the adjoining box.

"Will Handy, are you daft?" Bliss was in the passageway now, squawking theatrically. "Set down that pistol before you go and kill yourself! Can't a woman catch a wink? Been run half to death all day, I have, toting water and ale up and down that hill like some serving girl."

"Oh, I thinks I knows 'oo you been serving, miss." The voice of doom was mere feet away now. "Where's 'e at, eh? By God, this time, I mean to kill somebody."

Alasdair gingerly inched the stall door open and peeked out. *Christ Jesus.* Alasdair was not a small man, but Bliss's husband looked like a bad-tempered dray horse, big yellow teeth and all. He was sweating like one, too.

Bare from the waist up, save for his filthy leather apron, the smithy had rivulets running down his rough, bronze skin. Sprouting black hair covered his barrel chest, his tree-trunk arms, and most of his back. In one fist, he clutched a nasty-looking hand scythe, and in the other, a rusty old dueling pistol, its mate shoved down the bearer of his trousers.

Two guns. One shot.

Damn. Alasdair had excelled in mathematics at St. Andrews. He did not like his odds here. Christ, what a fix he'd gotten into this time. But he loved life too well to willingly give it up.

Bliss had wet one corner of her apron now, and was dabbing at a streak of soot on the big brute's face. "Shush, now, Will," she cooed. "There's no one here but me, aye?"

Alasdair eased the door open another inch, and waited until Bliss had the old boy by the arm. She was dragging him toward the door, so Alasdair waited until they'd turned the corner, then gingerly tiptoed out. And promptly stepped on a rake. A six-foot shaft of solid English oak popped out of the muck to crack him square between the eyes. Alasdair cursed, tripped over himself, and went sprawling.

"There 'e is!" roared the smithy. "Come back 'ere, you friggin' cur!"

Alasdair was reeling, but not witless. The smithy had thrown off his wife's arm and was barreling back down the length of the barn. Alasdair kicked the rake from his path, feinted left, then bolted past the brute. The smithy roared like a thwarted bull and turned, too late.

Alasdair burst out into the blinding sunlight just as a roar went up from the crowd in the meadow far below. An illegal and much-touted boxing match had drawn half the rascals in London to this little Surrey village, and the sight of a bleeding aristocrat being chased by a scythe-wielding blacksmith did not occasion so much as a glance.

Alasdair could hear the smithy pounding down the grassy hill behind him. Frantically, he searched the meadow for his companions. The smithy was grunting with exertion. Alasdair considered standing his ground. What he lacked in size, he just might make up in speed and skill. Still, old Will did have a loaded gun and a just cause. God mightn't be on Alasdair's side.

Alasdair reached the foot of the hill and began darting between the parked carriages. Fast footwork was not the smithy's forte, and he quickly fell behind. Alasdair circled half the meadow, dashing from carriage to carriage, urgently searching the sea of faces beneath the baking sun. The scents of damp grass, spilt ale, and fresh manure made for a sour miasma in the heat.

The jeers and groans of the crowd were audible now, punctuated by the rapid smack of flesh on flesh. One of the boxers staggered back, another roaring cheer went up, and in that instant, Alasdair saw his brother pushing his way out of the crowd, with Quin on his heels, still sipping a tankard of ale.

Merrick met him near a big, old-fashioned town coach. "What the devil's got into you?" he asked, as Alasdair dragged him behind it.

"And who was that Goliath on your heels?" added Quin. "Looks like he laid one right between your eyes, old boy."

Alasdair leaned against the carriage to catch his breath. "Let's just say it's time to go, gents," he answered. *"Now."*

"Go?" said Quin incredulously. "I've got twenty pounds on this fight!"

Merrick's expression tightened. "Why? What's happened?"

"Petticoat trouble again!" complained Quin. "Couldn't you cuckold someone smaller?"

Alasdair pushed away from the carriage, his gaze scanning the edge of the meadow. Merrick grabbed him firmly by the arm. "You *didn't.*"

Alasdair shrugged. "It was Bliss, the girl

12

who brought the ale," he said. "She looked as though she could use a few moments off her feet. A purely humanitarian act, I assure you."

"Good God, Alasdair," said his brother. "I knew better than to come along on this escapade wi—"

"Bugger all!" interjected Quin, hurling aside his tankard. "Here he comes."

Just then, a wall of sweating, grunting flesh came pounding toward them from the opposite side of the meadow, still waving the gun and scythe, which was glistening wickedly in the sun. "We'd best run for it," said Alasdair.

"I'll be damned if I'm running anywhere," said Merrick coldly. "Besides, I left the carriage at the King's Arms."

"One of his pistols is still loaded," cautioned Alasdair. "Perhaps I deserve it, Merrick, but do you really want the village idiot to kill some bystander?"

"Better to live and fight another day, old chaps," said Quin.

"Oh, to hell with it," snapped Merrick.

The three of them bolted toward the footpath. It snaked around the summit of the hill and up to the back side of the village. Here, people lingered all along the path, where shrewd tavern keepers had set up wagons and tents to sell meat pies and ale. Itinerant tradesmen and Gypsies had staked out ground, too, and were hawking all manner of handmade goods, tonics, and charms while, from the village above, the lively strains of a fiddle carried on the breeze.

Quin pushed on until the crowd thinned. Alasdair and his brother followed. In the next sharp turn, Quin was obliged to jump from the path of a thin man balancing a keg on one shoulder. Merrick followed suit. Unfortunately, Alasdair clipped the man's jutting elbow with his shoulder. The man stumbled, cursed, and dropped the keg, which went thundering down the path.

"Impressive footwork!" said Merrick snidely.

Alasdair cut a glance back down the hill to see that the smithy was gaining ground. A mere three feet ahead of him, the keg bounced off the path, exploding into beer and foam. The man who'd been carrying it apparently decided to throw in his lot with the smithy, and turned to join in the chase.

Around the path's next bend, a wagon painted in brilliant shades of green came into view. Beside it sat a large tent of stained and patched canvas. Quin leapt off the path and threw up the flap. "Quick," he ordered. "In here."

Merrick dived into the darkness. Alasdair followed. For a moment, there was nothing but the sound of their gasping breath. Alasdair's eyes were still adjusting to the light when a dusky voice came out of the gloom.

"Cross my palm with silver, Englishman."

He peered into the depths of the tent to see a Gypsy woman seated before a rickety deal table, one slender, long-fingered hand outstretched. "I — I'm not English," he blurted, for no particular reason.

She eyed him up and down, as if he were horseflesh on the block. "That is not entirely true," she said.

Alasdair *was* a quarter English on his father's side. He grew inexplicably uneasy.

"Cross my palm with silver," she repeated, snapping her elegant fingers. "Or perhaps you would prefer to leave? This is place of business, not a sanctuary."

"Oh, for God's sake, pay the woman," ordered Merrick, still looking through the flap. Beyond, Alasdair could hear the smithy arguing with someone — the chap who'd been carrying the keg, most likely — about what their strategy ought to be.

Alasdair dug deep into his coat pocket, extracted his purse, and laid a coin in the woman's hand.

"Three," she said with another impatient snap. "One for each."

Alasdair dug into the purse again.

"Sit," she ordered, after examining the coins. "All three sit. Those foolish men will not follow. They do not dare."

Quin and Merrick turned to stare at her.

She lifted one shoulder, and a curtain of shimmering black hair slid forward to shadow her face. "What?" she challenged. "You have somewhere else to go?"

Quin, by far the more tractable of the two, seized a couple of three-legged stools and did as she commanded. "Be a sporting chap, Merrick," he said. "What else have we to do for the nonce?"

Merrick approached the table and sat, still looking daggers at Alasdair.

"Your hand," she demanded.

Obediently, Alasdair extended it. The woman held it, palm open, and gazed at it for a time. As if to clear her vision, she rubbed at the lines with her thumb. Beyond the quiet of the tent, the world and all its clamor seemed to fade away. The woman pulled a tiny lamp nearer, and turned up the wick, flooding the tent with yellow light.

She was, Alasdair suddenly realized, quite breathtakingly beautiful.

"You have a name, Englishman?" she murmured, still staring at his palm.

"MacLachlan."

"MacLachlan," she echoed. "I think you are a bad man, MacLachlan."

Alasdair drew back. "But I'm not," he protested. "I'm a decent sort of chap, really. Ask — why, ask anyone. I have no enemies."

She looked up from his hand and lifted one thin, inky brow. "Like those men outside?" she asked. "They were your friends?"

Alasdair felt his face flush with heat. "A misunderstanding," he said. "Of sorts."

Her brows snapped together. "There are many kinds of bad, MacLachlan," she said, her voice low and throaty. "You have committed a multitude of sins."

"Ah, a priest now, are you?" It was Alasdair's turn to be sardonic. "Fine, I confess. Now tell my fortune, my lovely, and have done with it."

But instead, she laid his hand down and motioned for his brother's. Merrick narrowed his gaze. The Gypsy faltered. With his scarred face and cold blue gaze, Alasdair's brother presented a less than welcoming picture. In the end, however, he relented.

Again, she smoothed her thumb over the lines and mounds of his hand. "Another MacLachlan," she murmured. "With the devil's luck. And the devil's eyes."

Merrick laughed harshly. "Twice cursed, am I?"

She nodded slowly. "I see it here —" She touched a spot below his index finger. "And here." She stroked the very center, and despite his outward composure, Merrick shuddered.

"You possess a creative spirit," she said simply. "You are an artist."

Merrick hesitated. "Of a sort," he agreed.

"And like many artists, you have the sin of pride," she went on. "You have known great success, but no happiness. Excessive pride and a bitter heart have hardened you."

"Is that my future?" asked Merrick cynically.

She looked at him openly, and nodded. "Almost certainly," she said. "It has assuredly been your past." She pushed his hand away and motioned for Quin's.

"I've committed more than a few sins," Quin admitted, extending it. "I rather doubt there's room enough on my palm for all of them."

She bent over it, and made a *tch-tching* sound in her throat. "Impulsive," she said.

"You act rashly. You speak before thinking."

Quin laughed nervously. "I can't say you're wrong there," he agreed.

"You will pay for it," she warned.

Quin said nothing for a moment. "Perhaps I already have," he finally answered.

"You will pay for it again," she said calmly. "In the worst way, if you cannot right the wrong you have done."

"Which wrong?" he said on an uneasy laugh. "The list is long."

She lifted her gaze and held his. "You know," she said. "Yes, you know."

Quin twisted uncomfortably on the stool. "I — I am not sure."

The Gypsy woman shrugged, and stroked her index finger across the base of his thumb. "I see you have suffered a great loss recently."

"My father," Quin admitted. "He — he passed away."

"Ah," said the Gypsy. "What is your name?"

"Quin," he said. "Quinten Hewitt — or Wynwood, I should say. Lord Wynwood."

She made the noise in her throat again. "So many names, you English," she murmured, dropping the hand as if she had grown weary. "Go now, all of you. Go to

19

your carriage and leave this place. I can say nothing which will stop you from wasting your lives. Your fate is sealed."

Alasdair cut his eyes toward the tent flap.

"Go," said the Gypsy again. "The men have gone. They will not return. It is fate which will punish you for your sins this day, MacLachlan, not those bumbling idiots."

Merrick jerked to his feet. Quin gave an uneasy laugh. "Sorry, Alasdair," he said. "At least Merrick and I seem to have gotten off rather easily." He smiled at the woman, whose exotic beauty was decidedly growing on Alasdair.

"Easily?" she echoed. She lifted her eyes to Quin's and held his gaze. "But I have not told you your future."

It was true, Alasdair realized. She had said much, but portended little.

Merrick had turned his back to them and was again peering through the tent flap.

"Well, go on then," Quin encouraged. "What have we to look forward to, ma'am? Great riches? Exotic travel? What?"

She hesitated briefly. "This is no foolish parlor game, my lord," she answered. "Do you really wish to know?"

Quin faltered. "I — yes, why not?"

The Gyspy's gaze was distant. "What is the phrase you English say, Lord Wyn-

20

wood?" she murmured. "Ah, yes, I recall it. *Your chicks are coming home to roost.*"

"Chickens," corrected Quin. "I believe it's usually said to be chickens."

"Are you quite sure?" Her voice was suddenly sharp. "In any case, none of you shall continue to evade the consequences of your iniquities. None of you can continue to take and use and exploit, whilst paying no price. You must begin to pay for your sins. Fate will make this so."

"Iniquities?" said Alasdair. "Sins? Ma'am, those are harsh words."

"Call them what you will," said the Gypsy, with a shrug that set her long earrings jangling. "But you will pay, MacLachlan. And you will learn. And you will suffer in the doing of it. What is to come will be as real and as painful as that bruise between your eyes."

Merrick cursed softly, but did not turn around. "I grow weary of this Cheltenham tragedy," he snapped. "Let's be off."

"Wait a moment, Merrick." Quin was studying the woman warily. "Is this one of those Gypsy curses?"

At that the woman's eyes flashed. "Lord Wynwood, you are such a fool," she said. "You have read too many novels. The three of you have cursed yourself, with no help

21

needed from me. Now you must make restitution. You must make it right."

Merrick looked over his shoulder. "Utter balderdash," he snapped.

"Nonetheless, it shall be so," she said quietly.

An ill wind suddenly blew through the tent, chilling Alasdair despite the summer heat. He spun around to see that his brother had thrown open the flap and was striding back down the path. Quin shrugged, and followed.

Never one easily daunted — even, perhaps, when he should have been — Alasdair smiled, and slid onto the middle stool. "My dear girl," he said, leaning half-across the table. "Now that those Philistines have gone, I really must ask you — has anyone ever told you that your eyes are the color of fine cognac? Your lips like blushing rose petals?"

"Yes, and my arse is like two orbs of Carrera marble," she answered dryly. "Trust me, MacLachlan. I have heard them all."

Alasdair's smile melted. "Ah, a pity!"

The Gypsy woman gave him a bemused look and stood. "Begone with you," she said. "Get out of my tent, MacLachlan, and put away your well-worn charms. They do

22

you no good here and have caused trouble enough already."

Aladair hung his head and laughed. "It *has* been rather a bad day," he admitted.

For a moment, the Gypsy said nothing. "Oh, my poor, poor MacLachlan," she finally whispered. "Oh, I fear you do not know the half."

The chilling breeze touched the back of his neck again. But this time, when Alasdair looked up, his beautiful prophetess had vanished.

Chapter One

In which a Thunderstorm breaks

Upon returning to his town house in Great Queen Street, Alasdair waved away his butler's questions about dinner, tossed his coat and cravat on a chair, and flung himself across the worn leather sofa in his smoking parlor. Then he promptly slipped back into the alcohol-induced stupor which had served him so well on the carriage ride home.

A copious amount of brandy had proven necessary in order to endure the company of his traveling companions. Quin had become peevish about his twenty-pound wager, and grumbled all the way to Wandsworth. As for Merrick, Alasdair's younger brother needed no excuse to behave sullenly. It was his perpetual state of existence. At least the pretty Gypsy had called that one right, Alasdair mused, drifting into oblivion.

For a time, he just dozed, too indolent to rise and go up to bed. But shortly before midnight, he was roused by a racket at his windows. He cracked one eye to see that the unseasonable heat had given way to a brutal thunderstorm. Snug and dry on his sofa, Alasdair yawned, scratched, then rolled over and went back to sleep, secure in life as he knew it. But his lassitude was soon disturbed again when he was jolted from a dream by a relentless pounding at his front door.

He tried mightily to ignore it and cling to the remnants of his fantasy — something to do with Bliss, the beautiful Gypsy, and a bottle of good champagne. But the pounding came again, just as the Gypsy was trailing her fingertips seductively along his backside. Damn. Surely Wellings would answer it? But he did not, and the knocking did not abate.

Out of annoyance rather than concern, Alasdair crawled off the sofa, scratched again, and headed out into the passageway which overlooked the stairs. In the foyer below, Wellings had finally flung open the door. Alasdair looked down to see that someone — a female servant, he supposed — stood in the rain on his doorstep carrying, strangely enough, a basket of damp laundry.

Wellings's nose was elevated an inch, a clear indication of his disdain. "As I have twice explained, madam," he was saying,

25

"Sir Alasdair does not receive unescorted young females. Particularly not at this hour. Get back in your hackney, please, before you fall dead on the doorstep of pneumonia."

He moved as if to shut the door, but the woman gracelessly shoved first her foot, then her entire leg, inside. "Now whisht your blether and listen, man!" said the woman in a brogue as tart as Granny MacGregor's. "You'll be fetching your master down here and making haste about it, for I'll not be taking *no* for an answer, if I have to knock on this door 'til God himself and all his angels come down those steps."

Alasdair knew, of course, that he was making a grievous error. But drawn by something he could not name — temporary insanity, perhaps — he began slowly to descend the stairs. His caller, he realized, was not a woman, but a girl. And the laundry was . . . well, not laundry. More than that, he could not say. Halfway down the stairs, he cleared his throat.

At once, Wellings turned, and the girl looked up. It was then that Alasdair felt a disembodied blow to the gut. The girl's eyes were the clearest, purest shade of green he'd ever seen. Like the churning rush of an Alpine stream, the cool, clean gaze washed

26

over him, leaving Alasdair breathless, as if he'd just been dashed with ice water.

"You wished to see me, miss?" he managed.

Her gaze ran back up, and settled on his eyes. "Aye, if your name is MacLachlan, I do," she said. "And you look about as I expected."

Alasdair did not think the remark was meant to be a compliment. He wished to hell he was fully sober. He had the most dreadful feeling he ought to be on guard against this person, slight, pale, and damp though she might be. Somehow, beneath her bundle, she extended a hand. Alasdair took it, realizing as he did so that even her glove was soaked.

"Miss Esmée Hamilton," she said crisply.

Alasdair managed a cordial smile. "A pleasure, Miss Hamilton," he lied. "Do I know you?"

"You do not," she said. "Nonetheless, I'll need a moment of your time." She cut a strange glance at Wellings. "A *private* moment, if you please."

Alasdair looked pointedly down at her. "It is rather an odd hour, Miss Hamilton."

"Aye, well, I was given to understand you kept odd hours."

Alasdair's misgiving deepened, but curiosity overcame it. With a slight bow, and a flourish of his hand, he directed the girl into the parlor, then sent Wellings away for tea and dry towels. The girl bent over the sofa nearest the fire, and fussed over her bundle a moment.

Who the devil was she? A Scot, to be sure, for she made no pretense of glossing over her faint burr as so many did. She was dainty, almost childlike in appearance, save for her haunting green eyes. She could not be above seventeen or eighteen years, he did not think, and despite her damp, somewhat dowdy attire, she looked to be of genteel birth. Which meant the sooner he got her the hell out of his house, the safer it was for both of them.

On that thought, he returned to the parlor door and threw it open again. She looked up from the sofa with a disapproving frown.

"I fear my butler may have mistaken your circumstances, Miss Hamilton," said Alasdair. "I think it unwise for a young lady of your tender years to be left alone with me."

Just then, the bundle twitched. Alasdair leapt out of his skin. "Good Lord!" he said, striding across the room to stare at it.

A little leg had poked from beneath the smothering heap of blankets. Miss Hamilton threw back the damp top layer, and at once, Alasdair's vision began to swim, but not before he noticed a tiny hand, two drowsy, long-lashed eyes, and a perfect little rosebud of a mouth.

"She is called Sorcha," whispered Miss Hamilton. "Unless, of course, you wish to change her name."

Alasdair leapt back as if the thing might explode. "Unless I wish — wish — to *what?*"

"To change her name," Miss Hamilton repeated, her cool gaze running over him again. "As much as it pains me, I must give her up. I cannot care for her as she deserves."

Alasdair gave a cynical laugh. "Oh, no," he said, his tone implacable. "That horse won't trot, Miss Hamilton. If ever I had bedded you, I would most assuredly remember it."

Miss Hamilton drew herself up an inch. "*Me* — ? Faith and troth, MacLachlan! Are you daft?"

"I beg your pardon," he said stiffly. "Perhaps I am confused. Pray tell me why you are here. And be warned, Miss Hamilton, that I'm nobody's fool."

The girl's mouth twitched at one corner. "Aye, well, I'm pleased to hear it, sir," she answered, her gaze sweeping down him again. "I'd begun to fear otherwise."

Alasdair was disinclined to tolerate an insult from a girl who resembled nothing so much as a wet house wren. Then he considered how he must look. He'd been sleeping in his clothes — the same clothes he'd put on at dawn to wear to the boxing match. He'd had rampant sex in a pile of straw, been shot at and chased by a madman, then drunk himself into a stupor during a three-hour carriage drive. He had not shaved in about twenty hours, he was sporting a purple goose egg between his eyes, and his hair was doubtless standing on end. Self-consciously, he dragged a hand through it.

She was looking at him with some strange mix of disdain and dread, and inexplicably, he wished he had put on his coat and cravat. "Now, see here, Miss Hamilton," he finally managed. "I really have no interest in being flayed by your tongue, particularly when —"

"Och, you'd be right, I know!" The disdain, if not the dread, disappeared. "I'm tired and peevish, aye, but in my defense, I've been on the road above a sen'night, and another two days trying to find you in this hellish, filthy city."

"Alone — ?"

"Save for Sorcha, aye," she admitted. "My apologies."

Alasdair reined in his temper. "Sit down, please, and take off your wet coat and gloves," he commanded. When she had done so, he laid them near the door, and began to pace. "Now, tell me, Miss Hamilton. Who is the mother of this child, if you are not?"

At last, some color sprang to her cheeks. "My mother," she said quietly. "Lady Achanalt."

"Lady Acha-*who?*"

"Lady Achanalt." The girl frowned. "You — you do not recall the name?"

To his consternation, he did not, and admitted as much.

"Oh, dear." Her color deepened. "Poor Mamma! She fancied, I think, that you would take her memory to the grave, or some such romantic nonsense."

"To the grave?" he echoed, fighting down a sick feeling in the pit of his stomach. "Where the devil is she?"`

"Gone to hers, I'm sorry to say." Her hand went to the dainty but expensive-looking strand of pearls at her neck, and she began to fiddle with them nervously. "She passed away. It was sudden."

"My sympathies, Miss Hamilton."

Miss Hamilton paled. "Save your sympathies for your daughter," she said. "Her full name, by the way, is Lady Sorcha Guthrie. She was conceived at Hogmanay, over two years past. Does that jag your brain a wee bit?"

Alasdair felt slightly disoriented. "Well . . . no."

"But you must recall it," Miss Hamilton pressed. "There was a ball — a masquerade — at Lord Morwen's home in Edinburgh. A bacchanalian rout, I collect. You met her there. *Didn't* you?"

His blank face must have shaken her.

"Good Lord, she said you told her it was love at first sight!" Miss Hamilton protested, her voice a little desperate now. "And that — why, that you had been waiting all your life for someone like her! Mother was a brunette. Full-figured, and tall. Very beautiful. Good Lord, do you remember *nothing?*"

Alasdair searched his mind, and felt sicker still. He *had* been in Edinburgh some two years ago. He had taken the unusual step of going home for the holidays because his uncle Angus had returned from abroad for a brief visit. They had spent Hogmanay together. In Edinburgh. And there *had* been a ball. A raucous one, if memory served.

32

Angus had dragged him to it, and more or less carried him home afterward. Alasdair remembered little, save for the roaring headache he'd suffered the following day.

"Oh, well!" Her voice was resigned. "Mamma was ever a fool for a pretty face."

A pretty face? Was that what she thought? And who the devil was this Lady Achanalt? Alasdair wracked his brain, this time dragging both hands through his hair. The young woman was still sitting on the sofa beside the sleeping child, staring up at him. Her gaze was no longer so cool and clear, but instead weary and a little sad.

"Sorcha is precious to me, MacLachlan," she said quietly. "She is my sister, and I will always love her dearly. But my stepfather — Lord Achanalt — he does not love her. From the very first, he knew."

"That he was not the father?" asked Alasdair. "Are you quite sure?"

The girl's green gaze fell to the carpet beneath her soggy shoes. "He was sure," she whispered. "Because he and Mamma had not — or would not . . ."

"Oh, Lord!" said Alasdair. "What, exactly?"

"I don't know!" she cried, her face flooding with color. "I don't understand any of it. He *knew.* That is all Mamma would say. And

33

then one day, it just all blew up! She flung it in his face. She made it sound like a grand passion. Faith, did she never write to you? Nor you to her?"

Alasdair pressed his fingertips to his temple. "Dear God."

She looked at him sorrowfully. " 'Tis rather too late for prayers," she said. "Look, MacLachlan, the last two years have been the very devil for all of us. I did what I could to smooth o'er a bad business, but now, there is nothing more to be done. Mamma is dead, and it falls to you. I'm sorry."

The room fell silent for a moment. Alasdair paced back and forth before the hearth, the sound of his bootheels harsh on the marble floor. A child. An *illegitimate* child. Oh, God. This could not be happening to him. "How did she die?" he finally croaked.

" 'Twas a fever," she answered hollowly. "A very ordinary thing. She always wanted to die dramatically — *a poetic death,* she used to call it — but a fever went round the Highlands like a wildfire. It was God's will, I suppose."

Alasdair wondered if God hadn't had a little help from the lady's husband. "I am deeply sorry for your loss, Miss Hamilton," he finally said. "But I simply cannot take the child. Is that what you thought? That she would be better off here? Nothing, I assure you, could be further from the truth."

She looked at him strangely. "What I think little matters, sir."

But Alasdair was determined to throw off this treacherous burden. "I am persuaded that in your grief for your mother, you have been overcome by romantic notions, Miss Hamilton," he responded. "But I am a hardened gamester. A practiced wastrel. A womanizer of the worst order. The very last sort of man who ought to be rearing a child. Go home, Miss Hamilton. There was no passion, grand or otherwise, between your mother and me. Lord Achanalt is Sorcha's father in the eyes of God and the law. Indeed, I am sure he must be worried sick by now."

At that, Miss Hamilton laughed, a sharp, bitter sound. "Then you are the only romantic fool in this room, MacLachlan," she returned. "Worse, perhaps, than my poor mother. Achanalt cares not one whit for the opinion of the law, and in the Highlands, he might as well *be* God. Sorcha and I have no home. Do you not comprehend me, sir?"

Alasdair stopped in his pacing and turned to stare at her, clutching his hands behind his back to keep from putting a fist through something. "Good God," he whispered. "The man has turned you out?"

Miss Hamilton lifted one of her wrenlike shoulders. "Why should he not?" she answered. "We are neither kith nor kin to him. We share not one drop of his blood. We have no siblings, no grandparents. Achanalt owes us naucht. If you do not believe me, just write to him and ask. He'll readily tell you so."

Alasdair fell into a chair. "Christ Jesus, your mother died, and he . . . he just . . . ?"

"Our things were put out in the carriage drive before the doctor could declare her dead," said Miss Hamilton. "Fortunately, he was kind enough to take us up in his curricle on his way home. We have been living with his family all this time, a dreadful imposition."

Alasdair was appalled. "Achanalt has disowned the child, then?"

"He has not publicly proclaimed that she is *yours,* no," retorted Miss Hamilton. "He has too much pride for that. But his actions speak louder than words, do they not? Sorcha is at your mercy. You are her last resort."

"But — but what of your father's people? Can't they take you?"

She shook her head. "My father had no

family and little money," said Miss Hamilton. "Another pretty wastrel, I fear. As was Mamma's second husband. And her third. Mamma had a penchant for them."

"This Achanalt does not sound like a wastrel."

"No, just deceptively pretty. A dreadful misjudgment on her part."

"And you have . . . no one else?"

The girl gave a pathetic little laugh. "Mamma had an elder sister, but she went out to Australia over two years ago," she said. "I do not know if she means ever to return, or if she is even alive. I have written, but . . . I have no real hope."

"I see," said Alasdair, very much afraid he did.

Suddenly, the girl bent down to kiss the sleeping child. "I really must be away now," she said, coming to her feet and blinking rapidly. "I am so sorry, but I must."

Alasdair felt as if the earth just shifted beneath his feet. "Away?" he said. "Away to where — ?"

The young woman was blinking back tears now. "I'm to leave on the first mail coach this morning." She rummaged in her pocket and brought out a small brown bottle. "Now, Sorcha is teething," she hastily added. " 'Tis her last upper molar. If she cries and you cannot soothe her, just rub a little of this on the affected gum."

Alasdair's eyes widened. *"Rub — ?"*

Miss Hamilton gave him a watery smile. " 'Tis a camphorated tincture," she said. "Just poke your wee finger about in the back of her mouth until you find a hard spot. 'Twill be the tooth, trying to break through the skin. Trust me, if I can manage, you can. And then tomorrow, why, you can hire a nurse, aye? You will hire one, won't you? A very experienced nurse, mind. Sorcha is a good, quiet child. She'll be not a drop of trouble to you, I swear it."

Alasdair stared at the brown bottle she had pressed into his hand. "Oh, no, Miss Hamilton," he said, jerking unsteadily to his feet. "No, no, no. I am not doing this. I do not want this little brown bottle. I am not poking my finger anywhere. I am not feeling *gums.*"

"Oh, I imagine your fingers have been worse places," she said.

But Alasdair was so horrified, the insult barely registered. *She really was going to leave him.* For a moment, he couldn't breathe. The mantle of responsibility — the inescapable horror of it all — was settling over him now, and he could not seem to push it off.

His wet house wren was pulling on her gloves now and blinking back tears.

"But wait!" he protested. "This cannot be happening! What — who — where — do you mean to go?"

"To Bournemouth," she answered, giving her last glove a little tug. "I have been engaged as a governess there. Indeed, I am fortunate to have found a place at all. I have no experience. But Dr. Campbell knew the gentleman — a retired colonel — and made inquiries on my behalf. I have no other choice."

"No choice?" The concept was foreign to him.

Miss Hamilton looked at him rather solemnly. "I am, you see, quite destitute right now," she admitted. "But Sorcha is not, is she? She has *you*. Please, MacLachlan. You mustn't fail the child."

"By God, I'm not failing her!" he retorted. "I am not even *taking* her."

Miss Hamilton took two steps backward.

Alasdair was gaping at her. "But the — the child! Wait, Miss Hamilton! Surely you can keep her? She is — why, just look how small she is! Indeed, she must scarcely eat a thing!"

"Why must you make this so hard for me?" cried Miss Hamilton. "No family will

39

take on a governess with a small child. And they will think, of course, that she is mine, and turn me off at once."

Alasdair looked at her warily. "That's a very good point," he said. "How do I know she *isn't* yours?"

Suddenly, Miss Hamilton's eyes lit with ire. "Why, you selfish scoundrel!" she said. "Do you actually mean to continue to deny having had — had — *conjugal relations* with my mother?"

"Having what?" he echoed incredulously. "I deny even knowing how to spell *conjugal relations!* But if you're asking me if I gave the old girl a quick pump-'n'-tickle behind the draperies at some drunken New Year's celebration, then yes, I'd have to say that . . . well, that I might — perhaps — *possibly* have done. I cannot quite recall."

"My God," she whispered, horrified. "You really are a scoundrel, aren't you?"

"Guilty!" he cried, reaching heavenward with both hands. "Guilty as charged! And happy, madam, to be so!"

Miss Hamilton's lip curled scornfully. "I regret, sir, that I must do this to a child I love so dear," she said. "But being the illegitimate daughter of a scoundrel is better than anything the orphanage can offer her — and better than anything *I* can offer her, much as it pains me." She dashed away a tear, snuffled deeply, and snatched her soggy reticule from the sofa.

Alasdair caught her somewhere between the sofa and the door. "Miss Hamilton! Really! You cannot get me into this mess, then just waltz back out the door!"

Miss Hamilton spun round, and drew herself up a good three inches. "What got you into this mess, sir, was your . . . your *talleywhacker!* That, and a wee nip or two or twenty! So don't even think of casting the blame on me!"

But Alasdair had burst into laughter. "My *talleywhacker,* Miss Hamilton? Really!"

She drew back a hand as if she might slap him. "Do not you dare, sir, to make fun of me!"

Somehow, he stopped laughing, snatched the hand, and drew it swiftly to his lips. "There," he said. "I'm sorry. Let that be a kiss of peace. Now, surely, Miss Hamilton, we can work this out to both our advantages? Indeed, I see no problem at all."

She glanced at his bruised forehead. "Someone's conked you on the naper," she muttered. "And it has disordered your brain."

"Listen to me, Miss Hamilton," he protested. "You clearly do not wish to abandon

41

your sister. And I am a very wealthy man."

"Aye?" There was a hint of hope and wariness in her eyes. "Well, say away, MacLachlan. What is this fine notion?"

Alasdair shrugged innocently, and feigned his most angelic expression — the one which had never worked on Granny MacGregor. Miss Hamilton, however, was less hardened, or perhaps just desperate, for her eyes softened a bit. Good God, he was such a sham! And she looked dashed pretty when that quartzlike gaze melted.

"What if I bought you a cottage?" he lightly proposed. "A seaside cottage, perhaps? With, of course, a nice, er, annuity. You are very young, it is true. But with a little effort, I daresay you could pass for a young widow . . . ?"

Miss Hamilton shook her head very firmly. "Young widows — if they are respectable — are taken in by their husband's family," she said, rolling the *r* in respectable into a near growl. "Or by their own family. No one will believe that old widow-and-cottage nonsense, MacLachlan, and well you know it." Her voice was growing scornful again. "I'll be thought a common lightskirt, and Sorcha will be ruined."

"Now, now, Miss Hamilton. Surely you overstate the matter."

"You know I do not," she insisted. "Besides, Sorcha deserves a father, even a less-than-ideal one. And if she is to be thought a bastard, she might as well be the bastard of a *'very wealthy gentleman.'* You can afford to give her everything. You can clothe her and educate her. And then she will at least have a chance at a respectable life." Her eyes still leaking tears, she tore her hand from his, and turned away. Then, on a quiet sob, she started for the door again.

"Really, Miss Hamilton, you cannot leave me!" he said, following her. "Think of — why, think of the child! Think of the things she'll be exposed to under my roof! Why, I might let her play with pen-knives! I might put paregoric in her porridge! Why, I might even teach her how to count cards or — or load dice! Remember, I am a very wicked man!"

Miss Hamilton gave him a look that would have made his cock shrivel — if it hadn't already drawn up into a petrified nub at the beginning of this awful conversation. "Oh, you wouldn't dare!" she hissed. "Not loaded dice! That's a sad, sairie trick, MacLachlan."

Alasdair felt ashamed of the notion, for he'd never cheated in his life — well, only with other men's wives. Which was just what had landed him in this god-awful predicament. And as much as he wished to deny the child, Miss Hamilton had a convincing air of righteous indignation. Worse still, he had the vaguest recollection of having done something very, very wicked at that ball Angus had taken him to. There was a lingering sense of guilt.

He had always had a penchant for older, amply proportioned women — brunettes if he could get them. And apparently, he'd got himself one that Hogmanay. Christ Jesus, what had he said to that poor woman to get her to fuck him? And that's what it had been, too, he'd no doubt. Just a quick, raw fuck. No emotion. No thought for the consequences. Oh, God! Snatches of it seemed to dance in his head. He vaguely remembered the part about the draperies. Heavy velvet ones, soft on his backside. And the musty smell of old leather. Or was that some scrap of a memory from another sin, in another time and place?

No, the library, most likely. He'd always found empty libraries dashed tempting during balls and parties. He had probably enticed this Lady Achanalt person behind the curtains, murmured sweet lies in her ear, and promptly dropped her drawers round her ankles — probably even taken her standing up, too. It would not have been the first time for *that,* either.

"MacLachlan?" Miss Hamilton's sharp voice cut into his consciousness. "MacLachlan? Faith, man, you're crushing my fingers."

He looked down to see that he'd grabbed both her hands in his again. Suddenly, it struck him. "Miss Hamilton, why must you go to Bournemouth?"

"Because I must work!" Her tone was unflinching. "I'm destitute, MacLachlan, d'ye not comprehend?"

"But . . . but why can you not simply stay here?"

She drew back a good six inches. "Stay *here?* With *you?*"

Alasdair cut her a scathing glance. "Oh, for pity's sake, Miss Hamilton!" he said. "As — as my governess!"

Miss Hamilton arched one brow. "Well, I've no doubt your first one failed you miserably," she answered. "But you look rather too old and entrenched in wickedness now."

Alasdair scowled. "Oh, for pity's sake! For the child! The child! If — *if* — I'm to let her stay on, why can I not hire *you* to look after the little weanling? Who would know the difference? And who would be better qualified?"

That took her aback. "I — I —" Miss Hamilton blinked uncertainly. "But that's foolishness. Sorcha is not yet two years old. She needs a nurse, not a governess."

But Alasdair was determined to find a way through this quagmire of moral obligation. "Who says so, Miss Hamilton?" he demanded. "Who makes up these rules? Is there some governess's handbook I know nothing of?" He shot a quick glance at the sleeping infant. "Why, just look at her! Sharp as a tack, I've no doubt. All the MacLachlans are — well, most, anyway. Why, my brother Merrick could read by the age of three and do all manner of sums and such."

"So you admit, then, that the bairn is yours?" asked Miss Hamilton.

Alasdair hesitated. "I admit that it is remotely possible," he hedged. "I must write to Edinburgh and make some inquiries before I accept the full res-res — the full *resp-p-p*—" For some reason, his tongue could not quite shape the word.

"The *responsibility?*" supplied Miss Hamilton with mocking sweetness. " 'Tis a simple word, MacLachlan. Just six syllables. I'm sure you'll get the knack of it."

Alasdair was afraid she was right. "You seem to have all the qualities of a governess,

Miss Hamilton," he returned. "A shrewish tongue and a condescending attitude."

"Aye, and I thank you," she answered.

He studied her silently for a moment, cursing his own desperation. "So, what of my offer, then? How much does a governess earn, anyway? Just what is all this newfound *responsibility* going to cost me, even temporarily?"

She hesitated but a moment. "A hundred fifty pounds per annum would be fair."

"Bloody hell!" He tried to scowl. "Miss Hamilton, you are a dreadful liar."

She blinked innocently. "Then perhaps you could give me some helpful hints regarding that particular talent?" she suggested. "I'm told one ought to learn at the feet of a master."

Alasdair narrowed his eyes. "Look, Miss Hamilton, blackmail me over your salary if you must, but are you staying or not?"

She bit her lip and cast another glance at the sleeping child. "Three hundred pounds for the first year, payable in advance," she answered. "Nonrefundable, even if you change your mind. Even if you change your mind *next week*."

Good God, he'd be a fool to agree to such a thing! All totaled, the salaries of every servant in the house would barely equal *that*.

Alasdair was about to tell her to go to the devil, but just as he opened his mouth, the bairn let out a god-awful wail. The money forgotten, Miss Hamilton rushed to the sofa and threw back the blankets. Hastily, she lifted the child from her basket, settling her over her shoulder. Wild, red-blond curls spurted from beneath the child's snug wool cap.

"Whisht, whisht, wee trootie," Miss Hamilton cooed, rhythmically patting her back.

In response, the child made some happy, babbling racket. Then, just when Alasdair had begun to breathe easily again, the child lifted her head, and looked him squarely in the face. In that moment, he suffered another of those crushing, breath-seizing blows to the gut. He reached out and grabbed hold of a chair, wondering if his knees might give.

Miss Hamilton had turned around. "Faith, MacLachlan, are you ill?" she asked, hastening toward him.

Alasdair shook off the feeling. "I'm quite well, thanks." He released his grip on the chair. "It's just been a trying day, that is all."

"Och, 'tis that terrible bruise between your eyes, I do not doubt," warned Miss

48

Hamilton, all her o's coming out just like Granny MacGregor's. "The blood's all left your brain, man. Put some ice on it and take yourself to bed."

Alasdair shook his head. "I'll have this miserable business settled first," he insisted. "Now, as I was saying, I shall pay you one hundred fifty pounds —"

"*Three hundred,*" she reminded him. "Payable in advance."

It was robbery, plain and simple, but Alasdair hadn't much choice. "Fine, then," he muttered. "And you'll stay and see to the child until . . . until I think what next to do."

Suddenly, her face almost crumpled. It seemed most uncharacteristic, but thoroughly genuine.

"Oh, Lord!" he said. "What now?"

She drew a shuddering breath. "It just seems such a vast step," she admitted. "I was just taking hold of the fact that I must let my wee Sorcha go, and now this! I feel so ill prepared."

"Well, you bloody well don't haggle like you're ill prepared," he complained. "How would you like to be in my shoes? Half an hour ago, I was minding my own business and sleeping my way through the world's most delightful fantasy, when next I know, you and Lady Sorcha here are waltzing into the middle of my life. It's a damned inconvenience, to be frank."

Miss Hamilton did not look particularly chagrined. "What I meant was that this isn't what one would call a reputable household, is it?" she went on. "I shall be ruined, I daresay. On the other hand, I am not at all sure it much matters anymore."

Alasdair drew himself up rather straight. "This is a bachelor household, true," he admitted. "But I don't entertain my mistresses here, or go about seducing the servants, Miss Hamilton. And I certainly don't trifle with mere girls, if that is what you meant."

"I don't know what I meant!" said Miss Hamilton, patting Sorcha rhythmically on the back as she paced. " 'Tis half my problem. I've little experience in the ways of the world. Indeed, I knew almost nothing of child rearing until Mamma died. I have lived most of my life in small Scottish villages. I *know* there are things a lady oughtn't do, and I'm relatively certain that living under your roof is one of them. But you are offering me a terrible temptation: a way to stay with my sister."

Her sudden vulnerability troubled him, for reasons he couldn't explain. "Look, Miss Hamilton, if the child is to stay here, sooner or later, she will need a governess,"

50

he said. "If you are old enough to be a governess, then why shouldn't it be you? I have no female relations to fob her off on unless I send her back to Scotland — which, given the way gossip runs, is probably the last place she needs to be. So, have you a better idea?"

"No," she said, her voice very small. "None at all."

"Then I shall give you your three hundred pounds," he conceded. "And in return, you shall make my problem go away. Does that sound fair?"

Miss Hamilton sniffed. "Oh, I am going to regret this," she whispered. "I know it already."

Just then, the butler came back in with tea. Alasdair motioned the tray away. "We have a change of plan, Wellings," he said. "Be so kind as to take that up to the schoolroom."

"The *schoolroom,* sir?"

Alasdair smiled. "Yes, it seems I have acquired a . . . a ward," he answered, gesturing at the child, who had dozed off on Miss Hamilton's shoulder. "Arising, alas, from the sudden death of a distant relation. Miss Hamilton here is her governess." Alasdair bowed in her direction. "Wellings will have your baggage brought in and see you made

51

comfortable for the night. In the morning, he will introduce you to the staff. And then we will do" — he waved his hand vaguely — "well, whatever one *does* under such circumstances."

"And you will write to Edinburgh straightaway?" Miss Hamilton pressed.

"Straightaway," he agreed. And then Sir Alasdair left his new governess in Wellings's capable hands, and went upstairs to bed, no longer even remotely secure in life as he knew it. A child! In his house! And now, he was the last thing he'd ever wished to be. A father. Good God. *A damned inconvenience* did not begin to describe this.

The schoolroom, Esmée Hamilton soon learned, was occupied by a nine-foot billiards table, its green felt top almost bald from use. The nursery which adjoined it had long since been converted into a smoking parlor stuffed with worn leather furniture, and the shelves which should have held toys and books instead held stacks of hinged wooden boxes which Wellings called "Sir Alasdair's numismatic collections," whatever that meant.

Esmée was too tired to ask, so she just wrinkled her nose at the stale smell and followed Wellings, who was no longer so condescending. "And this way, ma'am, is the

52

bedchamber, which also opens onto the schoolroom," he said. "Will it do?"

Esmée laid Sorcha down on the bed and looked about. The room was not large, but it was high-ceilinged and airy. "Aye, thank you," she said quietly. " 'Tis lovely. I don't suppose you have any sort of crib or cradle?"

"I am afraid not, ma'am." But he helped Esmée position a large dresser drawer between two chairs near the bed.

She had become adept at such makeshift arrangements in the long weeks since her mother's death. It was that, in part, which had convinced her Sorcha must have a proper home. The child deserved a better, more stable life. And she deserved a competent parent, too. Esmée was not at all sure she met that qualification. Still, surely that brazen devil downstairs was worse?

After Wellings provided hot water and a profuse apology for the bed's not having been properly aired, he bade Esmée good night and pulled the door shut. Esmée went to it at once and turned the key. A sudden sense of relief mixed with sorrow surged through her as she stared down at the fine brass lock. Her mother was dead. Beloved Scotland was far away.

But for tonight, they were safe. For tonight, they had a proper bed, and every expectation of a proper breakfast on the morn. It seemed so little. And yet, it had come to mean so much.

Oh, how she wished she were older and wiser — and mostly the former. In eight more years, she would have an inheritance from her grandfather — a rather large one, she thought. But eight years was a long time. Sorcha would be almost ten. Until then, they had to live by Esmée's wits — a slender reed if ever there was one. Oh, if only Aunt Rowena had come home!

Esmée returned to Sorcha's side. The bairn was already sound asleep. Esmée sat down on the bed and tried not to cry. She was not qualified to take care of a child. And she certainly should not be here in this house. Even Esmée, gudgeon that she was, knew better.

Sir Alasdair MacLachlan was even worse than she'd been led to believe. He was not just a hardened rakehell; he was bold and unapologetic about it. And he was quite astonishingly handsome; too handsome for his own good — or any woman's peace of mind. Even when he was angry, his eyes seemed to be filled with laughter, as if he took nothing seriously, and though his hair had been a disheveled mess, the golden locks had gleamed in the lamplight.

Her stomach had done something very odd the moment he kissed her hand. She supposed that was just the sort of shivery, flip-floppy thing one felt when one was kissed by a practiced rake. Worse, he had not for one moment remembered Mamma. God, what an embarrassment that had been! But Esmée had parted company with her pride about six hundred miles ago, and she very much feared it was going to get worse.

Dead tired, yet filled with restless energy, she drifted back into the smoking parlor, where the light from a single sconce wavered, casting odd, shifting shapes up the walls and along the shelves. She flung herself down on the tatty old sofa and was immediately struck by a warm, already familiar scent. MacLachlan. Unmistakably. Then she saw the coat tossed so carelessly across a nearby chair. She tried to ignore the tantalizingly masculine scent which teased at her nostrils, and instead picked up a fine, leather-bound book from the untidy heap on the tea table.

She studied the small gold letters on the spine. *Théorie Analytique des Probabilitiés* by de Laplace. Esmée flipped it open, then muddled along in her bad French just far enough to realize that the author's theories, which had something to do with arithmetic, were far above her head. And far above MacLachlan's, too, she was sure. Perhaps the book had been left out as a sort of decorative pretense? But when she looked about the messy, malodorous room, she quickly cast that notion aside. No, there were no pretensions to refinement here.

Curious now, she picked up another. This book was very old indeed, its brown leather binding badly cracked. *De Ratiociniis in Ludo Aleae* by someone named Huygens. This one she could not read at all, for it was in a language she'd never seen. But again, it contained a great many numbers and mathematical formulas.

What on earth? She dug deeper. Beneath another six such books was a sheaf of foolscap, filled with chicken scratch and numbers. On the whole, it looked to be the ramblings of an insane mind — which fit what she'd seen of MacLachlan so far. But all the fractions, decimal points, and strange annotations were beginning to give her a headache. Esmée restacked the lot, blew out the sconce, and returned to Sorcha's side.

Relief surged at the sight of the child's face, so serene and happy. Yes, she had agreed to MacLachlan's outrageous proposal. What else was she to do? Leave Sorcha, merely to preserve her own good name? One could not eat a pristine reputation. One could not sleep on it or shelter under it. And who else would give them a home together?

MacLachlan might be a rogue and a scoundrel — he was without a doubt lazy and self-indulgent — but he showed no evidence of cruelty. That surprised her. In her experience, the handsomest men were often the cruelest. Was not Lord Achanalt a sterling example?

She let her gaze drift about the room, taking in the gold silk walls and the high, narrow windows with their opulent draperies. It was smaller, yet far more elegant than anything they'd had in Scotland. It was a miracle MacLachlan had not tossed them into the street. It was what she had expected; what she had steeled herself for. Indeed, it was just what her stepfather *had* done. For a moment, Esmée's anger got the better of her grief. Of Achanalt, she'd long expected the worst. But *her mother?* How could she just die and leave them to the mercy of that man?

As she undressed, Esmée noticed the ormolu clock on the mantel. Half past one. Her coach to Bournemouth would be leaving in five hours. If ever she were going to change her mind, the turning point was tonight. She might be a grass green girl from the Highlands, but she had every idea that once she remained alone in this house with a man of MacLachlan's repute, her employability in a decent household would be at an end. Worse, even in a state of dishabille, he was handsome. Dangerously so. Esmée did not like him, no. But her mother's blood coursed through her veins, and that, too, was dangerous.

But despite her fears, and her strange mix of grief and anger over her mother's death, there was a tenuous hope kindling in Esmée's heart. As she slowly bathed in the warm water Wellings had sent up, Esmée let herself savor the feeling. *He was going to do it.* MacLachlan was going to give Sorcha a real home. The very thought of it astonished her, and Esmée realized that in truth she had traveled all the way to London never expecting her bluff to work.

Oh, MacLachlan would not give Sorcha love, she thought, pulling her nightdress over her head. He would not nurture the child's soul. He would not be a father in any meaningful sense of the word. But he was not going to throw her out again, and Esmée had learned to keep her expectations low and rejoice at even the slightest victory.

Just then, Sorcha began to flail about with her left leg, tossing off her blankets. Esmée went to the makeshift cradle and bent down to tuck her blankets back around her. To her surprise, Sorcha was awake. At Esmée's appearance, she widened her startling blue eyes, laughed one of her gurgling, bubbling laughs, and clapped her hands together.

Esmée took the child's tiny hands in her own and felt Sorcha's fingers wrap round her index fingers, her grip warm and strong. "Are you happy now, my bonnie wee lassie?" asked Esmée, lifting one little fist to her lips for a kiss. "D'ye fancy this might be your home after all?"

"Be mo," agreed Sorcha, her gaze growing drowsy again. "Mo, mo, mo."

Chapter Two

In which Mr. Hawes lets the Cat out of the Bag

"Good God. You did *what?*" Merrick MacLachlan leaned across the breakfast table to stare at his brother.

"I told her she could stay," Alasdair repeated. "It was one in the morning, and there was the very devil of a thunderstorm on. What else was I to do?"

"Send her packing," advised Quin around a mouthful of kidney. "That's the oldest trick in the world, Alasdair. Can't believe you fell for it."

Merrick pushed back his chair in disgust. "That must have been one hell of a blow to the head yesterday," he said, going to the sideboard to refill his coffee. "Some tart shows up on your doorstep with a bairn in tow, tells you it is yours, and you just *believe* her?"

"She's no tart, Merrick. She's just a little wren of a girl." But Alasdair was suddenly very glad he had not mentioned the three

60

hundred pounds Miss Hamilton had extorted. He let his gaze drift round his well-appointed dining room, and wondered if his brother had a point. Or perhaps he was going a little mad. Somehow, he had believed that in the light of day, all of this would vanish like a bad dream. But it had not.

"Are you going to eat those?" asked Quin, pointing at the pile of kippers Alasdair had mechanically piled on his plate.

"Have them, by all means," offered Alasdair, too late, as it happened, since Quin had already forked half of them up. "Though how you can eat all that after the day we had yesterday, I cannot fathom."

"Cast-iron stomach," said Quin, finishing his eggs. "You're getting soft, Alasdair. Any more coffee, Merrick?"

Merrick filled Quin's cup, then returned to his chair. "What have you told the servants, Alasdair?" he demanded. "The house must be abuzz."

"The staff round here is beyond being shocked," he answered evenly. "I told Wellings the child was my ward, and he actually believed it. Especially since Miss Hamilton is so obviously Scottish and looks more like my daughter than my usual sort of lightskirt."

"But Alasdair," said Quin, "someone is bound to remember your trip to Scotland and put two and two together. You go so rarely."

Alasdair turned to face him. "Very rarely," he agreed. "I've been home but once in the last three years. But that particular year, if you'll recall, you and I spent the shooting season in Northumbria at Lord Devellyn's hunting box."

"Yes, I recall it," said Quin.

"And we'd meant to spend the holidays, too," Alasdair continued. "But then you and Dev found those two French girls in Newcastle, and I was odd man out, so to speak."

"We did offer to share," Quin grumbled.

Alasdair shook his head. "I decided I wanted to go *home*," he said. "Especially since I was already better than halfway there. And I hadn't so much as my valet with me."

"Good God, what is your point?" snapped Merrick.

"That no one save Quin and Devellyn are apt to remember I went within a hundred miles of Scotland that year — or any other recent year."

"I still say you must get rid of her, Alasdair," his brother warned. "Thus far, you've admitted no real responsibility — and even if you had, there's nothing this bit of baggage could do about it."

"God knows I don't fancy having a brat about the house, Merrick," said Alasdair darkly. "But I'm damned if I'll let the chit starve on my account. I remember too well what it was like to feel unwanted as a child."

"Father was strict, aye," said Merrick. "But we were never starved, Alasdair."

"Speak for yourself," his brother snapped. "There are many kinds of starvation."

"Well, best put her up in an inn, at the very least, until all this sorts out," said Quin, as if to forestall a quarrel.

Alasdair shook his head. "I haven't the heart," he admitted. "The bairn is barely past infancy, and Miss Hamilton is little more than a child herself. She seems so callow and tenderhearted. I rather doubt the chit's been south of Inverness in the whole of her life."

"A likely story," said Merrick. "You're a fool if you don't send the little jade *and* her child packing. Besides, Uncle Angus can tell you nothing. They sailed in April for the Malay Peninsula."

"Did they, by God?" asked Alasdair. "I'd forgotten."

"What does it matter?" challenged Merrick. "He'd likely tell you this Lady Achanalt is little better than a common tart, and that there is no way they can prove the babe is yours."

Alasdair pushed away his plate. "There, dear brother, is where you just might be wrong," he returned. "And I begin to resent your attitude." On impulse, he rang for one of the footmen, but the butler himself came back into the room.

"Yes, sir?"

"Is Miss Hamilton awake yet, Wellings?"

The butler's eyes widened. "Indeed, sir," he answered. "She rose before dawn and asked for a sheet of letter paper."

"Letter paper?" Alasdair echoed.

Wellings nodded. "She had a piece of correspondence she particularly wished to go out on the first mail coach to Bournemouth this morning," he answered. "I believe she is now in the schoolroom."

Ah, yes. Her retired colonel in Bournemouth. So she really was staying, then. Alasdair relaxed into his chair. "Fetch her down here, please," he said. "And tell her to bring the child."

A taut silence held sway over the dining room whilst they waited, but in just a few minutes, a soft knock sounded at the dining room door. Miss Hamilton came into the room looking even smaller than she had the evening before. The luminescent green eyes filled half her face, which was oval, and finely boned. Today she wore a brown wool dress which should have looked drab, but instead looked graceful. The shade perfectly matched her hair, which was twisted into a loose arrangement. The combination somehow emphasized her fine ivory complexion, and for the first time Alasdair realized that the girl was not plain at all. Instead, she possessed an elegant, subtle beauty — and it was a *woman's* beauty, not a girl's. The knowledge was a tad unsettling.

"Do come in, Miss Hamilton," he managed, as the gentleman rose.

She sketched an awkward curtsey and led the child forward into the room. This morning, the little girl wore a lacy frock over pantaloons gathered at the ankle with blue ribbons. She toddled forward unhesitatingly, pointing and chortling at something beyond the window.

"Miss Hamilton, my brother, Merrick MacLachlan," said Alasdair. "And this is the Earl of Wynwood. They wish to see the child. Would you be so kind as to show her to my brother, please?"

Miss Hamilton looked both discomfited

and confused, but obediently, she led the child round the table to Merrick. Merrick shocked them all by kneeling down to study her. "What is her age, please?" he demanded.

"She's to be two in October," said Miss Hamilton, who had begun to nervously toy with the strand of pearls about her neck. It was a habit he'd noticed, but not registered, amidst all of last night's uproar.

Merrick was still studying the child's face. In response, the child blinked and put a hand on his knee as if she meant to crawl into his lap. *"Gee 'atch,"* she said, her plump fingers reaching for Merrick's watch chain. "Pretty 'atch. Pretty."

Coloring faintly, Miss Hamilton forgot her pearls and hastened to lift the child away. "No, no!" squalled Sorcha, thrashing against her sister's arms. "Gee 'atch, Mae! Gee 'atch!"

"Whisht, now," cooed Miss Hamilton, bouncing the child on her hip. "Be a good girl."

Merrick stood, his gaze snapping to his brother's. "I take it you wished me to see the bairn's eyes," he said coolly.

"Aye, I did," admitted Alasdair.

"It proves nothing," said Merrick.

"Does it not?" asked Alasdair. "Where

were *you,* dear brother, on Hogmanay two years past?"

"Alasdair, don't be a fool," said his brother dismissively. "It certainly isn't mine."

"Well, those eyes are a dashed odd color," remarked Quin. "All a bit unsettling when one considers what happened with that Gypsy yesterday."

"We shall discuss this another time," said Merrick, still looking at Alasdair.

"I think we'll discuss it now," said Alasdair. "They are MacGregor eyes, are they not? As cold and ice-blue as any I've ever seen."

"Pale blue eyes are not unheard of," said Merrick. "It could be anyone's babe."

"I wish," snapped Alasdair. "But that particular shade is extremely rare."

"Perhaps discretion is in order, old chap," said Quin, flicking a concerned glance at Miss Hamilton.

But Alasdair was intent on his brother. "Merrick, don't be an ass," he insisted. "I've no interest in taking responsibility for the child of some woman whom I can barely remember bedding, but —"

"Och, a bed, was it now?" snapped Miss Hamilton, cutting him off dead. "As I heard it, sir, there was no bed involved in doing

67

the deed! 'Twas just a quick pump-'n'-tickle behind the draperies at some drunken New Year's celebration!"

Merrick and Quin turned to gape.

"Miss Hamilton!" Alasdair began, as she clutched the child tighter. "I say!"

"No, I've heard quite enough blather out of you three!" Miss Hamilton's creamy complexion had turned fiery pink, and she was quivering with indignation. "You people have the manners of swine. And Sorcha is not an *it,* if you please! She is your *daughter,* and she has a *name.* And I'll thank you to use it — all of you." Suddenly, she turned on Merrick. "And you, Mr. MacLachlan! I do not care for your manner one whit! Rest assured Sorcha could not possibly be yours. Even my mother, starry-eyed fool that she was, couldn't have been seduced by a midge-brained maundrel with nothing which might remotely pass for charm."

On that note, Miss Hamilton whirled about and strode from the room with as much grace as she could muster given the toddler balanced on her hip. Lady Sorcha, however, was reluctant to go. She strained to lean out of her sister's embrace, opening and closing her little fist in Merrick's direction. "No, Mae, nooo!" she shrieked, flailing wildly. "Gee me 'atch! Gee 'atch!"

As soon as they had disappeared from view, Quin collapsed into his chair with a paroxysm of laugher. Alasdair turned to look at him. "I am so glad you enjoyed that."

"Oh, she's so callow!" Quin could barely stop laughing. "So innocent! Just a little wren of a girl! Oh, Alasdair, you are in for it now."

"What the devil do you mean?"

"It isn't enough that you've been cursed by a Gypsy," Quin returned. "You've just been stuck with a ball of fire — and a dashed pretty one, too, especially when she blushes. I begin to think your eyesight has gone the way of your appetite, old chap."

Esmée rushed through MacLachlan's town house, the fine carpets and elegant staircase nothing but a blur as she flew round the newel posts, holding Sorcha close to her side. Dear God in heaven. Could there have been a worse time to let her temper get hold of her tongue? At least her trunk was not yet unpacked. It would save everyone time and effort when her arse landed in the street again.

She reached the nursery and burst through the door, only to come face-to-face

69

with one of the footmen. The worn leather furniture was gone, and servants were clearing the last of the boxes from the shelves. "Your pardon, ma'am," said one of them stiffly. "Wellings said Sir Alasdair wished the room cleared out."

Cleared out was an apt description, thought Esmée, looking about the room. Nothing but an old Pembroke table and two wooden chairs remained. Even the stench of stale tobacco was waning. "Thank you," she said to the footman. "I don't suppose there is any more appropriate furniture to be had?"

"Of what sort?" The low, rumbling voice came from behind her.

Esmée spun round to see that Sir Alasdair MacLachlan had followed her into the room. Her heart leapt into her throat. "I — I beg your pardon?"

"What do you need, Miss Hamilton?" he said more gently. "I shall send Wellings to fetch it."

Panicked, Esmée searched her mind. "Well, a . . . a worktable, I suppose," she answered, setting Sorcha down. The child went at once to her toys.

"Yes, go on," he said. "What sort of worktable?"

He did not mean to throw them out

70

again? "Something low enough for Sorcha to use?" she managed. "With small chairs? And — and a child's bed, perhaps?"

MacLachlan smiled, his brown eyes warming. "Miss Hamilton, you are ending all your demands with question marks now," he remarked. "It is most uncharacteristic of you. And surely Sorcha requires more than a table and a bed?"

"Why, I — I daresay she does," said Esmée, cursing her own stupidity. What *did* children need? She had but recently learned how to feed the child. How to keep her from tumbling into the fire. How to induce her to nap — well, sometimes. "Perhaps a high chair and a rocking chair?" she continued, struggling to remember what Lord Achanalt's nursery had contained. "And one of those odd little buggies one sees in the parks?"

"Ah, a yes, perambulator!" he said. "And a bigger, thicker carpet, perhaps? Just in case she decides to throw a tantrum?"

Esmée felt her blush deepen. "She is a bit spirited, aye."

MacLachlan flashed his too-charming, toe-curling grin again. "Ah, the truth will out, won't it, my dear?" he said. "Now, what was it you said last night? Ah, yes! *'A good, quiet child! Not a drop of trouble to you, I swear it!'*"

71

Esmée looked away. " 'Tis just the travel, I'm sure. The — er, the disruption in her life."

The smile softened at once. "Ah, well," he returned. "Better a racehorse than a dray horse, I daresay."

The footman departed with the last box and gently pulled the door shut. MacLachlan strolled deeper into the room. He stopped before one of the windows and stared down into the street below. "You do not like me very much, do you, Miss Hamilton?" he finally said. "Indeed, I think it safe to say you quite loathe me."

Esmée opened and closed her mouth soundlessly for a moment. "I — I apologize for my behavior earlier," she whispered.

He made a strange choking sound. A stifled laugh? "You do have a dreadful temper," he managed. "I'm not sure Merrick will ever be quite the same again."

"I cannot think what took hold of me."

The devil, she expected him to say. But MacLachlan turned to face her. "We did behave badly," he admitted. "We are none of us boorish by nature, I assure you. And Quin is actually quite kind. It is just this situation. Even you must admit how odd it is."

"Odd?" asked Esmée. "From what I have seen of life, I am more surprised it does not happen with greater frequency."

"You must have lived an unusual life, Miss Hamilton."

Just then, Sorcha tugged on her skirts. "Mae, tee *off!*"

Esmée bent down to see that Sorcha had pulled her doll's dress over her head. "You must unfasten the hook first, sweet," she said, kneeling down to show the child. "Like this."

The job done to Sorcha's satisfaction, the child toddled back to her small collection of toys, which Esmée had arranged on a small rug by the empty bookshelves. She did not seem particularly interested in MacLachlan. That was probably a good thing.

"What is that she calls you?" he asked curiously.

Esmée shrugged. "Mae, or something like. She cannot yet get her tongue round *Esmée.*"

MacLachlan was watching Sorcha as a naturalist might study a new species of beetle. Looking at his firmly chiseled profile, Esmée was struck again by how handsome he was. Oh, there were the usual signs of dissipation about his mouth, and a hint of world-weariness about his eyes. He was well on his way to becoming a wicked, worn-out

73

rip, and around the edges, he looked it. She had noticed it last night, in a purely clinical way, as one might when summing up one's adversary.

But strangely, at the moment, he did not quite seem like her adversary. Indeed, he seemed almost as confused as she. Perhaps he was. Both their lives had been thrown into total chaos by her mother's sudden death. All that she knew of child rearing she'd learned quickly, and very recently. It was more than a little daunting.

Suddenly, Esmée realized Sorcha was lifting her hand to her mouth. She'd already learned that that was never a good thing. "Och!" she said, rushing forward to snatch the child. *"A h-uile nì thun a' bheòil!"*

MacLachlan followed on her heels. When she snatched up the child, he pried something shiny from Sorcha's wet fingers.

"Nooo!" wailed Sorcha. "Gee to me! To meee!"

"Well, well!" MacLachlan murmured, studying the shiny object. "My missing Roman solidus."

" 'Tis what?" Esmée leaned over Sorcha's head to stare at it. "Oh, an old coin?"

"Very old indeed," agreed MacLachlan, tucking it away. Esmée released the wiggling child. With one last glare at

MacLachlan, Sorcha returned to her doll.

"What was that you said to her?" he asked. "Something about her lips?"

"Her mouth." Esmée frowned. *Everything to the mouth.* 'Tis just an old expression. Faith, MacLachlan, have you no Gaelic?"

He shrugged. "I had a little once, I suppose." He bent over and patted Sorcha's head awkwardly, as if she were a beagle pup. Still, it was an attempt at affection, Esmée supposed.

"Esmée," he repeated, returning his gaze to her. "That is a somewhat fanciful name, is it not?"

"Aye, my mother was a fanciful person."

"So I gathered," said MacLachlan, drawing her away from Sorcha's corner. "Your stepfather sounds like an ogre. How did a fanciful woman end up in such an ill-fated marriage?"

Esmée thought it a strange question. "My mother was always accounted a great beauty," she explained. "And Achanalt collected beautiful things."

"Ah, I see."

Inexplicably, Esmée went on. "At first, Mamma thought it quite romantic to be pursued by an older, wealthier gentleman. Too late, she realized she was nothing but a possession."

75

"He did not love her?"

Esmée looked at him oddly. "I think he loved her too much," she finally answered. "That sort of all-encompassing love which turns cruel when thwarted."

"And did she thwart him?" murmured Alasdair.

"I think she liked to make him jealous," Esmée admitted. "Sometimes even angry."

"How so?"

She lifted her shoulders. "After they married, he did not continue to pursue her," she admitted. "He did not cater to her whims or court her, believing, I daresay, that she was already his property. Unfortunately, Mamma took that as a challenge. Matters soon . . . escalated."

"And you were caught in the middle?" he said musingly. "That cannot have been pleasant."

She dropped her gaze to the floor. "Do not fash yourself over me, MacLachlan," she answered. "Your concern should be for wee Sorcha."

MacLachlan hesitated a moment. "Tell me, does the child — Sorcha, I mean — does she understand?" he asked. "Does she realize her mother is . . . gone?"

Slowly, Esmée nodded. "Oh, aye, on some level. She has not asked for her since

76

we left Scotland." She hesitated a moment, then added, "Do you accept, then, that Sorcha is yours, sir? From your remarks in the dining room, I collect you do."

He surprised her then by crossing the room to Sorcha's rug, and kneeling. The child looked up, giggled, and thrust out her naked doll. "Doll, see?" she said. "Mae gee me. See it? See?"

"Yes, I do see," he agreed. "She is a lovely doll. Here, shall we put her dress back on?"

"Put 'ack on," Sorcha parroted.

Methodically, he picked up the doll's dress and began to pull it back over her head. The child giggled again as he poked the arms through, and struggled to fasten the tiny hook with his large fingers.

"May I help?" asked Esmée. "I fear that catching those tiny hooks is something of an acquired skill."

MacLachlan looked up from the floor, and crooked one brow. "I daresay," he murmured. "It seems all my skill has been acquired in an altogether opposite direction."

Esmée was still searching for a proper setdown when MacLachlan returned the doll to Sorcha. He slid a finger beneath her chin, and lifted her gaze to his. "Did you look, Miss Hamilton, at my brother, Merrick?" he asked musingly.

"Aye, that one was hard to miss."

MacLachlan tweaked Sorcha on the nose, stood, and returned to Esmée's side. "But did you really *look* at him?" he pressed. "His features, you see, come from my mother's side of the family."

"He has 'MacGregor eyes,' you said," she agreed. "But I confess, I did not look closely." He stood directly in front of her now. And close. Too close.

"Frankly, his eyes can be a little un-nerving," said MacLachlan, leaning in an-other inch. "Like a wolf, staring at you from the edge of a wood. Ice-cold. Smooth and flat." She could feel the heat radiating off his body. "Now, your eyes, Miss Hamilton are beautiful, too, but in an entirely conven-tional way," he went on. "They are a sort of cool jade green, with little flecks of brown which one cannot discern until one is standing quite close."

Esmée took a step backward. "Do not be absurd."

"Ah, I cannot help it," he said. "Life is so often absurd. Now, Miss Hamilton, look into my eyes and tell me what you see."

"Into your eyes?" she echoed sardoni-cally. "They are just ordinary eyes." *God, what a liar she was.* His eyes were the color of sunlit whisky, golden and beautiful, rimmed with black, and his dark fringe of lashes rivaled her own. "Really, MacLachlan, have you a point?"

Suddenly, he smiled, and the strange moment was broken. "Not really," he confessed. "Perhaps I was just fishing for a compliment."

"Your eyes are brown," she said flatly. "A fine, fair color, aye, but as you say, quite conventional."

"Indeed, Miss Hamilton." He gave her a muted smile. "My eyes are nothing at all like young Sorcha's, and yet . . ."

"And yet what?"

He shook his head, and tore his gaze from hers. "It cannot be a coincidence, can it?" he said, his voice suddenly low. "I have never seen eyes like that on another living person, save my grandfather and Merrick."

A horrifying thought struck her. "Surely you do not mean to suggest that . . . that your brother — ?"

At that, MacLachlan threw back his head and laughed. "Good Lord, no!" he roared. "My brother has scarce left London this last decade. Indeed, he has scarce left his bloody *desk.* And, as you so succinctly pointed out, he would never trouble himself to charm a woman. He does not thrill to the chase, Miss Hamilton, as some of us lesser mortals do. If he gets it, I daresay he simply pays for it."

Esmée made a sound of irritation. "Mind what you say in front of the child!"

He lost a little of his color. "My apologies, Miss Hamilton," he said at once. "My wicked ways are hard to repress. And I keep forgetting that you are little more than a child yourself."

"Och, MacLachlan!" She looked at him chidingly. "I am twenty-two years old."

"Good Lord! Are you?" The shock must have shown on his face.

"Oh, aye. And I feel forty."

He smiled faintly. "Well, I very nearly *am* forty, and I cannot even remember being twenty-two," he returned, stepping back. "I should go now, if she has everything she needs?"

Esmée opened her hands. "I hardly know."

He smiled again, and this time, the smile reached his whisky gold eyes, crinkling them just a bit at the corners. "Has she any toys beyond those scant few?" he asked, tilting his head toward Sorcha. "Perhaps a rocking horse and a few books would be in order?"

Esmée nodded. "Aye, books and toys would be wonderful," she admitted. "We had to leave most of our things behind."

MacLachlan nodded. The fleeting intimacy was gone. He had drawn away from her and retreated inside himself. Good. That was good. She let herself relax.

"I shall be out until quite late in the evening," he said. "Perhaps . . . even later than that. But Wellings will go up to the Strand for you. Should you think of anything further, I shall put it on my list for him."

"Thank you," she said, following him to the door.

On the threshold, he stopped suddenly. "By the way, I almost forgot." He dug into his pocket, extracted a plump fold of white paper, and pressed it into her palm. "Three hundred pounds. In advance. I thought you would prefer cash, flinty-hearted Scot that you are."

His hand was warm and oddly comforting. "Thank you," she said.

Slowly, his hand slid away from hers, and the warmth was gone. "Now tell me, Miss Hamilton, is that your insurance policy?" he asked quietly. "Just in case I should change my mind about taking care of Sorcha?"

She dropped her gaze and said nothing. He had guessed, then.

He pulled open the door, then hesitated. "Well, you shan't be needing it," he said.

"Though I'm sure only time will convince you." And with that, Sir Alasdair MacLachlan was gone.

Alasdair escaped the house as soon as his letter to Uncle Angus was dispatched. He had the foresight, however, to order a suit of evening clothes sent across town to his friend Julia's house, since he had promised to escort her to the theater that night, and he'd no intention of going home again anytime soon.

Indeed, as he walked to his club in St. James's, Alasdair toyed with the notion of simply moving in with Julia and leaving the house in Great Queen Street to his female interlopers. But that would not do. He needed to keep one eye on his new governess, and Julia wasn't fool enough to have him anyway. Moreover, the house in Bedford Place wasn't even Julia's. It belonged to her friend Sidonie Saint-Godard, who had recently married the Marquis of Devellyn. Julia was at odd ends, too, having lost her best friend to the lure of wedding bells, just as he had. That, in part, was what had thrown them together.

Alasdair lifted his gaze to see St. James's Park ahead. The sun was unusually bright today, and the neighborhood nannies were out in full force, stiff white aprons flapping in the breeze, perambulators at the ready. He took the shortest route across the park's expanse, but halfway along the path, a young girl with bouncing blond ringlets dashed out in front of him, her eyes intent on the pull toy she dragged behind.

"Whoa!" said Alasdair, stopping abruptly.

Startled, the child almost stumbled, but an astute servant swooped down and snatched the girl up. "Begging your pardon, sir," she said, her face flushed. "The child was not watching where she was going."

Embarrassed, the girl clutched her pull toy and buried her head against her nanny's neck. It was a touching, simple gesture. "No harm done, ma'am," he murmured, removing his hat. "What is her name, pray?"

The nanny's eyes widened. "Why, 'tis Penelope, sir."

Alasdair looked round the woman's shoulder. "Hello, Penelope. What have you there? Is it a dog?"

"A horse," said the child sulkily. "A brown horse."

"Has he a name?"

"Apollo," said the child.

The poor nanny looked bewildered. She clearly was not accustomed to striking up conversations in the park with gentlemen who appeared to be unattached and childless. Time for the angelic smile, then. Alasdair flashed it, and the nanny's eyes began to melt.

Feeling more himself again, Alasdair poured on the charm. "What a beautiful child," he said. "And she obviously adores you. It is quite touching, ma'am, to see how she clings to you. Have you been with her long?"

"Why, all of her days, sir," said the nanny. "And her brother before her."

She was shifting her weight as if she meant to walk away. Just then, Penelope began to squirm. The nanny set her down. "We'll just be off, sir," she said. "My apologies again."

Fully recovered, Penelope had dashed a few feet down the path, her horse spinning merrily behind her. "You are going in my direction," said Alasdair to the servant. "Might I walk a little way with you?"

She shot him an uncertain glance. "Yes, sir. I'm sure you may."

"I know very little of children," he confessed, setting a pace in keeping with young Penelope. "How old is your charge, ma'am?"

"Why, she'll be six near Christmastime, sir."

"Ah," said Alasdair. "She still seems quite small. Is she about the right size for her age?"

The woman seemed to fluff up like an outraged hen. "Why, even a bit tallish, really."

"Indeed?" he murmured. "Has she a governess yet?"

"Oh, to be sure, sir," said the nanny. "But 'tis generally my job to take the children for walks and such."

"I see," said Alasdair. "So a governess *and* a nurse?"

"Aye, sir," said the servant defensively. " 'Tis a great deal o' work raising a child."

Alasdair pondered that for a moment. "She speaks very well," he said. "At what age do they begin to speak fluently?"

"Mercy, sir, have you never been around children?"

Alasdair smiled again. "A disgraceful shortcoming, to be sure," he admitted. "I had a younger brother, but not by much."

"Well, by three they're generally chattering like magpies," said the servant. "Before that, there's lots of babbling, much of it known only to them."

They continued their sedate promenade round the park, Penelope and Apollo in the lead, Alasdair and the nanny behind. The woman was gregarious enough, and Alasdair took the opportunity to ask all manner of questions about the mysteries of child rearing. She looked askance at him from time to time, but answered his queries thoroughly enough. Near the foot of St. James's Street, he tipped his hat, thanked her, and set a swift pace up the street to White's.

He felt a bit like an idiot talking to a stranger — a servant — in the park. But he wanted to *know*, damn it. He needed to understand what was to come of this strange, unexpected turn his well-ordered life had just taken. And for reasons he could not quite explain, he did not want to ask Miss Hamilton. She was not the enemy. No, not precisely. But already, it seemed as if she held the key to some important secret. Something held tantalizingly just beyond his reach.

This morning, he'd felt like a stranger in his own home. His smoking room was gone, his billiard table was shortly to follow, and in their place he was to have *females*, one of them very small and willful, and the other disconcertingly pretty, with eloquent all-seeing eyes, and the scent of the Highlands still clinging in her hair. Yes, better to be thought an idiot here, with a woman he did not know, than in his own home in front of his little spitfire of a governess and his own . . . *child.*

Good God! There it was again. Reality, intruding on what otherwise would have been a trouble-free life of ease and debauchery. Alasdair tucked his hat down to hide the mortification in his eyes and hastened his step toward the sheltering portals of White's. One little sin, and now all this! It really was too much to absorb in one day.

It was early afternoon by the time Esmée decided what her next step ought to be. Swiftly, she dug through their trunk and extracted Sorcha's walking shoes. She looked at them and sighed. Regrettably, the little leather boots were not as tidy as one would wish.

"Come along, my wee trootie," she said, hefting the child to her hip. "I'll no' have you looking like a dirty little jaudie out amongst these fancy English."

Together, they went belowstairs, Sorcha jabbering merrily about everything she saw along the way. On the last landing, she saw an oriental vase she took a sudden liking to. But when thwarted, she went rigid and began flailing and squealing, "Gee! Gee me!" at the top of her lungs.

Somehow, Esmée soothed her, but at the butler's pantry, Sorcha began to squirm to be put down. Her hands full, Esmée bumped the door open with her hip and started through. Unfortunately, she did not see MacLachlan's valet coming in the opposite direction. The swinging door cracked him hard across the elbow, resulting in a muffled curse.

"Och, what have I done!" said Esmée, hastening on through. A pile of cravats and a puddle of black wool lay scattered across the floor. "Oh, Mr. Ettrick! Do forgive me."

"Really, Miss Hamilton!" said the testy valet, seizing the trousers. "I just this instant finished brushing that set of clothes!"

Esmée had put Sorcha down, and was on her knees, trying to salvage the freshly starched cravats. "I am so sorry," she said, swiftly gathering them. "My hands were full. I did not see you."

Esmée stood, and laid the stack of cravats on the brushing table. Ettrick was shaking out the coat now, a lovely garment which looked to be made of premium superfine. "Well, I daresay there's little harm done," he said, picking a piece of lint from the hem. "Just a speck or two. Hawes, look sharp, man!" he called across the room to one of the footmen.

The footman looked up from his work at the opposite end of the long table. "What is it now, Ettrick?" asked Hawes irritably. "I've these boots to finish, haven't I?"

Ettrick shook the coat at him. "Sir Alasdair wants this delivered to Mrs. Crosby's house," he said. "Have it there by four or else."

"Oh, aye, I've nothing better to do than run all the way to Bloomsbury!" complained the footman.

"No, you've nothing better." Ettrick smiled sourly and hung the coat on a hook at the footman's end of the table. "And for pity's sake, Hawes, put a muslin sleeve over it this time."

Ettrick returned to the table and began inspecting the cravats. With one eye on Sorcha, Esmée picked up one of the many shoe brushes. Curiosity got the better of her. "Who is Mrs. Crosby, Mr. Ettrick?"

At the distant end of the table, the footman sputtered. Ettrick gave a weary sigh. "Mrs. Crosby is Sir Alasdair's particular friend."

"Aye, one of 'em!" interjected the footman. "You might as well tell the chit plainly, Ettrick, if she's to live here. Mrs. Crosby is an actress, and one of his mistresses. But you daren't say so past these walls."

Ettrick shot the footman a quelling look, but said no more. Hastily, Esmée cleaned Sorcha's shoes and made a retreat to the nursery.

A particular friend. *One of them,* the footman had said. So how many such "particular friends" would a man like MacLachlan have? He probably couldn't keep count. Obviously, he couldn't remember them all, which proved once again what a fool her mother had been to fall for his charms. And there lay a warning worth heeding where MacLachlan and his charms were concerned. His brown eyes melted, aye. But for anyone wearing skirts, most likely.

Exasperated with her line of thinking, Esmée forced the matter from her mind. She dressed Sorcha in a light pelisse and hat, put on her freshly cleaned boots, then informed Wellings that they were going out for a walk. Esmée was not at all sure what an English governess's duties were, but apparently taking one's charge for a stroll was one of them, for Wellings never lifted a brow.

"Go out!" said Sorcha, as Esmée carried her down the last flight of stairs. "Out, Mae! Me go out now!"

Wellings smiled indulgently at the child. "She knows her own mind, does she not?"

Esmée nodded. "Yes, and everyone else must know it, too," she muttered, putting the squirming child down so that she might fasten her own pelisse. "Can you tell me, Wellings, which way Mayfair would be? I confess, I became quite turned about in finding this place."

"We are rather off the beaten path, miss," he said, then gave her directions. Esmée realized at once it was too far for Sorcha to walk. But she dared not hire a hackney, and the perambulator had not come, so she set off, following the route the butler had given her. She would simply have to carry Sorcha when the child tired.

The air was blessedly cool and scented with rain. After crossing what seemed to Esmée like an almost frivolous expanse of parks, she reached the edge of Mayfair and soon felt more acquainted with her surroundings. She had been here twice before, and the elegant Georgian homes were starting to look all too familiar.

With Sorcha balanced on one hip and the old blisters on her feet rubbed nearly raw, she set off up the hill in the direction of Grosvenor Square. She had suffered a long, hard week on the road, followed by a disheartening two days in London, and already Esmée was beginning to hate England and everything in it. The only good to come of it, if one could call it that, had been Sir Alasdair MacLachlan. Still, she was quite sure she had no business living with the man and pretending to be her own sister's governess. Mamma would have scolded her soundly for such shocking behavior — though the irony of that fact was not lost on Esmée.

There would surely be talk when polite society learned that the wicked Sir Alasdair had suddenly acquired a ward. Esmée had thought to keep a low profile, but this morning's foray into the dining room had underscored the fact that she was, quite suddenly and unexpectedly, at the beck and call of another. She was a *servant.* Not even in her stepfather's home had Esmée been treated so condescendingly. Her palm still itched to slap Sir Alasdair's brother through the face. Lord Wynwood, at least, had been sympathetic. She had not missed the reproachful look he'd tossed in Merrick MacLachlan's direction.

Slightly out of breath now, Esmée had reached the glossy green door she sought and paused to shift Sorcha to the other hip. "Geen, Mae," she said pointing at the door. "Geen. See?"

Yes. Green. Just as it had been for the last

two days. And just as it had been for the past two days, the knocker was down. But Esmée had not walked so far for nothing. She stepped up, and hammered her knuckles on the solid wood slab. She could hear the sound echoing hollowly through the house.

"Damn and blast," she whispered.

"Damin bass," said Sorcha, mimicking Esmée's glower.

Oh, lud! Time to watch her language. "Aye, 'tis a very wicked door, is it not, wee Sorcha?" said Esmée, planting a loud, smacking kiss on the child's cheek. "Why does it never open for us?"

Just then a glossy red-and-black landau came rattling up the street, stopping at the house adjacent. A thin, dark man got out and barked at his driver to take the carriage round to the mews. The coach rolled away, and turned onto Charles Street. Intrigued, Esmée followed. A few yards down the hill, the coachman cut his horses to the right and turned into an alley. Esmée did the same.

Cleaving between the high brick walls, the unmarked lane was shadowy and cool. Esmée kept walking, counting off the houses as she went. The landau had stopped just a few yards in, and the coachman had leapt down to speak with a woman who stood on the pavement with a market basket swinging from her arm. Casting caution to the wind, Esmée rushed toward them. They noticed her at the same time, and turned toward her.

"I beg your pardon," said Esmée breathlessly. "Do you live here?"

"Aye, to be sure." The woman looked her up and down, clearly wondering why Esmée was calling in the yard rather than in the square.

Esmée shifted Sorcha to her other hip. "Can you tell me please if Lady Tatton still lives in the house next door?" she asked the woman breathlessly. "The knocker is down, you see, and —"

"Oh, yes!" said the woman. "Gone off to Australia, she has."

A sense of relief flooded through Esmée. "Thank heavens," she whispered. "I'd not heard from her in ever so long. Are there no servants in the house?"

Clearly certain he had nothing helpful to add, the coachman climbed back up and clicked to his horses. "There be but the Finches, the couple that look after the house," said the woman with the basket. "But Bess — that's Mrs. Finch — her mother fell ill in Deptford, and they went down Tuesday last."

"Oh," said Esmée, sagging with disappointment.

The woman took in Esmée's attire again. "Would you be wanting her ladyship, then?" she asked. "For so far as I know, she's not expected anytime soon, or not as Bess has mentioned to me, which I daresay she would have done."

"I — yes, I was looking for her," Esmée admitted. "But I have not seen her in some years."

"Aye, she went out with her daughter who was in a delicate way," said the woman. "Then the babe was sickly. Then came a set o' twins. And then, as Bess says, one thing led to another as such things will do, aye? But since she hasn't given up the house, she must surely mean to return."

On her hip, Sorcha was starting to squirm. "Abble, Mae!" she shrieked. "Gee abble!"

The woman took an apple from the basket, and held it out. "What a pretty little thing she is," she said, breaking into a smile. "And such rare blue eyes! Is this what you want, child?"

Sorcha squealed with glee, opening and closing her fingers as she had done earlier in the morning when she'd set her sights on Merrick MacLachlan's watch.

"Thank you, but you needn't," said Esmée. "She does not need it, truly."

"Oh, let her have it, do," said the servant, surrendering the red fruit into Sorcha's greedy little hands. "I just came up from Shepherd's Market, so 'tis fresh."

Unwilling to risk Sorcha's temper, Esmée thanked her. The woman smiled at Sorcha. "Such a pretty babe!" she went on. "Now, about Lady Tatton. I could pass on a word to Bess, if you'd wish?"

Esmée widened her eyes. "A letter," she said hastily. "I've a letter for Lady Tatton. Would you be so kind?"

The woman looked sympathetic. "Aye, I'll give it to Bess, ma'am, but so far as I know . . ."

"Yes, yes, I understand," said Esmée. "She is not expected. But will you ask Mrs. Finch to hold it for her? No matter when she might return?"

The woman took the letter Esmée dug from her pocket. "I daresay she could forward it, if you wish?"

Esmée shook her head. "That will take months, and I've already sent two, though I wonder if they got there at all."

The woman nodded sympathetically and returned her attention to Sorcha, who had already sunk her tiny teeth into the apple's

96

tender flesh. "Ah, such eyes!" she said
again. Then she smiled at Esmée knowingly. "From her father's side, I'm
guessing?"

"Oh, aye," said Esmée a little wearily.
"Definitely. From her father's side."

Chapter Three

In which Miss Hamilton is Taught
a lesson

Alasdair listened to the sound of Julia's breathing, soft and regular in the night as it had been for the last several hours. He found it a pleasant, soothing sound. Sleep had not come to him so easily. Restless, he had left the bed and moved to the chaise by the windows so as not to disturb her. He was staring down into Bedford Place and watching a blue-uniformed policeman pace sedately through the gaslight when suddenly, Julia's breath hitched.

"Alasdair?" she murmured, rolling up onto one elbow. "Alasdair, what is the time?"

"About four, I daresay," he responded absently. "Did I wake you, my dear?"

Julia rose, sliding into her wrapper as she crossed the room toward him. "What's wrong, Alasdair?" she asked. "You usually sleep the sleep of the innocent."

He laughed. "God has finally rectified

that error," he answered. "I've been up half the night."

"I'm sorry," she said. "Heavens, you're smoking. Rather early for that, is it not?"

"Or rather late, depending upon one's viewpoint." He caught her hand and drew her down beside him on the chaise. "I'm sorry, Julia. Shall I put it out?"

"You know you needn't." She pulled her legs up and tucked her wrapper around her toes. Julia was plump, pretty, and good-tempered, and Alasdair had enjoyed every minute he had spent in her company since meeting her some months earlier.

"Did you enjoy the play, my dear?" He rolled the ash off the end of his cheroot. "I thought your friend Henrietta Wheeler was magnificent."

"Pish, Alasdair!" said Julia. "You never even noticed her."

"What, when we went particularly to see her?"

Julia laid a hand on his cheek. "Quick, then, which character did she play?"

In the moonlight, he could not hide his chagrined expression. "I — oh, you are right, Julia," he admitted. "I fear my mind was elsewhere."

Julia shrugged amicably. "It does not signify," she answered. "But listen, dear boy.

Before you slip out into the night, I have something I wish to tell you."

Alasdair gave up and stubbed the cheroot out. He had taken a sudden dislike to it. "I have something to tell you, too, Julia. Please, let me go first and get it over with."

"Oh, God, I've been expecting this!" Julia's voice was tinged with wry humor. "What is her name? No doubt she is half my age *and* half my weight."

Alasdair grinned. "Not even a fraction of either, I'm afraid," he admitted. "And her name is Sorcha."

"Ah, a Scot, then!" said Julia. "Well done, my boy. Stick with your own kind, I always say. Now tell me, how long have you known your Sorcha?"

Dawn was flirting with the rooftops along Bedford Place by the time Alasdair finished answering *that* question. Early in his narrative, Julia had wisely gone to her side table and poured him a glass of his favorite whisky, which she always kept at hand. By the time his tale was told, she was pouring one for herself.

"Good Lord!" she whispered, turning from the table. "You really do think — ?"

Alasdair propped his forehead in one hand. "Julia, I have just the vaguest of memories," he said. "Memories of having done something I knew I would regret in the morning, if you know what I mean."

"Oh, too well!" she said sympathetically. "But Alasdair, you do so many wicked things, it could have been something else altogether."

He shook his head. "The child is the very image of my brother Merrick."

Julia made a clucking sound. "And this young woman, the sister. What of her?"

Alasdair groaned. "She is little more than a child herself."

"Indeed? How old?"

"Oh, seventeen perhaps? No, wait. Twenty-two, she said."

Julia laughed. "Heavens, Alasdair! She is a grown woman!"

"Hardly. The chit wouldn't weigh seven stone were she soaked to the skin, and she's as green as a girl from the Highlands could possibly be."

Julia shrugged. "My dear boy, by the time I was twenty-two I'd buried one husband and cast off two protectors," she said. "And as to naïveté, appearances can be deceiving. Now, I really must say my piece, Alasdair."

Alasdair waved his glass. "By all means. My life could scarce be more confusing."

But he was to be proven wrong on that score. Julia sat up very straight, set aside her whisky, and folded her hands in her lap rather primly. "This is quite shocking news, my boy," she warned. "You are not old enough to have an apoplexy are you?"

Alasdair scowled. "I am six-and-thirty, as you well know. Out with it."

Julia leaned across to kiss his cheek. "Alasdair, my dear —" She paused and drew an unsteady breath. "— I am . . . *enceinte*."

Alasdair dropped his glass. It landed on the carpet with a soft thud. "Oh, God, Julia." He squeezed his eyes shut. "You cannot possibly mean this. *No*. Have mercy."

She laid her warm hand on his knee. "I am not jesting, love," she said quietly. "I am stunned, of course, and my physician is still abed, recovering from the shock. But Alasdair, the babe is not yours."

He made some sort of choking sound and opened one eye. "Not . . . *mine?*"

Julia frowned at him. "Alasdair, my dear, we promised one another nothing save friendship," she answered. "Indeed, we go weeks without even seeing one another. Have *you* been faithful to me?"

He cleared his throat roughly. "I — well, I would have to say . . . that I am not perfectly . . ."

The grip on his knee tightened. "Alasdair, let me be blunt," Julia interjected. "I know all about Inga Karlsson and her little flat in Long Acre."

"Come, Julia! It was just a loan! I swear to God. We are just friends."

"As we are just friends?" she suggested slyly. "And we won't even talk about Lord Feald's wife. Or that tavern maid in Wapping. Or that French dancer. I know you can't help it. I know women adore you. Indeed, I don't know why you trouble yourself to hide any of it from me."

Alasdair swallowed. "I don't hide it," he lied.

Julia laughed. "You *do* hide it, my dear," she said. "You prevaricate reflexively, like some eight-year-old scamp when one asks him what he is doing, and in his first breath he says, 'Why, nothing at all!' And says it with such charm and innocence, one knows immediately he is up to some sort of wickedness."

"It just never crossed my mind, that is all," he swore. "How could I even think of Inga when I am with you?"

"Because Inga is blond, buxom, beautiful, and so thin she slinks like a cat when she walks?" Julia suggested. "Besides, she's at least two decades younger than I."

"I rarely go for that sort," said Alasdair truthfully. "Besides, Julia, what we have is something . . . special."

"Yes, I'm old enough to be your mother," she said dryly. "That's frightfully special."

He seized her by the arm. "You certainly are not," he responded. Then he looked at her with grave concern. "But you are a little old, Julia, to be with child. Good Lord. Who is the father? What are you going to do?"

"Pray," she said with a muted smile. "And the father is Henrietta's brother. We have been dear friends for twenty years, you know."

"Edward Wheeler, the playwright?" Alasdair looked askance at her. "Do you love him, Julia?"

She laughed, a light, tinkling sound. "Lud, what a question, coming from you! I respect and adore him." She set a hand on her abdomen. "And I want this child, Alasdair, if there is any way possible."

"Do you mean to marry him, Julia?" He scowled at her. "You should, you know."

Again, she laughed. "Oh, Alasdair!" she said. "What kind of rakehell *are* you? I begin to think you are not quite as advertised!"

"Don't tease, Julia. This is serious."

Her face fell. "I know," she said. "And I

do not know what I shall do. I've told Edward, of course. We are in quite a quandary. It would be terrible at our ages to rush to the altar, when my chances of carrying the child to term are . . . well, not good."

"God, Julia. I wish you all the best, of course."

She smiled a little sadly. "Another year or two, and it would have been quite impossible," she said. "Indeed, I thought it was something else altogether until the morning sickness struck."

Alasdair knew what she was getting at. Julia was forty if she was a day, probably more — possibly a *lot* more. She was a former actress, and knew how to disguise the signs. But with child? He was more than a little worried. "He will do the right thing?" Alasdair demanded. "Wheeler, I mean?"

"I think so," she said. "He's still in a state of shock. But I want the child, regardless."

He stood and kissed her hand. "You need a husband, Julia. I mean to insist on it."

She looked up at him with damp eyes. "Yes, you are probably right," she answered. "I will think on it, my dear."

"Do you wish me to have a little chat with Wheeler? By God, I will, and gladly."

Julia blanched. "Good Lord, no! What I am trying to say, Alasdair, is that we cannot continue to see one another at all." She dropped her voice to a whisper. "It would feel wrong, somehow, don't you see? So tonight was — well, just for *auld lang syne,* as you Scots might say."

Alasdair had reached for his shirt, and was pulling it on over his head. "So it's good-bye, then?" he said teasingly. "After all we have been to one another, I'm to be cast off like an old shoe, without a second thought?"

Julia's smile began to return. "Well, that would look a bit odd, wouldn't it? Since everyone knows we are dear friends."

Alasdair kissed her nose. "Dashed odd, old thing."

Her eyes sparkled again. "No, no, Alasdair, I could never completely cast you off," she said. "I just won't go to bed with you again."

"Ah, now *that,*" he said regretfully, "is a true loss!"

Esmée was standing at the schoolroom window, and staring down into Great Queen Street when she saw Sir Alasdair MacLachlan crawl gingerly out of a hackney cab and make his way up the steps. Though Esmée had taken breakfast some four hours earlier, MacLachlan was still wearing the evening clothes Ettrick had been brushing yesterday. Out all night, then — and God only knew where he'd left his other clothes. Well, she had suspected as much. All day yesterday, she had sensed his absence in the house. The strange feeling had carried into the night.

"Ma'am?"

She spun away from the window to see one of the footmen standing behind her.

"Where do you wish these?" The wooden chairs were so small, he held one in each hand.

Esmée's eyes widened. "Are there more?" The footmen had been carrying in furniture for the last hour.

"Yes, ma'am," said the footman. "Ten in total."

Ten chairs? "But that is wasteful," said Esmée. "What was Wellings thinking?"

"I'm sure I couldn't say, ma'am."

Esmée just shook her head. "Put them round the table with the other four," she said. "Then set the others against the wall, I suppose?"

And there was another problem. Just as MacLachlan had claimed, everything she said was beginning to come out sounding like a question. She knew how to be a lady, and give polite instructions to the servants.

But it was another thing altogether to be one of them, or almost one of them. The truth was, she was neither fish nor fowl in this very English house, she considered, turning back to the window. If there was anything Scottish about Sir Alasdair MacLachlan save his fondness for whisky, it had long ago vanished. A pity, that.

Just then, there was a sound at the open door. She turned again to see Wellings inspecting the furniture. "Is everything satisfactory, ma'am?" he asked.

"Aye, thank you." She motioned toward the nursery door, which was slightly ajar. "Sorcha is already napping in the little bed. But why so many chairs?"

Wellings lifted his brows. "I've no notion, ma'am," he replied. "Sir Alasdair decided to do the shopping himself yesterday afternoon. I suppose he wished to purchase everything the child might possibly need."

"I see." They did fit the room very nicely, Esmée secretly admitted. But it seemed extravagant, something no good Scot would condone. Perhaps MacLachlan was expecting a crowd. Perhaps he had a whole regiment of illegitimate children dotting London's landscape.

Wellings made a little bow. "Sir Alasdair asks that you join him for coffee in his study," he added. "In half an hour, if that suits?"

"I fear I cannot," Esmée answered. "Sorcha might awaken and —"

"Sir Alasdair says Lydia is to come up," he interjected.

Esmée had already met Lydia, the fresh-faced girl who brought up their tea and turned down their beds. Still, Esmée was surprised MacLachlan had troubled himself to anticipate their needs.

"Lydia is the eldest of eight," said the butler reassuringly. "She is extremely skilled with children."

Something inside her shriveled a little at that. Lydia could scarcely be less qualified than Esmée, could she? Perhaps Wellings already suspected his master had hired a fraud. Perhaps if she had not agreed to stay, Sorcha would have been given into the care of someone who knew what to do. Someone who was actually qualified to raise her. Until rather recently, Esmée had done little more than romp and play with her sister. It seemed such a luxury now. And a lifetime ago.

"Miss Hamilton?" said the butler. "The coffee?"

Her head jerked up. "Aye, then," she said. "In half an hour."

Lydia soon appeared with a basket of darning to occupy her time. Esmée went into her room to tidy herself. As she did so, she caught her reflection in the looking glass which hung above the washbasin. Two wide-set green eyes under dark, arching brows looked back. They were, she knew, her mother's eyes, and her finest feature.

Esmée had often been told she resembled her mother, but the thought frightened rather than comforted her — especially when she was around men like MacLachlan, and felt her pulse ratcheting wildly up. But her mother's hair had been a rich chestnut, whilst Esmée's hair was a nondescript brown, so fine and heavy it was forever slipping from its arrangement. Her nose was . . . just a nose, her chin just a chin, unlike her mother, whose features had been perfect in very way. Esmée had no charming tip-tilt or dimple or cleft to catch the eye.

Suddenly, she jerked back from the mirror. Good heavens, what a time to fret over her looks! Despite her slight stature and exasperatingly youthful appearance, she was of an age that put one firmly on the shelf, and that was not apt to change. Perhaps there had been a time when she had longed for a season in London. But her mother's marriages had taken them from one isolated estate to another, each deeper in the Highlands than the last, it seemed.

Although Lord Achanalt never invited Esmée to accompany them on their frequent travels, once or twice a year, Esmée's mother would take her to Inverness or Edinburgh to shop. And of course there had been houseguests and dinner parties. Until Achanalt put a stop to it, her mother had possessed a coterie of admirers, for she loved to make her husband jealous. But when Esmée finally began to press for more, her mother's bottom lip would always come out.

"Wait," she would say. "Wait until Aunt Rowena returns from abroad. Then you shall have a proper season, my love, I promise you."

I promise you.

But after burying three husbands too young, her mother had developed an entrenched fear of being alone. Esmée realized now she'd been the only constant in her mother's life. Achanalt, whom her mother had married when Esmée was sixteen, had quickly become dour and withdrawn. Within two years of the happy nuptials, the word *divorce* was already rumbling round the old castle.

"Aye, like a tomcat after his own tail, he

was," she'd once heard their head gardener cackle. "The auld de'il didna know what to do w' her once he had hold of her, and 'twas not near sae much fun as the chase." Which more or less summed up the whole of Lord and Lady Achanalt's romance.

Well, the "auld de'il" had never borne Esmée's presence with much grace. She had been strangely, perhaps foolishly, relieved when he'd put them out. Panic was a luxury she could ill afford, given the responsibility Achanalt had suddenly thrust upon her. Certainly she could not panic now. She simply would not allow herself to be unsettled by Alasdair MacLachlan, no matter how charismatic or handsome he was. And that thought reminded her that she was dawdling. Quickly, Esmée repinned her hair, and hastened down the stairs.

She found MacLachlan in his study as expected. He had changed into a dark green coat over a waistcoat of straw-colored silk and snug brown trousers. His starched cravat was elegantly tied beneath his square, freshly shaved chin. Indeed, he looked breathtakingly handsome, and his ability to do so after a night of debauchery somehow annoyed her. He ought, at the very least, to have the decency to look a little green about the gills.

Surprisingly, MacLachlan sat not by the coffee tray, but at his desk, his posture no longer loose and languid. Instead, he sat bolt upright, like a bird dog on point, fervent and focused. If he were suffering any ill effects from his night on the town with Mrs. Crosby, one certainly could not now discern it.

Upon coming farther into the room, she realized he was not working. Instead, he was intent on some sort of card game, his heavy gold hair falling forward, obscuring his eyes. Suddenly, with a muttered curse, he swept up the cards, then shuffled them deftly through his fingers in one seamless motion. He shuffled again, his every aspect focused on the cards, as if they were an extension of hands, which were long-fingered and elegant. And surprisingly quick.

She approached the desk, sensing the very moment when he recognized her presence. At once, he set the pack away and looked at her, something in his gaze shifting. It was as if she'd awakened him from a dream. He stood, and in an instant, the lazy, somnolent look returned to his eyes.

"Good morning, Miss Hamilton," he said. "Do sit down."

She moved to the seat he had indicated, a delicately inlaid Sheraton chair opposite the tea table. This room was beautifully decorated in shades of pale blue and cream. The blue silk wall coverings were accented by floor-to-ceiling pier glasses between the windows, and the creamy carpet felt thick beneath her feet. A footman carried in a small coffee tray and set it on the far end of the tea table. MacLachlan asked her to pour. The coffee was very strong, and rich, reminding her, strangely, of black velvet.

"Wellings tells me you took the child out for a stroll yesterday," he said. "I hope you both enjoyed it?"

For some reason, she did not wish to tell him about her visit to her aunt Rowena's. Perhaps because it made her look desperate and a little foolish. "London is a large place," she murmured. "But we had a pleasant outing."

"How far did you go?"

"Why, to Mayfair, I believe."

"A fine part of town," he remarked. "But I have always preferred the tranquility of this little neighborhood."

"Aye, 'tis much nicer here." Esmée sipped gingerly from her hot coffee. "Tell me, do you play at cards regularly, MacLachlan?"

There was a cynical look about his eyes today, and it made her a little wary. "I think you know I do, Miss Hamilton," he said in his low, husky voice. "How is it, by the way, that you keep making me feel as if I am still back in Argyllshire? I wonder you don't put an imperious 'the' before my name — *The* MacLachlan — as if I am the only one."

"To your clan, perhaps you are," she answered simply.

His eyes hardened. "I have no clan, Miss Hamilton," he said. "I have lands, yes, though nothing one would wish to boast about. My grandfather fought against the Jacobites, and for his service, he was tossed a bone, in the form of a baronetcy, by the King."

"Of England."

"I beg your pardon?"

"He was given a baronetcy by the King *of England.*"

MacLachlan lifted one brow. "A dyed-in-the-wool Highlander, are you?"

"Aye, and I dinna ken there was any other kind," she said in a thick burr.

He laughed. "So tell me, Miss Hamilton, are you one of those treasonous holdouts still toasting 'the king over the water'?" he asked. "Am I harboring a secret Jacobite?"

Esmée smiled faintly. "Perhaps you are harboring a stickler for historical accuracy," she suggested. "Do you wish me to call you Sir Alasdair?"

He shrugged, and began to stir his coffee with the same slow, languorous motions he seemed to use for everything else in life. Everything save his card playing. "I don't think I care," he finally admitted. "Call me what you wish. I am not a stickler for any sort of accuracy at all."

"I don't entirely believe that," she said. "I think you are a very accurate sort of cardplayer."

He looked up from his coffee and smiled thinly. "I collect you think little of my talent," he murmured. "But when carefully honed, Miss Hamilton, card playing is a skill by which an impecunious young Scot can make his way in this world."

"Aye, sair sarkless, were you?" She let her gaze drift to his elegantly cut coat, which had probably cost more than half her wardrobe.

"No, never quite that." His eyes glittered a little dangerously. "But now I am, as you recently reminded me, *a very rich gentleman.* And I can assure you I did not get that way by living off my tenant farms."

"Perhaps you got it by means of other people's weaknesses," she suggested. "Games of chance are inherently unfair."

"I don't care a jot about another man's weakness, Miss Hamilton, if he is fool enough to sit down at the table with me," he replied evenly. "And nothing is left to chance when I play. It is strictly a matter of probability and statistics — something so real and so tangible, it can be calculated on the back of an old newspaper."

"How ridiculous that sounds!" she returned. "You are just trying to paint up a vice as a virtue. Everyone knows card playing is a matter of luck."

"Do they indeed?" He reached behind him for his pack of cards. With an artful flourish, he fanned it across the tea table. "Pick a card, Miss Hamilton. Any card."

She scowled across the table at him. "This isn't a village fair, my lord."

"Are you afraid, Miss Hamilton, that despite your vast and worldly experience, you just might, for once, be wrong about something?"

She snatched a card.

"Excellent," he said. "Now, Miss Hamilton, you are holding a card —"

"How astute you are, MacLachlan."

Tension was suddenly thick in the room. "— A card which is either black or red," he went on. "It has a fifty-fifty chance of being either, does it not?"

117

"Yes, but that is hardly a matter of science."

"Actually, it is," he said. "And there is, of course, yet another variable."

"I should have imagined there were fifty-two variables."

The brow went up again. "Work with me, Miss Hamilton," he said. "The card you are holding is either an ace, a face card or a numbered card. At present, with fifty-one cards still facedown on the table, the probability of your holding an ace is four out of fifty-two. Not, admittedly, the best of odds."

"As I said, a game of chance."

He held up one finger. "And the probability that it is a face card is twelve out of fifty-two, is it not?"

"Well, yes."

"And the probability that it is a numbered card is thirty-six out of fifty-two, correct?"

"I daresay."

"Then I believe, Miss Hamilton, that you are holding a numbered card. That is a distinct probability, you see. And I shall venture to say, more specifically, that it is a red card."

Esmée looked at her card and blanched.

"May I see it, please?"

Reluctantly, she laid down the eight of

118

diamonds. "Still, it was just a lucky guess," she complained.

"The first supposition was not," he countered. "But the latter was. And that, Miss Hamilton, is the difference between probability and luck. Now, place your card facedown, and take another."

"This is absurd." But she did as he asked.

"Now, Miss Hamilton, you have just altered the probability," he said, his gaze locked with hers. "We now have but fifty-one cards, for your red eight is out of play."

At his insistence, they repeated the process a dozen times. On four of them, Sir Alasdair was wrong. Esmée tried to gloat, but regrettably, his accuracy improved with play, and after each card was laid aside, he would recite the new probabilities. Red versus black. Faces versus numbers. Soon, he was able to guess not just the color and style, but soon the suit, and eventually the number.

Esmée's head was swimming. But what was worse, no matter what was drawn, Sir Alasdair seemed to recall precisely what had been played, and knew, therefore, what remained. She thought of the pile of arcane, unreadable books she'd found in the smoking parlor. It galled her to admit that he must have read — and comprehended — every blasted one.

When he had guessed four cards in succession correctly, Esmée gave up. "This is all perfectly silly," she said, tossing aside her last card. "Surely, sir, you did not call me down here for a card game?"

He lifted one broad shoulder and swept up the deck with the opposite hand. "It was you, Miss Hamilton, who disparaged my means of making a living," he said calmly. "I am merely defending my honor against your cruel and scurrilous accusations."

Esmée laughed. "Surely you do not *live* by your wits?"

"You think I have none?" he challenged.

She hesitated. "I did not say that."

"But you did once suggest that I am little more than a — now, let me see — yes, *a pretty face,* was it not?"

"I suggested no such thing," she said, then realized she'd just lied. "Nonetheless, card playing is hardly an intellectual endeavor."

"Have you ever played *vingt-et-un,* Miss Hamilton?" he asked darkly. "Go back upstairs and get that three hundred pounds out of your inkpot or your hatbox or wherever it is you have secreted it if you are so sure, and let us put your high-minded assumptions to the test."

Esmée opened her mouth, then closed it again. With his golden good looks and raspy bedroom voice, MacLachlan was the very devil — worse, a devil who looked like an angel — and she had no doubt he would strip her of every ha'penny just to make his point. "No, thank you," she said. "I do not gamble."

"You gambled rather boldly, Miss Hamilton, when you came all the way to London with that child in tow."

"She is not *that child*," said Esmée. "She is —"

"Yes, yes," he interjected, waving his hand in obviation. "She is Sorcha. I recall it. Give me time, Miss Hamilton, to adjust to this vast change in my life."

They drank their coffee in silence for several moments, Esmée searching for some neutral topic, and finding none. "How is she?" he finally asked. "Sorcha. She is settling in well?"

"Oh, aye," said Esmée. "She's a resilient child."

"What do you mean?"

Esmée opened her hands expressively. " 'Tis hard to explain," she said. "But Sorcha is strong-willed, and she possesses a — well, a sort of trust in her own ability to charm everyone around her and get what she wants."

Suddenly, Sir Alasdair smiled, deepening the dimples on both sides of his too-handsome face. *"Hmm,"* he said. "I wonder where she got that?"

Esmée looked at him over her coffee cup. "Now that I think on it, sir, I'm afraid the poor child may have gotten a double dose."

"Ah." Languidly, he finished his coffee and pushed the empty cup away. "No doubt you are right."

Esmée felt suddenly churlish and unsporting. It wasn't his fault he'd been born handsome and charming, and knew how to put both to good use.

Absently, he drew a card from the spread, and began to flick it adroitly back and forth between the fingers of one hand, but his eyes never left hers. Esmée searched for something constructive to say. "Thank you for the furnishings," she blurted. "There seem to be a great many chairs. But it was terribly kind of you."

"Kind?" he echoed, still lazily turning his card. "I rarely do anything kind for anyone, Miss Hamilton. If I do, it is either out of self-preservation, or simply to please myself."

"I see." His disarming honesty perplexed her. "Which was it, then?"

"To please myself," he answered. "I

wished to see the warmth kindle in your eyes again when you thanked me — as you did just now. You have fallen, Miss Hamilton, into my trap."

"Kill them with kindness?" she murmured. "Well, 'twill take more than that, MacLachlan, to do me in. You ought to know Scots are made of sterner stuff."

"It is more my fear, Miss Hamilton, that hard work might do you in first," he said quietly. "I have it on the best authority that children should have both a governess and a nurse. Do you agree?"

Esmée was taken aback. "In a perfect world, aye."

Sir Alasdair twirled the card from between his fingers, and flipped it faceup in front of her. The ace of hearts. "Then may your world, Miss Hamilton, ever be perfect."

For a moment, she could only stare at his elegant, long-fingered hand, which was warm against the white starkness of the card. She was beginning to feel a bit unsteady. She did not like being alone with this man, his perfect hands, and his low, dark voice.

"What do you mean?" she finally managed.

"I mean to hire a nurse," he said.

123

"Wellings will have candidates in a day or two. Pick whomever you think best."

Esmée didn't know what to say. "That is generous, sir," she answered. "I hardly know what to say."

"How about *I shall be forever in your gratitude?*" he suggested. "Or *I am your deeply devoted slave?*"

Esmée did not like the way his words washed over her, warm and suggestive. "I think not."

MacLachlan gave his slow, lazy shrug. "Then perhaps you could simply pour me another cup of coffee," he proposed. "I emptied mine nearly ten minutes past."

Esmée looked down, mildly embarrassed at her oversight. His cup sat empty on the edge of the table. He lifted it, and thrust it in her direction. Instinctively, Esmée seized the pot. But somehow, the twain did not meet, and next she knew, MacLachlan had jerked back his hand, splashing coffee down his fine clothes.

"Christ Jesus!" he shouted.

After that, she was not perfectly sure what happened. She must have leapt from her chair. Somehow, she had her handkerchief, and was on her knees by his chair, dabbing impotently at his straw-colored waistcoat, never thinking what a fool she must look.

"Oh, I am so sorry!" Esmée scrubbed furiously at the silk.

MacLachlan had drawn back in his chair to survey the damage. "Bloody hell, that was hot!"

"Oh, have I scalded you?" she asked. "Are you hurt?" Inexplicably, Esmée wanted to cry. This felt like the last straw.

"I shan't be scarred for life." MacLachlan settled a warm, strong hand on her shoulder. "Really, Miss Hamilton, it is quite all right. Stop scrubbing, please, and look at me."

Esmée's gaze trailed upward. "Oh, no!" His cravat, too, was splattered. "Oh, this is ruined!" She plucked desperately at the folds as if drying it would help.

MacLachlan lifted her hand away and grasped it securely in his. "I've suffered worse," he said, leaning over her, so close his breath stirred her hair. "Now do get off your knees, Miss Hamilton, before someone barges in and draws a bad conclusion — which, given my reputation, might too easily happen."

She did not quite absorb his words. "I beg your pardon?"

MacLachlan sighed, then somehow pushed back his chair and drew her up with him. They were standing mere inches apart, her head barely reaching his chest, and her hand still caught in his. For a long moment, he was perfectly still, his gaze intent on their entwined fingers. "My dear Miss Hamilton," he finally said.

"Y-Yes?"

His mouth curled into a smile. "I think it safe to say you are the most relentless nail-biter I have ever known."

Her face already aflame, she jerked the hand from his and thrust it behind her back.

He seized hold of the other one and held it resolutely. "Indeed," he said, peering at it, "I am not at all sure these *are* fingernails."

She tried to extract her hand, but the scoundrel just grinned. "You have quite vanquished them, Miss Hamilton," he said, still looking at her fingers. "They are actually receding, like the French retreating from Moscow."

Esmée was still distraught over having doused him with hot coffee. " 'Tis a vile habit," she admitted, tugging at her hand. "I would I knew how to stop."

He lifted his gaze to hers and held it for a long moment. "What I would know," he said quietly, "is what it is that troubles you so much that you feel compelled to chew them to the quick."

He would not release her hand, though he

held it quite gently. "I just do sometimes," she said softly. "It means nothing."

"Esmée." The chiding affection in his tone unsettled her. "My dear, you really are troubled. Why? How can I help?"

Suddenly, she felt her chin quivering. "Do not you dare," she whispered, tearing her gaze away. "Do not you dare feel sorry for me."

His eyes heated. "I just want you to tell me what is wrong," he insisted. Suddenly, his tone shifted. "Is it me, Esmée? Do I . . . distress you?" At that, he dropped her hand and stepped back.

Oh, God. *It wasn't that.* Why did he even have to care? Why couldn't he be the insensitive lout she expected? How could he be so blithe one moment, and so compassionate the next? Suddenly, Esmée couldn't get her breath.

"It isn't you," she managed, her hand nervously toying with the strand of pearls at her neck. "It isn't you, and it isn't anything to do with you. Please, MacLachlan, just leave me be."

"I'm not sure I should." His voice was gentle but resolute. "You put on a brave face, my dear, but I begin to suspect a crack in that brittle veneer of yours. Are you in over your head?"

"I can manage!" she cried, dropping her hand. "I *can,* I swear it! Is that why you're hiring a nurse? You think I know nothing of child rearing? And the coffee — I'm sorry — I was careless." Her voice was taking on a frantic edge now, but she couldn't seem to stop. "It shan't happen again. And I can take care of Sorcha, too. I *can!*"

"Miss Hamilton, this is all so unnecessary," he said. "You are tired, homesick, and still grieving. Your mother is dead, and your responsibilities are grave. I am sure you must sometimes feel quite alone in the world. May I not show at least a little concern?"

She made a noise — a gasp? A sob? — she hardly knew which. And suddenly, she felt his arms coming around her, strong and sure. In that moment, it felt like the most comforting, most protective gesture anyone had ever made toward her.

Esmée shouldn't have done it, of course, but she let herself sag against the solid wall of his chest, which felt like the Rock of Gibraltar. He smelled of laundry starch and warm, musky male, and suddenly it was all she could do not to bury her nose in his sodden cravat and weep. She *was* homesick. She *did* miss her mother. And she was frightened. Frightened, perhaps, of herself as much as anyone.

"Esmée, look at me," he whispered. "Please."

She lifted her gaze to his, wordlessly pleading for something; she knew not what. His embrace tightened. His sinfully long lashes lowered just a fraction, his mouth hovering over hers. Esmée felt her blood quicken. She wanted to melt against him, to hide inside him. Instead she closed her eyes and parted her lips. As she'd somehow known it would, MacLachlan's mouth settled over hers, and a sense of inevitability settled over Esmée.

She turned her head, all but begging him to deepen the kiss. His mouth molded to hers, pliant and hungry. Something in Esmée's stomach seemed to bottom out. Her toes curled, and her breath seized. *Wrong. Oh, this was so wrong.* But an inexorable force drew her body fully against his. She gasped — or meant to — and felt the urgent press of his tongue draw across the seam of her lips. At his subtle urging, she let her head fall back, wantonly opening to him.

MacLachlan groaned, a low, agonizing sound, and slid his tongue deep inside her mouth. God, it felt so strange. So wonderfully sinful. Like nothing she'd ever felt before. Her breath came fast and shallow now. She rose onto her tiptoes, and let her hands slip round his waist, then up, up the warmth of his back, savoring his warmth and strength.

"Esmée." He whispered the word against her lips, then plumbed the depths of her mouth again. Beneath her hands, she felt the layered muscles of his back shiver, as if he were an impatient stallion.

She pulled her mouth away but a fraction. "Oh, God," she whispered.

His mouth left hers and skimmed along her cheek, all the way to her jaw, then along the row of pearls which encircled her throat. A warm, heavy hand slid down her spine, lower and lower, until it settled hotly over her hip, circling and massaging through the fabric of her skirts.

Oh, God, she was so tired of being alone. She craved the touch of another human being. She craved *this*. Esmée gave in to the urge to press herself against him. Vaguely, she knew what she was doing was wrong. Foolish. Still, she let her fingers curl hungrily into the silk which covered his broad back.

In response, MacLachlan shoved his other hand into her hair, his fingers threading through her tresses, stilling her to

130

his gentle onslaught. Ever so delicately, he had his way with her, sucking and nipping down the length of her throat, until his lips were set at the turn of her neck. Until she would have agreed to anything he asked. And yet, he hesitated.

"Oh, don't," she whispered.

"Don't — ?" The word held a wealth of agony.

Esmée tried to shake her head. "Don't *stop*," she choked. *"Please."*

But it was too late. His warm mouth was no longer pressed intently against her neck. The only sound was that of his breathing, which was rough and audible in the room. Slowly, he lifted his head to look at her. A brilliant shaft of late-morning sun slanted through the window and across his shoulder, heightening the gold in his hair. Bringing her back to her senses.

"Esmée." His eyes swam with despair. "Oh, Esmée. Oh, God. I am . . ."

She backed away slowly, mute and horrified. His hands slid down her arms, all the way to her elbows before falling away. His gaze tore from hers. Silhouetted as he was against the morning sun, MacLachlan looked like an angel. Like Lucifer come down to tempt and torment. And he had! Oh, heaven help her, what had she done?

Esmée turned and ran.

Lydia was on her knees in the school-room, stacking alphabet blocks on the worktable with Sorcha when Esmée burst back into the room. "Hello, Miss Hamilton," she said. "The young miss is awake now, and in a rare fine humor."

Esmée looked at her wildly. "Thank you," she managed. "I shall . . . I shall just be a moment."

Ignoring Lydia's questioning look, Esmée hastened past and into her bedchamber. She closed the door behind her and fell back against it. God. Oh, God. She covered her mouth with her hands. *What had she done?* She glanced almost desperately about the room and caught a glimpse of herself in the mirror opposite. Her hair was disheveled. Her face deathly white. Anyone with sense could see what she'd been about.

Esmée looked away. Dear heaven! And why was this room so cold? She shivered, and ran her palms up her arms. She could still feel the warmth of his hands high on her arms. Could feel them sliding reluc-tantly down, lower and lower, as she stepped back.

Esmée laughed bitterly. Well, of course he'd been reluctant to let go! She had been such an effortless prize. A ripe plum, dropped unexpectedly into his hands. What man would say no to something so easily tasted? Certainly, Alasdair MacLachlan wouldn't. He probably hadn't said *no* to an easy pleasure in the whole of his life. Now he would doubtless hope for more. And it was her fault. She had surrendered to her traitorous emotions.

Like mother like daughter.

Esmée's face began to burn with shame. That, no doubt, was just what MacLachlan would be thinking at this moment. And he would be right, too. That was Esmée's secret. Her fear. Her shame.

She would never be the beauty her mother had been. No, their similarities went deeper than that. A rashness of temper. A wit too quick. A tongue too tart. And the other. That aching hunger. That foolish loneliness which pierced the heart like a cold fear, overwhelming good sense and restraint. *Like mother, like daughter.* God, how she hated those words.

A sudden screech cut through her self-pity, snapping Esmée back to reality. Through the nursery, she could hear one of Sorcha's all-too-familiar tantrums inter-spersed with Lydia's firm voice. As usual, the rare fine mood had been short-lived, and now, something wasn't going Sorcha's

133

way. Perhaps she was not settling in so well after all.

Esmée dashed into the schoolroom to see that Sorcha had decided to clamber up on the window ledge. She had managed to take hold of it, and was flailing and kicking at Lydia for all she was worth.

"Let go, miss!" said the maid sharply. "You must let go!"

Sorcha screamed bloody murder.

Eschewing Lydia's restraint, Esmée simply grabbed the child around the waist, and hauled her ruthlessly backward. "No, nooo!" Sorcha screeched. "Look *out,* Mae! Look out!"

Esmée set her down forcefully. "Och, ye little jaudie!" she scolded, giving her a swat on the rump. "I am ashamed of you!"

In response, the child proceeded to stomp her way to the worktable and, with surprising strength, backhanded all her blocks into the floor. Chunks of wood flew and bounced, rolling into the corners and under the chairs.

It wasn't the end of the world. It wasn't even especially out of character for Sorcha. But this time, Esmée burst into tears. Lydia rushed to her side. "Oh, miss, I am so sorry," she cried. "I turned my back but an instant, and she got away. 'Twill never happen again, I swear it."

Esmée sobbed even louder. "But it will happen again!" she bawled. "Because I can't teach her any better! It just gets worse and worse! I don't know how to be a mother! I don't know what to do to make her behave!"

"Oh, no, miss!" said Lydia. " 'Tis naught to do with you, I'm sure. Truly."

"But she used to be such a good child," said Esmée. "Before her mother died, I mean. Yet these last few weeks, she is just getting worse and worse."

Lydia patted her sympathetically on the arm. "I'm sure, miss, that the child misses her mother," she said. "But 'tis unlikely that's her trouble. 'Tis just her age, more like. They get this way. A mind of their own, and all that."

"What do you mean?" sniffed Esmée.

"Oh, me mum used to call it the 'terrible twos,' " said the maid. "And an awful fright they are. Mum threatened to nail my twin brothers up in a barrel and feed 'em through the bunghole 'til they was three. Almost did it, too."

Esmée managed a weak smile. Lydia was just being kind, and she knew it. Esmée's tears began to fall anew. She could not escape the feeling that Sorcha's escalating

135

willfulness was all her fault. Still, Lydia did have a way with children. And God knew Esmée needed help.

"Lydia," she said, dabbing at her eyes with her handkerchief, "do you enjoy your work as a housemaid? Would Mrs. Henry let you take another job, do you think?"

But Lydia did not get a chance to answer. Sorcha had finally noticed Esmée's tears. She had toddled across the room and thrown her arms round Esmée's knees.

"No cry, Mae," she said solemnly. "No cry. Me be good."

Chapter Four

In which Sir Alasdair entertains an Important Guest

Alasdair stormed from his study, and watched in mute shock as Esmée bolted up the stairs. "Esmée!" he shouted after her. "I'm sorry! Stop! Wait! Damn it, get back down here!"

But Esmée seemed disinclined to take orders. Around the next turn, the drab gray skirts of her gown swirled out wildly, then vanished from view altogether. Damn and blast! He could not chase the chit up the stairs in front of the servants. And what would he do if he caught her? Kill her? Kiss her? What did he want?

He wanted his freedom back, blister it. He wanted every damned female — be they meddling and tempting, or toddling and squalling — out of his house and on the next mail coach back to Scotland.

He was not perfectly sure how long he remained at the foot of the steps, staring up into the twisting, turning ascension of balusters and treads, but when he returned to the world about him, he realized the longcase clock by the front door was striking noon, its mournful dole echoing up the stairwell.

Upstairs, he could hear Sorcha having another fit of temper, doubtless over something she'd been denied. She was a willful little minx, and he had no idea what ought to be done about it. Best leave *that* to Esmée — assuming she wasn't busy packing her trunks.

Suddenly, it all pressed in on him. Alasdair felt the need to escape. To flee from his own home, his own child, and all of his appalling mistakes. Just as he'd told Esmée from the first, he was no sort of father at all. And given how he'd just treated Esmée, not much of an employer, either.

Oh, he knew what was said of him. He knew respectable mammas pulled their daughters from his path, and that only his fortune and his charm kept society from branding him a total *persona non grata*. He knew, too, that Julia's stinging accusations were not far off the mark. He *did* lie and cheat where women were concerned. And he did sow his seed selfishly, rarely stopping to consider what the result might be, or who might suffer for it. Until today, however, he had not stooped to seducing innocent, fresh-faced virgins.

"Wellings!" he roared, starting down the steps. "Wellings, where the devil are you?"

The butler materialized just as Alasdair hit the last step. "I want my hat," he ordered, striding toward the door. "My hat and my stick. This instant."

Wellings's pace did not hasten as he fetched them. "You mean to go out, sir?"

"Yes, by God, to White's," he answered. "And I plan to be gone awhile. Perhaps all day — probably all night."

"But sir," Wellings gently protested, "Mr. MacLachlan is to take luncheon here."

"Then by all means, feed him!" Alasdair returned.

Wellings lifted his nose as if he smelled something offensive. "And your coat and cravat, sir. They are *soiled*."

Christ, the coffee! Alasdair went straight upstairs, ripping off his neckcloth as he went. When he came back down again, Wellings was still holding his hat and stick on the tips of his index fingers. Ignoring the butler's censorious glare, Alasdair allowed himself the pleasure of slamming the front door until the windowpanes rattled, then stalking off down the street like a spoilt boy.

Which, perhaps, he was. He simply did not know anymore.

It did not take Alasdair long to find Quin, and talk him into a night on the town — a night which started at two in the afternoon. They visited four or five of their favorite haunts, and as the evening came on, Alasdair had almost managed to forget the pesky females who had invaded his home. In fact, he had almost forgotten the awful thing he'd done to Esmée. *Almost.*

Eventually, of course, Quin wanted to go whoring — Quin *always* wanted to go whoring — but Alasdair didn't care if he never saw another female of any age ever again so long as he lived. So they split the difference and went to Mother Lucy's, a fine Soho bawdy-house and all-purpose hell. With her unshaved chin and burly arms, Lucy didn't really look female, but she employed a few more delicate creatures.

Seeing the way of things, Lucy sent Quin upstairs with one of her more practiced tarts, and settled Alasdair in the back room for a few hours of gaming and drinking — though ordinarily, Alasdair made it a point never to combine the two to any degree of excess. By midnight, however, he had made one hell of an exception. He was down by a thousand pounds, so cup-shot his clubs appeared to be turning into hearts, and unable to recollect so much as the name of the chap who was beggaring him.

Sometime in the wee hours of the morning, he felt Quin heave him into a hackney coach and send him bouncing home again. Someone — Wellings and Ettrick, he thought — hauled him up to his bedchamber, shucked him down to his shirt and trousers, then, surrendering to the forces of gravity, left him lying on his chaise without troubling themselves to draw his drapes.

Alasdair did not stir until sometime after daybreak, cursing the clean blade of light which cut across his eyes. The light did not oblige him by going away. Lord God, his head hurt. This serious drinking, he feared, might soon be the death of him. He needed to stick with the vices he was good at: high-stakes gaming and unrepentant womanizing. With a grunt of disgust, Alasdair rolled onto his side and drifted off again.

He had just begun to snore when something warm and damp touched his forehead. He jerked awake with a start to see a small, wet finger blurring before his eyes. "Wha—?"

Someone softly giggled.

Giggled? Alasdair forced his eyes into focus, only to see his brother staring up at

141

him from the floor. No, no. Too small. He closed his eyes, shook his head, and tried again. *Ah, the child.* The child that looked like his brother.

Alasdair was almost relieved. "You, is it, eh?" he asked her. "What are you doing there, crawling about on my floor?"

"Me gee up," said Sorcha, grasping the leg of his side table and pulling herself up.

"Oh, ho!" he said, stabbing a finger at the child. "Going to toddle about now, are you? Are you old enough to walk? Oh, yes! I remember now."

Sorcha seemed to find that supremely funny. She giggled and spit, pointing back at him.

Alasdair ran a hand through his hair. "Oh, aye, *mine* looks funny, does it?" he returned. "Have you seen yours? It is but three inches long, and sticking straight up. How do they put you to bed, eh? On that hard MacLachlan head of yours?"

Her eyes merry, Sorcha clapped a hand over her mouth and laughed again. "Me be go out," she said. "Mae go wee me. We go par'n ducks."

Alasdair couldn't quite make it out, so he changed the subject. "Look here, are you supposed to be on the loose like this?" he asked. "Oughtn't someone be after you?"

But Sorcha had begun to poke about on his table. The pocket watch she eschewed, going instead straight for the crown jewel. "Dink," she said, pinching the rim of his whisky glass. "Gi' me dis."

His whisky glass? Oh, holy damn. He had the vaguest recollection of ordering Wellings to pour him one. And of being argued with. Obviously, he'd won — then drunk not a drop of it before passing out again.

Sorcha was pulling the glass toward her. "Me tink it," she said. "Gi' me tink."

"Oh, no!" he said, setting the glass away. "That's not for weanlings like you, no matter what they taught you back in Scotland."

Sorcha screwed up her mouth, obviously getting ready to cut loose. Alasdair knew his head could not possibly take it. So he rolled to one side and hoisted the child onto his chaise. "Oh, come up here, then," he said, settling her across his lap. "And for pity's sake, don't squall at me. Now go to sleep. No child of mine ought ever be awake at such an ungodly hour."

Sorcha giggled again, then surprisingly, she settled back against him, curled her hand into a fist, and promptly closed her eyes.

Alasdair crooked his neck to look down at her froth of baby-fine hair, wild red-blond curls which tickled his nose and smelled of something fresh. Innocence, perhaps? The child was a snug, warm weight on his chest; a weight which was surprisingly effortless to bear. But she looked as if she meant to stay awhile.

"Now someone will come round to fetch you, won't they?" he found himself asking. "They won't just . . . *leave* you here, will they?"

Sorcha had tucked her thumb into her mouth. "Be mo," she said around it. "Me be mo."

Esmée had always been an early riser. In Great Queen Street, Lydia had standing orders to wake her each morning at half past six, so it was vaguely disconcerting when she heard her bedroom door open sometime before dawn. Drowsy and dreading the morning's chill, Esmée drew the covers over her head. But Lydia did not call to her, and Esmée gratefully drifted back to sleep.

Moments later — at least it seemed like moments — Esmée awoke to find her windows backlit by morning sun. "Good morning, miss!" said Lydia, energetically drawing open the first set of draperies. "A

144

fine, fair day it is. Young miss will be wanting a jaunt in the park for sure."

Esmée threw back the covers and set her feet on the plush rug beneath her bed. "I daresay you're right," she said on a stretching yawn. Then memory struck. "Lydia, did you come in earlier?"

Lydia turned from the next window. "Earlier than what, miss?"

"Before daylight, I mea—" Suddenly, Esmée froze, eyes fixed on Sorcha's new bed. "Oh, dear God."

Lydia let go of the next drapery cord and ran to the bed. Desperately, she patted the wad of covers as Esmée searched the room. "But how, miss?" asked the maid. "How on earth could she?"

"I don't know." Esmée headed into the schoolroom at a run. Lydia went directly into the nursery. Frantically, they searched, meeting at the connecting door.

"Nothing, miss," whispered Lydia. "Oh, dear heaven! Where can she have got to?"

Esmée was already throwing on her wrapper. "Go down the back stairs, Lydia," she ordered. "Ask Mrs. Henry to send up help. I'll take the front, and fetch Wellings."

Esmée hit the bottom staircase at a run. "Wellings!" she cried. "Wellings!"

He materialized round a corner. Esmée

145

grabbed him by the upper arms, looking, no doubt, like a madwoman. "Oh, Wellings, Sorcha is gone!"

"Gone?" The butler drew back an inch. "What do you mean *gone?*"

"From her bed!" cried Esmée. "Gone! I awoke and — and she just wasn't there."

Wellings paled. "That seems impossible."

"Kidnappers?" cried Esmée. "Oh, God! Have you any kidnappers in London?"

Wellings shook his head. "No one got into this house, Miss Hamilton," he said. "Nor out of it, either, I'll wager. She probably crawled out and landed on that hard head of hers, with no harm done."

"Oh! Oh, dear."

"She's somewhere near the schoolroom, I'm sure," Wellings assured her. "Let us go make a search of the closets and cupboards."

Together, they rushed to the schoolroom. Esmée's heart was in her throat. In short order, the entire floor was swarming with servants. Closets, cupboards, even the linen press was searched. There was no sign of Sorcha. Tears running down her cheeks, Lydia was soon searching corridors and corners which had already been checked twice, and Esmée was on the verge of being sick.

"Search the rest of the house and the gardens, Wellings," she whispered, her fingertips pressed against her mouth. "I shall go and tell him."

Wellings turned to look at her. "I beg your pardon, miss? Tell who what?"

"Sir Alasdair," she answered. "I must go and tell him that . . . that *I've lost Sorcha!*"

Wellings hesitated. "Miss Hamilton, you are in your night attire."

She looked at him a little wildly. "Aye, but he's seen such before."

"Nothing quite like that, I fear," murmured the butler, staring at her high-necked flannel wrapper. Esmée did not heed him, and hastened to the stairs. On the next floor, she rushed along the corridor to what she thought was the master's suite, then tapped lightly on the door, which was slightly ajar.

"Come!" cried a muffled voice.

Hand on the doorknob, Esmée hesitated. "Are you decent?"

"Not in the least," came the answer. "But I have clothes on."

She poked her head inside to see MacLachlan splayed out on a chaise near the hearth. Holding back tears, she approached. "I'm afraid, sir, that something dreadful has ha—"

It was then Esmée noticed the sleeping

child. On an incredulous gasp, she crept forward. Sorcha's little hand was curled into the thick hair of MacLachlan's chest; a very muscular chest, which was laid almost bare by his open shirt.

MacLachlan craned his head round the chaise to look at her. "Rendered you speechless again, have I?"

Spurred to awareness, she rushed toward him and snatched up the child. "Good God, what are you doing?" she cried, smoothing a hand down Sorcha's hair. "How dare you? Where did you get her? How long has she —"

"Whoa! Whoa!" shouted MacLachlan, holding out one palm. "Cease the inquisition, my dear! The child's been here half an hour or more, and came in of her own accord, so far as I know."

"Oh, aye! And you — you — you just *kept* her?" Esmée was indignant now. "And did nary a thing about it? It did not occur to you to ring for someone? To let someone know you had her?"

MacLachlan's eyes flashed darkly. "Did it not occur to *you,* Miss Hamilton, to keep the child where she belonged?" he returned. "Besides, she's my child, isn't she? I can have her wherever I bloody well please, can't I? This parenthood business runs both ways, my dear. You keep railing at me, and

148

I'll take the chit down to Crockford's for a hand of loo."

Still drowsy, Sorcha was scrubbing her eyes with her fists now. Esmée felt her face burning. "You — you would not dare!"

MacLachlan gave her a narrow, sidling look. "You don't know what I might dare," he warned. "I told you I wasn't a fit parent at the outset. Now take the child back to the nursery, and for God's sake, keep her there. Wait! How the devil did she get in here, anyway?"

Esmée stopped, her hand on the door, Sorcha still on her hip. "She climbed over her bed somehow," she admitted. "She was gone when Lydia came in to draw the draperies."

"So for all you knew, she'd flung herself down the kitchen stairs, or crawled out one of the windows?" he said. "Is that it?"

Esmée whirled on him. "I do not need you, sir, to point out my failings!" she exploded. "I am quite well aware of them. Aye, Sorcha could have come to a very bad end. Aye, 'tis my fault, and I am terrified, as I wish you were. But you aren't, are you? You think it all quite funny, do you not? Well, when you get done laughing, MacLachlan, you may come upstairs and dismiss me *if* you can stagger your way off

149

that chaise and up the stairs without breaking your damned fool neck!"

Alasdair stewed in his own juices for the rest of the day, angry with himself and angry with Esmée. She was right, of course. He should have rung for a servant the minute he saw the child. He should have known others would have been worried. In his weakened condition, it simply had not occurred to him — hell and damnation, he knew no more of child care than she obviously did — but he'd be damned if he'd admit it to Esmée, just so she could look down her perfect little nose at him.

He was almost relieved when his old friend Devellyn sent round a note asking him to meet him at White's that afternoon. The plan suited Alasdair perfectly. He needed some air, and Dev could always give a chap a good bucking up. Then, after a few hours in Dev's company, Alasdair would just find something else to amuse him. Perhaps he would fight down his newfound aversion to the female sex and spend a few hours between Inga Karlsson's perfect, milk white thighs. *That* would put Miss Esmée Hamilton out of his mind.

He rang for Ettrick and allowed himself to be bathed and dressed in sullen silence.

When at last his cravat was tied to Ettrick's satisfaction, Alasdair stepped back and studied himself in the mirror. "I apologize, old chap, for last night," he said quietly. "I was dipping rather deep, and I have the vaguest notion I behaved abominably."

Ettrick gave a muted, inward smile. "You took great exception to being carried inside," he agreed. "Then you did not wish to be undressed. Nor put to bed. Nor left without your whisky. In short, there were all manner of problems."

Alasdair set a hand on Ettrick's shoulder, made another terse apology, then went swiftly down the stairs and into the afternoon light. *All manner of problems!* What an understatement that was. And the most insurmountable problem of all was Esmée. That was what his anger — and even the quarrel over Sorcha — was all about.

He was still angry about what he had done yesterday. He didn't hold himself to a great many standards of decency, but *"thou shalt not trifle with servants"* was definitely on his list. Then again, she wasn't exactly a servant, was she? No. It was worse than that. She was a gently bred young lady. She was his own daughter's sister. And he had begged her to stay, even though he'd known how young and inexperienced she was.

For those reasons alone, he should be shot. Alasdair started across Princes Street, very nearly dashing out in front of a mail coach. The horses veered, harnesses jangling and hooves ringing wildly on the cobblestones. From the box, the coachman blared his horn. The riders atop jeered down at him as the blue beast careened round the corner.

Christ! Alasdair stepped back onto the pavement and pulled out his handkerchief. He'd broken into a sweat. He, Mr. Ever-Unflappable, who'd always thought to meet his Maker at the business end of some drunken husband's dueling pistol, not beneath the wheels of an ignominious mail coach. Which brought on another harrowing thought. *Sorcha.* He was, whether he wished it or not, responsible for the chit. His life and fortune were no longer his own to squander. What would happen to the child if he lay in the street at this very moment, drawing his last?

Sorcha would have her lovely sister's sympathy, his three hundred pounds, that ugly troll of a doll she kept stripping naked, and very little else. Once he was dead, Esmée couldn't prove the bairn was his — hell, she couldn't prove it now, and he was still alive. Illegitimate children had no rights save those expressly given them.

And the only way to do that was with a hawk-nosed, black-garbed solicitor and a ream of paper filled with legal claptrap, all of which he would have to read and sign but never fully comprehend. And that happy thought was the last nail in the coffin of what had otherwise been a promising afternoon — and it more or less extinguished any spark of interest in Inga's thighs or any other part of her anatomy.

Alasdair heaved a weary sigh, restored the handkerchief to his pocket, and pressed on to White's. Upon winding his way to the all-but-empty coffee room, Alasdair was oddly comforted to see his dearest friend seated at a table by the windows. The Marquis of Devellyn was not, however, fully conscious. No matter. Some of Dev's most enlightening counsel had been given whilst he was either half-asleep or in a drunken stupor.

There'd been grim rumblings over the years about tossing Devellyn out of White's altogether, but his father was a duke — a high stickler of a duke — so no one dared do it. Alasdair could see both sides of the argument. The marquis was, admittedly, a tad uncouth. At present, he had managed to tip his chair back on its hind legs whilst propping his own on the tabletop, boots nonchalantly crossed at the ankles. His head was flopped back, his jaw was dropped open, and he was making a sort of snorking sound in the back of his throat, like a rooting pig choking down an apple core.

Alasdair glanced round, saw no one about, and gave the tabletop a good swift kick underneath. Devellyn's heels bounced a good inch off the table. He awoke in a sputtering, cursing eruption, his chair clattering forward onto all its legs.

"You, is it?" he finally managed when his eyes fully focused. "Come looking for trouble?"

"Aye, well, you know what Granny MacGregor says," Alasdair mused, sitting down. "High jinks will e'er seek low company."

"God spare me Granny MacGregor!" Devellyn muttered. "What's the time?"

"Half past twelve. When did you drift off?"

Devellyn screwed the heels of his hands into his bloodshot eyes. "Don't recollect."

At last, a servant came in. Alasdair sent him scurrying out again. Devellyn looked as though he needed a pot of coffee. "I have shocking news," he said to the marquis.

"Nothing shocks me," Devellyn returned. "And it isn't news, either. Had dinner with

Quin last night. Gave me some tommyrot about the three of you being cursed by a Gypsy fortune-teller."

"Aye, well, my curse is named Sorcha," admitted Alasdair. *Or Esmée,* he silently added, depending how one looked at it.

"I heard," said the marquis. "What are you going to do?"

Alasdair lifted both brows. "My duty," he replied. "Much as it pains my oh-so-brilliant brother."

Devellyn shrugged. "Tell Mr. Oh-So-Brilliant to go frig himself," he suggested. "Then do what you know you must." He paused to yawn hugely. "Is she a pretty little thing?"

Slowly, Alasdair nodded. "Quite beautiful, really," he admitted. "But in a quiet, elegant way."

Devellyn looked at him oddly. "Never knew a two-year-old who could *be* quiet — elegantly or any other way."

Alasdair felt his face flush. "You meant Sorcha?" he muttered. "Yes, she's pretty as a peach. I thought . . . I thought you meant the sister."

"The sister!" Devellyn chuckled. "Thought she was the veriest shrew!"

Alasdair decided it was time to change the subject. "Where is Sidonie?"

"Oh, I had to come in a rush on business," he said. "My phaeton makes her ill now, so she'll come in Mamma's barouche next week. They are at Stoneleigh with Thomas and two pecks of yarn. Mama has taught Sid to knit!"

"Good God!" The notorious Black Angel, scourge of lamplit London, now thoroughly domesticated? Alasdair searched for something constructive to say. "Thomas must love having all that yarn about."

The marquis rolled his eyes. "I fear the little feline terror is otherwise engaged. One cannot step a foot into the lawns or gardens without squashing a dead rodent of one ilk or another beneath one's bootheel. Moles, voles, bats, rats, and worse. Sometimes he drags 'em up the front steps. Fenton fell over one yesterday. Likely heard him screaming all the way to Brighton."

Fenton, Dev's valet, had bad nerves and a weak stomach, but he could tie one hell of a knot in a neckcloth. Alasdair had long wished to lure him away, but honor forbade it. A chap might sleep with another man's wife and have society look the other way, but stealing a valet was indefensibly bad *ton.* Fenton would have to suffer the indignities of the countryside.

At that moment, the coffee was brought in. Alasdair stirred his, and it made him remember how he had done the same thing yesterday morning, and of what had happened next. But that would not do. He needed to stop thinking of Miss Esmée Hamilton in general — and in particular, of how small and round and plump her arse had felt beneath his greedy hand. And of how her lips had tasted; like sweet, molten —

"Sugar?"

Alasdair stared across the table.

Devellyn thrust the bowl at him again. "Sugar? Or not?"

Alasdair shook his head. "No, thanks," he managed. "Sidonie is well, I trust?"

Devellyn hung his head. "Hardly," he said. "Every morning she's hung over the chamber pot heaving up her breakfast. It is horrifying, Alasdair. *Beyond* horrifying."

Alasdair lifted one shoulder. "That's just the way of things, Dev."

"Yes, well, I have to watch it, don't I?" His face was a sudden mask of agony. "Watch it, and know that it is all my doing. Watch it, and know that the worst is yet to come. And that even after the worst is over, I'll still never be able to keep my cock in my trousers. And then we'll soon be right back

157

where we started."

Alasdair lifted one brow. "Thank you for sharing that cheering thought."

But Devellyn was not attending. "Alasdair," he said, leaning urgently forward, "I am not at all sure I can endure six more months of this."

Devellyn, normally about as sensitive as a dray horse, looked undone by his wife's pregnancy. It was beginning to make Alasdair acutely uneasy. He thought of the mysterious Lady Achanalt, and of what she must have endured. The poor woman had not had her child's father to lean upon during her confinement. She had had no husband, nor even a lover, with whom to share the worry or the joy — assuming there had been any of the latter. Quite the opposite, her husband had wished her ill. Once again, the guilt stung him.

"Tell you what, Dev," he said, leaning across the table. "All this yammering is for teary-eyed females. We ought to approach our troubles like men. We ought to go up to Duke Street, open a bottle of your cheapest brandy, and get ourselves properly pissed."

Devellyn was easily persuaded. They set off together in an amiable mood, and reached the marquis's rambling Mayfair mansion in short order. But almost as soon as the bottle was uncorked and the first dram drained, Alasdair remembered his pledge. His duty. His newfound moral obligation. Moreover, having barely recovered from the previous night's lark, Alasdair found that the taste of brandy was making his stomach churn.

"What is the name, Dev, of your solicitors?" he asked. "The ones in the City?"

Devellyn was studying his empty glass. "Brown and Pennington," he answered. "Gracechurch Street."

MacLachlan business, such as it was, was always handled in Stirling. Alasdair had never had much need for a local firm. "They are discreet?" he asked. "They can be relied upon?"

"Absolutely."

"Then I must go," said Alasdair, setting his glass down with an awkward clatter.

But Dev either did not hear or misunderstood. Clamping a smoldering cheroot between his teeth, the marquis picked up the bottle of brandy and aimed it in the general direction of Alasdair's glass.

By five o'clock in the afternoon, Esmée was on her fourth nursemaid and taking little comfort in the process. The latest applicant, Mrs. Dobbs, was a sweet, sunny-natured woman who seemed to have adored and catered to her every charge. Esmée did not have the heart to tell her that Sorcha could eat sweet nursemaids for breakfast and crush anyone's sunny nature beneath her dainty bootheel well before luncheon. This morning alone, she had upended her porridge onto the carpet, torn off her stockings and shoes in a fit of temper, scrubbed chalk all over the schoolroom walls, then tossed all of Esmée's extra hairpins in the closestool. Lydia, at least, knew what she was up against.

Esmée rose from the sofa in MacLachlan's study, still wishing Wellings had chosen any other room for the interviews. "I shall let you know," she said, extending a hand to Mrs. Dobbs. "Thank you for coming."

She rang for a footman to show the woman out, then tidied her papers and went downstairs to compare notes with Wellings. Perhaps he would have gained some insight which she had missed.

Regrettably, he had not. When she asked about Lydia, he agreed she might do. Esmée thanked him and turned to go. Just then, there was a knock at the door. Wellings opened it to reveal an attractive but decidedly middle-aged woman in a jaunty purple hat. She stood on the front step, a swath of muslin draped over her arm.

"Good afternoon, Wellings," she said brightly. "Is Sir Alasdair in?"

"No, ma'am." His voice was warm. "I'm sorry."

The lady stepped inside. "Oh, well! I just came by to drop this off." She handed her armful of muslin to the butler, then extended her gloved hand to Esmée. "How do you do?" she said. "You must be Miss Hamilton, the governess. How pretty you are! I'm Julia Crosby, a friend of Sir Alasdair's."

Stunned nearly speechless, Esmée took the hand. "Yes, I — I am," she said. "Miss Hamilton, I mean."

"How delightful!" Mrs. Crosby returned her attention to Wellings. "Will you see that Ettrick gets that, please? He'll know what to do with it."

The muslin sleeve obviously concealed clothing, probably the coat and trousers MacLachlan had left behind, though the woman was too tactful to say so. "Thank you, ma'am," said the butler. "Will you take tea or some refreshment before you go?"

"Only if Miss Hamilton will join me?"

Esmée opened her mouth, then closed it. "I should be pleased to," she finally said.

Mrs. Crosby smiled again, and it lit up the

room. Esmée had no trouble believing she was an actress, for she was beautiful and possessed what could only be called a commanding presence. She did not, however, look like Sir Alasdair's type. She looked older, even, than Esmée's mother had been, and was more than a little on the plump side, with a look of good humor about her eyes. Somehow, Esmée had imagined MacLachlan's taste ran more toward thin, catty, bad-tempered opera dancers.

She let her eyes drift over the woman again and felt a stab of envy. How dare MacLachlan kiss her with such passion when, not two days earlier, he'd been bedding someone who seemed so . . . well, so *pleasant?*"

Because he could. Because she'd let him. *Encouraged* him.

Abruptly, Mrs. Crosby cleared her throat.

"Well, then," said Esmée with false brightness. "Shall we go up to the drawing room?"

Together, they started up the stairs while Wellings went off to order tea.

"I hear Sir Alasdair was recently seen shopping in the Strand for children's furniture," remarked Mrs. Crosby, her tone mischievous. "Enough for an army of children, 'tis said. Quite a stir that's apt to cause."

Esmée glanced over her shoulder. "He

was supposed to have sent Wellings," she answered. "I cannot think why he didn't."

"Yes, Wellings is the soul of discre—"

Suddenly, on the stairs behind her, Esmée heard a startled cry. She spun about to see Miss Crosby sinking to her knees, one hand clawing into the carpet, the other clutching her abdomen.

"Wellings!" Esmée cried. "Wellings, come back!"

"Oh!" said Mrs. Crosby on a moan. "Oh, God!" Her face was white as death. Her jaunty hat had tumbled off and down the stairs.

Esmée knelt and clutched at the woman's hand. "What is it, Mrs. Crosby? Can you tell me?"

Suddenly, Wellings reappeared, one of the footmen on his heels. He took one look at Mrs. Crosby's face and glanced up at Esmée. "Take the back stairs," he said. "Tell Hawes to fetch a doctor. *Now.*"

"Strauss," rasped Mrs. Crosby, wincing. "Dr. Strauss. In Harley Street. Please."

The next few minutes were a flurry of activity. Esmée did as she was bid, sending Hawes across town on MacLachlan's best horse. Somehow, the men got Mrs. Crosby into bed and sent for Mrs. Henry. The elderly woman trundled in and out, looking very grim and sending the footmen scurrying up and down the stairs for all manner of potions and linens.

"Will she be all right?" Esmée asked, touching Mrs. Henry gently on the arm. "What is wrong?"

But Mrs. Henry would only shake her head.

It seemed an eternity until Dr. Strauss arrived. He was a round, elderly gentleman with wire glasses and a heavy accent. He and Mrs. Henry conferred in grave tones, then went in together. Not knowing what else she could do, Esmée dashed upstairs to check on Sorcha. Lydia was cutting strings of paper dolls, thoroughly captivating the child. Once or twice, Sorcha began to turn sulky, but Lydia persevered. Esmée lingered, marveling at how cleverly the maid averted Sorcha's tantrums.

Half an hour later, Esmée went back downstairs to see MacLachlan standing outside Mrs. Crosby's door with the doctor, their heads bent in quiet conversation. MacLachlan looked stricken. He saw Esmée and motioned urgently at her. "Miss Hamilton, what happened? Did she trip? Did she fall?"

"I don't know," said Esmée. "I do not think so."

The doctor was already shaking his head. "She says she did not," he said emphatically. "She reports a sudden onset of pain and a strong cramping sensation."

"Good God," MacLachlan whispered, dragging a hand through his hair. "Is there . . . any hope?"

The doctor looked pessimistic. "Some, perhaps," he said hesitantly. "The pain has stopped, and the child is not lost. Not yet, anyway."

The child? Mrs. Crosby was with child? Esmée's head began to swim.

Beside her, the men continued to whisper. Suddenly, MacLachlan's voice rose. "But what caused it?" he demanded. "And what is to be done about it? Should she remain in bed? Stand on her head? What?"

The doctor shook his head. "I cannot say what caused it," he confessed. "Her age is against her. You must know that."

MacLachlan was losing his self-control. "I *don't* know that!" he almost shouted. "Older women have children all the time."

"And they lose children even more often," countered the doctor. "It is nature's way."

"Why, my Granny MacGregor was nearing fifty when she had her last!"

MacLachlan roared. "And she can still strap me with one hand tied behind her back."

Dr. Strauss grasped MacLachlan by the elbow. "You needn't shout, Sir Alasdair," he said. "We'll do all that is possible, I promise. Now, if you'll permit, I must return to my patient."

"Yes, yes, fine," agreed MacLachlan, further disordering his hair. "We'll do . . . anything to help. *Anything.* You have to understand that. She wants this child so desperately."

The doctor already had one hand on the doorknob. "If the child is to have any chance," he said, "then she must remain perfectly still until the bleeding has stopped, which could be days or even weeks. Under no circumstances may she be moved beforehand."

MacLachlan swallowed hard, the knot in his throat sliding up and down. "I shall tie her down if I must."

"You shan't need to," said the doctor grimly. "She, too, will do anything. Now please, leave all this to me."

MacLachlan nodded, then turned to Esmée as if she were next on his list of Catastrophes to Be Dealt With. "You," he said decisively. "Come with me into the study. We've a little something to settle, you and I."

Esmée must have faltered.

MacLachlan's eyes narrowed. "Oh, come now, Miss Hamilton!"

The doctor had already vanished. MacLachlan seized Esmée by the arm and steered her almost roughly down the corridor. He pushed open the door, urged her inside, and slammed it shut.

"Good God," he said, exhaling sharply. "What a bloody awful nightmare this day has turned out to be!"

"Oh, aye, d'ye think so?" asked Esmée, her voice tart. "Then how would you like to have your womb tied up in knots like poor Mrs. Crosby, with your life's blood leaching out, and your child all but lost? *That,* MacLachlan, is what a nightmare feels like."

The muscle in MacLachlan's too-perfect jaw began to twitch. "I am not insensible to Julia's anguish," he gritted. "I would bear it for her if I could, but I cannot. All I can do is to try to be a good friend."

"Oh, would that every woman had such a friend!" she returned. "You are off gallivanting about town with a brandy bottle as your boon companion, whilst she is all but miscarrying your next child!"

Esmée had not sat down, a circumstance which MacLachlan either did not notice or

167

did not care about. He had begun to pace the floor between the windows, one hand set at the back of his neck, the other on his hip. His jaw was growing tighter and tighter as he paced, and his temple was beginning to throb visibly, too.

"Well?" she challenged. "Have you nothing to say, man?"

Suddenly, he whirled on her. "Now you listen to me, you spite-tongued little witch," he said. "And listen well, for I mean to say this but once: Julia Crosby's child is none of your business — nor any of mine, either, come to that."

"Aye, 'tis none of my business if you sire a bastard in every parish," Esmée returned.

"You're bloody well right it's not," he retorted. "And perhaps I have! But whilst I'm defending myself from your hot-headed notions, let me say that I have *not* spent the day idly drinking, either."

"Oh, faith! You reek of it!"

"Yes, and yesterday I reeked of coffee," he snapped. "Neither you nor Lord Devellyn possess a modicum of grace, it seems. He slopped brandy down my trousers."

Esmée didn't believe him. "Oh, aye, you've been gone all day, and when at last you come home, you smell as if you spent the afternoon in the gutter. What's anyone to think?"

He stabbed his finger in her face. "Miss Hamilton, had I any wish to be nagged, insulted, or upbraided, I would get myself a wife, not a goddamned governess!" he roared. "And besides that, you do not get paid to *think!*"

Esmée felt her temper implode. "Oh, no, I get paid to . . . to *what?*" she demanded shrilly, as he resumed his pacing. "Satisfy the master's base instincts when his itch wants scratching? Remind me again. I somehow got muddled up over my duties."

He spun about, and grabbed her by the shoulders, shoving her against the door. "Shut up, Esmée," he growled. "For once, just shut the hell up." And then he was kissing her, brutishly and relentlessly.

She tried to squirm away, but he held her prisoner between his hands. The harsh stubble of his beard raked across her face as he slanted his lips over hers, again and again, his powerful hands clenched upon her shoulders.

She tried to twist her face away. His nostrils were wide, his mouth hot and demanding. Something inside her sagged, gave way, and she opened her mouth to him. He surged inside, thrusting deep. Her

169

shoulder blades pressed against the wood, she began to shudder. There was no tenderness to his touch now, just a black, demanding hunger. Esmée began to shove at his shoulders, then to pummel them with the heels of her hands.

As abruptly as it had begun, he tore his mouth from hers and stared her in the eyes, his nostrils still wide, his breathing still rough and quick. And then, his eyes dropped shut. "Damn it all," he whispered. "No, damn *me*."

For a moment there was an awful silence. Then Esmée broke it. "I ought to slap the breath of life from you," she gritted. "Don't ever touch me again, MacLachlan. I am *not* Mrs. Crosby. I am not even my mother, lest you be confused. Now take your lecherous hands off me, or I'll be kneeing you in the knackers so hard you heave."

He pushed away from the door without opening his eyes. "Yes, go," he whispered, turning his back to her. "Go, for God's sake! And don't ever come in here again — no matter *what* I say."

The hinges squeaked in protest as she jerked open the door.

"Esmée?" The word was a raspy whisper.

Hand already on the doorknob, she turned.

170

Without even looking at her, MacLachlan withdrew a sheaf of papers from his coat pocket, and thrust them at her. "Put this in a safe place," he said. "And if ever you leave here, *take it with you.*"

Chapter Five

A Walk in the Park

The following fortnight passed with a strange sense of pessimism hanging over the house, as if Mrs. Crosby's collapse had set the entire household on edge. The lady herself remained ensconced in the bedchamber nearest the front door, her head and feet propped on small mountains of pillows. Each afternoon, Esmée would drop by and offer to read to her, but Mrs. Crosby always declined. She seemed almost embarrassed by her predicament.

Dr. Strauss came every day, *tut-tutting* over his patient in his strange foreign accent. And once, when Esmée failed to knock loudly enough, she found MacLachlan seated by Mrs. Crosby's bed, his head bowed so low it rested atop their clasped hands. It was a private, poignant scene. Neither noticed Esmée. She felt a stab of something which felt oddly like sorrow, then lightly closed the door.

Mrs. Crosby had other visitors, too. A couple by the name of Wheeler came every morning like clockwork. Mr. Wheeler, a handsome man of perhaps fifty, looked perpetually dyspeptic and worried. He also looked very familiar. Esmée was almost certain she'd seen him during Sunday services at St. George's, but his wife had not been with him.

And so it went, Mrs. Crosby slowly regaining her spirit and color. Three weeks to the day after her collapse, the Wheelers and Dr. Strauss arrived in Great Queen Street with a van and a canvas litter. Mr. Wheeler and one of the footmen carried Mrs. Crosby gingerly down the stairs, and the lady was at last borne home. MacLachlan was nowhere to be seen.

Indeed, save for the instance in Mrs. Crosby's room, Esmée had seen little of him. He had taken to staying out all hours each night and returning home in a disheveled state each morning. *"Shot in the neck again!"* she heard Ettrick whisper to Wellings one morning as the former headed upstairs with what looked like a glass of soda water and a pot of coffee. Even from a distance, Esmée could see that the lines of dissipation about his face had hardened and that he looked every one of the thirty-six years Lydia had casually ascribed to him.

At least he was more attractive than his brother. Save for their height and wide shoulders, there was not a drop of resemblance between the two. Where the former was handsome in a rakish, golden-god sort of way, Merrick MacLachlan was swarthy and dark-haired, with a nasty scar which ran the length of his jaw. He looked mean-spirited and a little cruel. Mr. MacLachlan lived, Lydia reported, at a "very posh place" called the Albany, an establishment which let suites of rooms to wealthy, unwed gentlemen of the *ton*. As a result, Merrick MacLachlan treated his elder brother's home, particularly the dining room, as if it were his own.

On those rare occasions when Esmée chanced to pass him, she took great pains to look down her nose at him. It was difficult, of course, since he towered above her. Still, she had managed to make her point. Merrick MacLachlan always bowed stiffly, then circled wide.

Sometimes Lord Wynwood accompanied him. Wynwood was warm, and his eyes were kind. He never failed to ask after Sorcha, and twice when he was waiting for MacLachlan to come down, he asked her to join him for coffee in the dining room. Wynwood was easy to talk to, and Esmée was glad to pass a few moments in his company.

Sorcha's moods did not improve, but Lydia was officially assigned the duties of part-time nursemaid. Each afternoon, Lydia would relieve Esmée so that she might go belowstairs and take tea with Wellings and Mrs. Henry, which was a welcome respite.

Oddly, during these times, a pattern began to develop. Esmée would go down the back stairs, and at almost the same moment, MacLachlan, apparently having coffee'd and soda-watered himself to a more sober state, would go up the front stairs to the schoolroom.

There, according to Lydia, he would simply sit and watch Sorcha play. In some faint hope that she could actually begin to *teach* the child, as a governess ought, Esmée had purchased chalk and a small blackboard. Regrettably, Sorcha had shown little interest in her alphabet. But she showed a great deal of interest, Lydia laughingly recounted, in the strange stick figures and surreal animals which MacLachlan sketched for the child's amusement. Other times, Sorcha would engage his help in dressing her doll or stacking her blocks.

Mid-October came, by which time a sort

175

of undeclared truce had developed between Esmée and MacLachlan. As if by mutual agreement, they avoided at all costs being alone with one another. This changed when, on one particular afternoon, Esmée went downstairs to tea, only to find it delayed by some minor crisis in the kitchens. She dawdled about the house for well over an hour, then gave up and returned to the schoolroom.

She peeked inside to see that MacLachlan was wedged into one of the small wooden chairs, and Sorcha was sitting on the tabletop. The other nine chairs, which had thus served as nothing but an extravagance, had mysteriously vanished. In the back of the room, however, someone had pitched a makeshift tent using an old brown blanket which looked suspiciously lumpy. Well. At least the chairs had proven useful for something.

She returned her attention to MacLachlan and Sorcha, who looked oddly incongruous together with his long, booted legs stretching almost the width of the table and Sorcha's flounced skirts spread round her like a princess.

Several books which Esmée did not recognize lay scattered about the table. Amongst them were some of the small wooden boxes which had formerly been shelved in the nursery, a few with their hinged lids thrown back. Sorcha and her father were peering into one of them. Just then, Esmée realized Sorcha was gnawing on something round and shiny.

"Och, what's she got?" cried Esmée, darting into the room.

MacLachlan looked up, and frowned. "Devil take it!" he said. "Hand that over, minx."

Esmée waited for the tantrum. Instead, the child dropped the object, spittle and all, into her father's hand, giggling as though it were a great joke.

Alasdair wiped off the object on his trouser leg. "Good Lord!" he said. "Another Byzantine Hyperpyron."

"Lud, another fancy coin?" said Esmée. "Where's she getting them?"

MacLachlan grinned a little boyishly and pointed to the open chest. "I am trying to instill in the child a proper appreciation of numismatics."

Esmée looked at him blankly. For an instant, she could not think beyond the twinkle in his eyes. Then, with every ounce of her self-possession, she jerked herself under control.

"Coin collecting," he said, obviously unaware of the effect he had on her.

She managed a nonchalant tone. "What, boxing up money?" She peered into one of the boxes. "I thought Scots came by that naturally."

MacLachlan threw back his head and laughed. "Most do," he finally answered. "But these, Miss Hamilton, are rare, old coins."

"Aye, then," said Esmée, setting one hand on her hip. "What's so rare about the one she's chewing on now?"

MacLachlan's brow furrowed. "Well, I'll be damned!" he said, snatching it.

"I be damn," said Sorcha.

The furrow deepened. "Don't say that."

"Don say dat," echoed Sorcha.

"Oh, aye!" said Esmée with asperity. "She's learning something, right enough."

MacLachlan gave a short, sharp sigh. "Don't rip up at me, Esmée! I'm trying."

Esmée smiled. "Aye, well, I know what they say about stones and glass houses," she murmured. "What else have the two of you been about?" She turned the slate toward her, and frowned.

"It is an opossum," said MacLachlan.

"See 'possum?" said Sorcha, stabbing at it with her index finger. "See?"

Esmée set her head to one side to better

study it. "An o-possum?"

"A North American marsupial," MacLachlan explained.

"Indeed?" Esmée peered at it. "It seems rather . . ."

"Ugly?" supplied MacLachlan. "You were thinking, were you not, that I lack talent? I assure you it is not so. Opossums are singularly unattractive creatures."

Esmée flicked a glance up at him, and smiled. "And what's this thing sprouting from its forehead?"

"Horn!" said Sorcha, pointing at it. "See? See horn?"

"I do see," murmured Esmée. "A *horned* marsupial? How perfectly fascinating."

MacLachlan smiled a little sheepishly. "No, a horn like . . . well, like a unicorn."

Esmée's smile broadened. "A unicorn?"

MacLachlan ruffled Sorcha's hair. "I had not forgotten, you see, that today is this imp's birthday," he answered. "Or, more honestly, I was informed of it yesterday by Wellings. I bought her a few new picture books by way of a gift. She was especially taken by that one about unicorns."

Esmée's smile faltered as she picked up the book. She had not imagined he would know or care about Sorcha's birthday. "I got her a wooden top," she said dumbly.

"And new mittens."

"Then she is a pampered little princess indeed," he answered. "And today the princess insists on having horns drawn on all her creatures."

Sorcha leaned over and stabbed at the blackboard with her finger, smearing the sketch. "Horn, see?" she said proudly. "Nucorns has horns."

In response, MacLachlan scooped her off the table and settled her onto his knee. "*Uni*-corns *have* horns," he corrected, dusting the chalk from her finger with his neckcloth. "But opossums — real ones, mind you — do not. That one is just to please you, silly."

Sorcha just giggled, and began to fiddle with MacLachlan's cravat pin. In response, he began to neaten her wild, curly hair, tucking it gently behind her ears.

Esmée looked back and forth between them, a strange warmth kindling in her heart. Unfortunately, it went straight to her knees, causing them to weaken. Oh, it was unwise to remain too long in this man's company! Unthinkingly, she snatched her hand from the back of MacLachlan's chair and drew back a pace.

It was, she later realized, a telling gesture, for suddenly, she was granted a reprieve.

180

MacLachlan kissed Sorcha and set her down. "There you go, minx!" He stood, and began closing up the wooden boxes. Sorcha peered over the edge of the table, her bottom lip slowly poking out.

"You are leaving?" Esmée murmured.

He cut her an odd, sidling look. There was a hardness in his eyes, and a tightness about his mouth, as if some unexpected pain had just struck him. "I expect I ought."

Esmée did not know what to say. Certainly, she did not wish him to remain. Yet Sorcha was obviously enjoying his company. Impulsively, she reached out a hand to touch his arm — to stop him, so that she might say . . . what?

Fortunately, he chose that moment to step farther down the table to pick up the last box. "I did not know you were a coin collector," she said inanely.

He smiled, but it did not reach his eyes. "Quite an avid one," he confessed. "A boyhood habit which is now something of an obsession — and a bloody expensive one, too."

Esmée considered that for a moment. The hobby seemed oddly out of character with the man she thought she knew. " 'Tis a rather intellectual endeavor, is it not?" she asked. "Coin collecting?"

He laughed without looking up from his boxes. "My father used to say it was nothing but a rich man's frivolity, and I daresay he was right," MacLachlan answered. "No, if you are looking for an intellectual in this family tree, Miss Hamilton, look to my brother. He got the brains and the business sense, whilst I got the looks and the charm."

Esmée did not know what to say to that. MacLachlan moved as if to pick up his stack of boxes, then stopped, his posture stiffening. "As to my charm, Miss Hamilton, I have not forgotten that I owe you an apology," he said very quietly. "My behavior some weeks past left much to be desired. I am sorry, and I ought to have said so sooner."

Esmée wished he had not reminded her of the unpleasantness in his study. "Let us speak of it no further," she said stiffly. "But you remind me that I have not thanked you for the papers which you gave me."

He cut a glance at Sorcha. "You understand them?" he murmured. "You have them in a safe place?"

She swallowed hard and nodded. It was very difficult, sometimes, to be as thoroughly angry with him as he deserved. He had a way of catching her heart off guard. "I have seen wills before," she answered. "I confess, it has lifted a great weight from my mind."

"That, Miss Hamilton, is what I was doing on the afternoon Julia was taken ill," he said, but his voice was flat. Emotionless. "My lands in Scotland are entailed," he went on. "They shall likely be Merrick's in the end, though he says he shan't accept them."

"I understand entailment," she said.

"But this house and all else will be Sorcha's," he went on. "Merrick will see to it, if . . . well, *if.* I know you don't care for him — I can't help that. But he is dependable. Sorcha shan't be left without a roof over her ever again."

Before Esmée could think of an appropriate response, MacLachlan had picked up his boxes and vanished.

Esmée did not see MacLachlan again until the following Sunday, and again, his appearance was unexpected. As had become her habit, she left Sorcha in Lydia's care whilst she attended morning services. St. George's had been Aunt Rowena's church, Esmée recalled, so she had begun attending it by default. Still, she felt a little out of place in such an elegant establishment.

On this particular Sunday, she spotted Mr. Wheeler in a pew near the front, but again, he was alone. The sermon was very dull, the congregation aloof when the service ended. Esmée walked back to Great Queen Street feeling homesick again, and thinking, strangely, of Mr. Wheeler.

In the late afternoon, Esmée dressed Sorcha in her best pelisse, and asked a footman to carry her little cart down the steps to the pavement. It was a cool day, the sky overhead ominously gray, and the air weighted with damp, but Esmée was desperate for some green, open space, even if was only St. James's Park.

"Go out!" Sorcha was chattering happily, pointing at her waiting conveyance. "Me go. Go park, Mae. Go park n'see ducks."

As it so often did, the child's joy buoyed Esmée's sagging spirits. She lifted Sorcha into the cart, buttoned her pelisse, and laughingly kissed her tiny hands.

Alasdair saw the winsome pair step outside as he approached his front door. Fleetingly, he hesitated, uncertain whether he ought to draw near, brush past, or simply leave as he had done last time. The decision felt painfully parallel to the choices which wanted making in his life just now; choices which had been weighing heavily on him.

He had begun this awful business by wanting nothing to do with the child. But that had quickly proven impossible. Already he had stopped waiting for Uncle Angus's letter and had surrendered all hope of escape. And strangely enough, he simply no longer wished to. Sorcha was a taking little thing. Headstrong and given to tantrums, perhaps. But she was *his,* and he was slowly coming to grips with what it meant to be a father.

No, it was not Sorcha who tormented him now. It was her sister. Esmée was not just earthy and beautiful; she was a Scot to her very core. Her voice, her demeanor, even her scent, stirred up old memories and left him oddly longing for something. His lost youth, perhaps. He wanted to lie with her in a field of heather and slowly draw the pins from her hair. He wanted to undress her, slowly and gently, so that he might see her alabaster skin against the greenery, and watch those all-seeing eyes drop slowly shut in surrender.

It was appalling. But apparently uncontrollable. He watched her now as she bent over to neaten Sorcha's blankets, and realized his mouth had gone dry. What in God's name had he been thinking to allow her into his home?

At the time, he'd been desperate, uncertain as to what to do and wishing only to cast off the responsibility he'd been saddled with. Esmée had seemed his only hope. Now she seemed his eternal punishment. Even now, he was held in thrall by the sway of her hips and the gentleness in her touch as she lifted Sorcha. The sudden surge of desire he felt for her seemed almost indecent. There was nothing erotic about a woman caring for a child, was there? Stranger still, the woman in question was better than a dozen years younger than he and about as green as a girl could get.

At least Esmée was not a silly female. That he could not have borne. Instead, she was resolute and pragmatic. She understood that life was sometimes hard. That it required one to make sacrifices. Yes, she knew, perhaps far better than he, for he was hard-pressed to think of one true sacrifice life had ever required of him — until now.

But Esmée knew nothing of the world; knew nothing of men like him. Had she a father or brother to defend her honor, Alasdair would have been called to account for his misconduct weeks ago.

Esmée was buttoning Sorcha's pelisse over her yellow muslin dress. The child sat upright, looking at her sister and prattling happily. In response, Esmée caught the child's hands in her own and lifted them one by one to her lips. At that simple gesture, something unfamiliar lurched in Alasdair's hard and selfish heart. He suffered an unexpected tug of yearning, but for what, he did not know. He felt, suddenly, as though he belonged to no one, and no one belonged to him.

He had become like a stray dog who longed for warmth and conviviality; one who peeked longingly through cracked doors and low windows at the outward manifestations of other people's contentment. The warm hearths. The happy laughter. A family dinner table, soft with candlelight. Things he'd never really believed mattered.

It was almost as if he were looking for a place to call home, which made no sense at all, for he had one. He had not felt such strange, mixed-up emotions since leaving Scotland. In the weeks since Esmée and Sorcha had come into his life, Alasdair had felt, inexplicably, more isolated than ever. Perhaps because he had begun to realize there was something actually worth missing.

On impulse, he removed his hat and approached.

Esmée was tucking a rolled blanket behind Sorcha. "Good afternoon, Miss Hamilton," he said. "You are off to the park?"

Her head jerked up, her color instantly deepening. "Indeed. We go every day."

"Yes, I sometimes see you leave." Thank God she'd no notion how often he stood at his bedchamber window trying to sober himself up and watching as her small, capable hands readied Sorcha for their jaunt. "It *is* raining a bit, you know," he added.

"Och, a wee mizzle, no more," she said. "I should hope I'm not so trimel-hearted as to be put off by a few clouds."

"No, no, I never dreamt that," he murmured. "Might I join you?"

She hesitated. "I fear you would find it exceedingly dull."

Alasdair studied her face very carefully. "Esmée, I think you must decide whether you wish me to be a parent or merely an income stream."

The remark sucked some of the wind from her sails. " 'Tis a choice which you must make, I daresay."

Alasdair covered her hand with his, stilling it on the handle of the buggy. "It is sometimes difficult," he said. "Especially

188

when I cannot bear to see you uncomfortable in my presence."

She flicked a dark glance at him.

"Save your daggers for someone else, Esmée," he said quietly. "I'll own my mistakes. And I swear that I will never again —"

"Go!" shrieked Sorcha suddenly. She seized the sides of her cart with both hands and gave it a good jerk. "Go! Go park! See ducks!"

Jolted from his abjuration, Alasdair laughed. "Self-centered minx!" he declared. "And irrepressible, too, I fear."

"Aye, she does try a body's patience," muttered Esmée.

Alasdair grinned. "I sometimes doubt a whole battalion of governesses could manage her," he said. "Did you see the hole she cut in the schoolroom draperies whilst Lydia and I were picking up her toys? The minx snatched up Lydia's scissors quick as bedamned."

Esmée did not chide him for the curse. "I have mended it," she said. "I believe it is not *too* noticeable."

"I scolded her," he said.

"As did I," said Esmée. "For all the good it did."

Alasdair threw back his head and laughed. "And after all our good intentions are spent, my dear, we are going to end up having to spank her quite mercilessly anyway — and probably for the next fifteen years. You know that, do you not?"

"Oh, aye, I do know it!" Esmée's gaze felt to the pavement. "But I cannot *do* it!"

Alasdair nodded sagely. "I quite understand," he said. "So we're agreed, then."

"Are we?" Her head jerked up.

"Indeed," he answered. "Lydia must do it."

"Oh!" said Esmée on a choke of laughter. "MacLachlan, you are shameless."

Alasdair smiled crookedly. "Yes, well, I warned you of that, too, didn't I?"

But Sorcha was tired of the delay. "Go! Go park!"

Alasdair leaned across, and chucked the child beneath what was still a sweetly babyish double chin. "Go *to the* park, impudent child!" he said. "Can you say that? Go *to the* park."

"Go to park," she responded. "Go to *now*."

Alasdair slapped his hat back on. "Miss Hamilton, our despot has spoken!"

Esmée found the walk to the park a little shorter, and a good deal more pleasant, than usual. Not far from the foot of Great

Queen Street, there was a broad sweep of stairs which constituted a shortcut to the street below, but she was always obliged to go round them. Today, however, MacLachlan simply picked up Sorcha's perambulator at both ends, and carried her down in his broad, strong arms.

Sorcha screeched happily and clapped her hands. When MacLachlan sat her down again, she held out her chubby arms. "Carry," she ordered.

MacLachlan surprised her by reaching down to do so. Impulsively, Esmée laid a hand on his shoulder. "You needn't," she said. "She will be fine."

He flashed his crooked smile again and lifted her out anyway. He settled Sorcha on his hip, and she circled one arm round his neck and used the other to point out familiar objects along the way. "Pretty dog," she said of a pampered-looking terrier they passed along Birdcage Walk. "Horses," she said of a passing carriage.

"*Black* horses," said MacLachlan. "Four of them."

"Back horses," echoed the child. "Four dem."

"And here come some *white* horses," he went on. "Can you say *white?*"

"White horses," responded Sorcha, stab-

191

bing her fat little finger in their direction. "Pretty."

Thus it went until they reached the center of St. James's Park. "Have you taken her to Hyde Park yet?" asked MacLachlan. "It is but a little farther on, and there will be some very fine horses along the bridle path."

"But have they any ducks?" asked Esmée with mock condescension. "Our despot must have her ducks."

"Oh, yes. And swans, too, usually."

"Sorcha calls them all ducks."

MacLachlan looked down at her and laughed, the lines about his gold eyes crinkling. "And so they must be, then."

Esmée was suddenly struck with how perfectly natural it felt to be walking by his side. Perhaps she oughtn't be doing so, but who was to see her? Who would care? Here in England, she was no one. Indeed, she *had* no one. Well, save Sorcha — and oddly, MacLachlan himself.

Perhaps it was just a foolish obsession which drove her, but she could not get him out of her mind. No matter how angry he made her, she could not stop thinking of him; him, as he was now, or as he had been that afternoon in the schoolroom with Sorcha. Nor could she forget the strange, wonderful sensations which went swirling through her each time their lips touched.

And sometimes — no, *often* — she dreamt of him. She would awake in a feverish heat, wishing desperately he would hold her again, their bodies pressed hard against one another. But that way lay madness — not to mention ruin and grief. There was another far wiser and far more legitimate reason to allow him to accompany them today, just as he had pointed out. He was Sorcha's father. He was *trying.*

She cut another sidelong glance at his well-chiseled profile and realized, suddenly and inexplicably, that in this moment, she was almost happy. It was a startling and somewhat disconcerting realization.

They soon reached Hyde Park, which Esmée had thus far viewed only from its southeast corner. MacLachlan pointed out the Duke of Wellington's grand house. "He claims to have spent sixty thousand pounds on its renovation," he said as they passed by. "And loves to complain of it to anyone who will listen."

"Aye, and a dreadful waste, it is, too," said Esmée. "Just think what such a sum would draw in the five-percents!"

"Ah, spoken like a true daughter of Caledonia," MacLachlan said, as they headed into the park's green expanse. He chose a bench situated above its curving pond, which he called the Serpentine.

Esmée tossed out a blanket to protect Sorcha from the damp. She refused it, of course, and instead toddled back and forth in the lush autumn grass, picking dandelions and bits of clover and placing them in untidy piles on the blanket. The sun was peeping through the clouds now. Already settled on the bench beside her, MacLachlan looked up at it, narrowing his eyes.

"I said the other day that I owed you an apology, Miss Hamilton," he said quietly. "I want to have done with it now. My behavior toward you on two occasions has been appalling. I have no explanation, nor any excuse that will suffice, but it shan't happen again."

Esmée had sensed his regret even as she had stalked out of his study that day. Nonetheless, she was surprised to hear him couch it now in terms of an apology. "You have not been alone in your bad judgment," she finally said. "I have made matters worse."

"I wish to God I'd never let you stay!" he said, his voice suddenly low and dark. "But I'm damned, Esmée, if I know what's to be done about it now."

"I wanted to be with Sorcha." Her voice

quavered unexpectedly. "You gave me that choice."

"And you do not regret it?" he asked. "You do not wish me to the devil?"

She was fidgeting with her pearl necklace again. Abruptly, she jerked her fingers away and clasped her hands together in her lap. "Perhaps I am not as innocent as you wish to believe," she whispered. *Perhaps I am just like my mother. Foolish. Romantic. A magnet for handsome rogues . . .*

Abruptly, he turned toward her on the bench. "Esmée, it is not too late for you," he said. "My grandmother is in Argyllshire and far removed from society, but I have friends who are well placed."

Esmée was confused. "What are you saying?"

"That you deserve something more than a life of drudgery."

"Caring for Sorcha is not drudgery," she said. "If you think me inadequate to the task, then speak it plain, MacLachlan."

Swiftly, he covered her hand where it rested on the bench and gave it a reassuring squeeze. "I meant only that you deserve a life of your own," he pressed. "Perhaps there is someone who might sponsor you. Perhaps Devellyn's mother, the Duchess of Gravenel? There must be *someone*."

She looked at him incredulously. "Aye, to do what?" she asked. "Truss me up in white satin and present me at court? Bring me 'out' and take me to Almack's?"

He shrugged. "Do you not want those things?"

"Oh, aye, once upon a time," she said mordantly.

Indeed, just a few months earlier, she would have jumped at such an opportunity. Then everything changed. It wasn't just her mother's death. It wasn't just Sorcha. It was everything. It was *him.* And he wished to be rid of her, while she was no longer so eager to go. The realization shook her.

"You are young, Esmée," he said — pointlessly, it seemed. What did her age matter to him? She watched the muscles of his throat work up and down. "You've no business living under the same roof with a bounder like me, let alone . . . let alone anything else."

Just then, Sorcha came up and opened her fist on MacLachlan's thigh, depositing a mangled bit of clover. "See?" she said. "Pretty, see?"

He seemed grateful for the distraction. "Oh, I see the prettiest blossom of all!" he cried, snatching her up and lifting her high. "And I have plucked her from the grass!"

Sorcha shrieked with laughter and allowed herself to be settled on his knee. Together, they observed the horses which came trotting past. "Back horse," said Sorcha.

"Black," he corrected. "And here comes a hard one. A dappled gray."

"A dabble gay," said Sorcha, pointing.

Esmée watched them, amazed by the change Sorcha's presence seemed to engender in MacLachlan. His eyes softened, and the hard lines of his face instantly gentled. Lips that were ordinarily curled with cynicism turned instead into a pure and honest smile, stripping away the years and tempering his jaded gaze.

So often in her darker moments, Esmée found herself wondering what she saw in such a hardened, practiced rogue. Suddenly, she knew. It was *this*. The change which came over him in such sweet and carefree moments. He was a different man. Sorcha was a different child. And Esmée — well, for good or ill, she was changing, too.

For almost half an hour, Sorcha sat thus, cheerfully jabbering about anything or anyone which passed by. When she tired of that, the child turned round and began to toy with the buttons of his waistcoat, actually managing to undo a couple.

MacLachlan just looked down at her indulgently. But eventually, Sorcha began to wriggle her way back down his leg. MacLachlan let her go.

Sorcha wandered a little down the hill and resumed her flower picking. MacLachlan's eyes stared almost blindly as another rider passed. "The fashionable hour approaches," he finally murmured. "The park shan't remain empty much longer. I should probably go."

His words made Esmée's heart sink a little. Without realizing it, she had begun to run her finger around the inside of her pearl necklace again. This time, unfortunately, something snapped. "Oh, no!" she cried, as pearls went flying. "Mamma's necklace!"

"Blast!" said Alasdair, as pearls went bouncing into the grass.

"Oh!" Esmée began to paw through the pleats of her skirt.

"Don't stand up," MacLachlan ordered. He was already on his knees, plucking pearls from the grass. "Hold on to what's left of the strand. Here, have you a pocket?"

"Yes, oh, thank you!" Esmée clasped the strand to her breast with one hand and took the pearls he handed her in the other. "It was Mamma's necklace from her come-out. She gave it to me when I turned seventeen.

Oh, what an idiot I am!"

"We shall find most of them," he soothed. "I know a good jeweler who can repair it."

But in a fraction of a second, the necklace was forgotten.

Esmée looked up and screamed.

Alasdair had no memory of leaping to his feet. Or bolting down the hill. The next moments moved as if he waded through water, even as the approaching phaeton flew across the earth. The occupants were chattering gaily, faces lifted to the nascent sun. They never looked at the path ahead. Never saw the child rushing toward the water, arms outstretched.

"Sorcha!" The word exploded from his lungs, lost in the sound of pounding hooves.

But Sorcha knew no fear. Everything happened at once. At the last moment, the horse shied toward the pond. The phaeton jerked right, almost overturning. Screams surrounded him. Esmée's. Sorcha's. The horse's. His own. Hooves flew, and Sorcha fell. And then he saw the wheel, relentlessly grinding. Somehow, he snatched her, and the carriage flew past, churning up bits of yellow muslin and lace. And then there was just the child, still and bloody in his arms.

Heart in his throat, he laid her down.

Esmée was still screaming Sorcha's name. On his knees in the grass, Alasdair cradled her face in his hands. "Sorcha!" he rasped. "Sorcha, open your eyes!"

"Oh, God! Oh, God!" Esmée fell to her knees beside him. "Oh, Sorcha!"

Alasdair felt faint. Men beaten near to a pulp in the boxing ring, or shot nearly dead on the dueling field, were nothing to this. It looked bad. Very bad. Blood streamed from a gash in her head. Her left arm hung at an awkward angle. Her muslin skirt had been half-torn from her dress. He had been too slow.

Esmée was sobbing hysterically now, and stroking the hair from Sorcha's forehead. "Is she . . . oh, God, *is* she?"

Alasdair had already set his forefingers to Sorcha's throat. "A pulse," he choked. "I feel it."

There were voices above him now, disembodied yet strident. He looked up to see the phaeton flying through the gates at the corner below, almost overturning as it lurched toward Knightsbridge.

"Gone to fetch a doctor," said a strained voice at his elbow. "Good God, we did not see her! I am so sorry. Oh, poor child!"

The screams had attracted a stout, blue-coated constable. He squatted beside

Esmée, holding on to her arm, restraining her from embracing Sorcha. "Now, now, miss!" he cautioned gently. "Mustn't move her a'tall. Wait for the doctor, now. He'll want to check her bones and such. Yes, there's a good girl!"

"But her arm!" cried Esmée, covering her mouth with both hands. "Oh, God! Look at her arm!"

"Happen it might be broke," agreed the constable. "But p'raps only yanked from its socket. Young bones mend, miss, and quick-like, too! There, there! Sit still now."

Instead, Esmée leaned forward, grasping Sorcha's tiny leg with both hands, as one drowning might cling to a bit of wreckage. "Oh, 'tis all my fault!" she wailed into the grass. "Oh, God! How could I? For a necklace! Oh, God!"

Acting on instinct, Alasdair turned and dragged her up and against his chest. "Hush, now!" he scolded. "If it's anyone's fault, it is mine."

"How can you say that!" Esmée sobbed into his cravat. "It isn't your job to watch her! 'Tis *mine!* Mine! And now look!"

"Hush, Esmée," he said again. "She'll be all right. She will. I swear it." He prayed to God he was right.

Just then, ever so faintly, Sorcha's lashes

fluttered. Alasdair felt a fierce, urgent warmth pressing against the backs of his eyes, and realized he was crying.

"Dislocated!" pronounced Dr. Reid gruffly as he straightened up from his patient's bed. "Dislocated, but not broken."

"Christ, that's my doing," Alasdair rasped, his eyes never leaving Sorcha's face. "That is — I think it must be. I remember yanking her — yanking her *hard.* And feeling something give. It felt sickening."

"A small price to pay," said the doctor emphatically. "Especially when that wheel was close enough to tear her clothes half-off. A dislocation is nothing compared to being crushed beneath a carriage."

Alasdair pinched hard at the bridge of his nose. "I — yes, I daresay."

Better than an hour had passed since the accident, though it was mostly a blur to Alasdair. One of the young bucks from the phaeton had turned up with the irascible Dr. Reid in tow. Alasdair knew him vaguely; the doctor had attended more than one dawn appointment in order to stitch up "some damned overbred fool," as he so charitably called the wounded. Blunt to a fault, Reid had no bedside manner to speak of — indeed, he'd already set Esmée on edge — but there was no one better at patching people up. And at this moment, Alasdair could have forgiven the devil himself, had he possessed that one skill.

Sorcha lay, limp and frail, on a bed which looked too large for her tiny body. The very bed, in fact, which Julia had so recently occupied. Reid had demanded the nearest bedchamber, and Alasdair had carried her to it. Sorcha had whimpered, but never opened her eyes. Now Alasdair and Esmée stood on opposite sides of the mattress, Esmée quietly weeping.

"But why won't she wake up?" Esmée whispered. *"Why?"*

The doctor was laying out a neat row of instruments on a fold of white linen. "Oh, she'll come round tomorrow, I daresay," he answered. "She'd likely have stirred by now, but I slipped her a dose of laudanum. No choice, really, with that arm hanging from its socket."

"Is she in pain?" asked Esmée fretfully. "Is she suffering? Good God, I need to know!"

The doctor snapped his bag shut and set it aside. "Doesn't feel a thing," he responded. "Though we're in for a long night. That gash was made by a flying hoof, but the skull is not fractured. She was lucky. If the blow had struck a temple, or the base of the skull, you'd have been burying her before the week was out."

Esmée made a little mewling sound, and buried her face in a handkerchief. Her hair had begun to tumble down, and her spirits had fallen with it. Alasdair tried to clear the knot from his throat. "And what of the arm, sir?" he asked. "What's to be done for it?"

"I've sent for someone," said Reid, extracting his pocket watch and peering at it. "An old sawbones I know. We must relocate the joint whilst the child is still unconscious. The pain is prodigious otherwise. It's a job best done by two, but my friend is in Chelsea setting a leg. He should be here by dusk — I hope."

"B-But what if he isn't?" cried Esmée. "What will happen? Can it wait? Should we send for someone else? Time is of the essence, is it not?"

Alasdair swallowed hard. "I . . . I could help, perhaps?"

Dr. Reid scowled impatiently. "Not necessary!" he said. "I shall ice the joint to bring the swelling down whilst we wait. Then I'll stitch up her head. What I need you to do, sir, is to take your wife to bed and pour her a generous tot of brandy."

Esmée crushed her handkerchief in one

hand. "But I am not — I mean, we are not — oh! We are sisters, Sorcha and I. Besides, I dislike brandy excessively. And I certainly cannot leave her. Indeed, I shan't!"

The doctor cut a grim look in Alasdair's direction, then jerked his head toward the door. Esmée sank down in a chair by the bed and laid her hand over Sorcha's. Almost unnoticed, the men stepped out into the hall.

"Take her upstairs, Sir Alasdair!" warned Dr. Reid as soon as the door was shut. "I'll not have womenfolk hovering about, crying and asking questions, when there's medical work to be done."

Alasdair hesitated. "I don't know," he said. "She's awfully stub—"

"Hell and the devil, man!" the doctor interjected. "Have you ever seen a dislocated shoulder replaced?"

Alasdair winced. "Yes, once," he admitted. "But we were all drunk as wheelbarrows."

"Then you know it's an ugly sight," gritted the doctor. "But first I've got to put about a dozen stitches in the child's head. And after all that, if there's swelling of the brain, I'll have to shave the child's head and trepan her skull. Now, do you want her witnessing *that*?"

"Trepanning?" he choked. He had heard about that horror from Devellyn. "Oh, God, no! I pray it doesn't come to that!"

Dr. Reid looked at him askance. "No, it won't," he grudgingly admitted. "I've seen enough such cases to know it. But mark me, that child won't so much as crack an eye before the sun's up. And if she does, I'll just have to sedate her again."

"Yes, I shouldn't wish her to suffer," murmured Alasdair.

"She *won't,* if I'm left to do my job properly," said Reid. "And the last thing I need is a fretful woman lingering over the bed all the livelong night and asking me every five minutes if the child is dead or alive or breathing too fast or thrashing too much or too pale, too hot, too cold, too — well, you take my meaning, I daresay!"

Alasdair relaxed a little. "You are staying the night, then?"

"If I'm left to do my work in peace, yes," said the doctor. "Now, do us all a favor, Sir Alasdair. Go upstairs, the both of you — and stay put 'til you're sent for."

Two minutes later, Alasdair was gently propelling Esmée from the room and up the stairs. "I wish to stay with Sorcha!" she protested, jerking to a halt on the landing.

"What if she needs me?"

He urged her toward the next flight. "She is in good hands, Esmée," he said firmly. "She does not need you."

Esmée looked as if he'd just struck her. "Aye, you'd be right!" she cried. "She *doesn't* need me, does she? I was of no use to her this afternoon. Just look what has happened!"

As he had in the park, Alasdair pulled her against him reflexively. "Shush, Esmée," he murmured against her hair. "Of course she needs you. But just now, the doctor must concentrate. He promises me she shan't awaken —"

"Aye, 'tis my very fear!" rasped Esmée.

"— because she's sedated," he swiftly finished.

Just then, Wellings came down the stairs. *"Whisky,"* he mouthed, as they passed. The butler nodded, and went on.

Once inside the schoolroom, Esmée began to roam restlessly about, her eyes darting from one vacant corner to the next. Even to Alasdair, the room felt cold and empty without Sorcha's cheery presence. He said nothing for a time, but merely watched Esmée, wondering, and yet knowing what was in her mind. She was blaming herself, just as he was.

He felt as if he'd aged a decade since that terrifying moment in the park. He remembered laying Sorcha in the grass, and feeling, fleetingly, as if his life had just ended. As if it were seeping away from him inexorably, in the very blood which covered his child. And in one stark instant of truth, he had realized just what Esmée had meant when she had spoken so poignantly of Julia's agony. To lose one's child! Could there be a deeper, more cutting pain?

Perhaps. Perhaps losing one's sister. Or one's mother. Poor Esmée. She had borne so much, and so stoically. He stood by the cold hearth, watching as she drifted through the room, picking up toys, then setting them down again, and neatening books which were already tidy, and all the while, silently weeping. Alasdair could bear her pain no longer. He went to her and took her hand lightly in his. "It isn't your fault, Esmée," he said quietly. "And it isn't mine, much as I'm blaming myself just now."

She looked up at him, blinking back tears. "But I was responsible for taking care of her!" she whispered. "That was my job. My duty as a sister."

There was a soft sound at the door, and Lydia came in with a tray. Wellings, God love him, had sent up a full decanter of whisky and two glasses, as well as a plate of bread, cheese, and cold meat, none of which would ever be eaten.

"Thank you, Lydia," he murmured. "You may work belowstairs the rest of the evening. Tell Wellings Miss Hamilton is not to be disturbed under any circumstance unless Dr. Reid sends for her."

Eyes sad, Lydia curtseyed, and went away. "Oh, Alasdair!" Esmée cried when the door was shut. "Oh, what have I done? What if she dies, too? I cannot bear it! I cannot!"

Alasdair knew better than to belittle her fear. He, too, was still terrified. And for Esmée, death was all too real. She had just buried her own mother, a woman who, by all accounts, had apparently been young and vibrant. She had lost a father, and three stepfathers. Now her sister lay still and pale as death. Life no doubt seemed very impermanent to Esmée. He was struck with the strangest urge to pull her into his arms and kiss away her tears. But it seemed wiser to dab them away with his handkerchief, then pour her a whisky, and press it into her hand.

"At least it isn't frog water," he said by way of apology. "Drink it."

"Thank you." Esmée sipped without hesitation and resumed her pacing. For long moments, she kept it up, pausing only to nurse her whisky. Alasdair considered leaving. Considered ringing for Lydia to come back. But he wanted — no, *needed* — to be with her. So he did neither, and doomed himself.

The sun had vanished from the sky, its rays warming the world beyond the school-room windows with shades of dusky rose. Darkness, and the intimacy which it so often brought, was but a moment away. Alasdair drained his glass, set it aside, and sent up yet another silent prayer for Sorcha's recovery.

"Och, what a soss I've made of this!" Esmée's voice came out of nowhere, thick and husky. "I never really learnt how to take proper care of a child. We were used to a gaggle of servants, Mamma and I. They did *everything*."

"I think you have done a fine job," he answered.

But she went on as if she had not heard him. "I suspected, of course, that Achanalt would put me out," she said, her voice taking on a hysterical edge. "But to put out a child? How could he? How? He must have known — oh, God! He must have known I was hopelessly incompetent!" She set down her nearly empty glass with an awkward clatter and let her head fall forward into her hands. "Oh, God, Alasdair! He must have wished for this!"

Alasdair went to her and set an arm about her shoulders. He was no longer certain the whisky had been such a good idea. "You need to sit down, Esmée," he said, looking impatiently about the room. "Good Lord, haven't we any normal-sized chairs?"

She lifted her head and looked at the little chairs as if she'd not seen them before. "In here," she answered, her voice throaty.

He followed her, foolishly, into her bed-chamber. There, the canopied bed had already been turned down, and a warm fire burned in the grate. But the other bed, the little bed he'd bought for Sorcha, stood empty. Esmée passed by it and blanched.

Alasdair took her by the elbow and urged her toward a pair of chairs which sat near the hearth. "Thank you," she said. "You are very kind. I don't know why I ever suggested otherwise."

Alasdair looked at her warily. "Even Old Scratch looks better through the bottom of a glass," he murmured. "Why don't you sit down, my dear?"

Instead, she slid her hands up and down her arms as if she were cold. "I cannot be still," she rasped. "I feel as if I might explode."

He took her gently by the shoulders. "Esmée, Sorcha will be all right," he soothed. "She *will*."

"Will she?" she cried. "Alasdair, how can you be sure?"

He tightened his grip, and gave her a little shake. "She will, Esmée. I know it. I believe it."

She sobbed, a deep, bone-shuddering sound, and fell against him, her arms going round his neck. And then he was holding her again, as he'd already done too often this dreadful day. Esmée was sobbing into his shirtfront as if her heart were breaking. Alasdair tightened the embrace and set his lips to her temple. "Whisht now, love," he whispered. "All's well. Trust me, Esmée. Just trust me."

Trust him? What in God's name was he thinking?

But instead of pushing him away in disgust, Esmée just swallowed hard and nodded. "When you say it, I believe it," she whispered.

She was a fool, he knew, to believe in him, the most resolute rotter in Christendom. But in that moment, he wanted her to believe. He wanted to deserve, just for an instant, the abject need he'd seen in Esmée's eyes. She set her cheek to his chest. "Oh, Alasdair!" Her plea was so soft, he could barely hear it. "Oh, just put your arms round me for a moment. Please."

So he encircled her in his arms and drew their bodies closer. He crooked his head, meaning to kiss her temple again. But she looked up at him instead, her damp eyes wide and searching. She made a little sound, a sweet, sudden inhalation, and somehow, he dipped his head. Their lips met — by accident, he would have sworn — and she let her weight sag against him, wordlessly pleading for something she'd no business having.

But there was, perhaps, a little sliver of decency yet left in Alasdair. He raised his head, and looked at her questioningly.

"Aye, Alasdair, I can hold my whisky," she whispered. "I'm not so tosie I don't know what I'm about."

Another tear leaked from her left eye, and impulsively, he dipped his head and brushed it away with his lips. Esmée made the small, plaintive sound again, and curled one slender hand behind his neck.

He let his eyes move over the pure ivory of her face, now tear-stained, and somehow convinced himself it would be ungentlemanly to refuse her a moment of consolation. So he let one hand slide from her shoulder down to the gentle sway of her back and spread his fingers wide, then eased his palm soothingly up and down, easing a little of his own fear as he did so. Burying his face in her hair, he drew in Esmée's sweet essence, that familiar scent of moor and heather. Of home. Of *her*.

Impatiently, she rose on her tiptoes and slanted her mouth over his, setting his head to swimming. Somehow, he managed to remember her innocence, and returned the kiss tenderly. But that was not quite what she wanted. Instead, Esmée opened her mouth beneath his, tempting him to take her.

Logic spun away. Alasdair slid inside her mouth, tasting the whisky on her lips. Her breath was like spicy fruit; a ripe persimmon, bittersweet on his tongue. Esmée's hands began to roam restlessly over him, her touch uncertain yet urgent.

Alasdair understood that sometimes harrowing experiences had an extraordinary effect on people. There was a sense of having been brushed by death, and often, a desire to obliterate the terror with some other — almost *any* other — sensation. But he did not explain this to Esmée, for he could not find the words. Instead, he set his other hand between her shoulder blades and began to pat her back in a gesture he hoped was more avuncular than avaricious.

Apparently, it wasn't working. She tore her mouth from his. "Alasdair," she choked. "Don't leave me tonight."

Her meaning was clear. "Ah, Esmée," he whispered. "It wouldn't do, love. You are distraught. And I am not for you. Remember, you don't even like me that well."

Anxiously, she licked her lips. "I was mistaken," she returned. "You make me afraid of myself, I think."

He kissed the turn of her jaw. "Be afraid of *me,* love," he whispered against her ear. "I'm no gentleman."

She arched her neck, all but begging his mouth to slide down the turn of her throat. "Just stay with me, Alasdair," she pleaded. "Make me forget this awful day. I can't be alone. Oh, I can't bear it. Not tonight."

Alasdair heard the little catch in her voice. He told himself that she was young and innocent, and that he needed to soothe her fear for Sorcha, without making his desire so bloody apparent. But that was the very trouble he'd been struggling with these last few weeks. Esmée was desirable — so much so that he'd been afraid to sleep alone in his own home. Afraid, really, that he wouldn't end up alone, for despite their fierce arguments, he had already felt the snap and crackle of passion between them.

Oh, yes, it was all too easy for a practiced rake to seduce an innocent. And it was particularly easy now, when they were both hurting, and afraid of being left alone with their fears. It was up to him to say *no*. But when she brushed her lips over his again, and slid her warm, slender hands round his back, he said *yes,* closing his eyes, and kissing her deeply, until her body came fully against his, and pressed artlessly against the bulge of his trousers.

What a naïve little fool she was! And what a cad he was. Suddenly, cool air breezed up his spine. She had tugged his shirt free. Her small hands were on him, warm and searching as they skimmed up the muscles of his back, setting him to trembling.

"God Almighty, Esmée," he choked. *"Don't."*

But Alasdair had no self-discipline, save his ruthless control at the card table. He refused himself nothing he wanted — and what he wanted now was Esmée. Which really wasn't anything new. So he let her slide the coat from his shoulders. Let her fingers skate round the bearer of his trousers. Let his hand ease down to the luscious curve of her arse. Let everything go to hell in a surge of overwrought fear and suppressed desire.

Esmée no longer kissed like an innocent. Instead, she was meeting his strokes with hers, languorously entwining her tongue with his. Blood began to pound in his temples, drowning out his good intentions. Tearing his mouth from hers, he shoved his fingers into her hair and drew back her head, brushing his lips down the tender flesh of her neck.

Esmée shuddered. "I want . . . oh, I want . . ." she whispered.

He knew what she wanted. And Alasdair had never been a saint. He undressed her with the efficiency of a practiced rogue, divesting her of gown and corset, chemise and drawers — everything, even what was left of her hairpins — all without taking his ravening mouth from hers.

Oh, he knew he was going to regret it; knew there was going to be a terrible price to pay. But he drew in her scent again, and let the strange mix of fear and desire swirl in his mind like a shimmering haze, obscuring his reason.

Esmée showed no embarrassment when his hungry eyes raked her bare body. Perhaps it was the whisky. Or perhaps just her earthy nature. He didn't care; he was mesmerized by the soft alabaster curves of her hips, her thighs, round swell of her breasts. She was small, so fine boned and delicate he feared he might break her. But her cool green eyes held his, as knowing and honest as the day he'd first met her. The heavy brown hair he'd once thought plain hung to her waist in a shimmering curtain which teased at her nipples. He buried his face in it again, drew in her scent of honey and heather, and was lost.

Later, he couldn't even remember undressing himself, or carrying her to the bed. But he remembered pressing her down into the white softness of the mattress and dragging his weight over her. Her breasts were surprisingly full, and when he set his hands firmly against her shoulders and took one in his mouth, Esmée arched beneath him and cried out his name.

Something hot and frighteningly possessive surged through him then, yet he was but barely aware of the danger. Esmée was all youth and beauty and innocence. And her innocence was his, it seemed, to take.

Esmée felt a sweet, hot heat go curling through her belly the instant his mouth touched her breast. Instinctively, she cried out, her body rising to his in a primordial sign of desire. She was not a total fool; she understood she was offering him something irrevocable. It did not matter. She wished to lose herself in this man's beauty; to let him ease her pain and obliterate her fear.

"Alasdair." Her voice was urgent in the gloom. "Alasdair. *Please.*"

Instead, he cradled her face between his hands, let his long lashes drop shut, and kissed her slow and deep. Esmée's head swam. His tantalizing scent — soap and tobacco, sweat and whisky — teased at her nostrils and made her stomach bottom out. She lifted one leg instinctively and curled it over his, drawing their hips together. But he pushed her leg away almost roughly and turned his attention to her other breast, his heavy golden hair falling forward, veiling his eyes.

For long moments, he suckled her, stilling her to his mouth with his powerful arms, and building her blood to a roaring boil. Oh, *this!* Yes, this was what she yearned for. With the weight of his body still sprawled over her, he drew the tip of one breast between his teeth. She gave a cry, soft and urgent, but it wasn't pain. It was . . . something better. Something heady and uncontrollable.

Esmée let her head tip back into the pillow, let her fingers curl into her palms, inviting him to do as he pleased as she watched from beneath her lashes. Oh, he was so beautiful, this lover she ought not have! But regret would wait until tomorrow. Right now, she needed to forget. Alasdair's body was slender and hard, sculpted into lean planes and taut curves. His arms and legs were layered with muscle and dusted with surprisingly dark hair. And the warm, silky weight which she felt between her thighs — oh!

"I want you," she said, barely realizing she'd said the words aloud.

In response, Alasdair trailed his mouth between her breasts and down her belly, then sat back on his heels. The heavy curtain of hair still hid his eyes, separating them. Novice and teacher. Slave and master. He had enslaved her against her will with his melting brown eyes and infinite beauty. He set his wide, warm hand on her belly, and Esmée trembled. With unhurried motions, his hand slid lower and lower, until his thumb inched into the thatch of curls below her belly. He stroked between the folds of her skin, and Esmée felt a tremor rock the bed.

He made a sound — an anguished groan

— and with one knee, urged her thighs wider. Then his hand slid between them, and he touched her again, gliding through her flesh, tormenting her past all bearing. "Ah, Esmée!" He sounded almost regretful. "Such a beautiful, sensual creature."

He set both hands on her inner thighs, pushing them farther, then bent his head and touched her with his tongue. "Ahh!" she cried, the pleasure so intense she wished to shut it out.

"Relax your legs, love." His voice was but a whisper. "Open for me, Esmée. Let me soothe you."

Let me soothe you.

She writhed beneath his touch. Oh, God. He could do it; she knew that much instinctively. But what was he offering? His hands pushed firmly on her inner thighs until she relaxed into the mattress, then his thumbs spread wide her flesh. His tongue slid deep, teasing at her wetness, heightening her desire, until it touched her very core and made her body tremble. And still, he tormented her, pleasuring her with light, little flicks, and then long, languorous strokes, until Esmée found herself shaking and shattering, and coming apart.

She returned to awareness in the dimly lit room to see Alasdair rise up on his knees.

When she saw the jutting length of his erection, she drew in her breath sharply. His head came up, and with a jerk of his head, he tossed the heavy gold hair from his eyes. His once-hidden gaze burned into her now, and with one hand, he touched himself, easing his fist along the impossible length of his flesh.

Esmée swallowed hard, then held out her hands, inviting him. Instead, he came down beside her, and curled one leg over her body. Sated and uncertain, she rolled onto her side, facing him. She thought he ought to be doing *something* — something more than just staring into her eyes — but she was unsure.

"Alasdair, I . . . I want . . ."

"Shush, love," he whispered, touching one finger to her lips. "I know what you want." He rolled closer, pushing her onto her back, then covering her body with his.

This was it, then. The moment every woman both craved and feared. But he did not put himself inside her body, as she expected. Instead, he kissed her again, opening his mouth over hers, abrading her face with the stubble of his beard, his nostrils flared wide, his breath coming fast and urgent.

"Touch me," he groaned, as if the words

had been dragged from the pit of his belly. "Esmée, touch me." Almost roughly, he took her hand and guided it toward his erection.

Esmée did as he asked, sliding her hand between their bodies. The weight of him felt like satin, but hard and warm, pulsing with strength. Tentatively, she stroked him as he had done, drawing her fingers firmly down his length. Alasdair came up on one elbow, and shuddered. "Again," he rasped, his eyes squeezed shut.

Esmée obliged him, marveling in the barely restrained power of his body. He trembled as if from his very core, then spread his mouth over hers again, kissing her deeply. Esmée felt a growing sense of power, a faith in her ability to give him pleasure.

Alasdair's long, elegant fingers curled over hers, easing her hand back and forth over his hot flesh as his tongue thrust inside her mouth. Again and again, she repeated the gesture, his hand over hers, his tongue sinuously curling around her own, his shudders deepening, until at last he tore his mouth away on a guttural sound. She stroked him once more, and his beautiful body bowed back, his mouth opening in a silent, triumphant cry. Then Esmée felt his erection spasm, again and again, until the warm wetness of his seed spilt across her belly.

Alasdair's deep sense of peace was not long-lived. After allowing himself the luxury of drowsing with Esmée in his arms for perhaps an hour, he began to stir, prodded by guilt and worry. Reluctantly, he slid away from the warmth of her body and returned with a damp cloth from the washstand.

She opened her eyes, and stiffened. "Sorcha — ?" she rasped, rolling up onto one elbow, and pushing the hair from her face.

"Nothing yet." He brushed the backs of his fingers along the turn of her jaw. "Rest, Esmée. It's late. I'll make sure Reid sends for you if there's any change."

She sat fully upright, and let the sheets fall. A less missish sort would have dragged them up to hide her nakedness, but Esmée seemed unconcerned. "Are you leaving me?" she asked, her eyes searching his face.

God knew he did not want to. "I'd best," he said. "The servants will be wondering."

"Alasdair —" she began, then halted. "I wish . . . I wish you to tell me *why*."

She was not referring to his leaving, and he knew it. Christ, it had been hard enough to do. Now he had to explain it? He bent one knee to the mattress, and sat down. "Esmée, you brought me great pleasure," he answered. "May we leave it at that?"

She shook her head. "No."

Absently, he tucked a curl behind her ear. "Esmée, you are very young," he began. She opened her mouth to speak, but he laid a finger to her lips. "And I have seen more of the world than a man ought."

Esmée's eyes hardened. "I'm inexperienced, aye, but not ignorant," she said. "There is a vast difference between the two."

He leaned across the bed, and lightly kissed her. "Is there indeed?" he said. "Well, we shall speak more of it tomorrow, Esmée, when we are not scared out of our minds."

She tore her gaze from his, and stared into the darkness of the room. "Did you not want me, then?" she asked. "Was it just me, throwing myself at you? Answer me that, MacLachlan."

So he was just *MacLachlan* again. "Aye, Esmée, I wanted you," he answered. "But wanting, and having the right to take, are far from the same thing."

She raked her hand back through her hair again. "I have been a fool, haven't I?" she whispered. "Sometimes I think I haven't the sense God gave a goose."

Alasdair didn't know what to say to that, but he understood the terrible weight of regret. He watched by the fire's light as she slid from the bed and padded across the carpet to the pile of clothing on the floor. She was so beautiful and so fragile. And yet the word beauty was inadequate, and her fragility was deceptive. He had taken not just pleasure in her arms tonight, but comfort, too. A sense of strength, and of being where he belonged. And yet he did not belong with Esmée. Certainly he did not belong in her bed.

Esmée returned with her drawers and chemise.

"Stay in bed, love," he urged her. "Try to sleep."

Again, the stubborn shake of her head, which sent her long, shimmering hair sliding over one shoulder. "I must go to my sister," she answered. "I shan't trouble Dr. Reid, I swear it. But I'll not rest tonight until I've seen Sorcha again."

Chapter Six

In which Lady Tatton is Aghast

Shortly after dawn the next morning, Alasdair arose from his own bed, feeling as if the Sword of Damocles hung over his head — two or three of them, actually. He had not slept to speak of. But to appease Ettrick, he'd taken off his clothes and put on his dressing gown. For about the fifth time since midnight, he hastened downstairs to check on Sorcha.

Dr. Reid roused in his chair and unfolded his hands from his belly. "She stirred a bit about an hour ago," he reported. "Her pupils are responding nicely, and the shoulder looks good. I think we are well out of the woods, Sir Alasdair."

"Oh, thank God." He went to the bed, and took Sorcha's tiny hand in his. The thought of the pain she must have suffered almost unmanned him. But she did indeed look different now, as if she were drowsing naturally. *She really was all right.* Relief began to flood through him.

The doctor rose. "I think she'll wake by

noon. Then we'll see if we can determine how much discomfort she's suffering. She'll likely be fretful for a day or two."

Alasdair smiled and let his hand play with one of Sorcha's fine, baby-soft curls. "Oh, Sorcha won't tolerate discomfort," he said with an inward smile. "And she'll communicate that quite forcefully."

"Hmph!" said the doctor. "Spoilt, is she?"

Alasdair shrugged. "I prefer to say *doted on.*"

Upon leaving the doctor, he choked down some dry toast and coffee, then dressed in haste. It was going to be one hell of a day. He knew what had to be done, and it left him a little ill, though whether from dread or anticipation, he was not perfectly certain. He was sorry, though — damned sorry for all of them — that he'd let it come to this.

In the entryway, Wellings handed him his stick and his hat. "Your brother was to take breakfast with you this morning, sir," he said with a sigh.

Alasdair looked at the butler incredulously. "Tell me, Wellings, is my brother not rich as Croesus?"

The butler inclined his head. "I believe so, sir."

"Then tell him to build *himself* a house,

and hire a bloody cook," Alasdair suggested, slapping his hat on his head. "Damned clutch-fisted Scot! If there's an emergency, I'll be in Oxford Street shopping."

Wellings' brows flew aloft. "*Shopping,* sir?"

Alasdair gave him a twisted grin. "Some things, Wellings, cannot wait."

It was a miracle. Or at least, it felt so to Esmée. By half past nine, Sorcha was wide-awake, raising the rafters and much of the staff. A little frantically, Esmée dandled the child on her knee, mindful of Sorcha's arm. It was not enough. Sorcha screwed up her small, pink face, and drew another deep breath.

"Porridge!" said Esmée to Lydia over the ensuing din.

"Porridge?" Lydia lifted the cover on the breakfast tray which Hawes had brought up, then hastened toward them with a spoon and bowl.

Esmée lifted the spoon, and the silence was instantaneous.

"Bite!" said the child, opening her mouth.

Esmée and Lydia sighed in unison.

"Spoilt!" grunted the doctor, who was dropping clanking bits of metal into his black leather satchel.

Lydia rolled her eyes.

"Now, nothing but that porridge and a bit of broth today!" Dr. Reid went on, shutting his bag with an efficient snap. "No running. No climbing. And for God's sake, no bathing. I'll be back first thing tomorrow. Until then, if she gets fretful, give her two drops of the tincture in that brown bottle, then let her sleep."

Esmée managed a weak smile. "Thank you, Dr. Reid," she said. "Lydia will show you out when you're ready."

But when the door closed behind them, leaving Esmée with nothing but her remorse and her sister to bear her company, the guilt set in anew. She thought of the ugly sutures in her sister's scalp, and for a moment, panic seized her breath. An instant's distraction, and now this! She was lucky the child wasn't dead.

Still, the knee-weakening sense of relief she'd felt this morning when Sorcha's eyes fluttered open had never fully overcome her dread. Apparently, it wasn't enough she'd been a fool where her sister's welfare was concerned. She'd been a fool over Sir Alasdair MacLachlan, too. She had allowed terror — and some nameless emotion she could not comprehend — to get a grip on her heart.

And what now was she to do? How did one go on after such a thing? There was no pretending it hadn't happened — and no pretending it wouldn't happen again if she remained here. She had all but begged him to take her to bed. And in so doing, Esmée had been a bigger fool than her mother had been. MacLachlan hadn't even needed to whisper sweet lies in her ear. She had just clung to him and begged him. What man would have said no?

Well, at least he had learned from his past mistakes. At least she would not be left carrying his child, like Mrs. Crosby and her own mother. For that small mercy, she ought to be grateful. He had also been amazingly tender toward her. He had made her feel desirable, and . . . almost loved. Those perhaps, were the greater dangers. She was too vulnerable. Too alone.

Oh, she should never have agreed to stay here! Yesterday, she'd proven worse than useless. Lydia was a far more competent caretaker than she would ever be. Lydia would never have let a child go running into the path of a flying phaeton.

It was time, perhaps, that Esmée accepted the awful truth — that she had stayed here with Sorcha out of pure selfishness. She was not qualified to be a nurse or a governess.

And as soon as Sorcha recovered from this horrific accident, then . . . well, Esmée could not quite bear to think of that just now.

As if to remind her of more immediate concerns, Sorcha began to squirm. Esmée bent her head, and gingerly kissed the child's bruised brow. "Och, my wee trootie!" she whispered. " 'Tis a sad, sairie mother I've made you!"

Sorcha looked up at her solemnly, and said, "Bite!"

Somehow, Esmée found it inside her to laugh. She dipped the spoon in the porridge, and resumed her task. But almost at once, Lydia returned, her eyes wide.

"Miss, I think you'd best go downstairs," she said. "There's a big black coach and four drawn up at the door, and a lady downstairs reading Wellings the riot act."

Esmée kissed Sorcha again, and passed her to the maid. "Who can it be?"

"No one as I ever saw before," said the girl, taking up the porridge spoon. "But I heard your name mentioned, miss, and Wellings is as white a shade of pale as ever a man could be."

"As I was saying, madam," Wellings voice echoed up the stairs, "Sir Alasdair is not at home. If you can but wait —"

"I certainly will not!" said an affronted female voice. "I have not traveled half the night to wait! Fetch me Miss Hamilton at once! I'll know the meaning of this scurrilous behavior!"

Esmée stood on the last step, frozen in shock. *"Aunt Rowena?"*

The lady's head swiveled round so fast her lavishly befeathered hat almost took flight. "Esmée!" she cried, rushing toward her. "Oh, Esmée! Dear child! What in God's name?"

Esmée embraced her aunt tightly. "You have come home!" she said breathlessly. "Oh, I'd begun to fear you never would."

"Oh, child!" said her ladyship. "Your letter was slow in reaching me, but I left as soon as Anne was well enough. Surely you did not think I would forsake you?"

"No, ma'am, but I did not know if you *could* come, nor how long it might take. And I wrote twice to you in Australia."

"Oh, the mail is so abysmally slow!" Lips pursed, Lady Tatton set her sharply away. "And I have been just sick with worry. Finch brought your last letter to meet me at Southampton, and I came straight here. Dear girl, we must *talk*. Tell this odious man to go away!"

Esmée looked at the butler. "Och, Aunt Rowena," she said. "You mustn't scold Wellings. He has been so very kind to me, and none of this is his fault."

"No, no!" said Lady Tatton. "I've every notion it is all your mother's fault! If good sense was weighed out in ha'pennies, Rosamund couldn't have bought herself a hair ribbon."

Esmée felt her face flush with color. "Come into the parlor, please," she said, going to the door and opening it. "Wellings, may I impose on you for coffee? Lady Tatton, you may have guessed, is my aunt, newly returned from abroad."

They were sequestered in the parlor for half an hour, most of that time spent in trying to bring Lady Tatton up to date on the disarray that had been her late sister's life. Lady Tatton cried most affectedly at the details of Lady Achanalt's death, but it was clear that her exasperation far exceeded her grief.

Rowena had been ten years her sister Rosamund's senior, and it had often fallen to her to extract her younger sibling from all manner of ill-thought scrapes. And after burning the candle at both ends through four marriages and twice as many *affaires*, it was not, Lady Tatton said, to be wondered at that the poor woman had succumbed to a fever.

Then Esmée tried to explain what happened afterward. The part about Lord Achanalt was not difficult, for her anger was still raw. But when she tried to explain why she had come to Sir Alasdair MacLachlan for help, and why she had remained in his home, it sounded perilously like one of her mother's ill-thought scrapes.

Her aunt was kind enough not to mention it. "Oh, my dear child!" she said, drawing out her handkerchief and dabbing at her eyes. "How could Rosamund have let it come to this?"

"I don't think she meant to, Aunt Rowena."

Lady Tatton sniffled pathetically. "I begged her, Esmée, to send you to me when you turned seventeen. But she refused me. She cried, and said you were too young. But you could have been married with a family by now. You could have had a dependable husband to take care of this mess, and dear Papa's money to ease your path through life. Instead, we have this!" She lifted her hands expansively. "Oh, it breaks my heart to think of you cast out of your home and left to live by your wits."

Esmée wasn't sure she had any wits, but

she held her tongue.

Lady Tatton let her gaze roam over the small parlor, the very room in which Esmée had struck her devil's bargain with MacLachlan. She thought of how he had looked that night; haggard, bruised, and unshaven, yet startlingly handsome just the same. She wondered now which of them had been in a greater state of panic. If the memory had not pulled so hard at her heartstrings, she might have been able to laugh.

Her aunt jolted her from her reverie. "Oh, I cannot believe you have been living in this den of iniquity," she said sharply. "Child, whatever were you thinking? And whatever was Alasdair MacLachlan thinking? Oh, that disgraceful scoundrel! An innocent young woman living under *this* roof? He assuredly knows better, even if you do not!"

"Well, I do know better," Esmée admitted. *Particularly after last night.* "But what else was I to do? I could think of nothing. And Sir Alasdair *is* Sorcha's father."

Lady Tatton sniffed a little pitifully. "Well, we don't really *know* that, do we, my dear?"

Esmée shook her head. "I heard Mamma throw it in Achanalt's face," she said for the second time. "She caught him in bed with one of the maids and flew into an awful rage. Why would she lie?"

"Oh, I don't know!" said Lady Tatton. "In any case, surely MacLachlan has no wish to raise the poor wee thing? Surely he can be persuaded to give her up? No one would think twice about Achanalt's having sent his daughter to be brought up by her aunt."

Esmée thought of the will MacLachlan had had drawn up, and of how he had looked at Sorcha in the schoolroom the afternoon they were bent so intently over his coin collection. And she thought of how he had bowed his head over Sorcha's limp body in the park, tears streaming down his face. Esmée had seen them, even through her own. Perhaps he *was* a disgraceful scoundrel. But even scoundrels could love their children, could they not?

"I am not at all sure he *can* be persuaded, Aunt," she finally answered. "Or even that he should be. He has grown rather attached to Sorcha."

Lady Tatton's visage darkened. "Well, I hope he hasn't grown rather attached to you!" she said tartly. "Your remaining here is out of the question. Indeed, we'll be hard-pressed to explain what you *were* doing here if rumors start to fly."

Aunt Rowena meant her to leave?

Well, of course she did! Esmée's last three letters had all but begged for Rowena's help, had they not? And what reason had Esmée to remain, other than her affection for Sorcha? Still, a small, silly part of her wanted to cry out that she *couldn't* go; that this was her home. But it wasn't. Indeed, it was the last place on earth she needed to be. And she was hopeless as a mother.

Worse, she seemed to have inherited her own mother's lack of common sense where men were concerned. And so she clasped her hands in her lap until her fingers went numb. "I was working here as a governess," she finally said. "That is the truth, and that is what I shall say."

"Oh, my dear, naive child!" said Lady Tatton. "Sir Alasdair is so shockingly *outré*. He is the worst sort of womanizer imaginable — when he isn't stripping young men of their fortunes."

"Perhaps the young men who are fool enough to sit down with him deserve what they get," said Esmée quietly, "if his reputation is so widely known."

Lady Tatton's shrewd gaze narrowed.

"Besides," Esmée quickly went on, "I really don't think anyone *will* ask, for Sir Alasdair does not go about in society very much, and we are quite some distance from Mayfair here. Moreover, I believe his servants are very discreet."

Lady Tatton sniffed again. "Yes, well, working in a house like this, they are probably required to be," she remarked. "How long, my dear, will it take you to pack your things? Mr. and Mrs. Finch are airing a suite of rooms for you in Grosvenor Square. I've told them to expect you, and the wee child, *if* Sir Alasdair agrees — which *I* think he will. And I hope you will own that I am just a tad more experienced than you in the ways of such gentlemen, using that term loosely, of course."

Esmée smiled a little weakly. She had forgotten how much her aunt talked. "Are you sure, ma'am, that this is what you want?" she asked. "I should not wish you to be embarrassed in any way by my presence."

"Nonsense!" said Lady Tatton. "You are my niece, Esmée, and much loved, as I hope you are aware. We'll just brazen out any gossip — my reputation is unassailable, you know — and you shall give me something to do in the spring."

"Shall I?" asked Esmée. "What?"

Lady Tatton's eyes widened. "Why, I shall bring you out, goose!" she said. "What else have I to do with Anne away, and her children all settled? You'll be in half-mourning, of course, so we can't cut such a *spectacular* dash, which, given your looks, we otherwise might have done. And you really are too old to be a debutant, in any traditional sense. But many gentlemen prefer older, more sensible girls."

"I — I beg your pardon?"

Lady Tatton patted her arm. "I'm trying to tell you we shall find you a good, staid husband nonetheless," she said. "Indeed, now I think on it, perhaps we oughtn't wait until spring."

"Oh," said Esmée softly. "No, I don't think —"

"Nonsense!" interjected Lady Tatton. "The sooner the better, before the gossip about Sorcha's situation leaks out."

Esmée pursed her lips a moment. "No, I am not at all sure I shall marry, Aunt Rowena."

"Not marry? But what of that generous dowry dear Papa left you?"

Esmée was beginning to wish Cousin Anne had had a few more children to occupy Lady Tatton. "I'm to have it anyway when I turn thirty, am I not?" she said. "I shan't need a husband then. Perhaps I shall become a bluestocking and retire to the country with a pack of hounds and a dozen cats."

Lady Tatton seized her hand and kissed it. "I can see I mustn't rush you!" she cried. "So we are agreed, then. We shall have quiet entertainments from now until spring — dinner parties and small, informal gatherings. You'll have a lovely time, I promise you. In no time at all, you'll have forgotten about this dreadful entanglement with Sir Alasdair MacLachlan. And if you should see him in town, my dear, you must at all cost turn your head and refuse to acknowledge him."

"Why, I cannot do that," she said. "He is Sorcha's father."

Lady Tatton pursed her lips again. "But he is not the sort of gentleman an unattached female *knows,* dear girl."

Esmée stiffened. "I cannot be cut off from Sorcha," she insisted. "Indeed, I won't be. Really, Aunt, that is too cruel."

Lady Tatton considered it but a moment. "Very well," she said. "The child has a nurse, I daresay? Perhaps she can bring her to visit in the mornings. Sir Alasdair, I collect, doesn't rise — perhaps doesn't even *return* — until well past noon, so it isn't as if he'd miss her. Trust me to think of something, Esmée. I would not for the world wish you or Sorcha unhappy."

They concluded their bittersweet reunion

with Lady Tatton going up to meet Sorcha, whom she declared a charming child. After clucking and cooing at the girl's wound, and vowing it would be her unalloyed delight to take the child in as her own, Lady Tatton finally rose and kissed her nieces' cheeks. She did not wish to leave Esmée behind, but finally bowed to Esmée's wishes in that regard and promised to return for her in the late afternoon.

Lydia showed her ladyship out.

Esmée sat down, and began to cry.

Unaware that his matutinal habits were being impugned by none other than that high stickler of the *haut monde,* Lady Tatton, Sir Alasdair MacLachlan walked briskly up his front steps but a scant three hours after going down them, feeling much more in charity with the world. His spirits had been buoyed by two vastly dissimilar circumstances. He had just passed Hawes, his second footman, out on an errand, and learned of Sorcha's demands for breakfast.

As to the second, he carried in his coat pocket two small jeweler's boxes, the contents of which he'd spent the morning choosing, and if the indulgences had left his purse several thousand pounds lighter, so be it. In the full light of morning, it seemed a small price to pay.

Wellings greeted him at the door.

"I hear we've good news upstairs," said Alasdair, cheerfully passing his hat and stick.

But Wellings looked instead as if someone had died.

"What?" cried Alasdair. "Good God, man! Is it the child? What?"

"We've trouble afoot, sir," he said gloomily. "There is a lady come to —"

"You!" cried a sharp voice from the foot of his stairs. "Sir Alasdair MacLachlan!"

Alasdair turned at once to see Lydia escorting a well-dressed lady. "Good God!" he said again. "Lady Tatton? Ma'am, is that you?"

Her ladyship bore down on him like a seventy-four-gun man-o'-war. "You may well ask!" she declared. "And now that you've done so, I wish a moment of your time."

Having already learned that women who invaded the sanctity of his home demanding a moment of his time rarely brought good news, Alasdair balked. "You have the advantage of me, ma'am," he said. "Especially since you are already *in* my house."

Lady Tatton put her nose in the air and marched into the parlor as if it were her own. Alasdair glanced at Wellings, who

243

looked as though he were trying to swallow a boiled lemon. *What the devil was going on?* Alasdair passed his two packages to his butler, enjoining him to lock them in the study desk.

"And what may I do for you, ma'am?" he asked Lady Tatton, stripping off his gloves as he came into the parlor. "I take it you are here on a matter of some urgency since we scarce know one another."

"I *don't* know you, sir," she said with asperity. "But this is a fine mess you've gotten us into, and I have come to sort it out."

Alasdair stopped in his tracks. "I beg your pardon?"

"My nieces!" she snapped. "The ones you are holding hostage!"

It was as if the floor shifted beneath his feet. *Lady Tatton's nieces?* Holy God. Somehow, he found the presence of mind to toss his gloves disdainfully down. "I was unaware, ma'am, that I was holding anyone hostage."

"You have caused inestimable damage, sir, to Esmée's reputation," said Lady Tatton. "Do not you dare get on your high horse with me."

Now he was rattled, and it took all his skill as a gambler to hide it. "You are the aunt, then, I take it?" he said lightly. "Returned at

244

last from points afar?"

She looked at him as if he'd lost his mind. "Of course I am the aunt! Never say you did not know!"

He twisted his mouth into a sour smile. "I did not know," he answered. "But it makes little difference to me. Sorcha is my daughter."

"And a sad shame it is, too!" said her ladyship. "Bad enough she be thought the daughter of that devil Achanalt, but you, sir, are beyond the pale."

Alasdair was swiftly losing his patience. This was not the happy occasion he'd expected his homecoming to be, and he did not like the comparison Lady Tatton had just drawn. "I hope, ma'am, that I am not sunk so low as a man who would put children out on the street to starve!" he snapped. "Now, have you a point? If so, make it and leave me in peace. I'm sorry for the loss of your sister, but Sorcha's paternity is none of your concern."

"Nonetheless, Esmée's welfare is," she returned. "And you, sir, have all but ruined her."

"Good God, what do you want of me?" he gritted. "I did not ask her to come here!"

"No, but you persuaded her to stay!" snapped Lady Tatton. "You knew she was innocent, and you knew she was desperate, and you took blatant advantage of those facts, without an iota of consideration for the damage you would be doing her good name."

Now her accusations were striking too close to home. "Wha—" His voice faltered. "What has Esmée told you?"

Lady Tatton looked at him suspiciously. "That it is all her fault," she said. "And none of yours. But I do not for one moment believe that. She is as green as grass, and you know it."

Alasdair tore his eyes from hers and stared into the depths of the room. For a moment, it was as if time held suspended, its passage marked by nothing but the ticking of the mantel clock. "Then I shall marry her," he finally said. "There need be no more talk of Esmée's ruin."

Lady Tatton gasped. "Good heavens!" she said. "Absolutely not!"

He returned his gaze to her face and forced his voice to hold steady. "It would make me the happiest man on earth," he said. He would not have wished such a thing on Esmée, but now that it had come down to it, Lady Tatton's cold recitation of his sins made it all the easier to do what he'd already known he must.

But Lady Tatton, it seemed, saw nothing easy about it. "Out of the question!" she snapped. "Unless you are telling me there is some reason why she would not make an eligible *parti* for someone else?"

Alasdair drew an unsteady breath. "Esmée would make any man proud," he answered. "And whilst I know I don't deserve her, I am the man accused of bringing about her ruin."

Lady Tatton's eyes hardened. "You would do nothing but make her miserable," she retorted. "You've already ruined her mother. Why should Esmée be forced to throw herself away on a gamester and a womanizer? On a man whose family is barely two generations removed from the croft? Perhaps my sister was a bit capricious, but our bloodlines go all the way back to the Conquest! Moreover, Esmée's beauty and deportment are beyond reproach. Yes, she would make any man proud. And if there is anything of the gentleman left in you, you will step aside, hold your tongue, and let someone worthy *have* her!"

Again, the long silence. Alasdair went to the window and stared down into the street. Again, he felt that quiet, quivering rage, and the impotent sense of something precious slipping from his grasp. That awful fear of losing something he'd barely known he wanted.

But Esmée was not about to be torn asunder by a carriage wheel. She was not bleeding to death. She was being offered an opportunity. A chance to become what she had been destined by blood and by birth to be. And he was . . . well, he was essentially what Lady Tatton accused him of being. He had no excuse for it, either.

As a young man, he had not been denounced or cut off by his father, as had his friend Devellyn. He had not endured the agonizing loss of a first love, as had been Merrick's fate. There was no dark, Byronic secret in his past, as with Quin. He was just a charming wastrel. Because that was what he'd chosen to be. And now, as he approached — well, if not the autumn of his life, then certainly a bloody late summer — he had little right to cry foul over it, or to drag youth and beauty and innocence down with him, simply because he had formed some pathetically adolescent tendre for a girl he didn't deserve. It would pass, and soon enough.

"You are persuaded, ma'am, that you can make a good marriage for her?" he finally asked, his voice hollow.

"I believe so," she said. "Do your servants talk?"

"They do not," he said firmly. "Moreover, they hold Miss Hamilton in the highest regard."

"Then I shall have her married by Christmas," declared Lady Tatton.

He detected, however, a moment's hesitation. He knew it boded ill. *And — ?*

Lady Tatton sighed sharply. "Of course, Esmée is reluctant to go without her sister. So I really think it would be best if you just let —"

He turned from the window, his face a mask of rage. "No!" he rasped. "*That* is out of the question! Do not you dare to ask it of me."

"I admit, it is an awkward situation," she said. "But the child is my niece, and —"

"The child is *my daughter!*" he interjected. "Mine! And I am quite capable, madam, of raising a child and of giving her life's every luxury. If Esmée wishes to leave me, take her, damn you! I can't stop her. But my child? No. Never."

Lady Tatton seemed to shrivel a little. "Well, the truth is, Esmée has put me off until this afternoon," she admitted. "I believe she means, Sir Alasdair, to speak with you."

"It is not necessary," he said, the words tight and clipped. "Indeed, I wish she would not."

"Just as I told her, but you know how she can be," said her ladyship. "And unfortunately, I cannot tell what is in her mind. It *might* be something very silly. So if she should say or do anything foolish, I beg you to remember your promise. I beg you to set aside your selfish notions, and for once, do what is best for someone else. Esmée's whole life has been fraught with disappointment. She does not need to find disappointment in her marriage."

Alasdair felt himself trembling inside with rage. "In other words, you mean for her to wed someone sober and respectable?" he gritted. "Someone who will help her take her proper place in society? And whether or not this much-vaunted husband stirs any passion in her heart, or has any appreciation of her strength of mind, or any respect for her independent spirit, is to be considered wholly secondary? I should think that damned disappointing!"

"Well!" said her ladyship. "I seem to have struck a nerve."

He had turned back to the window again, this time his hands clenched on the windowsill. "Lady Tatton, I fear you strain my limited civility," he said. "You have at least half your pyrrhic victory. You may take one of your nieces, and marry her off to the first worthy suitor that crosses your path. Now kindly *get out of my house!*"

He heard nothing more but the sound of the door latch clicking shut.

It was not long before Lydia returned to the schoolroom in another breathless, wide-eyed rush to warn Esmée that Lady Tatton had cornered Sir Alasdair on his way in the door. By that time, however, Sorcha had become fretful, just as Dr. Reid had predicted, and Esmée was obliged to pace back and forth through the schoolroom, patting the child on the back until she drifted off to sleep.

Heartsick over the choice which now seemed inevitable, and very much afraid her aunt had berated Alasdair unfairly, Esmée continued to pace, even after Sorcha was tucked into her little bed, and Lady Tatton's coach had vanished from the street below. She walked and she waited, her heart in her throat. Waited for Alasdair to come to her, all the while wondering what he would say.

It would be best, she supposed, if he said nothing at all. Had she not already acknowledged the wisdom — no, the *necessity* — of her leaving this place, even before her aunt's arrival? She could not continue to live here and be, in essence, a kept woman. Still, in her fantasies, Alasdair burst into the schoolroom, flung himself at her feet, and begged her not to go. In her more logical moments, she imagined him simply arguing with her, just as he had that first night, then wheedling from her a promise to stay.

But neither happened, and by luncheon — a meal she sent away before the cover was removed — she realized he did not mean to come at all. It was a lowering thought, but she could not go without speaking to him just one more time.

Esmée found him in his study. The door was closed, but she sensed his presence inside the room. It was as if she could smell his scent, familiar and comforting, in the corridor. She drew in a deep breath, then tapped lightly.

She heard his answering bark. "Come!"

Esmée stuck her head inside. "I hope I am not disturbing you?"

He looked up from his desk. "Oh, you is it, my dear?" Abruptly, he shut a drawer, but not before she glimpsed the two green velvet boxes within.

She came into the room, feeling suddenly awkward. "I understand you met my aunt this morning."

He had risen, of course, from his chair.

"What?" he said absently. "Oh, indeed! Lady Tatton. A most worthy lady."

"Aye, she is that," agreed Esmée. "But a bit of a dragon, all the same."

MacLachlan smiled. "In my experience, worthy ladies usually are."

Esmée tried to smile back, but it faltered. "You know, I daresay, why she came?"

MacLachlan paced to the window, one hand set at the back of his neck, the other at his waist. It was a sign, she'd learned, that he was either angry or troubled. But when he turned round and paced back again, he sounded neither. "Ah, Esmée," he said. "I collect you are to leave us."

"Am I?" she said sharply. "I had thought we might . . . discuss it first."

"Esmée!" He looked at her with chiding indulgence. "There is no question. You must go."

The world felt suddenly unsteady to Esmée, as if the floor beneath her feet was shifting in a way she'd not believed possible. "I *must* go?" she echoed. "You beg me to stay here, and now you can so easily send me packing?"

He picked up a penknife from his desk, and began to toy with it in a way that looked faintly dangerous. "I mean only that this is an unlooked-for opportunity," he said, slowly tilting the blade to the light. "Your aunt is well placed. She can give you entrée to a world most people can only dream of."

"*I* have never dreamt of it."

"Liar!" he said, still smiling. "What girl has not?"

"I am not a girl," she snapped. "If ever I was, my mother's death put an end to it."

"Quite right," he agreed smoothly — *too* smoothly for Esmée's liking. "You are a lovely young woman, full of grace, beauty, and potential."

"Alasdair, you don't understand," she said. "She wishes . . . she wishes me to *marry.*"

"Does she, by Jove?" For a long moment, he was silent. "And so you should, I daresay."

Esmée did not understand what was happening. "But — But what about last night?"

"What about it?" he asked coolly. "I was drinking, you know. I usually am."

Her eyes widened. "You are . . . you are saying you don't *remember?*"

"Not . . . er, completely," he said. "No."

Esmée threw up her hands. "Oh, *now* who is the liar?" she cried. "You drank little more than a dram! A good Scot puts twice that in his porridge of a winter's morn!"

He laid aside his knife and took her hands

in his. They felt bloodless. Cold, like his voice. "Esmée," he said. "We ought not even speak of last night. We must pretend it never happened, for your sake. We were all of us under such strain, doing and saying things, I daresay, we would otherwise never have done."

She looked at him accusingly. "I did naught I'd no wish to do!" she answered. "We made love, you and I. Oh, not, perhaps, in the usual way, no. But you cannot tell me it meant *nothing*."

"It *was* nothing, Esmée," he said gently. "You are young. You do not understand men, or how they —"

"Oh, aye!" she snapped, jerking her hands from his. "A silly chit, am I? Well, listen to me, MacLachlan, and listen well. I have grown quite tired of everyone telling me how young and stupid I am. I am neither, and we both know it. And I know this, too: You are trying to drive me away."

His eyes hardened. "No, I am merely accepting what you apparently cannot," he said in an arctic voice. "We have not been living in the real world, Esmée. We have grown close — *inappropriately* close — and I am to blame. It was a pleasant flirtation, no more. I should never have permitted you to stay here. And if you remain here, what

255

do you honestly think will happen between us? I need hardly tell you, my dear, that I am not the marrying kind."

She began to sputter with indignation, but he cut her off. "And if I am not the marrying kind, Esmée, then you need to find someone who is," he finished. "You are a beautiful, deeply sensual creature. Lady Tatton has come home, it seems, in the very nick of time."

Inexplicably, nausea gripped her. Esmée set a hand to her stomach. "My aunt — she put you up to this, didn't she?"

"Oh, for God's sake, Esmée! I'm half again your age!" He tore his gaze from hers. "Your aunt made me ashamed of myself."

"I don't believe you!" she retorted. "I think you are just trying to do the honorable thing."

Finally, he laughed aloud. "Oh, Esmée, I can hear society's collective giggling all the way from Mayfair," he said. "Sir Alasdair MacLachlan, sacrificing himself on the altar of a young lady's honor!"

"Oh, aye!" she said, sneering. "Make a great joke of it!"

But Alasdair pressed on. "Oh, you think me noble and good now, is that it?" he challenged. "Just because I held you, and helped you forget something horrible and tragic? If you think that, Esmée, then you are as silly and romantic as your mother. I took my pleasure from your body — and trust me, I did not leave your bed feeling good and noble. There is nothing at all of the romantic in me, Esmée. I live only in the here and now, not in dreams of some perfect future. Go. Go with your aunt, and make a life for yourself. Forget about me, and forget about Sorcha. Let Lady Tatton find you some well-mannered, respectable young man who can give you children of your own."

Esmée wondered if he'd lost his mind. "How — how can I?" she asked incredulously. "I am no longer innocent."

"Oh, trust me, my dear; you are the very definition of innocence."

"But after last night — I mean, what man would even contemplate — ?"

"You still have your virginity," he said.

"A technicality," she countered.

"Perhaps," he conceded. "But that little technicality is all that matters."

She fell quiet for a moment. She did not feel like an innocent. But otherwise, there was little in what he'd said that she had not already decided. Still, she had not thought to hear it spill so coldly and so logically from his beautiful mouth. A mouth which had coaxed and comforted and made languorous love to her but a few hours earlier. The very memory of it still made her shiver, and for an instant she feared she might make a fool of herself again.

Perhaps she was like her mother, God help her. All of her life, she had tried to be otherwise. She had tried to keep both her head and her heart safe, but Sir Alasdair MacLachlan had been her undoing. She wished to God she could blame him for it. Instead, she drew in a ragged breath. "Do you — do you think I am silly and romantic, then?" she demanded. "Do you think I am like my mother?"

Something inside him seemed to explode. "How the devil do I know?" he snapped. "I don't even remember the woman, you will recall. That's the sort of man I am, Esmée! There have been a hundred Lady Achanalts in my bed — lovers I never really knew, and whose names I don't even care to recall. The truth is, I barely know *you* — and obviously, you do not know *me*."

She felt hot, angry tears spring to her eyes, and blinked them back. "Oh, I know you, MacLachlan," she returned in a low, steady voice. "I know you better than you might wish."

"Come, Esmée! You have been here but a

few weeks. You know nothing of the world beyond Scotland. Take what is being offered you. Don't throw yourself away, girl, on a cad like me."

"How can I?" she retorted. "You have already said you do not want me."

He turned to the window and refused to look at her. "Esmée, please go to your aunt now," he said. "I have things to do."

"Aye, I shall, then!" she answered. "And fair fa' ye, MacLachlan! I mean to forget about you. Perhaps it won't even prove difficult —"

"Oh, it won't!" he interjected.

"Aye, you're right, I do not doubt!" she agreed. "But what I'll not be forgetting is my sister. You cannot cut me off from her."

He did not turn around, did not move from the window. "I have no intention of doing so," he rasped. "You may see Sorcha whenever you wish. Lydia will bring her. Just make the arrangements, please, with Wellings. As I said, I have things to do now."

Esmée stiffened her spine and went to the door, but at the last moment, another torment struck. "I wish to know one last thing," she said, her hand on the doorknob. "I claim the privilege of asking, as Sorcha's sister, if for no other reason."

"What?" he snapped impatiently.

"Are you going to marry Mrs. Crosby?"

He was so quiet and so rigid, she feared she had gone too far. "God, I hope not," he finally said. "But I suppose stranger things have happened."

"What is to come will be as real and as painful as that bruise between your eyes."

Behind him, the door slammed. Alasdair bent his head, shut his eyes, and pinched the bridge of his nose as hard as he could. But the beautiful Gypsy's words would not stop echoing in his brain

"You have cursed yourself, with no help needed from me. Now you must make restitution. You must make it right."

Good God, he was trying to make restitution! He was trying to make right whatever the hell it was he'd done so bloody wrong! But why did it have to hurt so much? Why wouldn't that goddamned voice leave his head? He *knew* what he had to do.

What did he have to offer a young lady like Esmée, anyway? His good name? His fine reputation? Oh, if he could have pointed to one thing — just one small thing — that Lady Tatton had been wrong about, perhaps he would have gone chasing after the chit. Perhaps he would have thrown himself at her feet and promised to be as good a husband as he possibly could be.

But Lady Tatton, damn her, hadn't been wrong. His only talents were his charm, his looks, and a steady hand at the gaming table. Just as he had said, he was not the marrying kind. Not really. He had never in his life been faithful to a woman, and though it now felt as if that had changed, how could he know? How could he be sure?

More importantly, what did Esmée deserve? Everything. The world. Her rightful place in society. A life of happiness and ease. A sober and respectable husband, just the sort Lady Tatton had promised to find.

Lady Tatton! Lord God Almighty! Never would he have dreamt his drowned wren was blood kin to such a pillar of English society. And had he known it, would he have treated her any differently?

Oh, he knew the answer to that one! It left him almost ill. He would not have let Lady Tatton's niece set so much as one toe into his parlor. He would have rousted every servant in the house from their beds and sent them out into the drenching rain to scour all of London in search of a suitable chaperone with a suitable roof beneath which she might shelter. Someone. Anyone. Dev's mother. Quin's sister. Julia. Even Inga would have been better than him, for God's sake.

Instead, he had treated Esmée like the near nobody he'd believed her to be. He now knew that Esmée was far from being a nobody. She was something extraordinary; extraordinary in a way which still eluded him. Extraordinary in a way which had nothing to do with class or social standing or Lady Tatton. And now he was being royally punished for his presumption.

Just then, he heard a heavy tread coming down the hall. He turned to see his butler on the threshold. "Yes, what is it, Wellings?"

The servant hesitated. "Sir, Miss Hamilton has asked that her empty trunks be brought down from the attics."

"Has she?" he asked. "Best get them down, then."

Wellings began to wring his hands. "But she says — well, she says that she is leaving, sir. Going to live with her aunt. Is that right?"

Alasdair smiled faintly. "I think it best, don't you?"

The butler colored a little. "I'm not sure I do."

Alasdair looked down to realize that he'd somehow got hold of the penknife again. His knuckles had gone white and bloodless from clutching it. "Miss Hamilton is not a slave, Wellings," he finally answered. "Do as she asks. *Please*."

Wellings crept closer to the desk, one eye on the knife, and laid before him a slender package wrapped in wrinkled white paper.

"What the devil is that?"

Wellings drew back. "I couldn't say, sir. Miss Hamilton bade me give it to you."

Alasdair looked at it again, and felt his heart lurch. "Wellings," he rasped.

"Yes, sir?"

He dropped the knife. "Tell Mrs. Henry to hire another maid," he said, as the blade clattered to the floor. "It seems Lydia will be moving up to the nursery full-time."

Still glowering, Wellings bowed himself out of the study.

Alasdair picked up the fold of paper, and weighed it in his hand. He closed his eyes, and willed himself to breathe. There was no need to open it. No, none at all. He already knew what he would find inside it. Three hundred pounds. In cash.

Esmée, it seemed, no longer needed her insurance policy. Indeed, she no longer needed *him*. His wish to be set free of his "managing female" had come true at last.

Chapter Seven

A new Girl in Town

It took Esmée all of three days in Grosvenor Square to realize that her life was no longer her own. It was, perhaps, just as well. The loneliness kept pressing in on her, but Lady Tatton's pace left one little time to brood.

All of Mayfair seemed to have simultaneously realized that her aunt had returned from abroad — and with her unwed niece in tow. A flurry of curiosity ensued, followed by a whirlwind of invitations to such quiet diversions as teas, literary readings, and dinner parties. But Esmée's heart was in none of it.

Her aunt sensed her melancholy, and at first asked a great many probing questions. When that did not work, Lady Tatton's solution was, of course, shopping. Lydia brought Sorcha two or three mornings a week, but afternoons were always devoted to Oxford Street.

Within the week, the first in an ocean of new clothing began to trickle into the house, and it soon turned into a torrent. Her own wardrobe, Lady Tatton complained, was hopelessly out-of-date from her years abroad. As to Esmée, she was treated to evening gowns and carriage dresses, pelisses, shawls, and shoes by the dozen, all done up in dark, subtle colors which Lady Tatton assured her were appropriate to a family still in mourning.

As they were unpacking the last of it, Esmée expressed doubt about a cloak of dark sapphire blue which her aunt's dresser had just laid out on the bed.

"Silly child!" said Lady Tatton, shaking the wrinkles out of an aubergine evening dress. "Your dear mamma has been gone many months now. And thank goodness the King died in June!"

Esmée's eyes widened. "I beg your pardon?"

Lady Tatton smiled. "Society quickly tires of muted entertainments and dark colors, my dear," she said lightly. "No one is apt to begin throwing stones at us, when we are all supposed to be grieving over the loss of our beloved monarch — and none of us really are."

"Och, I did not think —"

"And we are fortunate, dear child, that rich colors become you," Lady Tatton continued. "Thank God you are not a blonde."

She turned to her dresser with the aubergine gown. "Pickens! Press this next, if you please. Miss Hamilton will want it for Lady Gravenel's dinner party tomorrow. And the silvery gray silk shall do nicely for me."

Esmée drifted to the window, and stared out at the gated green expanse below. She missed Sorcha so dreadfully. Sometimes, late at night, as she tossed and turned in her bed, she feared she had made a mistake in leaving. And then Lydia would bring Sorcha to visit, and Esmée's eyes would go at once to the terrible wound on her sister's forehead. No. The truth was, she needed Sorcha far more than Sorcha needed her.

But what else was she to do with her life? The months since her mother's death had finally made her realize that it was time she got on with the business of living. And her protestations to Aunt Rowena aside, Esmée really did not wish to spend her life alone in a cottage full of dogs and cats. She wanted a family. She wanted children. And fleetingly — almost without knowing it — she had begun to want those things with Sir Alasdair MacLachlan.

The notion was laughable, of course. Had MacLachlan wished for a wife and a family, he could have — and *should* have — married Mrs. Crosby. Indeed, he ought to have done weeks ago. He did not want Esmée. She was lucky he had wanted Sorcha.

And so Esmée needed to make a life for herself and accept that those dreams would not be a part of it. She could not make the same foolish choices her mother had made. But to move on, she had to get out in the world. She had to meet people. She had to do precisely the things her aunt wished her to do. And yet, she was not at all sure she wished to attend another dinner party.

Lady Tatton had obviously put out the word — by whatever means matchmaking mammas and well-intentioned dowagers communicated — that her niece was in search of a husband. And she must have mentioned Grandpapa's dowry, too. There was no other explanation for the way in which unattached gentlemen had flocked to her side these last few days.

While she understood that her aunt's heart was in the right place, Esmée had little enthusiasm for the attention. Her thoughts, and apparently her heart, kept straying to . . . well, to someplace they ought not be. And yet, there had been no way to refuse the Duchess of Gravenel, who lived but two doors down the square.

Esmée had met the duchess the very day of her arrival. She had looked like a small blond sprite bounding down her front steps to embrace Lady Tatton as they climbed out of the carriage.

"Oh, Rowena!" she had exclaimed. "I thought you would *never* return! I have been waiting an age, it seems!"

Lady Tatton had been taken aback, too, for the duchess had apparently been firmly fixed in the country for some years.

"But we have reopened the house, as you see," said Lady Gravenel. "By the way, we are having a small dinner party next week. A very quiet affair. Both of you must come. I shan't take no for an answer! I shall find two more gentlemen to even up our numbers."

"We should be honored," said her aunt.

"And Isabel is coming to tea on Monday," said the duchess. "You must come, too, Rowena. It will be like old times! Miss Hamilton, do join us."

And so there had been no way out of it. Tea and dinner with a duchess! Esmée would have found it all quite daunting, save for the fact that Lady Gravenel had seemed so very pleasant.

The tea turned out to be a crush, and Isabel turned out to be the Countess of Kirton, a plump, pleasant dowager who lived but five minutes away in Berkeley Square. She looked Esmée up and down as if assessing her potential, then situated herself on a brocade sofa beside Lady Tatton, where they whispered furtively back and forth when they fancied no one was looking.

Esmée noticed that Lady Kirton kept patting her aunt's hand and giving her sympathetic, sidelong glances. And of course, there was the occasional furtive glance in Esmée's direction, a sure sign trouble was afoot. Had the ladies been five stone fatter and a little more garishly clad, they could have been a Rowlandson sketch entitled *Mischief in the Making.*

Just then, her thoughts were interrupted when Pickens came out of Lady Tatton's dressing room, the aubergine gown draped across her arm like a silken waterfall. It was so dark, it would probably look almost black in candlelight, and its utter lack flounces or ribbons, omitted in deference to mourning, served merely to make it more elegant.

"Oh, miss!" said the dresser, holding it out. "Isn't it the loveliest thing ever?"

Esmée managed to smile. "I've never seen a gown more beautiful." Even her mother's finest dresses would not have rivaled its quiet, understated elegance.

Pickens held it up in front of her and gestured toward the cheval glass. Esmée looked up and gasped. Her aunt had been right.

The rich color suited her dark hair and pale skin.

"Oh, miss!" said Pickens breathlessly. "You are going to cut such a dash tomorrow! I do hope you break someone's heart."

Esmée felt a strange sense of satisfaction stealing over her. She *did* look beautiful. Older, even a little taller, perhaps — and almost as pretty as her mother. So damn Alasdair MacLachlan if he did not want her. Someone else would; someone who would not call her a silly chit and throw her heart back in her face. And suddenly, Esmée decided to enjoy the hunt — or at least make a bloody good show of it.

Alasdair was in a back room at Crockford's with his brother and Quin when Lord Devellyn finally ran him to ground almost two weeks after his governess's abrupt departure. It was late, well past midnight, in fact, and Devellyn wanted his wife and his bed, in that order. But he was a man on a mission which would not wait.

He was also more than a little worried about Alasdair. Not without reason, as it happened, for Alasdair and Quin were half-sprung and tossing the ivory with a couple of slick Soho blacklegs.

"Fancy meeting you here," said Devellyn, sidling up to Merrick MacLachlan.

"Aye, fancy it indeed," Merrick returned. "I'd rather not be, but I'm half-afraid to leave. This is a pernicious shite-hole, you know."

"I do know," agreed Devellyn, tilting his head toward the table. "And they do, too, usually. What's wrong with Quin?"

Merrick lifted one shoulder. "His mother's bedeviling him. Wants him to find a wife."

"Yes, a dead father will tend to trigger that," said the marquis.

"And the devil's in *him* tonight, too." Merrick jerked his head toward his brother. "Ordinarily, he's never fool enough to play at hazard — nor even at cards, if he's foxed."

"Ah, well!" said the marquis. "You know what Granny MacGregor says. 'The worth of a thing is best known by the want of it.' "

Merrick's mouth curled sardonically. "Got you spouting her old saws now, has he?" he said. "And you are suggesting, I collect, that his pretty governess is the root of his trouble?"

Devellyn shrugged. "I suspect as much," he answered. "What does Quin think?"

"He's oblivious," said Merrick. "As to the

271

governess, I knew she'd be trouble from the outset."

"Did you indeed?" said Devellyn blandly. "I take it the old boy is in deep?"

Merrick shrugged. "Perhaps two hundred pounds," he admitted. "Even dog drunk whilst playing a pair of cheats, he is not a bad hand at hazard. Still, it is a game of chance, not skill."

"Yes, and it's time to put an end to it," said the marquess, striding up to the table. He set a heavy hand on Alasdair's shoulder. Alasdair looked up, his brow furrowing as if he couldn't quite focus on Devellyn's face. "I need to speak with you two," said Devellyn quietly. "A minor emergency."

Alasdair turned, swaying a little precariously. "Can't it wait, old chap? I'm down half a monkey, and about to give these chaps a proper thrashing."

Devellyn pulled a somber face. "Alasdair, I should hope a friend in need is more important than a paltry sum of money."

Alasdair considered it. "Of course," he said swiftly. "Gentlemen," he said, bowing to the Soho scoundrels, "I give you good night."

Quin, who had been flanking Alasdair, followed suit, and the four of them went in search of an empty table. After a bottle of brandy had been brought out, Devellyn leaned back in his chair, cradling his glass against his waistcoat. "Gentlemen, I need two brave and stalwart men," he said. "Volunteers, as it were, for a perilous mission. And I mayn't go home until I have them."

Alasdair set his glass down with an awkward clatter. "By God, I'll volunteer, Dev!" he said, reeling a little in his chair. "Damned if I'll ever leave you in the breach."

"Alasdair, I can always count on you," said the marquis. "Is there another among you so bold?"

Merrick made a skeptical sound. "Bold, my arse."

Quin, too, looked dubious. "What sort of perilous mission?"

Devellyn pulled a serious face. "A dinner party tomorrow night," he answered. "My mother's, to be specific. She's bollixed up her guest list, I collect, and come up two gents short."

"Now wait a moment, Dev!" protested Alasdair. "That's not per— per— *perilous!*"

"If you think that, Alasdair, then you don't know my mother's friends," said the marquis. "Besides, you owe the old girl. You practically stole Grandpapa's coin collection from her. Turning up at dinner is the least you can do — besides, you have already volunteered."

Merrick shoved his glass away. "Sorry, Devellyn, but I am engaged to dine with some American bankers tomorrow evening. The appointment was made months ago."

"I might have guessed," said Devellyn, setting down his glass and pushing away from the table. "Looks as though it falls to you, Quin."

"Oh, why not?" drawled Quin. "I've nothing better to do."

"Good man!" Devellyn grinned. "Six sharp in Grosvenor Square. And gird your loins, fellows. Every old tabby in town will likely turn up."

On the night of the duchess's dinner party, Lady Tatton took a sudden dislike to her silver-gray silk, throwing the house into a last-minute uproar. Whilst Pickens heated up an iron to press yet another gown, Esmée was dispatched to search for her ladyship's dark blue shawl and jet pendant. She quickly found both, then went downstairs to sit by the drawing room window, where she watched as one fine carriage after another drew up in front of Lady Gravenel's house to disgorge its well-dressed occupants.

In the end, they were a few minutes late. Lady Tatton offered her arm, and together they went down the street. "Now, there will be several eligible young men here tonight," said her aunt, still fiddling with the folds of her shawl.

"Och, Aunt Rowena!" said Esmée. "I'm not at all sure I've any interest in these eligible young men, fine though they may be."

"I comprehend, my dear," said her aunt, lightly patting her hand. "I comprehend. But one must try one's wings, mustn't one? Smile a great deal, and flirt a little, Esmée! Use your fan as I showed you. You must try to acquire a little town bronze before the season begins."

"Aye, so they're to be used for practice, are they?" murmured Esmée as they went up the steps.

"Exactly!" said her aunt. "For practice!"

The duke and duchess awaited them just inside a huge withdrawing room done up in the French fashion, in shades of gold and ivory, with elegantly inlaid furnishings and a great many gilt mirrors. Lord Gravenel, who was in poor health, sat beside his wife in a wheeled chair. Both smiled warmly as Esmée looked about in awe. But just as Lord Gravenel lifted Lady Tatton's hand to his lips, Esmée saw her aunt go quite rigid.

Esmée looked beyond the duke's shoulder. The air seemed to vanish from the room. *Oh, surely not!*

"My dear Elizabeth!" murmured Lady Tatton as the duke greeted Esmée. "Please tell me that is not Sir Alasdair MacLachlan just there, by your étagère?"

The duchess laughed. "Oh, come, Rowena, he is not thought *hopelessly* wicked, is he?" she asked in her light, tinkling voice. "I confess to a fondness for the scoundrel."

Rowena looked unconvinced. "When I left town, he was barely received."

"Oh, not much has changed," said the duchess airily. "There is always at least a titter of gossip whenever he turns up. But have pity, Rowena. The poor gentleman is here under duress."

"Under duress?" said Lady Tatton.

"My son twisted his arm," she answered, turning to Esmée. "Hello, Miss Hamilton. How lovely you look tonight."

But Lady Tatton was still focused on MacLachlan. "Yes, he is a friend of Devellyn's, isn't he? I had forgotten."

"Have you never met Sir Alasdair?" asked the duchess.

Lady Tatton hesitated. "Once, briefly," she said. "We are, I believe, distantly related. *Very* distantly." She paused to smile tightly. "Scots, you know! We are all kin if you go back far enough."

"Distantly related?" whispered Esmée as they walked away. "What can you be thinking?"

Rowena paused and made a fuss over rearranging her shawl again. "Esmée, I've reconsidered our strategy," she whispered. "What if Sorcha's situation becomes known? He has told his staff, you said, that Sorcha was the child of a deceased cousin —"

"Oh, no one believed that Banbury tale!" said Esmée.

"Nonetheless, it is our story now, and we must all stick to it," she answered. "It is always possible your name could yet get dragged into it. At least he is respectable enough to be invited *here*. And he probably *is* a cousin, were we to dig back far enough. We walk a fine line with this mess your mother has got us into. Now, *do* stop staring at him!"

"Aunt Rowena, I certainly am not!" And oddly enough, she wasn't. Once she'd gotten past the shock, she had torn her eyes away and forced herself to focus on the other gentlemen — the *practice* gentlemen — in the room. After all, she had already practiced on Sir Alasdair MacLachlan as far as she dared. The very thought of what they had done together cast a fine blush over her cheeks. And so it was that when her aunt dragged her a little deeper into the withdrawing room, and introduced her to two handsome, almost foppishly dressed young men, Esmée was looking quite her best.

"Lord Thorpe. Mr. Smathers." Esmée curtseyed at the introduction. "A pleasure."

Lord Thorpe bowed over her hand. "It is indeed," he said. "My dear Lady Tatton, town is so deadly dull this time of year. Why have you hidden this diamond from us?"

"Is this your first visit to London, Miss Hamilton?" interjected Mr. Smathers. "If so, please let me introduce you to my sister. She is an expert on all the not-to-be-missed sights."

The lady behind him turned round and smiled. Lady Tatton sent Lord Thorpe to fetch two glasses of sherry. Miss Smathers began to rattle on effusively about the British Museum. Esmée set her hand on Mr. Smathers's arm and did her best to ensure that Sir Alasdair MacLachlan saw that she was enjoying herself. She would be damned before she would let that arrogant devil imagine that she was wearing the willow on his account.

* * *

Lord and Lady Devellyn were watching the little drama which was unfolding across the ballroom, and wondering if they had heard Alasdair correctly.

"Good Lord!" said Devellyn. "*That* is your shrew?"

"The sister, yes," muttered Alasdair. "Miss Esmée Hamilton."

"Damn," muttered Devellyn. "Not quite what I had imagined."

"Why, she's lovely!" said his wife. "Have you ever seen such flawless skin and so much rich, dark hair? What must it look like down?"

Alasdair did not have to wonder. He knew all too well what it looked like down, a recollection which was making his palms sweat and his pulse race. He watched Esmée move through the crowd, her spine perfectly straight as she inclined her head and smiled, first in one direction, then the other, with more than one pair of male eyes following her as she did so.

Already that upstart Smathers had her hand on his arm, as if he meant to escort her to some empty corner of the room for a quiet little tête-à-tête. Alasdair watched in irritation as Lord Thorpe fetched her a glass of sherry and, with an ingratiating smile, moved to flank her other side.

"She puts me in mind of a sculpture I once saw in Venice," Lady Devellyn murmured. "A marble Madonna. Serene and lovely — but a little unyielding."

"Dressed a tad plainly," remarked Devellyn. "But elegant. Very composed."

She did indeed look composed, Alasdair would give her that. Her back was straight, her hair was twisted high to expose the slender turn of her neck, and despite her small stature, she moved like a duchess.

Just then the real duchess appeared at Esmée's side. Mr. Smathers and Lord Thorpe fell away, their smiles fading. Devellyn's mother took Esmée on one arm, Lady Tatton on the other, and started across the length of the room. Too late he realized they were heading in his direction.

"Lady Tatton," said the duchess brightly, "You remember my son, the Marquis of Devellyn?"

Alasdair stood in numb silence as all the introductions were made. When the duchess came to him, Lady Tatton acknowledged their acquaintance with a curt, "We've met."

He bowed low over her hand, then Esmée's, saying little beyond what was required. At first, he thought Esmée would not lift her gaze from the floor. Then, at the last possible instant, she did so, looking directly into his eyes, just as she had on the night they first met. The result was much the same. That disembodied slam, as if the wind had just been knocked from his chest. Her pure, green gaze, seeing through him. Stripping away his defenses in a chilling rush. It was as if she knew his every thought. Knew him perhaps better than he knew himself.

" 'Tis a pleasure to see you again, Sir Alasdair." Her faint burr melted over him, warm and evocative. He had missed the sound of it, he realized. Disconcerted by the contrast, he dropped her hand, and stepped abruptly back. She turned to Quin, and offered him a smile that was not altogether false. Then the trio moved on, leaving Alasdair to simply trail after them with his eyes.

The meal which followed was one of the most miserable affairs Alasdair had ever endured, so he spent the first three courses eyeing Dev nastily for having dragged him there. The crowd was small by Mayfair standards, and most were well acquainted. Around the long table, the dinner conversation was merry, punctuated by laughter so boisterous it would have been unseemly at a more formal affair. The duchess did know how to throw a party, Alasdair admitted.

He was seated between Sidonie and Isabel, Lady Kirton, the duchess's girlhood friend. Alasdair liked the matronly Lady Kirton immensely. She was a philanthropist who had friends from all walks of life, and despite her age, she was droll and full of mischief. Just a few months earlier, she had helped him perpetrate a hilarious hoax on the *ton* — a hoax which had laid to rest the notorious Black Angel, and enabled Dev and his bride to enjoy a marriage unburdened by the fear of Sidonie's past returning to haunt them.

Still, even Lady Kirton's amusing company could not pique Alasdair's interest tonight. He responded to her questions mechanically, until at last she turned her attention to the gentleman on her left, leaving him alone in the hubbub of dinner conversation.

Esmée, Alasdair noticed, had been seated between Smathers and a fellow by the name of Edgar Nowell, a bland, prosy fellow, who was known to be the duke's political protégé and topmost toady. Esmée's smile never faltered as she turned back and forth between them. Who would have dreamt such a dry stick could turn into a regular *bel esprit*?

Esmée was laughing at some jest Nowell had murmured rather too near her ear. Not to be outdone, Smathers attracted her attention by covering her hand where it rested on the table. It was rather a bold gesture. Esmée turned to him with a look of candid interest. Alasdair felt something strange twist and tighten in the pit of his stomach.

"Lovely, is she not?" murmured a voice near his ear.

Recalled to the present, Alasdair turned to Lady Kirton. "I beg your pardon?"

Her ladyship's eyes were bright and lively. "Miss Hamilton," she clarified. "I see she has caught your eye."

"Actually, my eye was drawn to her gown," he said coolly. "I cannot quite make out the color. It is not really black, is it?"

"Aubergine, I believe," murmured Lady Kirton. "The poor girl lost her mother in the spring. I met her last week at the duchess's tea, and again at a literary salon in Park Lane. We had a long chat, Miss Hamilton and I."

"I daresay she's charming."

Lady Kirton sipped delicately from her wineglass. "Lady Tatton tells me her niece shan't dance after dinner. Miss Smathers is to play a few country tunes on the pianoforte, you know."

"I was unaware," he answered.

Lady Kirton smiled. "I am sure the young lady would not be averse to taking a turn about the room instead."

Alasdair looked at her pointedly. "Again, I am afraid you've mistaken my interest."

Lady Kirton's eyes seemed to twinkle. "Oh! Did I?" She sounded suddenly dithery. "I should have worn my spectacles, I daresay. But there is no doubt the chit is a pretty thing — her mamma was a famous beauty in Scotland, you know — and her grandfather settled ninety thousand pounds on Miss Hamilton in his will, so I think she will do quite nicely, don't you?"

Alasdair thought his ears were failing. "I beg your pardon?"

Lady Kirton blinked owlishly. "Her mother was a famous beauty," she repeated. "Why, it's said the Earl of Strathan and the Duke of Langwell dueled over who was to get the last slot on her dance card at her come-out."

Alasdair shook his head. "No, the *will*. I thought . . . well, I thought her family was penniless?"

Again, the innocent blink. "Why, no indeed!" she said. "Oh, 'tis true her father wasted his fortune and died insolvent. But her maternal grandfather made a fortune in shipping. When he died, Rowena was already wed to the very wealthy Lord Tatton. And Rosamund, her sister, was married to — well, what can I say? To yet another pretty ne'er-do-well."

Alasdair smiled faintly. "That can be an expensive habit."

"Just what her father thought!" whispered Lady Kirton. "So being a good and prudent Scot, he put his disposable assets in trust for Anne and Esmée, his granddaughters, to be theirs upon their marriage, or their thirtieth birthday, whichever came first. So, which do you wager on?"

"Which do I wager on what?" Alasdair was confused.

"Which do you wager will come first?" her ladyship pressed. "Do you think there is even the slightest chance that so pretty a girl will remain unwed until she's thirty, now that she has finally come to town? To be sure, I do not!"

"I'm sure I don't know," he answered. He prayed to God she would wed. And the sooner the better.

Lady Kirton touched him lightly on the forearm and leaned nearer. "Someone really should warn her, though, about Mr. Smathers, do you not think?" she murmured. "She might be as green as she is pretty. And Lady Tatton may not know that Smathers recently had to mortgage his estate in Shropshire. I'm told he has suffered dreadful losses on the American stock market."

Finally, it dawned on Alasdair what she was saying. Smathers was a fortune hunter. And Esmée had a fortune. Good Lord! The chit would be like a lamb to the slaughter if her aunt did not keep both eyes firmly fixed upon her.

"Of course, there is always Lord Thorpe," whispered Lady Kirton. "A fine title, but his mother is *such* a dragon, and he is thoroughly cowed by her. Not being yourself on the marriage market —"

"Good Lord, no!"

"I thought as much," admitted her ladyship. "Therefore you would not know that Thorpe has been jilted by no less than *three* young ladies in as many seasons — driven away, they say, by the dowager, who provoked them to tears in turn. Can you imagine a more miserable existence for a wife?"

No, he could not. It sounded grim.

"And then there is Mr. Nowell," said Lady Kirton. "Just look how taken he is with her. Nowell is to stand for Stippleton next election, and it is a given that he will be elected to the Commons. Now, *that* is whom I should choose for her."

Alasdair dropped his fork. "I cannot believe you serious!"

Lady Kirton set her fingertips to her chest. "Why, I could not be more earnest."

"Nor could Nowell!" Alasdair returned. "Good Lord, Isabel, he is the single most boring human being I've ever had the pleasure to meet. Whoever marries him will likely fall asleep and drown in their tea before the wedding breakfast ends."

"Oh, dear, you might be right," she murmured. "What about Mr. Davies, then? He's Welsh, I know, but so devastatingly handsome."

"He has a mistress and three children in Spitalfields."

"Oh, dear! Mr. Shelby, then?"

"Hopelessly foppish."

"True, true! Sir Henry Bathstone?"

"He's bent in a different direction, Isabel. I hope you take my meaning."

Lady Kirton's cheeks turned pink. "Dear me! I think I do. Oh, I have it! Your friend Wynwood!"

"Out of the question," snapped Alasdair. "Quin has sworn off love."

"Oh, pish!" Lady Kirton struck him lightly on his arm with her fingertips. "Love has nothing to say in the matter. He *must* marry. I play whist with his mother every Wednesday."

"Do you indeed?" he said stiffly.

"Indeed, I do," said her ladyship with asperity. "And depend upon it, Quin will wed, and it will be soon. With his poor papa so recently in the grave, Lady Wynwood is quite beside herself. If Quin dies without an heir, everything goes to some third cousin once removed — a singularly unpleasant relation named Enoch Hewitt. A horrid name, is it not? It sounds as if one is trying to cough up something disagreeable."

"I don't think Quin cares who inherits what, Isabel."

"No, but his mother cares!" she returned. "And Quin would never leave her in such a precarious position. Nor will he deny her the grandchildren she yearns for, now that she's been widowed. Indeed, he has all but promised her he will marry next season, if not sooner."

"Good Lord! *Quin* — ?"

"Quin," said her ladyship firmly. "Indeed, now I think on it, they are perfect for one another! Lady Wynwood, you will recall, is Scottish on her mother's side. She will adore Miss Hamilton and her little eccentricities. I shall speak with Rowena at once."

Alasdair felt something like panic churning in his stomach. "Isabel, don't," he interjected. "Quin is — well, a bit of a rogue, you know. He won't be faithful."

Lady Kirton teased him with her eyes. "Oh, Alasdair!" she whispered. "There is no better husband than a scoundrel who has been reformed by a good woman. Miss Hamilton will have him wrapped round her finger in a fortnight. Besides, he is still quite young. What, not even thirty, is he?"

"Just nine-and-twenty," Alasdair admitted.

Lady Kirton's eyes brightened. "Perfect! Though she hardly looks it, Miss Hamilton is twenty-two. Really, Alasdair! We are quite a team, you and I. Every time we're together, we manage to do something ingenious. Shall I invite the four of them to the theater next week? Oh, Rowena will be so pleased we thought of this!"

Alasdair set down his wineglass, striking the rim of his plate. The panic had gripped his throat. Good Lord! *Quin?* That was the last thing Esmée needed.

Quin was devilish fun to carouse with, and the sort of fellow one was happy to account a friend — but one wouldn't wish him to marry one's sister. Certainly one would not wish him to marry the woman that one

. . . oh, hell and damnation! Quin was a roué and a rake and a hell-bent bounder. He had cut his teeth on some of the most wicked pastimes greater London could offer up. And he had a weakness for the worst sort of women imaginable. Any bit of muslin would do; the more base the better. Quin had no standards. And as far as morals went, he was no better than Alasdair.

Oh, Quin was a little younger — well, a good bit younger. And his title was very old and very grand — in other words, very English. But he was no richer. No better-looking. On the other hand, Quin did not yet have that hardened look about the eyes. His gaze was not yet so wicked and world-weary that mothers yanked their daughters from his path. Well, not always.

But what business was it of his? Esmée was not his problem, damn her. He had not invited her into his life — hadn't even invited her into his bed, no matter how frequently the idea had begun to cross his mind. Surely to God she'd know to steer clear of Quin? And if Lady Tatton had disapproved of *him* so thoroughly, she would like Quin little better. Well, good luck to the lot of them! Whatever the hell happened, it certainly wasn't his problem. Thus resolved, Alasdair snatched up his glass and drained it.

"Alasdair!" The whisper came from far away. *"Psst, Alasdair!"*

He turned to see Lady Kirton staring at him. She was motioning discreetly at his place setting. "Alasdair, dear boy!"

"What?"

Lady Kirton smiled. "I fear you have just finished off my wine."

"Really!" said Lady Tatton as she pulled on her gloves the following morning. "What has become of society whilst I was away? Sir Alasdair MacLachlan! At Elizabeth's dinner party! I thought it quite shocking."

Esmée looked up from her morning paper. "Aye, 'twas a surprise indeed."

Lady Tatton eyed her hat in the pier glass and tilted it a tad to the left. "And there was Isabel, such a clever, sensible woman, practically fawning over him during dinner! And that friend of his — Lord Wynwood — he used to be thought a scoundrel, too! Still, I *do* like his mother. One could not wish for better bloodlines. But Wynwood himself — ? Why, I am not at all sure that Elizabeth and Isabel are right to suggest . . ."

Esmée returned her gaze to her newspaper. "To suggest what, Aunt Rowena?"

"Oh, never mind!" She snatched up her

reticule. "Are you sure, Esmée, that you won't come along?" she said for the third time. "It is just a fitting, though *why* Madame Panaut wishes another one, and at such an early hour, I cannot think. But afterward, why, we could go down to Bond Street and look at those slippers you admired last week."

Esmée laid aside her paper and stood. "Thank you, no," she said. "Lydia is bringing Sorcha today."

"Oh, I'd forgotten," said her ladyship. "Do give the child my love."

Esmée kissed her aunt's cheek and saw her to the door. But Lady Tatton's carriage had scarce disappeared from view before another very familiar carriage came spinning round the square from Upper Brook Street. Lydia was arriving earlier than usual.

Grimond, the butler, had vanished, and Esmée did not ring for him. Instead, she threw open the door herself and went eagerly down the steps. But it was not Lydia who emerged from the carriage with Sorcha in her arms.

"Good morning," said Alasdair.

"Mae!" screeched Sorcha. "Look! Look! See dis doll? Pretty, see?"

Alasdair smiled dotingly and passed the child to Esmée. "Lydia was indisposed this morning," he said. "I decided to bring Sorcha myself."

"So I see," said Esmée weakly. "Will you come in?"

With Sorcha on her hip, she returned to the morning parlor and offered him a chair. He took it, watching her almost warily with his heavy, hooded eyes. Esmée sat down and settled Sorcha in her lap, a little troubled by how glad she was to see him.

Sorcha, however, was happily babbling about her doll. "See dress, Mae?" said Sorcha. "See dis dress? Got blue dress. She got shoes, too. And pretty hair."

"Heavens! So many new words!" Esmée kissed the child atop the head, taking care to avoid her injury. "Aye, 'tis a fine, fair doll. Is she new?"

"New," agreed Sorcha, tugging off one of the doll's satin slippers. "See stockin's?"

Alasdair cleared his throat. "I thought it was time she had another," he interjected. "This one came with an entire wardrobe. Sorcha seems to delight in dressing and undressing her dolls."

Esmée smiled. "Aye, her fingers are quite nimble now."

Alasdair cut Esmée an enigmatic glance. "How is it they grow so quickly?" he asked.

"Just this week she began speaking in complete sentences."

Esmée felt her chest suddenly constrict. "Aye 'tis worrisome, isn't it?" she said quietly. "It seems she was just a wee babe when our mother died. And now I look on her, and I see a little girl. The swiftness of it frightens me."

Alasdair smiled. "I begin to believe doubt is the curse of every parent," he answered. "But we must remember that Sorcha is not an eggshell, Esmée. She is tough and resilient. You once said as much."

Sorcha had the doll's dress off now. "Shiff, Mae," she said, flinging the dress into the floor. "See shiff? Take dis off. And drawers. 'Em off, too."

Esmée gave him a muted smile. "Her vocabulary is growing apace, too," she remarked. "She seems to have learnt all the words for ladies' undergarments."

He lifted one brow and flashed his irrepressible grin. "Ah, well. It was you, was it not, who said one should learn new skills at the feet of a master?"

Esmée looked at him chidingly. "Pray tell me about Lydia. I hope she hasn't taken the quinsy which is going round Mayfair."

"Worse, I fear." Alasdair winced. "A badly sprained wrist."

"Och! What happened?"

"The imp got away from her yesterday and bolted for the stairs. A tussle ensued, and I fear Lydia came out rather the worse for it."

Esmée felt a moment of panic. *Bolted for the stairs?* Oh, Sorcha was too headstrong by half! She could have been injured, too. And poor Lydia! Perhaps she was not so capable of managing the child after all? Esmée did not know whether to feel reassured or worried.

Alasdair read her mind. "Sorcha is a handful, Esmée," he said quietly. "For you or for Lydia. Indeed, a whole battalion of nurses would find her a challenge. But we cannot swaddle her in cotton wool."

"Aye, you're right." Gently, she touched the child's wound. "I was relieved when her stitches came out."

"Dr. Reid feels the scar will not be noticeable when her hair thickens," he said, as if reading her mind. "Do not worry over that."

Sorcha had squirmed her way out of Esmée's lap. She went careening across the carpet to her father, her doll in one hand, its shift in the other. Mere inches from him, however, her little legs stumbled and sent her flying.

In an instant, Alasdair had snatched her up. "Careful, minx!"

He set her on his knee, made a stern face, and gently chided her about the importance of not running in the parlor. Sorcha appeared to listen, her ice-blue eyes fixed on her father's face, her chubby hand still clutching the half-naked doll. Esmée realized that Alasdair's response — not to mention his reaction time — had become instinctive. Parental. He had become, somehow, a father, a truth which kept revealing itself in small, subtle ways.

No, she needn't worry quite so much about Sorcha. But she needed to worry a great deal about herself, and her heart.

His scold finished, Alasdair stroked the fine hair back from Sorcha's forehead. Sorcha turned and handed him the doll. "Take off," she ordered. "Take off dis shoe."

"This one is a little stubborn," he agreed, gently easing it off.

Sorcha made a happy noise and wiggled her way off his knee. Gathering up her doll and its clothing, she toddled off to a spot beneath the windows which Lady Tatton had designated as her play area. The child pushed the lid from a large wicker basket and began to toss the toys inside it onto the carpet.

"She seems very much at home here," he remarked.

"Aye, that one never met a stranger," said Esmée.

For a moment, they watched her in silence. The basket now empty, Sorcha plopped down on her rump and began to play.

Esmée's gaze remained fixed on Sorcha, but when she spoke, it was to him. "Alasdair," she said quietly. "Why have you come here?"

For a moment, she thought he mightn't answer. Indeed, when she looked at him, there was a hint of a challenge in his eye. "Doubtless your aunt will disapprove," he finally said. "But she is my child, Esmée. I have a right to be with her wherever she goes."

"My aunt is not at home," she answered. "And that is not what I asked."

His gaze faltered slightly. "I wished to give you something," he said, reaching into his coat pocket. He withdrew a slender box of green velvet and passed it to her. It looked familiar. Uncertainly, Esmée took it.

"Open it," he said. "Please."

Curious, Esmée did so. A lustrous strand of pearls shimmered inside. She lifted the clasp, and gasped. It was fashioned of ornate gold and encrusted with six diamonds. The pearls were precisely sized, and good deal larger than the ones she had lost. "Oh, how lovely!" she whispered. "But I cannot accept a gift from you."

"It is not a gift," he responded. "It is a replacement. I know it is not the same as having your mother's pearls back, but it was the best I could do in a hurry."

"These are exquisite."

Alasdair smiled a little regretfully. "I meant you to have them, Esmée, that very next morning. But when I got home from the jeweler's, Lady Tatton was there, and everything seemed to go to hell pretty quickly. I did not think of them again until . . . until I saw you last night. Your throat was bare, and I thought that you might — ah, well. In any case, they are yours now."

Esmée felt her cheeks flush. "Och, I cannot!" she insisted, closing the box and thrusting it at him. "I thank you. But I am quite sure Aunt Rowena would say 'tis improper."

His eyes flashed angrily. "And I am quite sure I don't give a damn," he answered. "Take them, Esmée. Please. I want you to have them. Besides, who will know they aren't the ones your mother gave you? One strand looks very like another."

Eyes wide, she shook her head. "*I* would know," she answered. "And I know you paid dearly for them, too. They are exceptionally fine, and perfectly matched."

"And they are yours," he said firmly.

Esmée laid the box in her lap. "Aye, then," she said. "I shall put them away for Sorcha."

"As you wish," he snapped.

"Alasdair, please," she answered. "Let us not quarrel."

He gave a curt nod and let his gaze drift back to Sorcha, who was building a circle of wooden blocks around the naked doll.

Esmée opened the box again, and stared at the pearls, willing away the tears which pressed hotly against the backs of her eyes. Why did his gift make her feel so wretched? There was such an ache in her heart, even as the gift weighed heavily in her hand. Was this all they would ever share? These moments of strained contact? These careful, muted words? A mutual concern for the child they both loved? It did not seem enough. No, not nearly enough.

She closed the box and somehow regained her composure. "I hope Wellings and the rest of the staff go on well?"

"Well enough," he answered.

"And Mrs. Crosby?" she pressed, her

voice surprisingly steady. "I hope she is fully recovered?"

He did not take his eyes from Sorcha. "I have not seen her in a day or two," he said. "But she seems much restored. Her color is good. She is putting on weight."

"I'm glad to hear it," she said honestly. "I was surprised to see you at Lady Gravenel's last night. Did you enjoy your evening?"

"Not especially," he answered. "Yourself?"

"I thought her very hospitable," said Esmée. "And kind to have invited me."

At last, he returned his gaze to hers, his eyes cool and unfathomable. "You seem to be invited everywhere," he remarked. "I gather Lady Tatton has you burning your candle at both ends."

"Aunt does wish me to go about in society a vast deal," she agreed. "She wishes me 'to take,' whatever that means."

Again, the strange, muted smile. "I think you know what it means," said Alasdair. "It means she really is determined to marry you off."

"Aye, 'tis what's done in London, is it not?" asked Esmée coolly. "One's family trots one out like a horse at Tattersall's, then arranges a match with a suitable gentleman?"

His eyes were hooded, his mouth turned up at one corner in a sardonic smile. "So I'm told," he answered. "But such worthy fellows rarely travel in my circles. At least the two of you are enlivening what would otherwise be a very dull time of year in Mayfair."

Esmée's eyes narrowed. "Faith, Alasdair!" she finally snapped. "What business is it of yours if we set the place afire? You disavow any regard for society. Indeed, you don't even live here! And yes, Aunt Rowena wishes to see me happy, and to her that means marriage."

He watched her warily for a moment. "But what does it mean to you, Esmée?" he asked, dropping his voice a degree. "I am just curious, you see. And it *is* my business, since whoever you marry will become, by extension, a part of Sorcha's life."

Esmée wished to quarrel with his logic — and wished to slap the mocking smile from his lips — but she could not quite find grounds for either. Instead, she sprang from her chair and began to pace the room. "You know that I would never wed a man who did not feel an affection for Sorcha," she insisted, her voice quiet with rage. "Not after all I have been through, so do not dare imply otherwise."

Alasdair had risen, of course, when she did. He stood now, broad and immutable, by his chair, watching her pace toward him. He no longer looked the part of the handsome, charming *bon vivant*. His eyes were hard and weary. His mouth was tight, his jaw so firm the muscle in it twitched faintly. At last, he gave a terse nod. "My apologies."

Too angry to face him, she turned away and crossed the room again. "And yes, I think I ought to be married," she went on. "You said as much yourself, if you will recall."

"Ought?" echoed Alasdair, ignoring her remark. "That sounds grim."

She crossed her arms over her chest and stared blindly through the window at the wrought-iron fence below. "I mean only that I wish to be settled," she answered, forcing her voice to sound calm. "I don't want to be like my mother. I don't wish for excitement or drama. I just want a life and a family of my own, Alasdair. I wish to *belong* somewhere, and I never really have. Can you not understand?"

At last, he seemed to hear her; to look beyond himself and his petty frustrations. "I would like to understand," he said quietly.

Without turning from the window, Esmée lifted her hands. "I have always lived in someone else's home," she whispered. "In someone else's *life*. I have always lived under the protection of one stepfather after another, in situations where I was tolerated — sometimes even welcomed — but 'tis not the same thing as truly *belonging* somewhere. You can have no notion, Alasdair, what that is like. It feels as if you are an extra carriage wheel. A dusty corner in an unused room. Useless. And I am sick to death of it."

"I'm sorry," he said, so close she jumped.

Esmée set her fingertips to her lips, willing herself not to say something even more pathetically stupid. She could feel the heat radiating off his body, he stood so close behind her. She drew in her breath when he set his hand on her shoulder. His touch was heavy, warm, and infinitely comforting, though she knew she should take no comfort from him.

"I am sorry," he said again. "Perhaps, Esmée, I understand more than you think."

She gave a sharp, bitter laugh. "Oh, I doubt it."

For a long moment, he was silent. "Esmée, you can feel useless, I have learned, even when you are living your own life," he finally said. "And living in a place you do, ostensibly, belong."

Her chin came up, and she looked at his

faint reflection in the window. "What is that supposed to mean?"

He lifted one shoulder, and dropped his gaze. "Oh, I don't know," he said. "I remember, occasionally, my boyhood in Scotland. I sometimes think that I never belonged there."

"But you had a home and a family."

"Oh, to be sure," he admitted. "But feeling as if one belongs is not so simple as that, Esmée. It is . . . it is so much more. And bloody hard to explain."

"I would like to understand," she pressed, echoing his own words.

Alasdair looked as if he wished he had not spoken. "It is just that I wasn't like anyone else in my family," he said quietly. "Scots are a sober, serious-minded lot, as you well know, and my family was more serious and sober than most. But I . . . well, I was neither. I was full of myself — and full of mischief and adventure, too. Full of the devil, Granny MacGregor used to say. I could never be serious two minutes running. I drank and gambled my way through school, and went on to worse when I got out. My father was deeply disappointed in me, so I came here to London and stayed out of his sight. It seemed to suit all concerned."

"Aye, but why?" she asked. "Young men

must sow a few wild oats, and you were intelligent enough, I'll wager."

"I had a head for numbers," he admitted. "A gift which I refused to cultivate, save at the gaming tables. But beyond that, I had no special talent, unless one counts charm and good looks. My father certainly didn't. He spent his every waking moment wondering aloud why I couldn't be more like my brother Merrick."

"He wished you to be like *Merrick?*" Esmée was appalled.

"My father thought Merrick perfect," he said quietly. "He was everything that I was not. He was not just intelligent, he was brilliant. Not just hardworking, but driven. He was the smart one. I was the charming one. In a family filled with brilliant, accomplished achievers, I definitely did not fit in."

Again, Esmée thought of the arcane books filled with complex computations which she'd found in his old smoking parlor. They had been well thumbed, and heavily dog-eared. They had not even been written in English, but rather in French, and perhaps Dutch or German. Yet someone had read them; studied them almost obsessively, and she was relatively certain it wasn't Merrick MacLachlan.

"Sometimes, Alasdair, I believe you take

pains to appear charming and facile," she remarked. "Sometimes, I think you try hard *not* to try hard."

He looked at her ruefully. "I'm just making a point," he said. "I spent the first fifteen years of my life convinced I'd been deposited on my parents' doorstep by Gypsies or some such nonsense. Until Granny MacGregor informed me she'd delivered me herself, which shot my lovely little fantasy straight to hell."

Esmée's shoulders sagged. "Och, that sounds sad!" she said. "Sad for both you and your brother."

"For both of us, indeed," said Alasdair. "Merrick was never a child, whilst I was rarely anything else. I would not trade places with him. No, not even now."

"Aye, you never go home to Scotland, do you?" she mused. "Someone — Wellings, perhaps — once told me that."

He let his hand slip from her shoulder. "No, almost never," he agreed. "I have never missed it. Not until . . . well, very recently. And now I wonder if there weren't some aspects of that dutiful, industrious life which I might miss just a little, if I would but let myself. Indeed, it no longer seems so grim as I once thought it."

There was a catch in his voice which

Esmée had not heard before. She turned to face him, setting her back to the draperies, expecting that he would step away. But he did not. Instead he held her gaze intently with his golden eyes; eyes which had never looked more serious. Or more wounded. He did not touch her, though the strange heat between them made her wonder if he might. She held her breath, and waited.

He did not touch her. Instead, he set his hand against the wall behind her and leaned into her. "Tell me something," he finally said, his voice oddly thick. "Are you happy here? Are you content, Esmée, with your choice?"

Her hand fisted in the drapery behind her. "With *my* choice — ?" Somehow, she choked out the words. "But I did not have a choice, Alasdair. Don't you remember? No one asked me what I wanted. No one ever does. And I am growing just a little tired of everyone else deciding what is best for me. I think you know what I mean."

Alasdair opened his mouth, then shut it again. He held her gaze warily for a long moment, his hand still braced beyond her shoulder. Esmée willed him to speak — then willed herself to break the silence — but no words came.

Her choice? What a joke that was. *He* was

her choice, though the realization brought her no joy. She burned to kiss him, or to slap him, or just to tell him to burn in hell. But she did neither. Instead, Sorcha saved her by shrieking with glee and sending a stack of blocks tumbling across the floor.

It was as if a spell had been broken. Alasdair dropped his gaze and drew away. "I am sorry, Esmée," he said again. But this time, she hardly knew what he was apologizing for. For wanting her? For *not* wanting her? Or something else entirely? Despite all her grand talk of wanting a life of her own, Esmée suddenly felt very young, and very inexperienced.

Alasdair had crossed the room to survey the damage. "Well done, minx!" he said, his voice composed. "How many did you have? Shall I count them?"

"Count dem," Sorcha agreed, pointing imperiously at the disarray.

He counted aloud, Sorcha repeating the numbers after him. "Eleven!" he finished as he restacked them. "What a great many blocks that is! And what a clever girl you are."

"Clever!" said Sorcha, knocking them down again.

Alasdair lifted her chin with one finger and swiftly kissed her atop the head. Then he stood and held Esmée's gaze, his expression guarded now. "I must go," he murmured. "Indeed, I did not mean to stay at all. May I return for Sorcha in two hours' time?"

Esmée focused her gaze on a point somewhere beyond his shoulder. "Yes, of course," she agreed. "Whatever is convenient."

He picked up his hat and stick, which he'd left beside the chair. "In two hours, then," he said with a curt bow. "Thank you. I shall let myself out."

And before she could think of anything haughty and dismissive to say, he had vanished.

Chapter Eight

In which Sir Alasdair gives Advice

to the Lovelorn

Sir Alasdair MacLachlan stormed out of Lady Tatton's house and down the street without any explanation to his coachman, who stood by his horses' heads, watching his master's backside as he strode off in the direction of Piccadilly.

Along the streets, the morning's costermongers were departing with their carts and barrows, giving way to the press of carriages which conveyed the aristocracy to their morning calls, and the shouts of newsboys as they hawked their lurid tales. A stabbing in Southwark. Rumors of Wellington's resignation. Another damned riot some damned place. Alasdair ignored it all.

Damn it, how dare she! How dare that mere chit of a girl make him question his own judgment! How dare she make him fear he'd made such a stupid, revocable decision! And how dare she look so damned beautiful and so damned angry, all in the same breath?

To his left, down an alley, someone tossed a bucket of water from a garret window. Somewhere, church bells were ringing. A disheveled young blade in a half-buttoned waistcoat lifted his top hat, greeting Alasdair by name as they brushed past one another. Alasdair pressed on, oblivious to the grind of daily life even as he shouldered through it.

Yes, damn and damn and damn her! Esmée Hamilton had become the bane of his existence; an existence he'd once thought comfortable and uncomplicated. Well, by God, it was neither now. Perhaps it never had been. And now that the scales had been lifted from his eyes; now that he began to comprehend the sheer triviality of the life he'd been living, he had to do something — for Sorcha's sake, if not his own. He had to think about the future and stop obliterating life's nothingness with cheap pleasure and costly improvidence. It was going to require an awful lot of effort, something Alasdair did not normally exert.

At the corner of Mount Street, he turned on impulse toward Hyde Park, hunching his shoulders against the sharp autumn air. He had not thought to bring his greatcoat. Indeed, he had not *thought* at all. If he had considered for one moment the folly of his errand to Grosvenor Square, he would have sent someone else. Wellings. Hawes. Anyone could have accompanied Sorcha in the carriage.

It was a short walk in an ill wind, but he ignored the blasts which kept gusting down his coat collar. Indeed, it felt almost invigorating to be cold. He felt as if he'd been caught in a hot, emotional rush for weeks now. Ever since Esmée Hamilton, damn her, had inveigled her way into his home and his heart. A curricle came tooling down Park Lane, harnesses jangling. He jerked back onto the pavement and watched it roll past, its wheels flinging up bits of mud and manure. It was not an especially close call, but it reminded him yet again of the hazards which seemingly surrounded him.

Once inside the park, he headed directly to the bench near the Serpentine; the very bench where he and Esmée had sat on the dreadful day of Sorcha's accident. The day everything had changed. And nothing had changed. Absently, he prodded at the turf with his shoe, and to his shock, saw a pearl in the matted grass beneath. It was filthy. He picked it up, rolled it between his fingers, then dropped it into his pocket anyway. A keepsake. A reminder, perhaps, that he'd best be keeping his wits about him.

No, he'd had no business going to Lady Tatton's. But damn it, he had wanted to see those pearls around Esmée's neck. He had wanted her to wear them every evening as she was wined and dined by the highest of the *haut monde.* He had wanted to take a secret pleasure in knowing that it was his gift which encircled her throat, even as other men drank in her quiet beauty. It was a small, pathetic thing, to be sure. But he had wished it nonetheless.

Well, it did not matter. She was not going to wear them. For whatever reason. He watched dispassionately as a gull wheeled over the Serpentine, piercing the air with its forlorn cry. The bird had likely been blown about by last night's squall and was now just a little lost. Alasdair knew the feeling. He thrust his hand into his pocket, and felt about for the comfort of his little pearl.

Esmée was sorry when Alasdair's coachman rang the bell two hours later and asked for Sorcha. He carried the child down to the waiting carriage and handed her through the open door. From the gloomy depths, Alasdair reached forward to take her, the familiar signet ring on his left hand catching the midday sun as he did so.

313

He did not acknowledge Esmée's presence in any way. Indeed, he did not even lean forward far enough to reveal his face. She felt the warm weight of tears behind her eyes and spun around, ruthlessly shutting the door. The situation felt suddenly so ugly to her, as if she and Alasdair were some miserable married couple trotting a beloved child back and forth because they were too antagonistic to live beneath the same roof.

After brooding on it for a time, she was mercifully distracted by an afternoon filled with surprises, some more pleasant than others. The first was a bouquet of yellow roses from Mr. Nowell, along with a note asking her to drive with him in the park the following afternoon. The second was an invitation from Miss Smathers to accompany her and her brother to an exhibit of new landscapes at the Royal Academy.

She was penning acceptances to both when her aunt returned from Madame Panaut's with a bandbox containing a beautiful dress of dark, bronze-colored satin.

"It perfectly matches your hair!" her aunt declared. "Oh, I knew it would! I asked *Madame* to make it up as a surprise."

Esmée fingered the exquisite fabric. "Aunt, you are too kind."

But Lady Tatton brushed aside the

314

remark. "Now, we have only to get it fitted, and you may wear it to the theater next Wednesday."

"To the theater?"

Lady Tatton smiled knowingly. "We have been invited to share Lady Kirton's box," she said. "And I am most keen to go. She has invited Lady Wynwood and her son. I wish to see what that young man is made of."

"But the theater?" said Esmée again.

"Well, it is not as if we're to see a farce," said her aunt. "We're to see *The Wicket Gate*, an adaptation of *The Pilgrim's Progress*, a most upright and edifying work."

Esmée thought it sounded deadly dull. She was also reluctant to spend an evening with Wynwood and his mother. Even the ten minutes she had spent strolling on his arm after dinner in Lady Gravenel's withdrawing room had severely taxed her conversational skills. She had been unable to keep from imagining what Alasdair might have told Wynwood about her. Then there was that embarrassing memory of her outburst in the dining room not so many weeks ago.

Dear heaven. She had called Mr. MacLachlan a midge-brained maundrel, and told Lord Wynwood he had the manners of pig. The latter had not been true. He had been the only one of the three gentlemen *not* to behave as if she and Sorcha were pieces of furniture, to be discussed, and even quarreled over, as if they had no feelings of their own. And afterward, he had been perfectly pleasant. Why did it trouble her now?

At Lady Gravenel's, Wynwood had tried to entertain her. He had asked after Sorcha, and told her a funny story about his boyhood in Buckinghamshire, and about some of his less scandalous adventures with the jaded-looking Lord Devellyn and the brothers MacLachlan. But just when Esmée felt she might grow at ease in his company, she had noticed the way Lady Wynwood's keen eyes kept following the two of them around the room.

"Why, Esmée!" Lady Tatton's voice jerked her back to the present. "What have you here?"

She turned to see her aunt standing by the writing desk. "Oh, invitations," she answered. "I thought I should accept both."

Lady Tatton fanned Miss Smathers's card back and forth. "Now, why do I wonder if this invitation was sent at someone else's behest?" she teased. "Perhaps *Mr.* Smathers?"

Esmée smiled. "I daresay you are right," she admitted. "At least poor Mr. Nowell had the nerve to send his own."

Lady Tatton plucked it from the desk. "Riding in the park with Nowell!" she chirped. "I think you should accept, my dear. He's too monotonous to marry, but the connection cannot hurt."

Just then, the butler entered, carrying a silver salver with two cards. "A lady and a gentleman to see you, ma'am."

Lady Tatton tossed down the invitation and snatched up the cards. "Oh, lud, 'tis Wynwood! And his mother!" Her head jerked up. "Quick! We must receive them in the drawing room!"

At Esmée's confused hesitation, Lady Tatton seized her by the elbow and dragged her toward the door. "In two minutes, Grimond! Oh, dear, Esmée! Is that a smudge on your dress? Here, take my handkerchief. Dust it off. Quick! Quick! Now, stand very straight, if you please. Height becomes you."

Esmée followed her into the parlor and stood very straight. "But why are they here *now,* if we are to go to the theater together on Wednesday?"

She did not have to wonder long. Lady Wynwood, a tall, slender reed of a woman,

317

hastened into the drawing room in a rustle of silk and kissed Lady Tatton's cheeks. Lord Wynwood made his bow to Esmée, a bemused half smile on his face.

"Oh, Rowena!" said Lady Wynwood, clasping her chest. "The most dreadful thing! Cook has come down with that quinsy which is going round!"

"Oh! Oh, my poor dear!" Lady Tatton seized her hand and patted it.

"You don't know the half!" she wailed. "I've a dinner party set for Monday! Oh, *will* you give me the instructions for that poultice you mentioned last night?"

"The boiled onion wrapped about the throat? But of course." Lady Tatton went to a small desk in the corner, and Lady Wynwood followed. "Now, it must be very hot," said the former, pulling out a sheet of letter paper. "Hot enough to draw the poison, mind! But not hot enough to blister."

Esmée smiled at Lord Wynwood and motioned toward the chairs which flanked the hearth. "Will you sit down, my lord, whilst this terrible tragedy is averted?"

Wynwood's blue eyes flashed with merriment. "Miss Hamilton, I do like your sense of humor," he said. "I think it was the first thing I noticed about you."

Esmée tossed him a skeptical glance. "How perfectly astonishing," she remarked. "I should have thought it was my habit of having histrionic outbursts in front of people I hardly know."

He threw his head back and laughed again. The two ladies at the writing desk turned round to stare. "I think you make my point, Miss Hamilton," he answered. "Your sense of humor is perfectly irrepressible, even when you're in a temper."

"Oh, I was very angry that day," she admitted.

"It is not the norm for you, I am sure," he went on. "I think you are probably a very good-natured person at heart. God knows Merrick could provoke a saint, and Alasdair is almost as bad."

"I try to maintain a positive outlook, Lord Wynwood," she said. "Though it has been hard of late."

His face fell. "You miss your sister, do you not?" he answered. "I can understand that. She is such a little angel."

"Actually, she is an utter hellion." Esmée smiled tightly. "But I miss her anyway. Desperately. Until now, I have never been away from her. It has been harder than I expected."

"Ah, my sympathies, Miss Hamilton,"

said Wynwood. "Your predicament is a difficult one. Perhaps I can help take your mind off your troubles for one evening. I understand Lady Kirton has invited you and your aunt to attend the theater with us on Wednesday. Dare I hope that you will join us?"

"Yes, I believe we mean to," she said. "Though I confess an unfamiliarity with the play."

Wynwood smiled dryly. "*The Wicket Gate?*" he said. "I believe it is designed to elevate our morals. I only hope that mine do not crack under the pressure."

Just then, Lady Tatton closed the desk drawer and began folding the paper. Lord Wynwood rose. "I must go," he said. "Mamma is having one of her fragile days. I have offered her my arm for the afternoon."

"How good of you," said Esmée.

Again, he flashed his bemused smile. "Sometimes a man must own his responsibilities," he said. "Whether he wishes to or not."

In a few short moments, Lord and Lady Wynwood were saying their good-byes and promising to see them on Wednesday. "There!" said Lady Tatton, as Grimond pulled shut the drawing room door. "I thought that went very well."

"You thought what went very well?"

Lady Tatton drew back a pace. "Oh, you do not for one moment believe that nonsense about the onion, do you?"

Esmée blinked. "Should I not?"

Her aunt patted her gently on the arm. "Ten to one, the cook has nothing but a sniffle," she said. "Did you not see how Lady Wynwood eyed your attire? My draperies and decor? Even the cut of poor Grimond's coat? Next she'll be rubbing my silver to see if it's plated. No, she wished to catch us off guard. Lady Wynwood is beginning the vetting process."

Esmée was aghast. "The *vetting* process?"

"Oh, indeed," said Lady Tatton. "She wishes to reassure herself that you — indeed, that *we* — are good enough for her son."

Esmée was good enough, at the very least, to go riding the following afternoon with Mr. Nowell, who shocked her by arriving in Grosvenor Square in a dashing new cabriolet with a pair under the pole. Perhaps she had misjudged the young politician? She had initially believed him earnest, but dull as ditchwater.

Unfortunately, on closer acquaintance, she realized his earnestness was intact, and bordered on pomposity. On the way to the park, he treated her to a rant about Wellington's foot-dragging over parliamentary reform. As they drove along Rotten Row, the topic turned to his traitorous support of the Catholics. Apparently, the end of English civilization as they knew it was upon them, and it was all the Prime Minister's fault.

Esmée, who had more than a little sympathy for the Catholics, did not bother to ask Mr. Nowell's political view on England's treatment of its more northerly neighbor. Their opinions on that subject would most almost certainly diverge, and Mr. Nowell, she had decided, was not worth the argument. But after tooling the length of the park, he surprised her by dropping the subject of politics altogether and asking if she would like to see his new house.

"Not that it is quite mine yet," he admitted almost shyly. "Indeed, it isn't even finished."

Esmée was intrigued. "How far away is it?"

"Not far at all," he said. "Near Chelsea."

Esmée agreed with alacrity, though she wasn't perfectly sure where Chelsea was. After scarcely two months in London, she had grown weary of trotting round the same old streets and parks, and waving to the same silly people.

The streets leading away from Hyde Park were not crowded, and Nowell set his horses at a surprisingly good clip. Esmée clapped one hand on her hat and sat back to enjoy the drive. On the outer fringes of Belgravia, they began to see beautiful new mansions in various stages of construction. "My house is farther on," Nowell said, as the glorious white edifices breezed past.

Soon the white mansions vanished. Mr. Nowell made several turns, and they began to pass an occasional open field, tidy church, or quaint manor house — sometimes even a row of shops; the odds and ends, Esmée supposed, of little villages destined to be swallowed up by greater London. Eventually, terraced facades of brick came into view. These houses looked a little like those in Mayfair, but more modern and more imposing. After passing along several finished dwellings, Mr. Nowell turned into what was soon to become, so far as Esmée could surmise, an elegant close.

The dusty, cobbled space was abuzz with activity. Men wielding shovels, hammers, and trowels were everywhere. In one corner, two surveyors were setting up tripods. Farther along the close sat a cart laden with mortar, a dray stacked with brick, and even a glossy black curricle with a groom carefully attending it. Nowell pointed across the close to a soaring edifice of brick-and-marble glory. The house appeared complete from the exterior, but was surrounded by piles of stone and dirt on one side and an incomplete foundation on the other.

"Number Four, Ballachulish Close," said the young man proudly.

Esmée was impressed. Mr. Nowell was not, it seemed, in need of a fortune — unless it was to pay his mortgage. She shut away that bit of cynicism, and smiled. "Ballachulish Close," she echoed. "That's Scottish."

Nowell nodded. "The architect who conceived and built all this is a Scot," he said. "A singularly moody fellow, but a genius nonetheless. Won't let them lay so much as a brick without his approval, and manages the design, the financing, every little detail, personally. Worse than crazy Cubitt up in Belgravia, I reckon. I'm to take title on December 1, if the poor devil can bring himself to part with it."

"How lovely it all is!" said Esmée. "And I've never seen so many workmen in one place at one time."

Nowell's expression turned fretful. "Perhaps this isn't a proper place for a lady to visit?"

"Nonsense," she returned. "Still, I daresay we ought to go. Aunt will be wondering where I am."

Nowell snapped his reins, and attempted to turn his cabriolet amidst all the carts and drays. In the process, he edged perilously close to the black curricle. The groom jerked to attention and watched Nowell assessingly, as if daring him to so much as scratch his master's fine conveyance.

Esmée exhaled a little sharply as Nowell cut the turn with only two inches to spare. "You needn't worry," he said calmly. "It's Mr. MacLachlan's, and believe me, he can easily afford a score of 'em."

Esmée's grip tightened on the side of the cabriolet. "I — I beg your pardon?" she managed. "It belongs to whom?"

Nowell was still working his way around the close. "Merrick MacLachlan, the famous architect," he said absently. "He and his brother are the investors behind all this. But wait — you are distantly related to them, are you not? That is to say, Lady Gravenel mentioned something to that effect."

"Aye, distantly, perhaps. I'm not sure."

Esmée looked back at the close, and almost as if she'd willed it, Merrick MacLachlan came round the corner of Number Four and stepped carefully over the low foundation adjoining it. His dark coat and waistcoat were immaculately brushed as always, but his trousers were covered in dust to the ankles. His face was fixed in its perpetual glower, the nasty scar across his cheek stark and taut. And worse, he was not alone.

"Good afternoon, gentlemen," said Nowell, as the men approached the curricle. "Miss Hamilton and I were just admiring the house."

The brothers exchanged glances and greeted them with cool politeness. "Well, you may trot out here and look about all the livelong day, Nowell," Merrick added, "but the house won't be ready 'til December, and wishing won't make it otherwise."

Nowell looked at Esmée a little sheepishly. "I have made rather a pest of myself," he admitted. "Tell me, Sir Alasdair, has your brother enlisted your help in his architectural endeavors?"

Alasdair gave a bark of laughter. "For your sake and his, Nowell, you'd best hope not."

Merrick MacLachlan shifted his gaze

from Alasdair to Esmée uncertainly. "It's as well you're here, I suppose," he said to Nowell. "Penworth is inside, torn between two different chimneypieces I designed. I prefer one, he prefers the other. Do you wish to choose for yourself? It will likely ruin your shoes."

Nowell glanced back at the house almost covetously, then hesitated, but whether over the propriety of leaving Esmée alone or the welfare of his shoes, she could not say.

"Alasdair will hold your horses," said Merrick.

"Oh, nothing would give me more pleasure," said his brother.

Covetousness won out. Nowell leapt down. "I shall return in a jot, Miss Hamilton!"

Critically watching his departure, Alasdair gave a sour smile. "I don't think your aunt would approve of Mr. Nowell just now, do you?"

"She wasn't overfond of him when I left," Esmée admitted breezily. "I believe I am merely to practice my feminine wiles on him until something better comes along."

Alasdair shot her another dark look, but somewhere along the way, it turned into a spurt of laughter. "Oh, she said that, did she?" he asked. "Good God, I have thrown you into the clutches of a true Machiavellian."

Esmée looked imperiously down at him. "Aye, so you have," she retorted. "And I'm glad to hear you admit 'twas your own doing."

His eyes narrowed, and his perfectly chiseled jaw twitched. "Don't cut up at me, Esmée," he warned. "No one put a skean to your back — neither to go, nor to flirt so outrageously with these fools."

Esmée lifted her brows. "Flirt outrageously?" she echoed. "Really, Alasdair, I think you give my feminine wiles more credit than 'tis warranted. And as to that skean, I could have sworn I felt it draw blood."

He turned his head away, and the knuckles holding the horses' harness went white. "I see," he gritted. "And who is to be the next spider in the web?"

"Your friend Wynwood, I collect," she said airily. "He is to take me to the theater Wednesday night."

She heard him curse softly. "Quin?" he responded incredulously, his head swiveling round again. "To — to the theater?"

"Yes, but it will be hard for me to *flirt outrageously* with the poor fellow," she went on. "It is a very moralizing sort of play, so I daresay I shall be obliged to leave my fan at home, wear a demure neckline, and confine myself to mild coquettishness. For propriety's sake, you know."

"Good God," he responded. "You are — but you are going to see *The Wicket Gate*?"

"Aye, what of it?" she answered, dropping her voice to a more serious tone. "Really, Alasdair, I cannot quite make out what it is you wish me to do. I thought I was to get out of your hair and find myself a husband, and yet nothing I do to that end seems to please you."

"But *The Wicket Gate*," he said again. "That is — is — oh, never mind!"

"You did not answer my question," she said.

He flicked another of his dark looks up at her. "What I wish you to do, Esmée, is go straight home when that lack-wit Nowell comes out," he said. "And don't tell your aunt you've been out here. A building site is no place for a lady."

Esmée cast an uneasy glance toward the house. "I did begin to wonder at it," she admitted. "I never seem to know what's expected. I was used to doing as I pleased in Scotland."

"This isn't Scotland."

"Aye, I'd noticed," she returned. "Besides, you seem almost as out of place here as I do."

He was no longer looking at her, but instead letting his eyes run over the distant piles of rubble and brick. "I am out of place," Alasdair agreed. "But Merrick has a notion to build one of these modern monstrosities for our grandmother. She's having none of it, of course. So it falls to me to make peace and explain to Merrick why one of his ideas is thought less than brilliant."

"Oh, I'm sure that concept is hard for him to grasp." Esmée looked up and squinted against the sun. "Your grandmother is in Scotland, is she not? Why should she wish to leave?"

Alasdair shrugged. "It is a colder, harsher life there, isn't it?" he replied. "But she more or less manages my estate for me. She has command of a drafty old castle and a whole army of servants. No, I do not think she would willingly give up such independence for a little warmth and a few modern conveniences."

"Good for her!" said Esmée.

He looked up at her appraisingly. "You would do the same, wouldn't you?" he murmured. "You would go home in a flash if you could."

She was silent for a moment. "I no longer

have a home to go to," she said simply. "And I could not bear to be so far away from Sorcha."

One of the horses shifted a little restlessly, and to soothe him, Alasdair began to stroke him from neck to withers with slow, almost mesmerizing motions. "If you are trying to make me feel guilty, Esmée, it won't work," he finally said. "I am her father, and any sort of father is better than none at all."

Esmée stiffened. "Did I say otherwise?" she asked. "I never even knew my father, and I would not wish that on Sorcha. I have never so much as suggested she should leave you."

"No, but your aunt did." Alasdair was still stroking the horse, as if he did not wish to hold her gaze. "Esmée, why did you not tell me you were an heiress?"

She blinked in mild surprise. "An heiress?" she echoed. "Why, I'm not, really. Am I? I mean, I suppose that I will bring wealth to my husband if I marry. But that money does me not a jot of good now, does it?"

"But you are still an heiress."

Suddenly, the devil seemed to gig Esmée. "Rethinking your haste, Alasdair?"

He looked up, his eyes hardening. "That remark does not become you, Esmée," he snapped. "I am trying to do what is best for you and for Sorcha."

"Aye, there it is again!" said Esmée. "That overweening paternalism! Poor little Esmée! So young! So naïve! We must do what is *best* for her!"

Alasdair suddenly exploded. "God damn it, what do you want of me?" He lifted one arm so violently the horses started. "Just tell me, for pity's sake! And be careful what you wish for!"

Esmée was still clinging to the side of Nowell's cabriolet, and staring at his face, which had gone stark with anger. "Nothing," she finally whispered. "I want nothing."

"Aye, if you're smart, you don't!" he agreed. "It is one thing, Esmée, to rely upon your looks to find yourself a husband. But when money comes into play — well, you need be excessively careful. That is all I'm trying to say. Fortune hunters are a clever lot. Be on your guard."

Just then, Merrick stepped outside. Nowell followed, gingerly picking his way down the steps, and along the boards which fashioned a sort of path into the close. Esmée watched him almost dispassionately. "What do you think, Alasdair?" she murmured. "Is my handsome young suitor a fortune hunter?"

His face looked bloodless now. "Nowell?" he answered. "Not so far as I know."

Esmée turned on the seat to squarely face him. "And what of Mr. Smathers?" she asked, forcing him to hold her gaze. "Or Lord Thorpe? Or your friend Wynwood? Tell me, Alasdair, what would you advise? You seem to have such a strong grasp on what is best for me."

His eyes flashed again. "Fair enough, then," he answered. "Since you asked, Smathers is a fortune hunter, Thorpe is a mamma's boy, and Nowell is about as exciting as watching herring pickle. I'm shocked, honestly, that your matchmaking aunt cannot reel in a better fish."

"You did not remark upon Lord Wynwood," she said quietly.

He tore his gaze away. "I cannot," he said quietly. "He is a friend. But if he marries, Esmée, it will be out of duty."

"And not love?" she asked. "Is that what you meant to suggest? For if it is, feel free to dance at our wedding. I am not looking for love. Not any longer."

Alasdair turned away and said no more. Merrick and Nowell had finished their conversation and were striding toward them now. After a curt thanks to Alasdair, Nowell climbed up, clicked to his horses, and set off. At the last possible moment, Esmée turned on the narrow seat to look back. Merrick MacLachlan had vanished. But Alasdair still stood in the cobblestoned close, watching them as they rolled away.

The streets leading to the theater on Wednesday evening were choked with carriages for a quarter mile in all directions. Esmée tried to stare out the window without appearing to gawk like the rustic she secretly was. All of London, Aunt Rowena claimed, was attempting to attend the opening night of *The Wicket Gate*, lest they be viewed as less pious or less saintly than their neighbors. Some even expected to be entertained.

For Esmée, however, such a trip to the theater *was* the evening's entertainment, for she had never seen a real play, save for a traveling theater company at a village fair one summer. Once inside the theater, they were shown to their box, a lavish little nook done up in wine-colored velvet. Esmée, it seemed, was to sit in the front of the box with Lord Wynwood, whilst the three ladies took the rearmost seats, where they immediately fell into whispered gossip about everyone and everything around them.

Wynwood was all that was polite, offering to fetch refreshments, ensuring she had the best possible view, and making light conversation whilst they waited for the lights to go out. And yet she sensed that he was ill at ease. His gaze kept drifting around the theater, and his conversation felt forced.

Esmée did not have long to ponder it. Behind her, the whispers were growing in heat and intensity. Esmée strained to hear the words.

"Why, the audacity!" her aunt murmured. "Ever the peacock, isn't he? And *she* means to play more than one role tonight, I'm guessing."

Lady Kirton's voice was quiet but calm. "Actually, I believe that is the sister on his arm," she responded. "And the Karlssons really are quite good actresses. I met them once, you know."

"Oh, horrors!" said Esmée's aunt. "You are speaking of that dreadful incident at Drury Lane, are you not? When that Black Angel person was murdered?"

"She shot herself, Rowena," corrected Lady Kirton. "It was an accident."

"Still, Isabel, one must admit you were in the wrong place at the wrong time," said Lady Wynwood. "And then to be detained by the police — and with those infamous Karlsson sisters! — really, my dear, I should have fainted, I am sure!"

"The sight of blood does not make me faint, Gwendolyn," said Lady Kirton calmly. "Nor does having to visit a police station with a pair of actresses. We were all three witnesses to the accident, and we all three did our civic duty. I thought them very kind."

Lady Wynwood ignored the tactful overture. "Nonetheless, Wynwood, I hope and pray, would never make such a spectacle of himself as *he* is doing! Indeed, I should hope Wynwood would not acknowledge her at all!"

Beside Esmée, Lord Wynwood seemed to sink lower in his chair. Esmée wanted to look about and see just who was provoking such fervent disapproval, but by then, the lights were going out.

Due to the play's length, there was to be no prelude, so Esmée slid eagerly forward in her seat. Lord Wynwood leaned over to whisper in her ear. "Have you read Mr. Bunyan's famous allegory, Miss Hamilton?"

In the gloom, she gave him a self-deprecating smile. "I tried," she confessed. "I believe I made it as far as the Valley of the Shadow of Death, then decided poor Christian would have to soldier on to his eternal reward without me. Did you finish?"

He laughed softly. "It may surprise you to learn that I have read every word of *The Pilgrim's Progress* twice," he said. "Both times at knifepoint — a penknife, that is, since my tutor was a notoriously hard-minded fellow. So if you have questions, feel free to ask me."

From the general direction of the pit, a strain of almost celestial music rose, swelling to a crescendo as the curtain slowly rose on its shrieking mechanisms to reveal the chorus.

"Good God," whispered Wynwood, wincing. "They ought to oil those pulleys."

The chorus consisted of a trio of beautiful, white-clad angels bearing flaming torches. The centermost angel, a tall, breathtaking beauty whose white-blond hair hung below her waist lifted her torch and stepped forward. In unison, they began to speak, portending in dire, theatrical voices the many tribulations and temptations which were to come. Soon the actor playing the role of Christian the Pilgrim stepped forward and began the first act.

The work was ingeniously put together. Only the essential elements of the novel's plot had been retained. The three beautiful angels remained stage right at all times, cleverly bridging the scenes whilst holding

337

their burning torches aloft until Esmée felt sure their arms must have gone numb.

Esmée remained on the edge of her chair as their intrepid hero faced down the deceit of Mr. Worldy-Wiseman, and traveled through such temporal hazards as the Slough of Despond and Doubting Castle on his journey to reach the Celestial City. But soon, the allegory lost her interest, and Esmée began to look about the theater for distraction.

She did not have to look for very long. At that very moment, Christian exited stage left, the chorus of angels stepped back, and the curtain began to descend, the mechanical protestations of its rings and pulleys even more shrill than when it had risen.

Esmée relaxed. Intermission was beginning. Behind her, the ladies began to whisper excitedly again. Wynwood stood, and bowed. "Your pardon, Miss Hamilton," he said quietly. "I see someone to whom I must pay my respects."

After being enjoined by his mother to fetch refreshments as he returned, Wynwood pushed his way through the heavy curtains behind them. The three ladies resumed their chatter. Alone in the front of the box, Esmée amused herself by looking about at the beautifully dressed people who sat in the boxes opposite. Just then, she heard a sharp gasp behind her. As if her gaze had been directed by the sound, Esmée looked up and to the right, and felt her heart lurch.

Alasdair. Alasdair, who was being joined by Lord Wynwood. And Alasdair was not alone. Someone — a very beautiful someone — sat beside him. She was dressed all in red, with a red plume in her hat. It was, Esmée realized, the lithe, blond angel from the chorus. She was smiling up at Wynwood, an exultant expression etched upon her face.

Wynwood stepped past Alasdair and kissed the hand she languidly offered. The actress let the hand drop, and returned her gaze to Alasdair, seductively dropping her lashes even as she looked at him. Esmée felt a painful stab of envy. The woman was very beautiful, and Esmée was still trying to comprehend how she could have reappeared so quickly, and in an altogether different costume, when she heard Lady Wynwood again.

"And just what does he think he is doing?" she demanded. "I vow, I ought to — ought to —"

"Ought to what, Gwendolyn?" interjected Lady Kirton gently. "Spank him?

Scold him? He is a grown man, my dear. And she is going to be a very famous actress someday. Besides, she is Sir Alasdair's guest, not Wynwood's."

"She is his *mistress*," corrected Lady Wynwood. "Or one of them, and everyone knows it."

"No, I don't think so," said Lady Kirton. But even she sounded confused now. "I think it is the angel in the chorus who is — or perhaps *was* — his mistress. That is her sister who is sitting in his box."

Sisters thought Esmée. There were two? That brought her no comfort.

"Oh, dear," said Lady Tatton. "This is very awkward."

"Yes, and Sir Alasdair is your cousin!" remarked Lady Wynwood, as if she sought to spread the blame around.

"Well, I am not at all sure he —" Lady Tatton's words broke off. "Well, he is not close kin, at any rate. A fifth cousin, perhaps."

By now, Lord Wynwood had vanished from Sir Alasdair's box. Alasdair and the blond actress — the angel's sister — were whispering intently. Esmée sat quietly, her hands folded demurely in her lap. But beneath her ladylike gloves, her knuckles were white with anger. His mistress, was she? Or his mistress's sister? Indeed, she would not put it past Alasdair MacLachlan to have sampled both!

She spent the next ten minutes stewing until Wynwood returned, his big hands filled with stemmed glasses. He passed them round to the ladies, glancing down at Esmée with a look of mild chagrin. She forced herself to smile, and thanked him. The lights were beginning to dim again. Wynwood took his seat just as the squeaking pulleys began their ascent, hauling the curtain back up.

Poor Christian was center stage, bent beneath his burden, and looking dreadfully glum. The chorus was stage right this time. Again, at the precise moment the curtain revealed them, the three angels stepped forward, their flaming torches in hand, their white robes swirling ethereally about their feet.

But this time, something went awry. The rightmost edge of the curtain did not rise in proper synchronization with the angels' movements. The center angel, the taller of the three, hesitated when the curtain brushed her forehead. In confusion, the second faltered, catching her foot in her pooling skirts. The third angel soldiered on, stepping determinedly forward to hoist her torch as planned — and in the process, set the curtain afire.

For an instant, everyone froze. Then the first angel looked up, and screamed. The curtain burst into full flame, which hastened its way in all directions, snapping and crackling as it consumed the fabric. Pandemonium exploded. "Fire! Fire!" someone screamed.

Christian tossed down his heavy knapsack and hurled himself into the pit. The angels followed, white skirts billowing as they leapt from the stage. In the audience below, men and woman ran screaming for the doors. Wynwood had seized Esmée's arm. "I realize Mr. Bunyan wished to warn us of the perils of hellfire," he said. "But this seems a bit much."

"Oh! Oh dear!" cried his mother. "Oh, Quinten, we are going to die!"

Lady Kirton had the curtain drawn back and was pushing Lady Tatton through.

"Esmée! Where is Esmée!" Lady Tatton shrieked. "I shan't leave without her!"

"I have her, ma'am," Wynwood shouted. He had his mother by the arm now, too. Smoke was beginning to roil in the air. "Press on, ladies, please. Quickly."

"Oh, Quinten!" his mother wailed. "You haven't an heir! Oh, oh! I told you to get married! Now look! We are going to die!"

"Mamma, for God's sake *move!*" he insisted, propelling her forward as he dragged Esmée behind. "Follow on Lady Tatton's heels. Go! Go!"

They worked their way toward the upper balcony, the crowd thickening as they went. Shouts and screams were everywhere. Lady Tatton looked back periodically, her face white with panic, as if to ensure Esmée followed. Lady Wynwood was still shrieking above all the other shrieking women.

"Oh, all shall be Cousin Enoch's now!" she cried. "Vile, odious man! Oh, we are going to die!"

Inside the upper lobby, the crowd was near impenetrable. Ladies were pushing and shoving to get down the narrow twin staircases, while gentlemen — the true ones, anyway — stood to one side. Wynwood was frantically pushing the women closer. The stench of burned fabric filled Esmée's nostrils. True panic edged near, but she fought it down.

When they reached the top of the steps, Wynwood stood aside. "Urge them on, I beg you," he said to Esmée. "Keep Lady Kirton in front — she won't lose her head — and keep the others between you!"

Nodding, Esmée started down the stairs,

coughing against the smoke. But she could feel a little air stirring in the stairwell, a good sign, she prayed. Urgently, she pushed the ladies toward it. But halfway down, the smoke became almost impenetrable. Suddenly, as they neared the bottom, Lady Wynwood froze. "Quinten?" she cried. "Oh! Where is he? I won't go on without him!"

"Please, ma'am," said Esmée firmly. "Move on, then the gentlemen may follow."

Lady Wynwood's face was stark with fear. "No! No! I cannot leave him!"

"Move on, you damned cow!" shouted an angry voice. In the roiling smoke, a man's arm thrust over Esmée's shoulder, giving Lady Wynwood a violent shove.

Situated perhaps four steps up, Lady Wynwood pitched forward into the haze, practically taking the others down with her. Esmée tried to catch her, but the man shoved Esmée from his path, too, slammed her hard between the shoulder blades. She stumbled, fell, and a terrible pain shot through her left leg. Everyone was screaming and tumbling.

Esmée rolled to one side at the bottom of the steps, skirts tangling about her knees. The crowd continued to trample past. Chaos was everywhere. More men were thundering down now. Everyone was shouting out orders and directions.

"The door! The door!" someone cried. "It's that way!"

Esmée rose onto her arms and called out. No one heard. She tried to get up, but a shaft of pain stabbed her knee. The thundering footsteps went on. Somewhere in the distance, glass shattered. In the haze, she seized hold of something — the stair rail, perhaps — and debated whether to drag herself up, or try to crawl beneath the smoke. Suddenly, a ghostly shadow moved from the opposite stairwell toward her.

"Esmée?" She would have known his voice anywhere. "Esmée! Good God! Are you all right?"

Strong, solid arms slid beneath her, lifting her almost effortlessly from the floor. "Oh, Alasdair," she said. "Oh, I am glad to see you!"

"And I you," he said, glancing over one shoulder. "Ilsa, I have her!" he shouted. "Go on, get out! Find Inga!"

The woman in red materialized from the smoke, coughing. "Ya, we find you outside," she managed. "Your friend, she is good?"

"Yes, go!" He was shouldering his way through what remained of the crowd. The woman in red pushed past them, vanishing into the haze. "Turn your face into my coat, Esmée," he ordered. "Don't breathe the smoke. What happened?"

"I wrenched my knee and fell down the last of the stairs," she said, her words muffled against his broad chest. "A man shoved us out of his way."

"Bastard!" he gritted. "Where the hell is Quin? Where are the ladies?"

"I do not know," she answered, coughing. "Perhaps he passed me in the smoke? I think the others got out."

Suddenly, a flood of fresh air hit them. *The door!* A few more long strides, and Alasdair burst through it, swishing her skirts round one of the columns which lined the theater's facade. The crowd had spilt into the intersection and beyond. Smoke billowed from the theater's doors and windows. Esmée lifted her face from Alasdair's coat to see clusters of hacking, soot-stained people everywhere. From the coffeehouses and taverns nearby, customers had flooded forth to offer aid, or just to gawk. But no one was lingering long. Fires could spread too quickly.

Esmée looked about in vain for her aunt. Just then, a cart loaded with men came rattling up the street. "Make way!" they shouted. "Make way for the fire brigade! Make way, now!"

The crowd in the street split like the Red Sea. Alasdair reached a flight of stone steps leading up to some sort of building, then carried her up to the top, as if she weighed nothing at all. "We should be safe here for now," he said, settling her on the top step. "Esmée, listen to me. Which way did your aunt go?"

"Through the door we used, I think," she managed between coughs.

Just then, a strange-looking contraption, like a steam engine on wheels, came rumbling past, drawn by four stout dray horses. The men on the cart leapt down, and began to rush to and fro, barking orders and waving madly at the man driving the steam apparatus.

Alasdair returned his attention to her. His face was stark with worry and streaked with soot. Backlit by the haze of smoke and flame, he again put her in mind of some fallen angel. Her angel — for tonight, at least. "I'm not sure how long we can safely remain here," he said. "You cannot walk. I am afraid to leave you, or I would go back and search for the others."

Esmée considered it. "I think they *must* have got out that door," she said. "There was no place else to go but in that direction."

He knelt and stared at her knee. "How badly are you hurt?"

" 'Tis but a sprain," she answered. "And you?"

He smiled crookedly. "Well enough, for a man who's had the life scared out of him," he said. "I pray God everyone got out of that hell alive."

As if to punctuate his description, an upstairs window suddenly blew, raining glass upon the street. A fireball roared out behind it, then receded into smaller flames, which began to lick their way up what was left of the wooden frame. Esmée stared up at it and felt a frisson of fear run down her spine. She had made a lucky escape. What if Alasdair had not come? Would anyone have heard her cries? Would she have been able to limp out? Crawl out? It was too horrible to contemplate.

"Alasdair," she said quietly. "Were you looking for me in there?"

"Yes."

"Why?"

"Why?" He stared at her a little oddly. "Because . . . because I thought . . . oh, I don't know. I saw Quin pushing you from the box, and I just thought . . . something was wrong. I felt uneasy. That's all."

"Uneasy," echoed Esmée.

She had had a brush with almost certain death, and all that had saved her, perhaps, was the unease of a man who had cared enough to come looking for her. A premonition, so to speak, from someone who professed to live only in the here and now, and who insisted he had nothing of the romantic in him.

Well. Esmée was not sure she believed that any longer. But what could she do about it? He was convinced, so no one else's opinion much mattered. The futility of it all seemed to well into a deep, sorrowful knot in her chest. She glanced up again and gave a sharp cry. "Och, Alasdair, your hair — !" she began. "Oh, 'tis . . . 'tis so . . ."

"What's wrong?" Awkward as a boy, he ran one hand through it — or what was left of it — and paled.

She closed her eyes, and nodded. "Aye, 'tis badly singed," she whispered. "I'm afraid there shan't be anything for the ladies to run their fingers through for at least a fortnight." She did not realize she was crying until he sat down on the step beside her.

"Esmée, Esmée," he soothed, circling a strong, solid arm round her. "Oh, Esmée,

349

never mind my hair. I don't give a damn about it. Now don't cry, love. All's well. We're safe. Your aunt is safe, too. Trust me, all right? I'll find her, I swear it."

"I know." She sobbed. "I do. Trust you, I mean."

He pulled her firmly against him and ran one dirty knuckle beneath her eye, which only made her cry harder. "You've had a terrible fright, that's all."

Esmée shook her head, her disordered curls dragging on the wool of his coat. It wasn't just the fright, or the fire; not even the fact she did not know where her aunt was. It was him. *Them.* She opened her mouth to tell him so, but just then, a shout sounded from the street below.

"Miss Hamilton, thank God!" Lord Wynwood bounded up the steps toward them, then faltered. "Miss Hamilton, are you all right? Alasdair, what's happened?"

Alasdair set her away, and stood. "Miss Hamilton has wrenched her knee," he said. "She will need a doctor."

"Oh, Lord Wynwood!" Esmée interrupted. "Thank God! Have you found the others? Have you seen my aunt?"

"They are well, and waiting for us down by the Lyceum, along with my coach," he answered. "You were very brave, Miss

Hamilton, to keep them moving. Alasdair, where is Miss Karlsson? Oughtn't you see to her?"

Alasdair seemed to go rigid. "Ilsa is fine," he said stiffly. "But Miss Hamilton cannot walk. She can hardly be left alone, Quin, in such dangerous circumstances."

Wynwood knelt to look at Esmée, who still sat upon the steps. "My dear girl," he said. "Are you in pain?"

" 'Tis a wee sprain, no more," she answered.

Wynwood looked sympathetic. "This must be the worst theater engagement you've ever endured."

"Well, so far, 'tis the only one," Esmée confessed. "At least it shall be memorable, aye? And I think I can walk, if I have someone to lean on."

"Nonsense," said Alasdair. "I shall carry you down to the Lyceum."

But Lord Wynwood had already scooped her up in his arms, quite as effortlessly as Alasdair had done. For a moment, the gentlemen eyed one another almost warily. Then Wynwood gave a tight nod.

"I'm off then, old chap," he said coolly. "Must get the ladies safely home. Shall I see you at White's for a brandy after?"

Alasdair shook his head. "No," he said.

"No, I think not tonight, Quin."

Then Alasdair went rapidly down the steps and vanished into the chaos of the streets.

Despite his mood — a miserable mix of despair, jealousy, and rage — Alasdair forced himself to search for Ilsa. Regardless of whatever Quin had meant to suggest, Alasdair did feel a duty to ensure the sisters returned home safely. Fortunately, Ilsa had found Inga and the other two angels in Broad Court, still dressed in their white robes and halos, and leaning against the bow window of a tavern. It made for an interesting picture, to say the least.

They were suffering very little, for the tapster and most of the male patrons had rushed out to press cider and wine into their hands. In her sooty white robe, Inga looked beautiful as always. He was almost sorry he was not actually keeping her in that little flat in Long Acre. He should have liked to go home with someone besides himself this dreadful night.

Ah, but Inga would expect a little more than a sympathetic shoulder, and he had nothing more to give. So Alasdair kissed her on the cheek, sent the four of them off in his carriage, and set out on foot for home.

He drifted back past the theater to see that the steam engine had been fired up, and was belching more black smoke than the theater itself. No water yet spewed forth, and the blaze looked to be dying of its own accord. He stopped to make inquiries of a portly constable who was keeping a watchful eye on the scene.

"Why, bless me, sir, but everyone's accounted for!" he answered, whipping off his tall hat. "A proper miracle, it is. And naught but the stage and half the upstairs gone, unless the fire catches up again."

Alasdair thanked him, then hesitated. The man looked dashed familiar. " 'Tis Simpkins, sir," he said without prompting. "From Hyde Park."

Simpkins. Ah, yes! The day Sorcha had been injured. "I remember," said Alasdair. "And I am remiss in not thanking you sooner for your help."

"No thanks necessary, sir," said the constable. " 'Tweren't as if I did much. I do hope the child goes on well?"

"Another miracle," he said. "She remembers nothing and has only a scar to show for it."

The constable smiled and set his broad hands on his belly. "And your lovely wife?" he asked. "My heart broke for her, it surely did. Such a pretty, sweet-natured thing she seemed, and took it terrible hard. A Highland Scot, weren't she, sir? I did notice the lovely accent."

"A Highlander, yes," murmured Alasdair. Again, he found himself fighting down a cold, crushing disappointment — the same emotion he'd felt watching Quin bound up the steps after Esmée tonight. "But the child's governess. Not my wife."

The constable looked confused. "Well, beg pardon, sir," he said, scratching his head. "I just thought — or somehow took it into my head that — well, in any case, I'm glad all's well."

Alasdair thanked him again and headed home at an even brisker pace. They'd all lived through the fire, thank God, but otherwise, this evening could hardly get worse. *His wife.* What a conclusion to draw. He was too old to be Esmée's husband. Wasn't he?

Oh, he knew some lecherous old dogs who made a sport of marrying women young enough to be their children — younger *than* their children, often enough. Such men sought out the girls who had little choice. The naïve young misses just up from the country, whose fathers had gambled away the family farms or lost their dowries at faro. The very thought of what they must endure made his flesh creep. No, women did not willingly enter into those sorts of marriages.

But that wasn't exactly the case here, was it? Esmée was but fourteen years his junior. She wasn't dowerless. She was not young enough to be his daughter. Well, not quite. And Esmée seemed perfectly willing to be courted by Quin, who was not yet thirty. Thirty seemed reasonable. *Six*-and-thirty did not. Why? It was just six or seven years. It was nothing. Why did it trouble him so?

Because of Sorcha. Because of how she had been conceived — or with whom, perhaps, was the better way of looking at it. It seemed wrong to wish to bed Lady Achanalt's daughter, given what had happened between them, even if he did not really remember the doing of it. Good Lord, had he actually impregnated the poor woman, then married her, as any decent man would do, that would have been the end of it. The church would have forbidden him Esmée forever. She would have been considered his child, just as Sorcha was.

But he had not needed the church's refusal. He had refused Esmée without any help at all. He had refused to so much as discuss her own future with her. She had

355

come to him for advice, and he had practically laughed in her face. He had thought it best for her that they sever all contact, and a keen blade always cut cleanest. So he had sliced apart their relationship. That had been his choice, he reminded himself as he hastened across the vast darkness of St. James's Park.

And now, Quin had stepped in. And if Esmée were truly serious about Quin, then Alasdair would have the pleasure of going through the rest of his life imagining what Esmée looked like in his best friend's bed. Her *husband's* bed. Every bloody time he saw them together.

He had wanted her to wed. The sooner the better, he'd told himself. He had gone so far as to warn her away from fortune hunters like Smathers and boors like Nowell — not that she had thanked him for it.

Good Lord, he needed the evening to be over. He dashed up Cockpit Stairs and hastened toward Great Queen Street. He felt an almost desperate need for the solace of his own home; for a few moments of peace and quiet in which to nurse a whisky or two or six. But it was not to be. He heard Sorcha's screams before he'd so much as knocked on the door.

Wellings let him in. "A nightmare, sir,"

he intoned. "Young miss has been inconsolable for the last ten minutes or more."

He went upstairs to find Lydia, still in her nightcap, pacing back and forth with Sorcha, who was flinging herself about in her nurse's arms, and squalling until she could scarce get her breath. Lydia — not to mention her still-splinted wrist — probably couldn't take much more.

"A nightmare, sir," Lydia said over the racket. "Or some sort o' colic, per'aps? She awoke in such a state, I can't think what else it could be."

Alasdair held out his hands just as Lydia turned. "Sorcha, my love," he said, when the child's wild eyes caught his. "What's all this, *hmm?* Come to me, minx."

The child held out her arms demandingly. "Mae!" she squalled, her face red and swollen, her nose dripping like a tap. She all but crawled into his arms, and deliberately turned her back on Lydia. "Mae!" she squalled again. "Me go Mae. Go *now!*"

He looked at Lydia. "She wants Miss Hamilton, I collect," she said almost apologetically. "She's been squalling for her off and on since she woke."

Alasdair began to pace the floor of the nursery, rhythmically patting Sorcha's back. "Why don't you go downstairs, Lydia and warm some milk?" he said gently. "And tell someone else to carry it up so you can rest that wrist. I'll manage here." Indeed, Sorcha was already quieting.

Lydia curtseyed. "Yes, sir, as you wish," she said. "But . . . but she's making a mess, sir, on your fine coat."

Alasdair looked down to see his lapel was smeared with tears and something a good deal worse. "Ah, well, this coat was never a favorite," he answered, sighing. "Why don't you put on enough milk for three, Lydia? It feels like an awfully long night."

Lydia curtseyed again and went out quietly.

And that was the end of his whisky. It was to be warm milk in the nursery instead. And the funny thing was, Alasdair didn't really care. He was more concerned for Sorcha, who was still sniveling against his lapel. The child felt wet and feverish, but from her fear and her tantrum, he thought, rather than illness. But he wasn't perfectly certain. Still, he went to the window, drew the drapes, and threw up the casement anyway. Cool night air washed over them, the breeze so strong, it teased at what was left of his hair.

Sorcha seemed somewhat appeased. She had set her stained and swollen cheek against his coat, and her sobs had subsided into shuddering hiccups. For a long moment, he simply stood there, looking down at the darkened streets of Westminster, drawing in the brisk night air and wondering if he was making his child ill. Perhaps she would take pneumonia. Perhaps she already *had* it. Good Lord, where was Esmée when you needed her?

Gone, that's where. Sent away, by his own hand, God help them all. And as he stood there, feeling his child quake and his own heart break, he realized, suddenly and awfully, that it just might have been the biggest mistake of his life.

"Mae," Sorcha whimpered, curling one tiny fist into his lapel. "Me wants Mae."

Alasdair bent his head and set his lips to her forehead. "I know you do, love," he whispered. "I know you do. And I'm afraid, my little minx, that I do, too."

Chapter Nine

In which Miss Hamilton receives
A Bold Proposal

The following day, Esmée was in the morning parlor with her leg propped up on a little footstool when her aunt rushed in to tell her that Lord and Lady Wynwood had come to call. "Grimond is bringing them up shortly," she said, looking anxiously about the room. "I did not think you ought to walk into the withdrawing room. Will this do, do you think?"

Esmée smiled and laid aside her needlework. "This is a pretty, cozy room, Aunt Rowena," she said. "You worry too much."

They were shown in, and at once, and Lady Wynwood swept across the room to bend down and kiss Esmée's cheek. "Oh, my poor, poor child!" she said. "Oh, I do hope the pain is not unbearable."

Esmée widened her eyes. "Why, there's no pain to speak of, ma'am," she said. "I'm a wee bit hobbled, but I'll be fit to dance a jig by week's end."

Lady Wynwood straightened up, but her hand still covered Esmée's on the chair arm. "What a dear, brave girl!" she announced, placing the other hand over her heart. "Wynwood, is she not courageous? And to look so serene and lovely after all we endured last night!"

Lord Wynwood tried to urge his mother toward a chair. "All that I endured, ma'am, was the ruin of my evening slippers traipsing about the streets after you," he said. "Now if we should sit down, perhaps Lady Tatton can be persuaded to serve us a cup of coffee."

Lady Tatton was easily persuaded, and the coffee was brought in short order. Initially, the talk was of the theater fire: who had been where, what they had worn, said, or done. But soon, Lady Wynwood let the topic drop and looked at Lady Tatton with spurious innocence. "Well, that's old history now, is it not?" she said. "Rowena, I was wondering if I might prevail upon you to show me your garden."

"My garden?" said Lady Tatton. "But Gwendolyn, this is November."

"Your spring bulbs," said Lady Wynwood swiftly. "I wish to see how your gardener has laid their beds in for the winter. Everyone says you have the loveliest daffodils in town. Mine always fail so utterly! I am convinced it has something to do with the wintering."

"Well . . ." Lady Tatton rose slowly. "I shall just go and change my shoes, then."

"An excellent notion!" Lady Wynwood jerked to her feet, clutching her reticule. "I shall help you."

Esmée, who had been watching this exchange in mute amazement, turned to Lord Wynwood as soon as the door closed. He was hunched awkwardly in his chair and pinching his nose in a valiant attempt not to laugh.

"Miss Hamilton," he finally said, when he had regained his composure, "I daresay you understand why we've been left here alone."

She gave him a bemused smile. "I'm not sure I understand anything anymore, Lord Wynwood."

"I believe I am now expected to ask permission to pay court to you," he said. "My mother wishes me to marry, and I believe she has settled on you as the perfect wife."

Unconsciously, Esmée imitated Lady Wynwood's overwrought hand-over-the-heart gesture. "My goodness," she managed. "This seems . . . very sudden."

"You did not know that I was expected to marry soon?"

Esmée smiled a little tightly. "Oh, I shan't insult your intelligence by claiming *that*," she said. "Aunt Rowena knows every worthy bachelor from Penzance to Newcastle. But why me?"

He opened his hands expansively. "Why not you?"

Esmée felt her face heat. "Well, I am new to town," she said slowly. "And a Scot. Then there is the unfortunate situation with Sorcha. I do not delude myself, my lord. I know that gossip about the circumstances of my sister's birth is inevitable. I cannot think your mother wholly unconcerned on that score."

Wynwood flashed a crooked smile. "My mother suffered a terrible fright last night, Miss Hamilton," he replied. "Her life passed before her eyes, and at the end of that inauspicious vision, she realized most acutely that there were no grandchildren. My marriage has suddenly become her most pressing priority. To that end, she has settled on you and damn the consequences."

"Why?" asked Esmée quietly. "Because I am convenient?"

"No, because I like you," he said, his expression honest. "And she knows that you are not a silly, simpering fool like most of the chits who'll be on the marriage market next season. Those sorts would be easier for me to refuse. And for all that you don't look it, you are a woman, not a girl."

Esmée's gaze fell to her hands, which were clasped in her lap. "I feel very like a girl sometimes," she confessed. "I wish I had been more in society. I wish I understood how the world works."

Wynwood leaned intently forward in his chair. "Your aunt and my mother believe we would make a good match, Miss Hamilton," he said calmly. "What do you think?"

"I can't think," she answered. "This all seems too fast. And you do not even know me, my lord. We have scarce exchanged a dozen words."

He gave her another muted smile. "In the weeks since we became acquainted, Miss Hamilton, I have come to esteem you highly," he answered. "You have a kind heart, and you love your sister. You are gracious, well bred, and obliging. Those are qualities I seek in a wife."

"Do you really wish for a wife at all, my lord?" she gently challenged.

He lifted one shoulder and tore his gaze from hers. "I am a practical man, Miss Hamilton. My father died some months past, and it is my duty to beget an heir as soon as possible. Indeed, my mother's future is somewhat uncertain until I do so. And for all my wicked ways, Miss Hamilton, I do love my mother. And I will do my duty."

Esmée gave a pathetic laugh. "Aunt Rowena keeps reminding me that a man who treats his mother well will treat his wife well."

His smile deepened. "What of you, Miss Hamilton? Do you not wish for a family?"

"Sorcha and Aunt Rowena are my family," she said simply. "If I have no one else, my love for them will sustain me."

"That is in part what motivates my offer," he said. Then abruptly, he bowed his head. "I beg your pardon. I have not yet made my offer, have I? Miss Hamilton, will you do me the honor of being my wife? And please carefully consider what is best for your sister before you answer."

"What do you mean?"

"I am already aware of Sorcha's parentage," he continued. "You need make no awkward explanations to me. I understand the delicacy of your situation and respect you all the more for it."

"I thank you," she said quietly.

"Indeed, were Alasdair to agree to give your sister up, nothing would better please me," Wynwood continued. "But he won't, and I would never ask it of him. Still, if Sorcha should end up spending a vast deal of time in our home, or is treated like a cherished niece or godchild, who would question it? Alasdair and I have been close friends for many years."

Esmée marveled at the beauty of his argument. If she were Lady Wynwood, she could come and go in Sorcha's life often and with ease, and no questions would be asked. That would be the most wonderful thing imaginable! But if married to Wynwood, she would also see a great deal more of Alasdair. Suddenly, she felt the hot press of tears behind her eyes. She set the back of her hand to her lips and tried to force them down.

Lord Wynwood started from his chair, then halted uncertainly. "I beg your pardon," he said again. "I am behaving as if all this is a given. Nothing is settled, nor need it ever be. The wishes of your aunt or my mother are secondary. I would account myself fortunate simply to be your friend."

His kindness made it worse. "The problem is, Lord Wynwood, that I do not love you!" she cried. "Indeed, I cannot. I feel very sure of that. I can say no more, except to explain that — well, that I am probably far less innocent than any gentleman would wish his bride to be."

Fleetingly, his serene smile faltered. "Ah, I collect there has been someone before me," he said quietly. "I understand that better than you might think. And alas, Miss Hamilton, I do not love you either. But I do like you very much. I like your honesty and your plain speaking. And I certainly do not require a virgin in my marriage bed."

Esmée paled. "Oh, 'tis not tha—"

"Please, say no more," he interjected, holding up his hand. "I should rather not know. Let us agree to keep our pasts in the past. Indeed, given my reputation, many would wonder at my audacity in offering for you."

Esmée snagged her lower lip between her teeth. "A great many men seem to be considering it," she answered. "But I daresay 'tis that little word *heiress* which attracts their attention."

He smiled dryly. "I do not need your grandfather's money, Miss Hamilton," he said. "If you accept me, we will arrange to have it set aside for Sorcha or one of our children."

One of our children.

Oh, Esmée wanted children! Wanted them desperately, even if she wasn't very good at raising them. But she was not at all sure she could want Lord Wynwood, no matter how kind or handsome he was. Long moments passed, punctuated by the tick of the mantel clock.

"You are uncertain," he said, fracturing the silence. "Do you not wish to marry?"

"Oh, yes," she admitted. "I do."

He smiled. "Well, a betrothal is not binding on the lady," he reminded her. "I can put Mamma off until the season ends, and it is perfectly reasonable for you to wait a full year after your mother's death. If, at the end of that period, you are still uncertain, cry off."

"Cry off?" she interjected. "I could not!"

"Oh, I'll give you a good excuse," Lord Wynwood reassured her. "I'll do something wicked enough to make sure no one calls you a jilt. Indeed, I might well do so without even trying. I have a way of bollixing up my life sometimes."

"Well," said Esmée, drawing in a deep, ragged breath. "Then I suppose . . . I suppose my answer is *yes*."

Wynwood smiled, and it looked amazingly sincere. "Miss Hamilton," he said, "you have just made me the happiest man on earth."

She looked askance at him. "Please," she

said, "let us begin as we mean to go on. Let us always be honest with one another."

His smile faded very little. "Well, the happiest man in Mayfair, then," he corrected. "Now I wish to beg a favor of you, if I may?"

"But of course," said Esmée. "You have only to ask."

"Mother wishes to retire to my estate in Buckinghamshire until spring," he went on. "It is but a few hours' drive from town. As soon as she is settled, she wishes to give a dinner party in our honor. A quiet affair for our closest friends and family only. She wishes everyone to meet you, especially her brother, Lord Chesley, who owns the estate adjacent. You will like him very much — everyone does. Would you be willing to come?"

Esmée opened and closed her mouth soundlessly. It seemed too soon. She was not ready. But she *had* agreed. "Yes, of course," she finally said. "I should be honored."

"Excellent!" he said, swiftly rising. "I must go and give Mamma the good news. She will be so pleased. And she will be a good mother-in-law to you, Miss Hamilton, I promise. She will know her place. And should she forget it, you may depend upon me to remind her."

"Thank you, Lord Wynwood," Esmée managed. "You are very kind, I'm sure."

Swiftly, he seized her hand and kissed it fervently. "You must call me Quin now," he said. "Or Quinten, if you prefer."

"Quin, then," she said. "And I am Esmée."

"Esmée. That is lovely."

And just like that, the deed, it seemed, was done. Lord Wynwood — *Quin* — kissed her hand again, as if for good measure, then left her sitting just as she had been upon his arrival; her leg propped on the footstool and her mind in a secret turmoil.

"Paper! Paper! Get it 'ere!" The newsboy's voice rang clearly in the sharp autumn air. "Prime Minister steps down! Read all about it!"

About to turn the street corner into St. James's, Alasdair hesitated, then dashed between a gap in the stream of horses and carriages to fetch a paper instead. Lately, very little of current affairs interested him, but the sudden shakeup in government could have piqued a dead man's curiosity.

"Paper! Paper! Get it 'ere!" cried the boy, palming Alasdair's coins without missing a beat. "King accepts P.M.'s resignation! Read it 'ere! All the details!"

Alasdair snapped open his freshly inked copy and set off again in the direction of White's.

"What do you think, MacLachlan?" asked a voice from behind him. "Is Wellington finally done for?"

Alasdair turned to see one of the young pups from his club dogging his heels. "So it would seem," he said, as the lad fell into step with him. "Off to White's, are you?"

The lad nodded effusively. "Mustn't miss the excitement," he said. "A banner news day, ain't it? First Wynwood, now this."

Alasdair abruptly halted on the pavement. He had not seen Quin since the fire, some three days past. "First Wynwood *what?*" he asked, looking pointedly at the lad.

The young man was turning faintly crimson. "Well, I don't know, precisely," he answered. "I heard he was to be married. Tenby said it was in the *Times* this morning." He paused to gesture at the paper. "I daresay it's in that one, too, if it's true. Let's have a look, shall we?"

The ground shifted beneath Alasdair's feet. "Later," he managed, stalking off in the direction of his club. He could not bring himself to utter another word to the lad, who hastened to keep his pace. *Married.*

Good Lord, Quin was to be married? Alasdair felt suddenly ill. His hand clutching the paper had gone cold and bloodless. There was a roaring in his ears, as if he were about to faint, though he was not. The traffic beyond faded from his consciousness.

Quin was to be married. Oh, he'd known that was inevitable. But surely *she* had not . . . ? No, not so soon. Not this fast. Not before he'd had time to so much as think . . .

But Quin, it seemed, had not been busy thinking. He had been acting. Alasdair went up the short flight of steps and was met by a porter, who threw open the door. "Good morning, sir," said the servant as he took his hat. "An eventful day, is it not?"

"So I keep hearing," said Alasdair, setting off in the direction of the coffee room. It was blessedly empty again. He took a table, and waved off the servant who approached. The lad — Frampton or Hampton or some damned thing — had disappeared. Alasdair spread open the paper, no longer interested in Wellington's fate, but in something altogether different. He thumbed quickly to the page where such acts of folly generally appeared. And there it was. In black and white, quite literally.

He blinked his eyes, and tried to focus.

But the words danced about in bits and pieces. *The honor of announcing . . . wedding in the spring . . . daughter of the late Countess of Achanalt . . .*

He tried to make sense of it, but it was as if he were surfacing from a nightmare, caught in that netherworld between sleep and wakefulness; a world which one struggled to escape because nothing made sense. Just then, someone cleared his throat sharply. Alasdair looked up to see Quin bracketed in the doorway, his chin down, his gaze faintly rueful.

"Frampton said he'd followed you in," he remarked. "Am I to have your congratulations, old chap?"

For two heartbeats, Alasdair couldn't find his tongue. "I am not perfectly certain, Quin," he answered stiffly. "Why the devil am I reading about this in the paper? Do I not deserve the courtesy of a private word?"

"Mother couldn't hold her horses," Quin answered, propping one shoulder casually against the doorframe. "Seems the fire frightened her out of her wits, and she decided she'd much rather be a dowager countess than a dead one, with Cousin Enoch inheriting all. She took a liking to Miss Hamilton and seized upon the notion. And, I must confess, I am not displeased."

"Oh, well, jolly good then!" said Alasdair mordantly. "I'm glad your mother is happy in her choice. But did it ever occur to you, Quin, to discuss it with me first?"

"Why should I?" he asked frankly. "Esmée is nothing to you. *Is* she? I mean, I thought you wished to be rid of her."

"Good God, she is Sorcha's sister!" Alasdair said in a low undertone. "And she is my . . . she is someone for whom I feel at least partly responsible. Yes, of course she is something to me."

Quin approached the table. "She is damned lucky her reputation wasn't ruined by you," he said, his voice quiet but unmistakably reproachful. "Honestly, Alasdair, what the deuce do you care? You wanted her wed and out of your hair. Soon she'll be both."

Alasdair had left his seat and begun to roam restlessly through the room. "Why, Quin?" he rasped. "Of all the marriageable women in London, why Esmée? Can you tell me that? *Can* you?"

Quin seemed taken aback. "Well, I — I like her, Alasdair," he answered. "She's sensible."

"Sensible?" echoed Alasdair incredulously. "If by that you mean she'll turn the other way when it comes to your whoring,

Quin, you may be in for a rude awakening. Scots are not known for their forgiving nature."

Quin set a heavy hand on Alasdair's shoulder. "Careful, old chap," he growled. "The state of my marriage, and what does or does not occur within it, is not your concern. I shall give her children, fine homes, and a title. Trust me, she shall have no cause for complaint."

Alasdair was quiet for a moment. "And what of love, Quin?"

"Yes, what of it?" Quin sneered. "I just said I mean to get children on the girl, for God's sake. That will suffice. No, I don't love her, and she doesn't love me. Neither circumstance is apt to change."

"Has she told you that?"

Quin colored faintly. "It's none of your damned business, but yes. She has."

Alasdair swallowed hard. Tried to think. He felt as if he were drowning. "Are you sure, Quin?" he choked. "Are you sure this is what she wants? Her . . . her aunt did not coerce her?"

"Her aunt knew nothing of it until the matter was settled," his friend returned. "Lady Tatton was thrilled, of course. No, Esmée was not coerced. My God, Alasdair! What is your problem? Are you playing dog in the manger here? If you wanted her, damn it, you had every opportunity."

"I am her sister's father, Quin," he gritted. "Not to mention almost a decade and a half older than she. What I did or didn't *want* is a moot point."

"Yes, you're bloody well right it is," Quin agreed. "Because she has accepted *me*." He threw himself into the chair in which Alasdair had been sitting and watched his friend pace for a moment. "Damn it, I thought you would be pleased. I thought this would be good for Sorcha. For all of us, really."

Alasdair paced the floor, back and forth between the windows, but Quin said no more. "You do not deserve her, Quin," Alasdair finally said. "You know you do not. You cannot go to her with a whole heart and love her as she ought to be loved."

"Because of Viviana, you mean?" The sneer was back, tenfold now.

"Because of her, and because of all the women after her," said Alasdair. "Good God, you could pave a road to hell, Quin, with the women you've kept and the whores you've had. Esmée is an innocent, for pity's sake! Think what you are doing!"

But Quin was giving him a suspicious sidelong look now. "She tells me she is not all that innocent," he said in a remarkably quiet voice. "Is there something, Alasdair, which *you* ought to be telling me?"

Alasdair held his gaze for an eternity. "Be good to her," he finally gritted. "That is what I am telling you. Be good to her, Quin, or I swear to God, I won't even trouble myself to call you out. I'll just put a knife between your goddamned ribs."

Quin clamped his hands on his chair arms, as if restraining himself from violence. Alasdair wished he would not. He wished Quin would just come at him with his fist flying, so he would have some semblance of an excuse for beating the very devil out of him.

But he was not to be that lucky. Instead, Quin rose and bowed. "Mamma is giving a dinner at Arlington soon," he said in a voice of calm reserve. "It is for close friends and family only, to celebrate the betrothal. I wish you and Merrick to attend."

"I should rather not," he answered. "I cannot speak for my brother."

"I'll see to Merrick," said Quin smoothly. "But it will look very odd if you are not there. You are one of my dearest friends, Alasdair. Besides, Mamma has come by some story that you are Esmée's distant relation."

"More of Lady Tatton's mischief, I collect," said Alasdair tightly.

"It is just as well," said Quin. "Now, for the sake of our long friendship, Alasdair, will you come?"

Alasdair lifted one shoulder. "I shall think on it," he said.

Esmée spent the days which followed hobbling about on Lord Wynwood's arm. They drove in the park, visited the zoo, dined with friends, and attended a new exhibit at the British Museum. Despite the sadness which hung over her, Esmée found it easy to be content in his company.

Wynwood was kind and friendly, and he did not seem to require very much of her. Indeed, she liked him so well, she was beginning to feel the slightest stirring of guilt. Surely, somewhere, there was the perfect woman for Wynwood? Someone who could give him the love and devotion which he deserved?

Their betrothal had taken society by surprise. There had been some standing wagers, she belatedly learned, in the betting book at White's which heavily favored the possibility that he would never wed at all. Her aunt had not been wrong, it seemed, about his reputation as an unrepentant womanizer. But when Esmée teased him about it, Lord Wynwood's eyes crinkled merrily, and he just laughed.

Most of Esmée's mornings were devoted to Sorcha, but she did not see Alasdair at all. She wondered what he thought of her betrothal. A childish little part of her hoped it stung him just a bit. But perhaps he was unaware of the announcement? More likely, his thoughts were simply elsewhere — with Mrs. Crosby, perhaps, where they certainly should be. Then there were his two blond actresses.

In the cold light of day, she tried to think of it all with dispassion. She tried to block out all memory of her first bittersweet weeks in London, when just passing him on the stairs could make her temper flare and her heart flutter, all at the same time.

Now, however, when Alasdair's name was mentioned in her presence, she schooled herself to react with polite indifference. She managed it quite convincingly. But at night, her strategies were not so successful. At night, she thought of his forbidden kisses and fervent embraces. She thought of the way his hands had trembled the first time he touched her. His had been the touch of a practiced libertine, yes. But there had been awe and delight in it, too.

From the very first, her womanly instinct had told her that Alasdair was not indifferent to her. She wondered what that meant and why he would not talk with her about it. For all her twenty-two years, she felt almost as green as Alasdair accused her of being. But in truth, what was there to talk about? He was "not the marrying kind." And she — well, she was just a gudgeon. She had done such a foolish, foolish thing in falling in love with him.

The second week of her betrothal took a slightly different turn. She saw a little less of Lord Wynwood, and when she did see him, he seemed oddly distant. The change was so marked, she wondered if he had somehow sensed her obsession with Alasdair. But when she expressed concern that perhaps they had moved too quickly, Lord Wynwood merely laughed, and gave her a silly, smacking kiss on the cheek.

It was wholly out of character with the discontent she saw in his eyes. Worse, it was a dreadful letdown after Alasdair's tempestuous embraces. And slowly, it began to dawn on her that this was the man with whom she would soon share a bed. She was not at all sure she could.

Once, Esmée started to talk to Aunt Rowena, but the words simply would not come. She thought, too, of calling on Mrs. Crosby, but that seemed a rather desperate, childish thing to do. What could she learn from the poor woman? The truth? That might be worse than confusion. And Mrs. Crosby had her own problems so far as Esmée could see.

Thwarted, Esmée began to write Alasdair letters informing him of her betrothal; the first stiff and formal, the second almost companionable, and the third feverish and pleading. She was ashamed of each, and tore them up in turn. There was no point. He did not want her, and she had no business with him. And so Esmée did nothing but trot about town with her hand on Lord Wynwood's arm, whilst her wrenched knee healed, and the trip to Buckinghamshire edged nearer with every passing day.

"Oh, I say!" exclaimed Lady Tatton, her head half-out the carriage window. "Arlington Park is a splendid estate!"

From her side of the carriage, Esmée could see nothing but acres and acres of finely landscaped parkland, which was dotted with herds of deer, glistening little lakes, and the occasional picturesque folly. The rambling little village of Arlington Green had vanished near the gateposts a quarter mile earlier. Esmée's aunt, however, apparently had a stellar view as they approached the main house, for she was describing it now in every detail.

"Oh, it is Palladian, Esmée!" she pronounced. "Three — no, four — stories tall if one counts the dormers! Heavens, they must have twenty bedchambers. And the brickwork! Oh, that exquisite shade of warm, deep red. There is a double staircase from the entryway. And a huge fountain in the center of the carriage drive. Oh, my dear, do look!"

Esmée would have looked, had her aunt's befeathered hat not been blocking her view. Still, she could bestir little enthusiasm for the grandeur of Arlington Park. Indeed, this entire affair seemed somehow surreal to her. She felt as if she were living someone else's life — wearing their elegant clothes and mingling with their fashionable friends, whilst she was still just Esmée, the girl who had landed, angry and frightened, on Sir Alasdair MacLachlan's doorstep almost a lifetime ago.

Within a few minutes, however, her new life returned to the forefront, and the grandeur of Arlington was rising up before her. Lady Wynwood was coming down the wide, curving steps with her arms thrown wide. In a flurry of activity, cheeks were kissed and luggage unstrapped. Servants in fine livery were everywhere.

Inside, it was worse. Some of Wynwood's relations had arrived before them, and were impatient to meet the fiancée they'd never thought to see. So Esmée was soon being led round on his arm, being introduced to what appeared to be an army of aunts and cousins.

"You must be tired from your journey, my dear," said Wynwood, staving off an especially persistent aunt who wished to show her the gardens. "Forgive my enthusiasm. Mamma is scowling at me. Doubtless she wishes to show you and Lady Tatton to your rooms now."

Esmée's "rooms" consisted of a bedchamber, a dressing room, and a small sitting room. Her aunt had the connecting suite. In the center of Esmée's bedchamber sat an elegant canopied bed hung with silks in gold and ivory. Adjacent was a massive marble fireplace in which a fire already crackled, warding off the country chill. Dinner was to be served at six.

Only a few members of the immediate family had arrived today, she had been informed. Wynwood's uncle had been back in England but a few days and was resting at his nearby estate. The remainder of the guests would arrive the following day for the more formal dinner to come.

If the crowd in the drawing room constituted "a few" of the family, Esmée wondered what a full house would look like. Lord Wynwood was but one of two children. Esmée had somehow concluded that his family was small. It was not.

In fact, Lady Wynwood bragged, she also had six sisters, two aunts, and an uncle, all of whom had families. Wynwood's great-aunt, Lady Charlotte Hewitt, lived in the gatehouse. And Wynwood's sister, Lady Alice, had three children of her own. Moreover, Lady Wynwood's unwed brother, Lord Chesley, also had a houseful of guests at *his* estate. It was more — *much* more — than Esmée had bargained for, but she vowed to see it through.

After bathing off the day's grime and combing out her hair, she drifted to the window. For a time, she simply stood there, just looking out across the formal English gardens and wishing she was back in Scotland with her mother. A lifetime ago, Esmée had yearned to come to London to meet people and, eventually, to find a husband. But now that she'd accomplished both, it brought her no satisfaction. She had not counted on falling in love with a scoundrel — a scoundrel who did not, it seemed, love her back.

It was cold by the window, and Esmée still wore her shift. Absently, she reached for the shawl she'd worn on the drive and tossed it haphazardly over her shoulders. Just then, she heard a sound, and glanced over her shoulder to see her aunt coming briskly into the room through the connecting door.

"I've asked Pickens to press your dark blue," she began. "Will that do, do you think?"

Esmée turned from the window. "Aye, nicely. Thank you, Aunt Rowena."

Finally, her aunt looked — really looked — at her. At once, her face fell. "Oh, my dear child!" she said, hastening across the room. "Where are your stockings? In that shift and shawl, with your hair down, you put me in mind of an orphan."

Esmée managed a weak smile. "I *am* an orphan, Aunt."

Lady Tatton was already bustling her away from the window. "Not that sort of an orphan," she declared. "Now put on your wrapper and sit down here by the dressing table, my dear. I shall comb out your hair whilst Pickens finishes the ironing."

Obediently, Esmée sat. Lady Tatton picked up the brush and set to work. "Now you must tell me, Esmée, just what is on your mind," she began. "You look perfectly wretched. Are you having second thoughts? It is quite natural to do so."

"It isn't second thoughts, exactly," Esmée explained. " 'Tis just that there seem to be a great many people here and such a fuss being made over this betrothal. And this house. It seems so large."

"But your stepfather's house was large." Her aunt kept drawing the brush rhythmically through her long hair. "Most Scottish estates are quite comparable, are they not? For example, I understand that Castle Kerr is one of the finest homes north of York."

"Castle Kerr?" said Esmée. "I never heard of it."

In the mirror, she saw her aunt watching her assessingly. "It is the seat of the MacLachlans of Argyllshire," she answered. "It is Sir Alasdair's home. Did you not know?"

Esmée watched a faint blush creep up her cheeks. "He never spoke of it," she responded. "But Scottish estates are not so formal, are they? Indeed, they do not seem so to me. But this house demands formality. I feel . . . I feel no *warmth* in it."

Her aunt drew the brush through Esmée's hair in a long, soothing stroke. "Esmée," she finally said, her voice very quiet, "why did you accept Lord Wynwood's proposal?"

Esmée jerked her head up and held her aunt's gaze in the mirror. "I — I thought it was best," she said. "I like him, and 'tis quite a good match. You said so yourself. And it will make things so much better for Sorcha."

"For Sorcha?" Lady Tatton's voice was arch. "What on earth has Sorcha to do with this?"

Esmée explained Wynwood's argument. "Even you must admit, Aunt Rowena, that if we go on as we are, someone is bound to wonder who she is," Esmée concluded. "At present, she visits infrequently, and most of the houses in Grosvenor Square stand empty. But in a few months, town will be abuzz, will it not?"

"Yes," Lady Tatton reluctantly admitted. "I fear I cannot fault Wynwood's logic."

Esmée held her aunt's eyes in the mirror. "But . . . ?" she asked leadingly.

Lady Tatton laid the brush down with a loud clatter. "My dear child," she began, "you simply cannot live your life for Sorcha. You have devoted entirely too much of yourself to the needs and whims of others.

Rosamund kept you too long in the Highlands, holding you captive to her hysterics and fancies."

"But Mamma did love me," said Esmée, blinking back a sudden tear. "I know she did. She was just frightened, I think, of being alone."

Her aunt's eyes had darkened. "Rosamund wasted her life grasping at straws," she countered. "She was always searching for someone to cling to; always certain that abandonment was just round the next corner. I vow, sometimes I think she willed widowhood upon herself. And the irony of it is, if she'd just married the first man she fell in love with, none of this would have happened, and you would not be in this mess."

Esmée forbore to point out that had her mother married someone other than her father, *she* would not exist at all. "What first man?" she asked instead. "Who was he?"

But Lady Tatton was biting her lip now and looking very much as if she wished she had not spoken. "I don't think Rosamund ever said," she answered. "Indeed, she mentioned it but once or twice. Still, it weighed on her, I collect."

Esmée was surprised. "This man, did he

not love her? Did he not wish to marry her?"

"Why, I gather he did," answered her aunt. "But he was the adventurous type — a seaman or an explorer or some such thing — and he would not give it up. Rosamund couldn't have that. She needed security. She needed someone to dance attendance upon her. So I collect she decided that her adventurer was a bad bargain, and like to die of a tropical fever, or in a typhoon, or some such thing. So that was the end of it."

Esmée let the irony of it sink in. "Aunt Rowena," she finally asked, "why are you telling me this?"

"Oh, child, I have no notion!" Rowena reached over Esmée's shoulder and tucked a stray curl behind her ear. "Well, I think that what I am trying to say is that the heart does not always steer us wrongly."

Esmée's eyes widened. "Does it not?" she asked sharply. "I always thought Mamma's heart got her into trouble."

"Oh, no! That was her brain!" said Lady Tatton. "Rosamund *thought* too much."

"Did she?" Esmée considered it. "Aye, I wonder if you mightn't be right."

Lady Tatton hesitated a moment. "Oh, God, I do hope I don't regret this," she muttered, almost to herself. "I pray I have not steered you wrongly. But the truth is,

389

Esmée, that sometimes we can let logic —
or worse, our fears — guide us too far off
course. Sometimes the heart knows best.
You have not seemed yourself these past
two weeks. Wynwood is a good catch, but I
suppose it is possible that he is not the right
one."

Esmée shrugged. "Most women would
think me mad not to want him."

Lady Tatton smiled indulgently. "Well,
just give it time, my dear," she advised.
"And promise me that you won't do anything . . . well, *rash*."

Esmée felt the dreadful weight of guilt
settle on her shoulders. Her aunt had
worked so hard, and behaved so generously,
in order to ensure a good future for Esmée.
"Yes, I do promise," she answered. "I
shan't embarrass you, Aunt, by doing anything impulsive."

"No, you are too sensible for that," said
her aunt. "I oughtn't even have mentioned
it. And in time, you'll be convinced of the
rightness of this match, I hope."

Esmée was very quiet for a moment. "I
hope so, too," she answered. "But . . . but
what if I am not?"

Lady Tatton patted her soothingly on the
shoulder. "Well, if you have really given it
time, dear, yet in the end, he does not suit,

why, we shall just throw our fish back into the sea," she declared. "There will be talk, of course, but frankly, his reputation is not the best. I think we'll weather the storm."

"I cannot imagine doing such a thing to Wynwood."

Lady Tatton smiled tightly. "It would not be ideal," she agreed. "But better that than a marriage which will make you miserable. Now, Gwendolyn — well, *she* is quite another kettle of fish. I should be in her black book for a month or two. I might even have to grovel a bit."

"Oh, Aunt, I should hate to embarrass you!"

"I should hate it, too," said Lady Tatton briskly. "But I shall survive, and so shall you. *If* it comes to that, which I pray it doesn't. Now, child, where are the pearls which your mother gave you? I vow, I've not seen them in an age."

"My pearls?" Esmée's gaze fell to the portmanteau beside the dressing table. She was still mulling over what her aunt had said about the head and the heart. "Why, my pearls are in a green velvet case," she finally answered. "Just there, in the pocket of my portmanteau."

"Excellent!" said her aunt, reaching for it. "Tonight I am going to ask Pickens to put your hair up very high, in a style suitable to a young woman about to be married. And for that, you shall definitely want pearls."

Esmée smiled. "Thank you, Aunt Rowena. Perhaps it will make me look older and taller?"

"Oh, to be sure!" Lady Tatton snapped open the green velvet case and gave a sharp exhalation. "Merciful heavens, child! Why did you not take these out sooner?"

Esmée thought of her mother's first love, and of opportunities lost. "You know, I am not perfectly sure why I haven't worn them," she answered. "Perhaps it was foolish of me. Perhaps I ought to have been wearing them every day."

"I should say so!" said her aunt. "Why, they are perfectly breathtaking. I had quite forgotten what Rosamund's old pearls looked like."

The following day's journey was not an especially pleasant one for the MacLachlan brothers, neither of whom wished to travel into the wilds of Buckinghamshire, yet for entirely different reasons. Indeed, they had waited until the last possible moment to leave London, as if hoping divine intervention might strike. It did not. Worse, the November day was cold and overcast, and by the time they reached the border, the winter's sun had all but vanished, and a chill had settled over the carriage — a chill which was matched by Alasdair's mood.

"You aren't making this miserable journey any more agreeable, you know," said his brother from the shadows opposite. "Recall, if you will, that I am the moody, sullen one. You are supposed to be blithe and charming."

Alasdair glowered into the shadows, unable to make out his brother's face. "Bugger off, Merrick," he grumbled. "There! Charmed, damn you?"

Merrick just laughed.

"Besides, you abhor these sorts of things." Alasdair regarded him with suspicion. "Why are you even going?"

Merrick lifted one shoulder. "It is rather like watching a rioting mob or a hanging," he remarked. "The horror of it all is perversely compelling." Then, deftly, he changed the subject. "What is the time, anyway?" He tugged out his pocket watch, flicked it open, and tilted it toward what was left of the light.

"A quarter to four," muttered Alasdair. "Am I right?"

"To the very minute."

"Aye, and I'm counting every bloody

one," he complained.

"Alasdair," said his brother sharply. "Why are *you* going to this dinner?"

Alasdair could not hold his gaze. "I'm damned if I know."

The carriage turned, and the hedgerow fell away, allowing the feeble daylight to make its way through the window. Alasdair toyed with the thought of lighting one of the carriage lanterns, but he found the darkness oddly comforting.

Merrick had begun to absently polish his watch with his handkerchief. "Lord Devellyn reminded me of something the other day," he remarked. "It was one of Granny MacGregor's wiser adages. *The worth of a thing is best known by the want of it.*"

"Utter drivel," said Alasdair. "Or in this case, it is. And I know, Merrick, what you are getting at. Devellyn does not trouble to keep his opinions to himself."

Merrick cocked one of his harsh black brows. "Does he not?"

Alasdair stared at his brother for a moment. "It did not require Esmée's leaving me, Merrick, for me to comprehend her true value. She is well worth a man's fortune. But I do not need you to lecture me about decorum or restraint, as I suspect you are considering."

"I, lecture?" Merrick laughed again. "In this case, I might rather suggest that perhaps you've exhibited a tad too much restraint. I confess, I cannot fathom the attraction, but if you wanted the chit, why didn't you just go after her?"

Alasdair considered denying he'd considered it. But what was the use? To Merrick, he had always been an open book. "I am too old and too jaded," he remarked. "And she has seen too little of the world."

"Oh, come now!" said his brother. "You haven't yet seen forty. And Miss Hamilton is not exactly a naïve little miss."

"Merrick, I had an *affaire* with the girl's mother!" Alasdair felt his temper slip. "An *affaire* I don't even remember, and I left her with child. A child which I'm now left to raise. Esmée's sister, for God's sake."

"Did that bother Miss Hamilton?" Merrick pressed.

"Good Lord, Merrick," he answered. "She is twenty-two years old. What does she know?"

"Oh, a vast deal, from what I have seen." At last, Merrick seemed satisfied with the sheen on his timepiece. "Moreover, men often father children out of wedlock," he went on, tucking the watch away. "I could name you a half dozen well-placed men of my acquaintance who are — if you'll pardon the term — bastards. And yet all have done well in life. They have position and money. They have married well."

"Men, yes," Alasdair reluctantly admitted.

"Women, too," his brother insisted. "Acknowledge the child, Alasdair. Spoil her. Pamper her. Trust me, the world will treat her as *you* treat her."

"At present, Sorcha is too young to understand," said Alasdair. "But when the time comes, I shall certainly acknowledge her. As to how she is dealt with, if the world treated her as she is treated in my house, the child would be Queen of England."

The carriage slowed to take another turn, requiring Merrick to steady himself against the side. When he spoke again, his voice held an air of boredom. "I thought Miss Hamilton's betrothal came rather suddenly," he remarked. "Was she pressured into it, do you think?"

Alasdair fisted his hand, and wished for something to smash. "Quin swears not," he answered. "I daresay that's true. She does not bow to pressure especially well."

"I wonder she settled so quickly, then," Merrick returned. "It seems uncharacteristic, and Quin does not have an exemplary reputation."

"No, damn it, he doesn't," gritted Alasdair. "I cannot imagine what Esmée was thinking. I am half of a mind to ask her. I *thought* she would find someone worthy. Someone steady and dependable."

"Ah, I see," said Merrick. "You had a plan, then. Did you convey that plan to Miss Hamilton?"

"I gave her advice, yes," Alasdair responded. "What else was I to do?"

"What else indeed?" said Merrick mordantly. "I hope, dear brother, that you do not mean to cause a scandal tonight. You and Quin are old friends."

"I don't need you to remind me of that, either," snapped Alasdair. "There will be no scandal."

Merrick fell silent for a time, but it did not last. "Tell me, Alasdair, did Miss Hamilton return your — ah, what shall we call it? Your esteem?"

Alasdair lifted one shoulder lamely. "For a time, I believe she felt something of a sentimental attachment to me," he admitted. "But as I said, she is young. And now she has her aunt to turn to."

"Alasdair, she is not young," Merrick countered. "Most females her age are married, and many have children. Quin thinks her clever and sensible. Has he been courting an altogether *different* Miss Hamilton?"

Alasdair merely glowered at him across the carriage.

"Alasdair, if you wanted the chit, why —"

"For God's sake, Merrick, shut up!" Alasdair interjected. "Whatever I *should* have done, it is too late now."

Merrick shook his head slowly. "Alasdair, I suppose nothing is certain," he said again. "Not until the vows are spoken. Just be careful. I know the temper you possess under all that well-polished charm."

Suddenly, the carriage went rumbling over what sounded like a bridge. Alasdair looked out to see the pretty village of Arlington Green flying past, then the carriage slowed to turn in at a familiar-looking gatehouse.

"We are almost there," he said quietly. "We must all endeavor to remember that this is to be a joyous occasion for Quin."

His brother made no answer.

Ten minutes later, their footmen were putting down the steps and unloading the bags. Alasdair looked up to see Quin hastening down the curving staircase, his expression as dark as the dusky sky.

Apparently, the joyous occasion had already suffered some sort of setback. Against his will, Alasdair's hope sprang forth. Could Esmée have come to her senses?

As he alit from the carriage, Quin caught Alasdair's gaze with eyes which were hard and cold. He seemed incapable of speech.

"Quin?" said Alasdair, putting a hand on his friend's shoulder. "Quin, old chap, what's wrong?"

"Nothing," he snapped. "At least — well, I hope it is nothing."

"You looks as if you've just seen a ghost," said Merrick.

"Not a ghost," he murmured. "Not yet, anyway." But Quin had cut a dark, suspicious look in the direction of the wood; the wood which separated his estate from that of his uncle, Lord Chesley.

"Your uncle is at home?" asked Alasdair lightly.

"Indeed, the prodigal returns." Then, as if to force a brighter mood, Quin slapped Alasdair convivially between the shoulder blades. "Look, old chaps, pay my blue devils no heed. I'm imagining things — bridegroom's nerves, and all that rot, eh? Come in, and help me wash it all down with a glass of good brandy."

Chapter Ten

In which Sir Alasdair proves there's nothing like a Good Book

"Are you ready, my dear?"

Esmée flicked a quick glance up at the mirror. Behind her, Lady Tatton stood in the connecting doorway, resplendent in her dark green silk gown and matching plumes.

Pickens laid aside the leftover hairpins, and Esmée stood. "What do you think?" she asked, smoothing her hands down the front of her dinner gown.

Lady Tatton hastened forward. "Oh, how lovely!" she exclaimed, motioning for Esmée to twirl about. "My dear Pickens! You have quite outdone yourself!"

Indeed, Esmée had hardly recognized the young woman who looked back at her from the mirror. That woman looked — well, like a woman. Tall, and somehow more sophisticated. The dark gray silk she wore was simple, but cut low on her shoulders, with the barest hint of sleeves. About her neck, she again wore Alasdair's pearls, and in her hair, a second strand, loaned by her aunt, which Pickens had cleverly twisted into Esmée's upswept arrangement.

"I have a gift for you," said Lady Tatton, holding out her hand.

Esmée looked at the tiny velvet bag. "Aunt, you mustn't."

"This is a special occasion," her aunt insisted. "Aren't you going to open it?"

Esmée unthreaded it, and dumped the contents into her hand. A pair of pearl drop earbobs tumbled out, swinging from large, white diamonds. "Oh!" she said breathlessly. "Oh, how elegant they are!"

"And now they are yours," said Lady Tatton, plucking one from her palm. "I wore them when I married Tatton, and they are very precious to me. Here, let me put them on for you. Wynwood will wish his future bride to look elegant and sophisticated."

Esmée felt her eyes tear up. She wished the occasion felt as special to her as it clearly did to her aunt. "Aunt Rowena, I ought not take anything else from you," she said when the last was on. "You have been so very generous."

"And I shall endeavor to always be so," said Lady Tatton, stepping back to survey her work. "Now, my dear, let us go downstairs and face the future boldly on."

From the corridor, Esmée could hear the soft sound of violins resonating up from the drawing room. Lady Wynwood had insisted on a string quartet. "For ambiance!" she had said. "And dear Chesley does so love his music."

"I saw the Lord Chesley's barouche draw up a few moments ago," whispered Lady Tatton, as they went down the wide, curving staircase. "Now remember, he is Gwendolyn's younger brother, and she quite dotes on him."

Esmée had often heard Wynwood speak of his uncle. "Surely he is not that young?"

"Oh, heavens no!" said Lady Tatton. "Fifty now, perhaps? He is a world traveler, and a great patron of the arts both here and on the Continent."

"Och, I shall have nothing to say to such a man!"

"Nonsense!" said her aunt. "You'll charm him."

In honor of the occasion, Lady Wynwood had thrown open the withdrawing room and the two elegant parlors adjoining it. Black-clad footmen seemed everywhere, floating through the crowd with trays of champagne that glistened gold beneath the light of what seemed to be a thousand candles. Silver had been polished until it gleamed, and the fine oriental carpets had been beaten half to death, Esmée was sure. The wealth and grandeur of the Hewitt family was indisputably on display tonight.

The drawing room was already filled with people, most of whom Esmée had already met. There were, however, a few neighbors whom she did not know. She was being taken round the room on Wynwood's arm to meet them when she felt him stiffen abruptly.

Esmée's gaze followed his in the general direction of the string quartet. An opulently dressed middle-aged gentleman stood nearby, accompanied by three other people, none of whom looked like neighbors or relations.

"Is that your uncle, Lord Chesley?" Esmée asked. "I am very eager to meet him."

"I shan't interrupt him just now," said Wynwood coolly. "Let me return you to your aunt, my dear. Mother is looking daggers at me. I must have forgotten to do something."

Esmée did not see Lady Wynwood anywhere in the room, but she rejoined her aunt, who was holding court on the opposite side of the windows. Esmée sat quietly by her aunt's side as a gaggle of garden-minded ladies debated the merits of various manures. Sheep seemed to be coming out on top, so to speak.

Bored, Esmée began to let her gaze drift round the room. Lord Chesley had bent down to consult with the cellist. Lady Wynwood had returned, and was now speaking with Chesley's friends. Her son was nowhere to be seen.

Just then, Esmée felt someone's gaze burning into her. She turned to glance over her right shoulder, and her heart seemed to stop. Sir Alasdair MacLachlan stood in the wide doorway beyond the crowd. His long, lean figure filled the space. He was dressed in solid black, a glass of sherry held loosely in his hand. Almost mockingly, he lifted it, tilted the rim in her direction, then drained the contents.

For an instant, Esmée could not catch her breath. Until this moment, she had not truly believed he would come to Arlington Park. But not only had he come, his brother stood in the shadows behind him. Why had he done so? Did he mean to torment her past all bearing? She wished she had not worn his pearls. They seemed to be burning into her bare flesh now, just as his eyes had done.

Esmée turned back to the ladies' conversation, her cheeks faintly hot. Good Lord, she was being ridiculous! The three men were best friends. Why *wouldn't* Alasdair be here? It was time she grew accustomed to the fact that he was going to be a part of her life if — no, *when* — she married Lord Wynwood. Impatiently, Esmée shook off the doubt, and looked about the room for something to distract her.

Chesley's three houseguests were interesting. Esmée forced herself to focus on them. The party consisted of a frail, older gentleman whose black evening coat seemed too large for his body. He had a beaklike nose, the weight of which seemed to tip him slightly forward, stooping his shoulders. Beside him stood a nondescript gentleman of perhaps thirty years, who behaved with great deference to the elderly man.

The third guest was the most interesting of all. She was a beauty — and definitely not English. She was tall; taller than either of the men. Her inky hair was drawn tightly back from a face which was both fine-boned and vibrant. Her eyes were even blacker than her hair.

She stood beside the elderly man, holding a stemmed glass of what appeared to be champagne, and regarding the roomful of guests from beneath a pair of slashing black eyebrows. She wore a dress of dark red silk cut low across her slender shoulders, and a pair of ruby drops the size of Esmée's thumbnails dangled from her ears. A black cashmere shawl draped from her elbows, as if placed just so by an artist. The only thing about the woman which was not utterly perfect was her nose, which had a tiny knot halfway down the bridge.

Wynwood's great-aunt leaned near. "Have you met Contessa Bergonzi yet, Miss Hamilton?" asked Lady Charlotte.

Esmée turned to look at her. "Contessa Bergonzi?"

"An opera singer," the old lady added slyly. "But she married well. She arrived just last week from Venice with her father, Umberto Alessandri."

"Umberto Alessandri?" Even Esmée had heard of the famous Italian composer. "What on earth are they doing here?"

The old lady's eyes twinkled. "Wasting Chesley's money," she answered. "He wishes to commission an opera."

"An opera?" Esmée echoed.

The old lady sniffed. "Chesley's a dilettante," she responded. "Always dabbling in this and that, and throwing money at these temperamental artist types. *Continental* types. I daresay you know the sort I mean."

"I — yes, I daresay," murmured Esmée.

The old lady rose, looking very frail as she did so. "Come along, girl," she ordered in a tone that was decidedly *not* frail. "I shall introduce you."

Esmée had little choice.

"Chesley!" said the old lady, as they drew up near the orchestra. "Chesley, forget that silly music and come here at once."

He stepped from the midst of the musicians and came toward them with an indulgent smile. "Aunt Charlotte!" he said, lifting her hands in turn to his lips. "My dear, you don't look a day over seventy! And who is this young beauty? Pray do not tell me she is my nephew's intended."

"Of course she is, you fool," said his aunt. "Make your curtsey, girl, to your silliest in-law-to-be."

Esmée did so. "Good evening, my lord."

"Oh, cruel, cruel world!" said Chesley. "The beautiful ones are always taken."

Aunt Charlotte cackled, her humped shoulders shaking with mirth. "You've never been in the market for a female in your life, Chesley," she answered. "Now introduce the chit to your musical friends."

Lord Chesley slid a hand beneath Esmée's elbow, and steered her in the direction of the striking, dark-haired woman. "My dear, may I introduce my nephew's intended bride, Miss Hamilton?" he said. "Miss Hamilton, the Contessa Viviana Bergonzi di Vicenza."

Esmée made a quick curtsey. "It is an honor, ma'am."

The contessa observed her with bold, dark eyes. "My felicitations on your betrothal, Miss Hamilton," she said in careful but perfect English. "I wish you many years of happiness in your marriage."

Esmée felt awed by the woman. "Thank you, my lady."

The contessa's dark gaze swept down her again. "You must forgive us for intruding on what was obviously meant to be a family celebration," she murmured. "Chesley did not perfectly explain the occasion."

"Oh, don't rake me over the coals, Vivie," said the earl. "I can't keep up. What difference does it make?"

The contessa turned her penetrating gaze on Lord Chesley. "Why, none at all, I'm sure," she said coolly. "Miss Hamilton seems all that is amiable."

Just then, they were called to dinner.

"Thank God!" said Aunt Charlotte. "I'm famished. Come along, girl. You can acquaint yourself with the others after dinner.

Oh, I do hope Mrs. Prater has made her famous curried crab tonight."

But Esmée did not have to wait until after dinner. Instead, she found herself seated beside the pale young man who had come with Lord Chesley. The contessa was seated some distance away. Lord Wynwood sat to Esmée's left, at the head of the table, but he seemed disinterested in polite dinner conversation. Esmée's aunt sat with Sir Alasdair MacLachlan to one side, and the Contessa Bergonzi directly opposite, and she looked none too pleased about either.

The young man beside Esmée breathlessly introduced himself as Lord Digleby Beresford, younger son of the Marquis of Something-or-Other. Esmée was beginning to lose track of who was who, and her brain was now jettisoning the names of anyone not actually present. Lord Digleby, thank heaven, did not require much of her. He seemed content to rattle on about himself and about his work with the great Signor Alessandri.

"You are a composer, then?" asked Esmée, surprised.

The young man blushed — for about the third time since the soup course was served. "I am indeed, Miss Hamilton," he said with an air of confession. "Well, primarily a librettist. *Nel Pomeriggio* is to be my first full opera, and Chesley was bound and determined I should have help with the score."

"Chesley was determined?"

Again, the blush. "He is my patron, Miss Hamilton," said Lord Digleby. "All the famous composers have them, you know."

Esmée rather thought that patrons were for starving artists. If Lord Digleby was the son of a marquis, it seemed unlikely he fell into that category. "Well, I hope you are finding inspiration for your work here in Buckinghamshire," she murmured. "It certainly is lovely."

Lord Digleby, it seemed, was indeed inspired. He was happily ensconced, he explained, at Chesley's country house for the duration of his creative efforts. Signor Alessandri had been coaxed from Venice to advise him, based on Chesley's kind assurances that Digleby's was a rare talent.

Secretly, Esmée wondered if having now met the young man, Signor Alessandri and his beautiful daughter weren't ready to flee rural England on the first boat back to Venice. But perhaps Digleby was really quite good? In the midst of pondering it, Esmée again felt the heat of someone's stare. She cut a swift glance down the table to see Alasdair staring boldly — and quite perceptibly — in her direction. Quickly, she looked away, and felt warmth spring to her cheeks.

What an awful coil! The arrogant devil she both loathed and desired would not take his eyes off her, whilst the man she was to wed seemed all but unaware of her existence.

Soon came the worst part of all. Lady Wynwood asked the guests to drink a toast to the happy couple. Esmée sat quietly by as the entire table lifted their glasses, and shouted "To Esmée and Quin!" That happy moment was followed by a round of good-natured jests from the gentlemen, and a series of warm wishes from all the ladies. Esmée sat through it all feeling like the world's worst fraud, and watching Wynwood smile mechanically down the table at his guests.

But dinner did not last forever, nor did the coffee and impromptu dancing which followed it. This time, however, Wynwood remained at her side until the guests began to straggle from the room, led off by Great-aunt Charlotte. Wynwood surprised Esmée then by taking her hand and leading her from the drawing room and into a quiet alcove near the library.

"You must be tired, my dear," he said,

entwining her hand in his. "You look as though you long to go up to bed."

"Aye, desperately," she admitted. "But I shall wait awhile yet. I would not have your mother think me ungrateful."

Wynwood was silent for a long moment. "Esmée, I —" He stopped abruptly, and shook his head. "I have not been very attentive tonight. It is unforgivable. Yet I ask your forgiveness. I shall try to be a better husband than fiancé."

Esmée held his gaze, and carefully considered her next words. "My lord, rest assured that if you are having second thoughts —"

He cut her off sharply. "Absolutely not," he said. He tried to smile with some success, but his eyes were wan.

"You look tired, too, my lord," she said. "Did you not sleep well last night?"

The smile deepened into something more sardonic. "Not especially, no," he said. "Look, there are Mamma and Lady Tatton at the foot of the stairs. Everyone is going up, it seems. You should go, too. Sleep well, my dear."

Mechanically, Esmée turned her cheek for his kiss, then stepped out into the corridor and followed the remaining guests up to bed. But she wondered even as she did so if Lord Wynwood was secretly glad to be rid of her for the evening.

At the top of the stairs, she bade her aunt good night.

"Shall I send Pickens to you, my dear?" asked Lady Tatton. "You look all in."

Esmée shook her head. "I will manage," she said. "Good night, ma'am. And thank you."

She retired to her room, and began to undress. It had not been a pleasant evening. She released the clasp at the nape of her neck and let Alasdair's pearls slither into her hand. They puddled in her palm, warm as the tears she had shed for him. As heavy the heart in her breast.

But her heart was safely hidden, and her tears she had always shed in private. She let the pearls pour through her fingers and onto the dressing table. She could not bear to see the green velvet box again. Pickens could put them away tomorrow.

Slowly, methodically, she stripped away the rest of her clothes and tossed them onto the divan. She could not escape the feeling that tonight had been a disaster for Wynwood, too. She had made a mistake, she feared, in accepting him. What he had said was quite true. He had *not* been attentive — and the worst part of it was, she had not cared. It would have made no difference. She could not have told from one moment to the next when he was in the room or out of it — though she could have said to the very inch just where Sir Alasdair MacLachlan had stood at every instant.

No, she did not yearn for Wynwood's companionship. Her stomach did not turn flip-flops at the merest sight of him. And it never would. Well. She had wanted a marriage of the head, not the heart. Perhaps yearning and flip-flopping were too much to hope for.

Esmée took down her hair, then crawled into bed with a novel she had brought from London, but tonight, it seemed banal. She read the third chapter for the second time and finally comprehended that it was not holding her interest. Her mind kept returning to Alasdair. To the sardonic look on his face. The way he had lifted his glass as if wishing her well, even as his eyes had mocked her.

She closed her book with an angry snap. He was *not* indifferent to her. She sensed — no, she *knew* — he was not. But he was also "not the marrying kind." He had used that as an excuse when he'd sent her away — and she believed him. He was six-and-thirty, and if rumor could be trusted, had never so much as considered marriage. So what did he want? Lord, what did *she* want? To be the next Mrs. Crosby?

Esmée hurled the book across the room with unrestrained violence. It flew open, smacked against the opposite wall, and slithered into the floor. She realized with a start that it had felt *good* to do something violent. Perhaps it was time she began giving in to her impulses more often. She wished she could toss Alasdair out of her head so easily.

She looked again at the ormolu clock by the bed. She knew she would not sleep another wink in her present state of agitation. Silently, she slid from the bed and drew on her wrapper. Surely there was something worth reading in that vast library of Wynwood's? Preferably one of those fat mythological tomes about Amazons who pitched uncooperative men into vats of boiling oil. Or was she mixing up her mythology and her history? No matter. She liked the notion of boiling oil.

Carrying an extra candlestick, Esmée made her way back down the grand staircase, which was lit by the occasional sconce. She turned into the corridor which led past the withdrawing room, the morning parlor, and on to the library, carefully counting off the doors. Yes, this one.

She pushed the door open on silent hinges, and was surprised to find that a fire still burned in the grate. Intending to light her candle, she started toward it. Too late, she realized that the room was occupied.

"Looking for Wynwood, m'dear?" asked a dry, laconic voice from the hearth.

Alasdair sat in a large high-backed chair, his feet propped up on a table, and a glass of something golden dangling from his fingertips. Esmée looked down at him pointedly. "No, astounding as it may seem, I was looking for a book."

Alasdair unfolded himself from the chair and stood. "Then by all means, choose one," he said, waving his hand about the room. "I believe there are some eight thousand volumes here."

Esmée peered about at the shadows. "Are you alone?"

Alasdair came toward her with a bitter smile. "Merrick and Quin found my company disagreeable," he said. "They wished me to the devil and went up to bed."

Esmée refused to budge. "Well, you have been disagreeable," she said. "You've looked daggers at everyone all evening. I don't know why you came if all you mean to do is quarrel."

Alasdair rocked back on his heels and

studied her. "Are we quarreling, Esmée?"

She cut him a quick, sidelong glance. "What would we have to quarrel over?"

"Ah, what a question that is," he said, setting his glass aside. "Sorcha? The weather? Your choice of husbands?"

Esmée held his gaze quite steadily. "Have you some sort of quarrel with my choice?"

For a moment, his expression shifted. There was something . . . something different in his eyes tonight. Sorrow? Regret? He was not drunk, she thought. Indeed, she had the strangest impression he'd been nursing the same glass of brandy since dinner.

She gentled her own expression and approached him, setting a hand on his arm. "Alasdair, perhaps I have made a mistake," she said quietly. "I do not know. I know only that it is something Quin and I must work out for ourselves. But I won't hurt him, Alasdair. And I shan't disappoint my aunt, either."

"So you mean to go through with this foolishness?"

She lifted one shoulder. "Perhaps it has gone too far to stop," she answered. "And frankly, no one has given me reason to do so."

The emotion in his eyes darkened. "Tell

417

me something, Esmée," he rasped. "Does Quin know about us?"

"Us?" Her voice was arch. "There is no *us*, Alasdair. You could not have made that more plain."

"Damn it, you know what I meant," he said. "Does he know we were lovers?"

Esmée felt the blood drain from her face. "You — why, you said there was nothing between us!" she choked. "You told me I was a virgin and free to marry where I pleased."

His jaw tightened. "Not to marry someone like Quin!" he returned, seizing her by the shoulders. "Esmée, he is little better than I! Besides, you do not love him."

"Love!" she said disdainfully, jerking her gaze from his. "I begin to think you know nothing of the word, Alasdair."

His hand, cold as ice, cupped her chin, forcing her face to his. "Look me in the eyes Esmée," he growled. "Look me in the eyes, and tell me that you love him, and I swear I'll never touch you again."

"I don't want to love him!" she cried. "Oh, Alasdair, can't you see? All I can hope for now is to marry with my head, not my heart! I don't want to be a fool like my mother, falling imprudently in love and wedding one pretty scoundrel after the next."

His eyes searched her face. "But Esmée, that's just what you are doing," he whispered. "That's just what Quin is."

She looked at him boldly, her words angry and impetuous. "Do you desire me, Alasdair?" she demanded. "Is that what this is about? If it is, why not just have me? What would it matter? Lord Wynwood made it plain he did not require a virgin in his bed."

His fingers slid round her cheek, then into her hair. "I ought to, by God," he growled. "I ought to drag you down onto the floor this very minute, Esmée, and have my way with you. If you mean to throw yourself away on a worthless scoundrel, it might as well be me."

If it was meant as a threat, it didn't work. Instead, his words sent a shiver of raw lust down her spine. And like a fool, she couldn't keep her temper and her frustration from flaring. "Go on," she challenged. "Do it. I *dare* you."

His hand fisted angrily in her hair. "You silly little fool!" he choked. "And you are ten times a fool to remain alone here with me."

She felt her whole body begin to tremble with rage and thwarted desire. "Stop pretending I don't know what I want," she hissed. "And stop pretending I don't know *you.* I know the scent of lust on your skin. The heat in your eyes. I know you want me. God knows I want you, fool that I am."

Alasdair heard the passion and anger in her words, and knew he should walk away. This was dangerous ground. Esmée belonged to another. To a *friend.* But in the end, desire overcame honor. Bracketing her perfect face between his hands, Alasdair slanted his mouth over hers, and kissed her hungrily. Esmée goaded him, kissing him back with equal abandon, no longer his little innocent.

She allowed him every liberty, opening her mouth to his tongue and tasting him deeply in return. Fleetingly, he tried to think. Tried to stop. But Esmée had come fully against him, tempting and tormenting him with her lithe, round body. When he hesitated, she coaxed him, sliding her tongue provocatively along his. When he tried to pull away, she slid her hands round his waist and up his back, her touch warm and sure beneath his coat.

"Alasdair." With lips like honeyed satin, she tempted him, wrapping her body round his, binding them together, heart to heart. At last, she tore her mouth from his. "Oh, Alasdair, make me forget you," she begged. "Take me. Take this terrible craving and sate it. I don't want to feel this way anymore."

"Esmée, love," he whispered into her hair, "it doesn't work that way. It only gets worse."

"Try." Her lips moved lightly across his throat. "Oh, just try. Just once."

His mouth sought hers, and she kissed him again, exultantly and openly. All the impossibilities fell away. His good intentions crumbled. He bent her back, reminding himself of how small she was. He felt tall and a little awkward, like a boy again. But he was no boy. He'd bedded more women than he could count. But tonight, he was going to bed Esmée — and she would be the last. No matter what happened.

"Nothing is certain," his brother's voice echoed. *"Not until the vows are spoken."*

She gave a little moan of pleasure, and she slipped one finger beneath the bearer of his trousers. Just one teasing, tormenting finger. She wanted him. He had always wanted her. And they had this moment, if nothing else.

"God, Esmée." It was a whisper. A plea. He needed her, and he was so bloody tired of fighting it. He let his lips slide down the tender flesh of her throat, drawing in her

421

heathery scent as if it might be the last breath he drew. She smelled of warmth. Of comfort and joy. Of home.

"Alasdair," she pleaded. "Please."

Somehow, he found a shred of self-control and lifted his head without quite looking at her. "Esmée, are you sure?" he whispered. "I would sooner die than hurt you."

" 'Tis the not having you, Alasdair, that hurts me," she answered, sliding her hands higher still. "I've tried not to want you, but the ache never leaves me. I think it might, if . . . if you just . . . ."

"Oh, Lord." He closed his eyes and bent his forehead to her shoulder. "I'll burn in hell for this."

She turned her head and brushed her lips along the shell of his ear. "I'll make it worth the trip."

He lifted his head, and looked at her. The warmth kindling in her eyes was no reflection of the fire. It was a woman's knowledge. A woman's power. It was real, and it was dangerous, and it was for him. She was no girl; he wondered he'd ever thought so. He stroked his thumb along her cheek, but it was not enough. She turned her face into his open hand, her mouth still open and seeking. Lightly, she touched his palm with her tongue and muttered something soft and needy.

He pulled her roughly to him again and pressed his body to hers in a way which made plain his intentions. With his fingers sliding into the hair at her temples, he cradled her face in his hands, still kissing her, still drowning in her. He could feel her skin heating. Her heart beating. Faster and faster.

She delved deep into his mouth with her delicate tongue, and he began to tremble in her arms. Desperately, his hands went to the tie of her wrapper, loosening it with unsteady fingers. Her hands did not shake. They slid boldly up his chest and over his shoulders, pushing his coat to the floor.

His waistcoat followed. His cravat yielded to her small, clever hands, a stitch ripping as she pulled it from his collar. Behind them, the fire snapped, exploding into a hundred tiny sparks. Alasdair felt alive. Exhilarated. Like a man given a second chance at life. There was a throbbing — a mystical, driving drumbeat — pounding in his blood and his brain. He pushed her wrapper away and followed suit with her nightgown.

Oh, sweet heaven! She was as naked beneath as the day God had made her. He let his hands slide over her, down her, shaping her every hollow and curve, worshiping the thing of beauty that she was. But Esmée was impatient, as if fearing sanity might reclaim her. With urgent motions, she pulled at his shirt hems, still kissing him, hot and openmouthed.

He loosened the fall of his trousers and pushed everything — drawers, shoes, everything — off in an awkward jumble, leaving him in nothing but his shirt.

She returned her mouth to his at once. When he slowed fleetingly, she made a sound of desperation. "Don't slow down, Alasdair," she begged. "Don't think. Don't let me think."

He was so easily convinced. Pressing the weight of his arousal against her, he slid his hands to her buttocks and lifted her against him. She pulled at him, urging him down. Somehow, he guided her down onto the Persian carpet, setting her back to the fire's warmth. Esmée was all softness and beauty. Sweetness and heat. Her bare skin glowed in the firelight. His pulse pounded in his head and throbbed in his groin. She rolled onto her back and shoved his shirt over his head.

Awkwardly, he helped her strip it off. She slid one hand round the curve of his buttocks and pulled him onto her body. He went willingly now, pinning her to the carpet with his weight and pushing her legs apart with his knee. Forcing himself to slow, Alasdair slid one hand down her belly and eased a finger into her womanly heat.

Esmée thought she would explode the moment Alasdair touched her. She lay pinned beneath him, her body aching and throbbing. His mouth found her breast, suckling hotly. Raw need surged through her like nothing she'd ever known. Over and over he drew her nipple between the sweet heat of his lips, nibbling and tasting as his finger circled the center of her desire. Esmée was left writhing and gasping. And then ever so gently, he bit down, forcing her to stifle a cry of pure desire.

Perhaps she was a wanton. Perhaps she was worse than her mother. It did not matter now. Nothing mattered except the awful ache between her legs. "Oh, now!" she choked, tilting her head back. "Let me — give me — oh, God!"

With his finger, Alasdair touched the hard nub of her arousal, making her hips jerk. She opened her legs wider, begging him. "Slow down, love," he crooned, his lips teasing at her earlobe. "Let me touch you. Let yourself feel it. Here — yes? Umm."

Esmée strained against his hand, unable

to still her body. Her head swam with the scent of him. Soap and sweat. Male musk and luscious warmth. She wanted to drown in it.

"Oh, so beautiful," he whispered. "Let me make it perfect for you, Esmée love."

"It — it — it's perfect now," she choked. "I'm — I can't . . . *Please.*"

He raised up on one elbow, watching her face as he touched her. His eyes held hers, hard and dark by the glow of the dying fire. The long, sleek planes of his body were sculpted by the shadows. Then he bent his head and kissed her again, pushing his tongue deep into her mouth, tasting her deeply. He made a sound, a groan, and against the flesh of her thigh, she could feel the burning weight of his erection. The thought of it frightened her. Thrilled her.

He was still touching her, but it was not enough. *Madness.* Oh, such madness. Esmée circled his tongue with her own and tilted her hips eagerly upward. Another finger slipped inside, spreading her wide. His thumb eased higher, teasing the tip of her need, torturous and more demanding now.

"Do you want me inside you, love?" he rasped. "Do you ache for me?"

"Yes," she whispered, riding greedily

down on his hand. *"Yes."*

To her shock, he bent his head, and his tongue trailed fire up her throat. He nuzzled her earlobe, then sucked it lazily between his teeth, matching the rhythm of his mouth to the touch of his thumb. Esmée arched off the floor again.

At last, Alasdair sat back on his knees. His erection rose between them, a shaft of warm, silken flesh. Tentatively, Esmée slid her fingers around it, marveling at the size and the strength. Alasdair shuddered and let his head tip back. Intrigued, she eased her hand down to the base, then up again. He made a growling sound deep in his chest, and one tiny pearl of moisture beaded from the tip. Esmée touched it with her thumb, circling it gently around and around the satiny head of his erection.

The gesture seemed to meet with Alasdair's approval. His eyes were squeezed shut now, his nostrils flared wide. Suddenly, his head came up, his hair falling forward to shadow his eyes, which were hot and intense. She could see the depth of his need in them.

"Come inside me, Alasdair," she whispered. "Do it — *please.*"

She couldn't catch her breath. She really feared he was going to stop. And yet to go on was insanity. An insanity she craved, no matter the ruin it might bring. She could think of nothing save him; of his touch, his mouth, his essence.

Wordlessly, he set one muscular arm above her shoulder, and with the other hand, pressed his male hardness slowly but insistently into her. Esmée closed her eyes and forced her legs to fall apart, relaxed and welcoming. The pressure was daunting, but she never once considered stopping. Right or wrong, this was inevitable. It was meant to be. Slowly, oh so slowly, he sheathed himself, rocking backward and forward, each stroke deeper than the last.

A sharp, sudden pain made her cry out. His eyes snapped open, urgent and questioning. Esmée slid her hands around his hips, curled her fingers into the hard, sculpted muscles of his buttocks, and urged him deeper. The pain did not matter. He drew back and entered her again on a guttural cry. A sound of triumph. She rocked her hips experimentally forward. He filled her. Claimed her — at least in this one moment. He set the pace, a rhythm of pure pleasure. Esmée met him stroke for stroke, feminine instinct guiding her.

Soon the pain was forgotten. Instinctively, Esmée curled one leg round him and dragged herself hard against him. The feeling building inside her was uncontrollable. She urged him deeper. Faster. There was something — oh, something wonderful just beyond her reach. Esmée closed her eyes, and begged him for it with words that were hungry and incoherent.

Alasdair obliged her, driving himself madly back and forth. Sweat beaded on his brow. One drop fell between her breasts, warm and enticing. Something inside her broke away, and flew to him — her heart, she thought. "Look at me, Esmée," he commanded. "Look at me. Come to me, love."

His dark, smoldering eyes held her prisoner. And then he drove into her again, and Esmée's world exploded. Her entire being throbbed and cried out. Light surrounded them, melted over them, warm and pure. She felt his seed pump hotly into her, heard his guttural cry of joy. And she fell back onto the carpet, spent and glorious.

Alasdair fell across her, the weight of his body pressing her down. "Oh, Esmée!" he said as he gasped for breath. "Oh, love."

Esmée must have drowsed for a time, gloriously sated and almost content. Eventually, Alasdair rose from the rug to turn the lock. Oh, what fools they had been! But better late than never. He returned, and tucked her back into her nightdress, then pulled on his clothes.

She knew they should not remain here, stretched out before the dying fire like lazy cats. She waited for Alasdair to tell her so, but he did not. Instead, he rolled onto his side and drew her body back against his, encircling her waist with his arm. They did not speak — perhaps because they were both too afraid.

Behind them, the fire was all but dead now. A sense of near peace stole over her as she listened to the soft, rhythmic sounds of Alasdair's breathing. The arm which bound her to him seemed to fit so naturally. She could not even kiss Lord Wynwood without automatically turning her cheek. And yet she could bind herself to this man with an ease which she should have found alarming.

She was not alarmed. Instead, there was a sense of inevitability about what they had done. She had believed him a scoundrel from the very first, and she had not been entirely wrong about that. But he was so much more. The blithe charm and physical beauty were unmistakable, but there was a rock-hard foundation of honor beneath it all. Perhaps she had inherited her mother's impetuosity. Perhaps she was letting her heart rule her head. She simply did not care anymore.

Quietly, she turned in his arm to face him. In the gloom, she could just make out that his eyes were open, and soft with sleep. Impulsively, Esmée reached out and traced its shape of his sinfully beautiful mouth with the tip of her finger.

She had done something so irrevocable, some would even say dishonorable, that it seemed incomprehensible to her. And yet she did not regret it. God only knew what she would say to Lord Wynwood.

"He will likely call me out before all's said and done," said Alasdair, as if reading her thoughts. "I would, were I in his position."

Esmée shook her head. "He does not love me enough to trouble himself."

"Then he is a damned fool," said Alasdair, rolling away from her to stare at the ceiling. "A bigger fool, even, than I have been."

Esmée drew back to study his face, but he said no more. Oh, God, how she wished he would simply say what was in his heart, whatever it was. But her betrothal to his best friend hung between them, an awful, unspoken thing, and the next step was hers. She knew what it had to be, too, but the doing of it was her duty, not his.

For a long moment, his eyes held hers almost beseechingly. But what did he want? What was he asking? He tore his gaze away, as if whatever he had seen there wounded him. Instead, he took her hand in his and entwined their fingers together. He pressed his lips to her knuckles and refused to look at her.

"There is a part of you which must hate me, Esmée," he said, "for what I have done to Sorcha. To your mother. To you. I have lived my entire life with a cavalier disregard, never thinking the damage my carelessness might do another. Some might say that my making love to you tonight was but another example of that."

"Oh, Alasdair! Don't speak of it. Not of Mamma, nor of Quin. Not even Sorcha. Let us just pretend for a few moments that none of those complications exist. That it is just us, here, like this."

"But they do exist." In the gloom, his eyes drifted over her face. "Will you ever be able to look at me with Sorcha and not feel a moment's bitterness? You said there was '*no us*,' Esmée, and there isn't — or shouldn't be — because I was trying so hard to make it right for both of you. I was trying to give you the life you were meant to have, and to give Sorcha the father every child deserves. But

432

it is so bloody hard. If I had met someone like you a decade earlier, perhaps I would not have wasted so much of my life."

"Perhaps you ought to stop wasting it now," she suggested. "But that is a discussion, I daresay, for another time and place."

There were a great many other questions she wished to ask him, too. But those questions would wait. Tonight was for cherishing the moments they had together. Tomorrow was for making things right with Wynwood, and asking his forgiveness. After that . . . well, life was unpredictable.

Alasdair drew his arm tight again and set his lips to her forehead. Esmée vowed not to think about the future, or of the painful task which lay before her. Instead, she tucked her head on his shoulder and forgot about scurrying back to her room as she ought to have done.

Just then, a noise beyond the door made her jump. Alasdair pressed his lips to her ear. "Shh," he whispered. "A servant."

Esmée's heart leapt into her throat. "Good heavens! At this hour?" She heard it then, a racket which sounded like the scrape of the shovel on the hearth. The clank of a bucket being moved about.

"Damn, they'll be here next," said Alasdair. "And wondering why they're locked out. Quin must have bloody insomniacs for servants." Silent and sleek as a cat, he rose and swiftly neatened his clothing.

Esmée felt a moment of panic. "How will we get out?"

Alasdair offered his hand. "This way," he whispered, pulling to her feet. "There is an old butler's pantry which leads to the parlor. Let them figure out how the door got bolted."

Hitching up her wrapper as they went, Esmée hastened after him. The pantry opened silently, but the room beyond was devoid of all light. They slipped inside, and Alasdair set an arm about her waist. "Stay close to me," he mouthed against her ear.

With great care, he wound them around the furniture. In the room behind them, Esmée could hear the servants — two of them, debating about the locked door. A very close call. On the opposite side of the room, Alasdair opened the door which gave onto the main passageway, then peered out.

"It's clear," he whispered, tucking her wrapper close about her neck. "Go, love. You mustn't be seen with me."

Esmée was loath to leave him, and he sensed it. Swiftly, he kissed her, hot and openmouthed. "Oh, Esmée, Esmée!" he whispered, his lips pressed feverishly to her throat. "What is to become of us?"

A sense of urgency drove her. "I do not regret it," she whispered hurriedly. "Please, Alasdair, tell me you feel the same."

She felt the heat of his eyes on her, even in the dark. "I *do* regret it, Esmée," he answered. "But God help me, I would do it all over again."

"As would I," she said simply. "Oh, what a soss we've got ourselves into!"

His hands tightened on her waist. "Esmée — I — oh, God, I have no right to ask anything of you just now," he rasped. "Indeed, I won't. Do what is best for you, my girl. Take care of yourself. Take care of your heart."

Esmée considered telling him it was much too late to take care of her heart. It had long been his. But the awful task which lay before her was heavy on her mind now. "We will see one another tomorrow — or rather, today — will we not?" she said hastily.

He shook his head and dragged in his breath roughly. "Merrick leaves for London at first light," he answered. "I must go with him."

"Must you?"

He ran a hand through his disordered hair. "I think it the only honorable thing to do, under the circumstances," he said hollowly. "I cannot bear to remain here, partaking of Quin's hospitality — and his fiancée."

Esmée shook her head. "Alasdair, it isn't like that."

The clanking and scraping in the library had begun now. Somehow, they'd unlocked the library, and would be moving on soon, perhaps in this direction. Alasdair opened the door again and gently pushed Esmée out. She hesitated an instant, then considered the risk she was running. With one last glance over her shoulder at Alasdair, Esmée left.

She made her way quietly through the house and up the stairs, certain she would sleep no more that night. Instead, she slipped back into her room, lit the lamp, and curled up on her bed with the same dull novel which had sent her downstairs to begin with.

Alasdair was not going to ask anything of her, he had said. She was to do what was best for her. But the decision had been made a lifetime ago, it seemed, and what she cared most about was Alasdair. That much had never really changed, and never would change. Which meant that everything else — Wynwood, Mrs. Crosby, Aunt Rowena, Sorcha, *all* of it — would somehow work out. It had to. It just had to.

Chapter Eleven

In which Contessa Bergonzi
draws her Weapon

When the horizon began to show the first hint of daylight, Esmée rose and went to the window to wait for Alasdair's carriage. She did not have to wait long. With her fingertips pressed lightly to the glass, Esmée watched as his baggage was loaded. Then Alasdair and his brother came out, flanking Lord Wynwood, and shook hands all around.

At the last instant, Alasdair hesitated, then grasping Wynwood's right hand again, he set his left upon his shoulder, as if reassuring him of something. They exchanged a few quiet words, then the men climbed in, the coachman clicked to his horses, and the carriage spun away.

That was it, then. Alasdair was gone. Esmée turned from the window and began to lay out her clothes. With any luck, most of the other guests would still be abed, and there was no putting off what she had to do this day. Reluctant to ring for a servant, she bathed in the previous night's cold water. Her body, she noticed, was sore, and there was just the slightest hint of blood when she washed. Alasdair had been gentle, but no matter. Her body was forever altered. Forever his.

She would certainly never be Lord Wynwood's, she thought as she dressed and twisted up her hair, and the sooner she told him so, the better. And yet, he had been exceedingly kind to her. She wished very much that she could love him; that she need not humiliate him. The thought brought a tear to her eye. She rummaged through her valise, extracted a handkerchief, and went out into the passageway. There, she hesitated. Perhaps she would find Wynwood in the breakfast parlor?

The breakfast parlor was indeed occupied, but not by Lord Wynwood. "Good morning, Lady Charlotte," she said.

"Why, good morning, Miss Hamilton," said the elderly woman. "And what is this 'lady' nonsense? You must call me your great-aunt now."

Esmée smiled weakly. "Thank you," she said. "You are very kind."

Lady Charlotte laughed. "I see you are an early bird like me. All the others will be abed

438

for another hour. May I pour you some coffee?"

Esmée hesitated on the threshold. "Actually, I was looking for Lord Wynwood. Have you seen him?"

The old lady's eyes twinkled mischievously. "Oh, he came in for coffee, then scuttled off to his study," she said. "He's still in there, I do not doubt. Do you know how to find it?"

Esmée twisted a little desperately on her handkerchief. "I do not," she confessed. "Could you please direct me, ma'am?"

Lady Charlotte set her cup and saucer down. "It would be easier to simply take you there," she admitted. "This is an inexcusable monstrosity of a house. I should know. I grew up here."

She set off down the corridor at a pace which seemed too brisk for a woman of her advanced years. "The study is in the very back of the house," she said over her shoulder. "In the oldest part, overlooking the rear gardens. Quin hides there when he wishes to escape Gwendolyn's whining."

Esmée followed along, her dread deepening as Wynwood's great-aunt turned left, then right, then trotted up a little flight of stairs, along a crooked passageway, and back down an even shorter flight of stairs.

They passed a pair of housemaids assiduously engaged in sweeping the carpets, then suddenly, a huge slab of solid oak appeared around a corner.

"And here it is!" Lady Charlotte whispered, gleefully pushing the door open against a gust of cold air. "Nowadays, I can forget my own name, Miss Hamilton, but I have not forgot —"

The old lady froze on the threshold.

A woman lay sprawled across the desk in the center of the room, forced down by a man who was violently kissing her. The woman was kicking and flailing like a tigress, but the man — *good God, Lord Wynwood* — held her pinioned by both wrists.

Somehow, she jerked her face away. *"Fa schifo!"* she spat, jerking up her knee as if to do him serious injury. *"Sporco!* Get off me, you bastard English pig!"

With a muttered curse, Wynwood half lifted his body from hers. Only then did Esmée see the riding crop clutched in her glove. The woman lashed it hard across Wynwood's face, sending bright red blood spattering across his linen. Neither seemed aware of the two ladies in the doorway. Not, that was, until Wynwood's great-aunt fainted dead away.

Silent as a stone, the old lady collapsed, slithering into the floor with remarkable grace. Esmée must have screamed. The housemaids appeared from nowhere. The woman — Contessa Bergonzi — shoved Wynwood away and rushed toward Charlotte, tripping over the hem of her riding habit as she came.

The contessa fell clumsily to her knees, but did not heed it. "Quin, you fool!" she cried, trying to push the hair back from Charlotte's face. "*Basta! Basta!* Now you have killed your aunt!"

Esmée had her fingertips on the old woman's throat. "Her pulse is fluttering," said Esmée. "But she is not dead."

Wynwood still stood as if frozen. Behind him, a French window stood wide-open, the cold air from the gardens streaming in. "Shut the window," Esmée snapped at one of the maids. "Wynwood, send someone to fetch a doctor. For God's sake, *hurry!*"

Wynwood leapt into action. Charlotte emitted a pitiful groan. "No . . . no doctor," she managed.

"Oh, *poveretta!*" the contessa was murmuring, still stroking the old lady's face. "Oh, *non ci credo!*"

When Esmée next looked up, Wynwood was gone. The two housemaids were staring after him, eyes wide and mouths gaping. Dear God. They must have seen everything.

The doctor was not long with Lady Charlotte. "Nothing is broken," he pronounced to the crowd which waited in Lady Wynwood's sitting room. "But her pulse is still erratic, as it has been this last decade or better. I wish her to have a day's bed rest, and her usual heart tonic. Tomorrow she'll be her old self, and may return home, I hope."

"Oh, thank God!" Lady Wynwood clutched a crumpled handkerchief to her breast. "Oh, I feared the worst."

"Mark me, Gwendolyn, it was the blood!" asserted the elderly gentleman beside her. "Charlotte never could abide the sight of blood!"

"No, I think it was her weak heart," said Lady Wynwood. "She overexerted herself, perhaps."

Reflexively, Lord Wynwood ran his finger along the wound on his cheek. He had been pacing the floor ever since his great-aunt had been carried up by the footmen. His sister, Lady Alice, was scowling at him from the corner and twisting her own handkerchief into knots.

"Remember, Helen, how Charlotte

fainted and fell out of the dogcart that time we ran over a squirrel?" the gentleman continued to a woman on his other side.

"Oh, heavens yes!" said the round, silver-haired lady — another great-aunt, Esmée thought. "Charlotte needed six stitches!"

Esmée cleared her throat. "This was a terrible accident, too," she remarked in a clear, carrying voice. "Really, Wynwood, you ought not creep up on people like that. The contessa jerked instinctively, just as anyone would do."

The room fell silent for a moment. Lady Wynwood eyed Esmée very oddly over her handkerchief. "Yes, a dreadful accident!" she finally echoed. "We are lucky Great-aunt Charlotte did not break a hip, Quin. Do have a care next time!"

"I'm sorry," he said for about the tenth time. "I'm just so bloody sorry."

The doctor looked faintly embarrassed. "Well, I'd best be off then," he said. "I'll look in on Lady Charlotte tomorrow, just in case. She isn't getting any younger, you know."

The excitement over, the early risers began to trickle from the room and make their way down to breakfast. Lady Alice dragged her mother out, mumbling something about the children. The contessa had already excused herself, leaving Wynwood's study the way she'd apparently entered it, through the French window which opened onto the gardens. Everyone else was yet abed. Nonetheless, the gossip would likely be running rampant before noon, despite Esmée's efforts at obfuscation.

Soon, Esmée and Lord Wynwood were alone in his mother's sitting room. It was time to do what she'd come downstairs to do. She turned to see that he was still staring blindly out the window, as if unaware of her presence.

She went to him and set a hand on his shoulder. "I fear there will be gossip, my lord," she said quietly. "But perhaps we can counter it. We must continue to assert that silly accident story."

Lord Wynwood refused to look at her. "Esmée, I can explain."

"No, don't," she said. "I would really rather not discuss it."

"I don't blame you," he whispered. "I am such a fool — and worse, I've humiliated you. Can you ever forgive me?"

" 'Tis not a matter of my forgiveness," she said quietly.

"If you think that, my dear, then you are a fool, too."

Esmée drew a deep breath. "I ought to explain, Wynwood, that I came looking for you this morning to tell you . . . to tell you that I cannot marry you," she went on. "I made a grievous error in accepting your offer. I apologize."

He threw back his head and gave a bark of bitter laughter. "I am not surprised you'd wish to cry off now," he answered. "What an embarrassment this will be! And I believe it is I who owes the apology."

"You are not listening, my lord," she said firmly. "I was coming to tell you I wished to cry off the betrothal. I am sorry I interrupted you in . . . in whatever it was you were doing —"

"Ruining my life," he interjected. "That's what I was doing."

Esmée shrugged. "In any case, it had nothing to do with my decision. I mean to tell your mother so as well. I would not have her think you responsible for my choice."

Wynwood's shoulders sagged. "I will send a notice to the *Times* this afternoon," he said, dragging a hand through his already disordered hair. "No one will be surprised. My dear, I am sorry this has ended so badly."

"Don't be so sorry," she whispered. "Trust me, I never should have said yes. Something . . . something happened last

445

night to convince me of that."

Wynwood tore himself from the window and began to pace the room. "I thought it a good match, Esmée," he said, his tone almost mystified. "I persuaded myself we could make a go of it, you and I. I was a fool to imagine I could — or would ever — oh, damn it, why didn't I just listen to Alasdair?"

"To Alasdair — ?"

"He told me from the very first I was not good enough for you," Wynwood admitted. "And I knew, even then, he was right. I thought perhaps you might make a better man of me. But it isn't working, is it? Even Alasdair can see it. Last night, he read me the riot act, then tried to thrash me into a bloody pulp."

"Alasdair? But — but why?"

"He thought I wasn't paying enough attention to you," Wynwood answered. "He thought you looked unhappy. He wanted me to call off our wedding, but I refused, of course. How could I? A gentleman may not do such a thing." He flashed her a crooked, bittersweet smile. "But now you have done it for me."

Esmée dropped her gaze to her feet. "Aye, and I think it best," she said. "We do not perfectly suit after all."

For a time, he simply watched her without speaking. "Are you a secret romantic at heart, Esmée?" he finally asked, his voice musing. "Do you believe there is but one perfect partner for all of us?"

"I — yes, I begin to believe that might be so," Esmée admitted.

He turned again to the window and braced his hands wide on its frame. He stared into the distance so long, Esmée wondered if she ought simply to slip out. "I do not know, Esmée, what there is between you and Alasdair," he said quietly. "Certainly it is none of my business now."

She began to interrupt, but he turned and threw up a staying hand. "Please, just let me speak."

Esmée owed him that, at the very least. "Yes. Of course."

He looked at her almost pleadingly. "All I am saying is that if there is even a scrap of sincere regard between the two of you, I urge you not to let it go. Not until you are sure nothing more can be made of it. For once you let go of that tiny scrap — by accident or by design — it is sometimes gone forever."

Esmée could not look at him. "That is good advice, I am sure," she answered. "Now, if you will excuse me, I must go and tell my aunt what we have decided."

"I shouldn't wish her to be angry with you," said Wynwood. "Tell her the truth, by all means."

"The truth is that we do not suit," she said again. "We never did. We are meant for other things, you and I. We were fools ever to think otherwise."

He smiled at her almost wistfully. "Little Esmée," he murmured. "Always the wise one. Why is it that we cannot love one another? It would make life so much easier, would it not?"

She returned the smile ruefully. "Aye, but I begin to think we do not get to choose whom we love," she answered. "And that life was not meant to be easy." Then she stood on her tiptoes and lightly kissed his cheek.

Feeling very much as if she might cry, Esmée turned and hastened from the room. Aunt Rowena would surely be awake. She believed her aunt would support her choice, but by now, Esmée's nerves were so thoroughly rattled, she wished this next step over with quite desperately. Regrettably, she was not quick enough in her errand.

Esmée went into her aunt's bedchamber as soon as her knock was answered. Her face a mask of indignation, Lady Tatton sat stiffly in bed with a breakfast tray laid out before her. It looked as though Pickens had carried up the tale of Lord Wynwood's indiscretion along with her mistress's morning chocolate.

"Don't speak!" ordered Lady Tatton, holding up one dainty hand. The lace which cascaded from her wrist trembled with indignation. "This is an outrage. An insult. Do not even *think* of defending him! I always said Wynwood was a rogue and a scoundrel, did I not?"

"You did, Aunt," said Esmée in spurious deference. "I cannot say I was not warned. I've cried off the engagement, and I'm sure 'tis just as well."

"Good girl!" said her aunt. "Oh, the gossip we shall endure! Oh, Lud, I feel one of my headaches coming on. Pickens, my vinaigrette! And we return to London this afternoon. Get everything packed up. I shall speak with Gwendolyn as soon as I can collect myself."

Esmée went to her aunt's bed and settled herself on the edge of it. "Pray do not quarrel with Lady Wynwood over this," she begged. "She can no more control her son's behavior than . . . than you could my mother's."

Lady Tatton sniffed, but her indignation

faded. "True, very true!" she agreed. "Still, it is a terrible insult he's done you. And with an opera singer! A foreigner! The rumors are running wild already."

Esmée covered her aunt's hand on the counterpane and gave it a light squeeze. "I was going to cry off anyway," she insisted. "I really was. I had decided I could not go through with it and was working up the courage to tell you."

"The courage?" Lady Tatton echoed incredulously. "Oh, my dear child! I would never press you to marry a scoundrel."

Esmée managed a weak smile. "I know," she answered. "Now, if you will excuse me, I have some packing to do as well. And I must say, Aunt Rowena, that I will be very glad indeed to see London again."

"*Hmm,*" said her aunt with a suspicious, sidelong glance. "I did not realize you had developed such a fondness for town life, my dear."

Chapter Twelve

In which Captain MacGregor

explains Everything

Esmée awoke in Grosvenor Square the following morning with a strange mix of both dread and expectation hanging over her. Something was about to happen. She could feel it in her Scottish bones. Unable to settle her nerves, she dressed and went downstairs to pace the floor in the family parlor until Grimond came in with a large silver tray.

"Would you care for some coffee and the morning's paper, miss?" he asked politely. "Her ladyship is still indisposed with her headache and means to stay abed awhile."

"That would be lovely," said Esmée. At least it would occupy her mind.

Esmée settled down on the settee, spread out the paper, and began to read another day's worth of speculation over Wellington's resignation. Then it occurred to her with a strange, sinking sensation that the word of her broken betrothal might possibly have made it into the papers. Lord

Wynwood had been very insistent about sending it straightaway. It had felt as if he wished the awful episode over and done with almost as much as Esmée did.

The scent of fresh ink assailed her nostrils as she flipped through the pages, searching. It did not take her long to find what she sought. Wynwood must have sent a fast horse to London. The announcement was succinct, and printed near the top of the page. And that, Esmée concluded, was the end of what had probably been the shortest engagement in the history of the *ton.*

Lord, the gossip it would spawn! No wonder her aunt had a headache. For that, at least, she was sorry. Esmée picked up her cup, eyes still on the page, and sipped tentatively at the hot coffee. It was a bit of misjudgment, however, for in the next breath, she choked it back up again.

With a precarious clatter, she set her cup down, shoved it away, and spread the newspaper fully open. What the devil was that printed just below Wynwood's announcement? A familiar name. *Edward Wheeler.* But the article could not be right. It made no sense. She read it again, every word. This time, sudden knowledge slammed into her. Alasdair's warning that awful day they had quarreled came back to haunt her.

"Julia Crosby's child is none of your business — nor any of mine, either, come to that."

Oh, God. What an idiot she was!

Quickly, she refolded the paper and went out into the passageway, where the butler was arranging a vase of flowers. "Grimond, I am going out for a long walk," she muttered, hastening toward the stairs.

It took Esmée but a moment to gather her cloak and reticule, but she was well beyond Mayfair before her left hand stopped shaking. In her right fist, she still carried the newspaper. Mr. Wheeler was a successful playwright; that much she had known. Now the rest of it was falling into place.

Henrietta was Wheeler's sister. Not his wife. *Mrs.* Wheeler was Miss Wheeler. How had she concluded otherwise? Oh, she had been such a fool, and in more ways than one.

It was time she and Alasdair had a long talk. She intended to give him no choice in the matter. She would lay siege at his doorstep if she had to. And in the end she would have her way, or die trying. This was her life. It was time she took charge. Just as her aunt had said, she could not keep living it for the benefit of others.

It was a little appalling to consider, but

even if Julia Crosby had been carrying Alasdair's child, Esmée had just about decided that all was fair in love and war. But even that impediment no longer existed. She was glad. She was relieved. No, she was *ecstatic.* Sir Alasdair MacLachlan might be a rake and a rogue and a charming scoundrel, but by God, *he was her scoundrel* — and she meant to have him.

The wind whipped at her face and tore at her cloak as she took the shortcut across the park, which was almost empty. The streets, too, were quiet. In Great Queen Street, nothing stirred, save for the skirling dead leaves, and a short, thickset man who was alighting from an elegant traveling coach at the foot of the street. Ignoring him, Esmée hastened up Alasdair's steps and dropped the knocker determinedly.

Wellings threw open the door, and his face broke into a smile. "Why, good morning, Miss Hamilton. Here to see the young miss, are you?" His smile faltered a bit. "Oughtn't you have sent for Lydia?"

"Aye, but I don't want Lydia or Sorcha." Esmée was already sliding out of her cloak. "I want Sir Alasdair. Wake him up at once, Wellings. And tell him I shan't leave until he comes down and speaks with me."

Wellings hesitated. "I'm afraid he is not

in, miss," he replied. "Sir Alasdair went out in his curricle not ten minutes past."

Esmée brandished her newspaper, but just then, there was another abrupt knock at the door. Wellings frowned. "Excuse me, miss."

He opened the door to reveal the thickset gentleman who had been alighting from his carriage farther down the street. The stranger held a bicorn in his hands, and his barrel-shaped chest filled the door.

"I beg your pardon," he said in a thick Scots burr. "Is this MacLachlan's residence? I seem tae have blown off course by a hoose or two."

"A *hoose?*" said Wellings.

"A *house,*" whispered Esmée.

"Ah." Wellings cast a quick look down the man's attire. "I'm afraid Sir Alasdair is out."

The man put down his hat and began unbuttoning his sweeping greatcoat. "Och, a pity!" he said, then he turned to call through the door. "Carry in my chest and portmanteau, Winters," he ordered one of the footmen. "Seems we've found the laddie."

Wellings looked affronted. "Does Sir Alasdair expect you, sir?"

"Oh, I doot it!" he said, slipping out of his coat to reveal the smart blue naval uniform underneath. "But he'll have me nonetheless, and no choice in it, for I'm his own blood kin. Captain Angus MacGregor at your service. Now, which way lies the Admiralty from here?"

Wellings pointed in the general direction of Whitehall. "Er, it's that way, sir," he said. "Just round the corner, really."

"Excellent! Excellent!" said MacGregor. "I'll stop by there tomorrow."

The captain's servants were carrying in his baggage now, and having heard the magic words — *blood kin* — Wellings was giving orders about what was to go where. Esmée was simply taking it all in, her eyes wide.

Regrettably, Alasdair's uncle was one of the most unattractive men she'd ever laid eyes on. The captain was not as short as he'd first appeared, but he was built like a bull. His hair was a wiry tangle of bright red and gray, which sprouted in all directions, whilst his skin was dark and deeply etched, like shoe leather left too long in the weather.

He was short a few front teeth, and his nose had obviously been broken — twice, if Esmée was any judge. It was also mottled and peeling, as if he'd suffered a recent sunburn, and one of his eyes had a terrible squint, putting Esmée in mind of a pirate without his eye patch. Suddenly, Captain MacGregor turned them both on her.

"And who would you be, miss?" he asked, narrowing the squint. "And are ye goin' out, or comin' in?"

"Coming in," she said a little archly. "I'm waiting for Sir Alasdair."

The captain eyed her up and down. "Aye, aren't we all?" he said in his deep, rolling burr. "Now, you've a familiar look about you, lass. Wha' was the name again?"

"Hamilton," she said, sketching a stiff curtsey. "Miss Esmée Hamilton."

"Oh, aye! The Hamilton lass!" he said, scrubbing at his stubbled chin with one hand. "The laddie told me you were here."

"I'm not *here*," said Esmée irritably. "I mean — I am here. But only to pay a call."

"Are you indeed?" said the captain. He turned to Wellings, who had dispatched the other servants. "Fetch us a pot of strong coffee and a wee nip o' whisky, will ye? Miss Hamilton and I will entertain one another 'til my nephew sees fit tae return."

"But it's half past nine, sir."

"Aye?" The captain squinted at him. "What's your point?"

Wellings blanched, and looked at Esmée. Esmée shrugged. She wasn't sure about Alasdair's uncle's plans, but whisky or no,

457

she wasn't stepping a foot out of Alasdair's house until she had spoken with him. "We'll be in the parlor, Wellings," she said. "Coffee would be lovely."

The captain's heavy tread followed her into the parlor. She was surprised to learn that Alasdair had mentioned her name to his uncle. Why on earth would he have done so? A little desperately, she searched her memory for any reference to an Angus MacGregor and came up with nothing.

She laid down her newspaper, motioned him toward a seat, and took the chair opposite. The captain sat down and slapped his knees heartily. "So you'd be Rosamund's eldest, eh?" he began. "You've the look of her, too, and no mistake."

Startled, Esmée blinked. "You knew my mother?"

"Oh, aye!" he said. "Scotland's a small place, society-wise. And a rare beauty she was, too. Never met a woman who could hold a candle to her — though I tried hard enough, by God!" The captain laughed and shook his head, as if caught in some remembrance.

Esmée lifted one brow. "How did you know her?"

"Why, I met Rosamund at her comeout," he said. "Did she never mention me?"

Esmée shook her head. The captain's face fell. "Oh, I was smitten!" he went on. "As was every red-blooded man who clapped eyes on the lass. I'd been made lieutenant by then, and was very cocksure of myself, as only a young officer can be."

The remark made Esmée smile. "Yes, I think I know."

The captain's gaze turned inward. "Of course, by the time I arrived, Rosamund's card was full. That took the wind out of my sails. Then a pair of drunken lordlings commenced squabbling over who was to have the next dance, and I saw my opportunity." He looked up at Esmée and winked with his good eye. "Rose slipped out to the garden with me, and let the lordlings feud on."

Esmée's smile faltered. "That sounds almost romantic," she remarked. "Did you eventually sail away and never see her again?"

"Oh, Lord no!" said the captain. "Courted her desperately for a month or more, I did. Even proposed marriage, imprudent as it now seems. Now, don't laugh, miss! I cut a dash in my salad days. Had all my teeth and a head full of fine red hair."

Esmée studied him, trying to imagine the young man he'd once been, but it was a struggle. "And what happened?"

"Oh, Rose was too wise tae have me," he answered ruefully. "Said she wouldna' wed a sailor, and I was too stubborn to give it up. Can't say as I blame her, looking back. Many a fine laddie went off to sea and never came home again."

Suddenly, Esmée remembered something. *Could this be the man Aunt Rowena had spoken of?* Her mother's first love? It seemed impossible. And yet . . . not. For all his ill looks, the captain was clearly a charmer. Esmée clasped her hands in her lap and drew a deep breath. "If it makes you feel any better, Captain MacGregor, I think my mother remembered you with great fondness."

The captain grinned widely. "Oh, aye, she did that!" he said with another saucy wink. "Forever tormenting me o'er it, she was, and scolding me for my choice. O'course, I'd scold her back and tell her the choice had been all hers, and none o' mine. And so it went, lassie. But we remained good friends after a fashion."

"Oh." Esmée sat up a little straighter. "You — you kept in touch, then?"

The captain shrugged. "Aye, as well as a seafaring man can do," he said. "A letter now and again, and we'd run up on one another every two or three years — Scotland's a small place, as I said — but I could ne'r catch her between husbands. 'Twas a sad irony, I once told her, that all her fine, land-bound dandies died on her, whilst I kept hale and hearty and got uglier by the day."

"Did you — did you still wish to marry her?"

Again, the shrug — but just one shoulder this time. "Oh, aye, in my fancies," he said. "But 'tis probably just as well. Rosamund was a rare handful. We'd likely have killed one another if ever we'd made a proper match instead of just the occasional . . . well, never mind that."

Just then, there was a noise from the corridor, and Alasdair strode in, stripping off his gloves as he came, his face a little windburned. "Esmée!" he choked, throwing his arms wide.

On instinct, Esmée leapt up and rushed into them.

"Oh, my dear girl," he said into her hair. "They said you'd gone out for a walk. You oughtn't have come here, you know. Why didn't you wait for me?"

Esmée set him a little away. "I am tired of waiting for you, Alasdair," she said. "You are very slow."

Suddenly, the captain cleared his throat. "What does a hearty old tar have to do,

461

laddie, to get a mug o' coffee in this hoose?"

Alasdair turned, his expression incredulous. "Angus!" he cried, crossing the room in two strides. "What the — ?"

His uncle stood, and they clasped hands warmly. "I came, laddie, soon as I got your letter," he said, his face suddenly somber. "Aboot the bairn, I mean. Sorry tae be so long a' coming."

Alasdair set a hand on his uncle's shoulder. "Ah, it little matters now," he said. "We've got it all settled."

Angus flicked a glanced at Esmée. "Aye, that much I can see," he remarked.

Alasdair actually blushed. "Besides, Angus, you did not need to come all the way to London," he added. "A letter would have sufficed."

Angus looked back and forth between Esmée and Alasdair. "Aye, well, I'm no' sae sure aboot that," he said. "It might require a wee bit more finagling."

Suddenly, Esmée was struck with an awful sense of foreboding. She edged closer to Alasdair, who was staring at his uncle a little oddly. Just then, Hawes came in with the coffee and whisky, but no one paid it any heed.

"Well, I'm listening, Angus," said Alasdair, when the footman had gone out again.

Angus gestured at Esmée. "Aye, and so is she," he said. "But 'tis no talk for a lady's ears."

"Say away, Uncle," Alasdair commanded. "If it's important enough to bring you all this distance, then Esmée needs to hear it."

His uncle lifted his shoulders, and spread his hands wide. "Well, the truth is —" he began, then he halted, and heaved a weary sigh. "Aye, the truth is, laddie, aboot the wee bairn — well, she's no' yours. I canna' think how this mixed-up sosserie came to be, and I'm sorry you've had the de'il scared out o' you on my sairie account."

"Not . . . not *mine?*" said Alasdair. "But she is. Esmée said so. You are mistaken."

Angus slowly shook his head. "Nay, laddie," he said. "D'ye not remember? The bairn's my get, and I'll not fob her off on you. 'Twouldn't be fair."

Esmée glanced at Alasdair, who had lost all his color. "But — but that's quite impossible!" she said. "I *know.* I was there."

"Ah, were ye now, lassie?" asked the captain slyly. "I dinna remember it that way."

Esmée felt her face flush with heat. "Sorcha is Alasdair's child," she insisted. "I was there when my mother confessed it."

"Och, *confessed it,* did she?" said Angus.

"And what were the circumstances?"

Esmée's blush deepened. "She caught Achanalt in . . . well, in an embarrassing position with one of the kitchen maids," she admitted. "One who was especially pretty and flirtatious — we always had to keep an eye on her — and seeing the two of them like that, why, it just set Mamma off. She was livid. We all heard the quarrel."

"Aye?" said the captain. "In a taking, was she? Go on, then."

Alasdair crossed his arms over his chest. "Why must the two of you rehash old history?" he demanded. "I've no wish to hear it. I don't care who was swiving the kitchen maids. And by the way, Angus, Sorcha has not been *fobbed off* on anyone."

But his disputation went unheeded. Esmée's words were tumbling from her mouth, and she seemed unable to stop them. "I — I rushed into the room," she said. "To tell them the servants were listening. The girl was still naked, with his bedsheets wrapped round her. I threw her out. They paid me no heed; they were still at one another. I turned round and saw Mamma strike him. It — it went downhill from there."

Alasdair made a disparaging sound. "How the devil could it?"

"Oh, easily!" said Esmée. "He accused her of carrying a bastard in her belly. He said he'd known it for months. And then she — dear God, she spat in his face and admitted it! She said she was glad, and wished him to the devil."

Angus nodded at the last. "Aye, angry, and wishful o' hurting him any way she could, eh?"

"Oh, aye," admitted Esmée. "Wild with anger."

"Aye, that sounds like Rosamund," he says. "And I'm no' a thing to be jealous of, am I?"

Esmée looked at him oddly. "What do you mean?"

"Why, look at me!" said the captain, pointing at one of his missing teeth. "What manner o' jealousy would I inspire, eh, with my paunch and my teeth and my grizzled red hair?"

Alasdair gave a bark of bitter laughter. "Oh, I cannot believe this!"

"Aye, believe it, laddie!" said Angus. "She's caught Achanalt poking a buxom young maid, and she's tae retaliate with . . . what? With *me?* An old salt who's been twenty-five years on the sea and lost what little looks he e'er had? No, better to throw the handsome young laddie here in his face.

Besides, Alasdair was aboot seven hundred miles away by then. Me, I like tae go home from time to time, and Rosamund was fond o' me. She would have hated to see my head on a pike."

"But how?" cried Esmée. "How in God's name could she do such a thing to Sorcha?"

Alasdair sat down on the sofa and dropped his head in his hands. "This is not true," he said. "It is not."

But Angus was pacing back and forth now and ignored him. "In her mind, lass, Rose wasn't thinking o' the child," he said. "She just wanted revenge. And she dinna expect to die, either. Like all of us, she thought she'd have time to make things right. That's my guess, anyway."

Esmée sat down beside Alasdair. "Dear God!"

"No!" said Alasdair sharply. "I — I *remember,* Angus. Why are you saying such things?"

Angus stopped pacing, and looked down at him. "What d'ye remember, laddie?"

Alasdair shrugged. "Well, being pretty well castaway," he admitted. "And . . . and doing something I knew I would regret. Something shameful."

"Aye, laddie, you nearly did!" said Angus, cutting another swift glance at Esmée.

"What?" said Alasdair. "*What?* Was there something worse?"

Angus tilted his head. "Well, not precisely *worse,*" he said. "But are you sure you want me tae tell it?"

"Oh, why the hell not?" said Alasdair, throwing up his hands.

Angus was chuckling to himself. "You tried to take a piss in Lady Morwen's potted palms."

Alasdair's head jerked up. "I *what?*"

"Och, sotted as a sow, ye were," Angus continued. "And desperate to make water. Said you were going to the gents' room, but I saw you take the wrong door. You staggered through some curtains behind the musicians' dais, tripped over a violin case, and somehow dropped your drawers, then couldna' get 'em up again."

Alasdair emitted an awful groan. "Oh, Christ," he said. "The curtains — were they heavy? Velvet?"

"Aye, mayhap."

Another groan. "Did — did anyone see —?"

Angus slapped him cheerfully on the shoulder. "No, but 'twould have been quite a shock to the womenfolk if the drapes had been drawn whilst your trews were round your ankles," he said. "But not tae worry. We hitched everything up again, and 'twas then I realized 'twas time to take our leave of Lord and Lady Morwen before one of us got shot, for I well knew what I'd been aboot."

The humor of the situation was lost on Esmée. She was half in a panic. *Captain MacGregor was her mother's lover?* Good Lord. It was beyond belief. Her mother had always preferred handsome, faithless wastrels. A short, squat, grizzled old sea captain with a face like a well-worn saddlebag was inconceivable. And now, what would become of Sorcha? How could this have happened?

Suddenly, she remembered all the callous things she'd thrown at Alasdair. "Oh, Lord!" She pressed her hands to her cheeks. "What a bloody awful mess I've made of all this!"

"No, lassie, 'twas your mother that made it, God rest her."

Esmée did not heed him. "Oh, Alasdair! I owe you a most profuse apology."

Angus looked at her oddly. "Why?" he said. "What did *you* do?"

Esmée stared at the carpet. She felt a little sick. "I — I said some terrible things," she whispered. "Some things I can't bear to think back on."

But Alasdair seemed disinterested in her

apology. He was still watching his uncle warily. "Angus, are you sure?" he asked, his voice a little hollow. "I've spent these last months coming to grip with what I thought was the truth. That child is precious to me."

"Aye, laddie," he said wearily. "I'm sure."

Esmée set her hand on Alasdair's arm. "Sorcha does have those MacGregor eyes," she mused. "And I think your uncle might be right about Mamma, too. It sounds just the sort of overwrought, shortsighted thing she would do. And then there was something Aunt Rowena said — oh, but never mind that! I am just so sorry, Alasdair, for the ugly things I said."

Alasdair turned to face her and took both her hands in his. "But you weren't far off the mark, my dear," he answered. "I suppose I must accept that what my uncle says is true. He has no reason to lie. But the awful truth is, it could just as well have *been* me. Perhaps I'm off the hook — now, the first time I'd as soon not be — but how many other times have I been guilty of just such a thing? How many, Esmée? I can't even count them."

Angus was watching them curiously. "What d'ye mean, laddie, 'as soon *not* be'?"

Alasdair turned to face his uncle and set

his jaw in that hard, stubborn line Esmée had come to know too well. "Angus, I want no trouble with you," he began. "But it is like this: Possession is nine-tenths of the law. I'm not giving her up. Not without a fight."

Angus drew back in shock. "You're wishing to *keep* the bairn?" he said. "But I thought Miss Hamilton was raising her."

Esmée sniffled pathetically. "Well, I was," she said. "Until my aunt Rowena found out."

Angus chuckled quietly. "Aye, Rowena!" he said. "I remember *her,* too."

"Angus, damn it, this is not funny."

Angus lifted his hands expressively. "Ah, well, laddie! Ye know what your granny MacGregor always says: One way or anither, your chicks will come home to roost. But somehow, this one came to roost with you by mistake."

Alasdair's brow drew into a knot. "Did Granny really say that?"

"Oh, aye, a thousand times!" said Angus.

Alasdair fisted both his hands. "Well, she roosted here, and by God, she's staying here," he said. "I've raised the child as mine. I'm the only father she's ever known — God knows Achanalt never spared her a thought — and I tell you, I shan't give her up."

It was slowly dawning on Esmée that Alasdair was entirely serious. He really did *not* want off the hook. Indeed, he was quite angry. The muscle in his jaw was having spasms now.

Angus sat down and scratched his grizzled head. "Well, well, what's best done?" he muttered. "God knows a sailor can't raise a child — I had no intention of it, anyway. And I want the best for the wee thing, o'course. But laddie, the truth is —" Here, he gestured at Esmée again, "— *She's* got more rights to the bairn than you or I, come to that. And 'tis womenfolk that know what's best for children."

"*I* know what's best for Sorcha," Alasdair snapped, his jaw still firmly set. "I understand her. Esmée and I will raise her together."

Angus looked befuddled. "Thought Esmée was living with Rowena."

"Yes, and that's the next problem I mean to fix," said Alasdair, scrabbling through his pocket and extracting a small velvet box. It was green, just like the one her pearls had come in, only smaller. He slapped it down beside the unused coffee service and shot Esmée a look that dared her to contradict him. "But we'll be having *that* discussion in private," he added.

"Ah!" said Angus, slapping his knees and standing up again. "That would be my cue tae get upstairs with my whisky."

Alasdair waved him toward the door. "Yes, yes," he said. "By all means, go."

Angus stopped beside Esmée and laid a gnarled hand on her shoulder. "Now don't fret, lass," he said. "I'm a wealthy man, and I'll do right by the bairn. I needed an heir anyway."

Esmée just stared at him. "B-But what are we to tell Sorcha?"

Angus gave her an avuncular pat. "Why, when she's of age, you can tell her whatever you please — or nothing a'tall!" he said. "She can be just Lady Sorcha Guthrie, your dear, wee sister. Achanalt is na' apt to gainsay that; not publicly, and if he does, I'll kill 'im. Or you can tell her she had two parents who loved each other very much, but bollixed up their lives, yet still wanted the very best for her. Or if you truly wish it, why, you can just change her name and tell her she's yours and Alasdair's — which she will be, aye?"

Esmée opened her mouth, then closed it again. "Well. At least we have . . . alternatives."

Angus paused just long enough to give her another wink and snatch the whisky decanter. "Aye, so bide your time," he advised. "But either way it goes, lassie, a child does need two parents, aye? And parenthood has verra little to do with who begat you and a vast deal to do with who loved and cared for you."

Slowly, she nodded. "That is very true."

Then, quietly, Angus left, closing the door behind.

Alasdair watched him go in disbelief. "Well," he said, reaching for her hand, "this has been one hell of a day, and the morning's but half-gone. What do you make of it, my girl?"

"I believe, Alasdair, that I am in shock." Esmée, too, was still staring at the door. "Just imagine! Captain MacGregor *and my mother?* But it does indeed seem that he was her long-lost love. It all quite boggles the mind."

"Aye, well, my mind's been boggled for weeks now," Alasdair returned. "But what's this lost love business?"

Esmée turned on the sofa, and set her hand against his cheek. "Oh, just a silly, romantic story Aunt Rowena told me," she murmured. "Something of a cautionary tale."

Alasdair watched her a little warily. "Ah, I see," he murmured. "And what was the moral of the story?"

Esmée leaned closer and kissed him lightly on the lips. "That one should always trust one's heart," she said. "Because sometimes, the first love you find is the right one, and you should hold on to him with all your strength."

"Ah!" said Alasdair. "Is that so?"

"It is," she said certainly. "My mother did not do that, and it may well have been the cause of all her unhappiness. I hope to do better. I hope to seize what is meant for me and hold to it no matter what. Perhaps I shall have a happy life. Perhaps I shan't turn out like my mother after all."

Alasdair stroked the back of his hand over her cheek. "My dear girl, you aren't *like* anyone I've ever known," he whispered. "You are just Esmée. And you are perfect."

Esmée managed a watery smile. "Well, you are *not*," she said. "You are hopelessly flawed, and very, very wicked. Unfortunately, I seem to find the combination irresistible."

Alasdair was holding her gaze gently. "Oh, Esmée, I have been such a fool," he answered. "And it did not take Angus's coming here to teach me that."

Esmée gave him a muted smile. "Yes, 'tis true. You have been a fool."

A teasing glint flashed in his eye. "But perhaps we should begin at the beginning," he went on. "Esmée, what are you doing here? You shouldn't have come alone, you know."

"Yes, I believe you mentioned that earlier," she remarked, picking up her newspaper.

"What's that?" he asked. "Today's paper? How odd. That's the same one *I* read before bolting off to Grosvenor Square."

She shot him a coy look. "Then you will have noticed, I daresay, that my betrothal to Lord Wynwood is at an end?"

His expression saddened. "I saw it and went directly to your aunt's house, only to find you gone," he said. "I won't pretend, Esmée, that I'm not glad. And I shan't let the opportunity to win you pass me by a second time. I'd hate to saddle you with a rogue like me, but I mean to do it if you'll let me. I love you, my girl, with all my heart."

"And I love you," she said, taking both his hands in hers. "Indeed, I came here with every intention of throwing myself at you most wantonly. I know it's a dodgy business, MacLachlan, consorting with a man of your ilk, but 'twould be best if you just gave in gracefully. I mean to have you no matter *what* it takes."

He flashed his most charming grin. "Oh, it won't take much," he answered. "Especially if you mean to do it wantonly." Suddenly, the grin fell. "I just . . . well, I just hope Quin will not hate me."

"Oh, I think Quin has other fish to fry," she murmured. "Indeed, he barely noticed my leaving."

"The devil!" said Alasdair. "I don't believe you."

Esmée gave him a sly smile. "Oh, you may well believe it," she said, snapping open the paper. "But that, I daresay, is another tale for another time. Now, as to this paper — what really got my attention was *this*."

"Ho!" he said, following her finger down the page. "Well, I'll be damned! I never got that far before dashing off to your aunt's house. I'm glad to see Wheeler did the right thing by Julia. That will save me a dawn appointment."

Impatiently, Esmée tapped on the announcement. "Alasdair, why did you not tell me Henrietta Wheeler was Mr. Wheeler's *sister?*"

He looked at her blankly. "Why should I?" he answered. "I scarcely know the woman. What difference does it make?"

Esmée lifted one shoulder. "Oh, never mind!" she said. "So Mr. Wheeler is the father of Mrs. Crosby's child?"

"So Julia says," answered Alasdair. "What, are you still trying to pack that off on me?"

Esmée shook her head. "I guess I did not believe you."

Alasdair scowled at her darkly, then just as suddenly, his face fell again. "Well, the truth is . . . oh, Esmée, the ugly truth is, it just as easily could have been mine," he said. "I take no pride in saying it, either. But it *isn't,* and I told you so. Now Julia is Mrs. Edward Wheeler, and I wish them both very happy."

Esmée felt a little nonplussed. "Well, that was simple enough," she said. "So tell me this, Alasdair — what's in that box?"

Alasdair dropped his gaze, his dark lashes fanning across his cheeks. "Something I bought for you long ago," he said. "Before your aunt came and turned my life upside down."

"*Before* my aunt came?" she echoed. "How intriguing! Am I to have it now?"

"No," he said, picking up the box and giving her just a peek of what was inside — the flawless sapphire-and-diamond ring which had set him back a bloody fortune so many weeks ago.

Her eyes widened at the sight. *"No — ?"*

"No." He snapped the box shut. "First you must agree to marry me and help me raise Sorcha and the other nine children we are going to have."

"Must I?" she asked, reaching for the box. "But why nine?"

Alasdair slid the box behind his back. "To fill up all those empty chairs in the schoolroom," he confessed. "A good Scot would never let them go to waste, now, would he?"

Esmée drew back and frowned. "That's just what I thought when you bought them," she said. "But surely you . . . you did not plan . . . ?"

"Oh, I've never planned a thing in my life!" he returned. "But Granny MacGregor says the mind works in mysterious ways."

Esmée reached behind him and snatched the ring. "Oh, Alasdair, I am not marrying you for your mind," she said, distracted by opening the box. "And certainly not for your granny's old adages. But this ring — ! Oh, my love! Now, *that* is another thing altogether! For this, why, I would almost — *almost* — marry your uncle Angus."

With a muttered oath, Alasdair pushed her back onto the sofa and dragged his body half over hers. "Oh, no, my little Highland lass," he said in a mocking burr. " 'Tis MacLachlan or no one for you. I'll not take a chance on losing you to another man ever again."

Esmée looked up from beneath her half-lowered lashes. "Will you not, then?" she asked, rubbing her thigh suggestively against his — and to quite good effect.

"No, not in a thousand years," he vowed. "Or a thousand years after that."

A slow, satisfied grin spread over Esmée's face. "Then get up and bolt that door, MacLachlan," she whispered, lowering her lashes fully. "You've got nine empty chairs left — and you've wasted far too much time already."

About the Author

During her frequent travels through England, **Liz Carlyle** always packs her pearls, her dancing slippers, and her whalebone corset, confident in the belief that eventually she will receive an invitation to a ball or a rout. Alas, none has been forthcoming. While waiting, however, she has managed to learn where all the damp, dark alleys and low public houses can be found. Liz hopes she has brought just a little of the nineteenth century alive for the reader in her popular novels, which include *The Devil You Know*, *A Deal With the Devil*, and *The Devil to Pay*. Please visit her at www.lizcarlyle.com, especially if you're giving a ball.